MIKE ASHLEY is an author and editor of over eighty books, including many Mammoth titles. He worked for over thirty years in local government but is now a full-time writer and researcher specializing in ancient history, historical fiction and fantasy, crime and science fiction. He lives in Kent with his wife and over 30,000 books.

Also available

THE MAMMOTH BOOK OF

DICKENSIAN WHODUNNITS

Edited by Mike Ashley

CARROLL & GRAF PUBLISHERS
NEW YORK

Carroll & Graf Publishers
387 Park Avenue South, 12th Floor
New York, NY 10016
www.perseusbooks.com

First Carroll & Graf edition 2007

First published in the UK by Robinson,
an imprint of Constable & Robinson Ltd 2007

ISBN-13: 978-0-7867-1971-6
ISBN-10: 0-7867-1971-0

Printed and bound in the EU

Contents

Copyright and Acknowledgments

Introduction:
Dickensian Crimes

Mike Ashley

Even if we've never read anything by Charles Dickens, there can't be many of us who don't know the names of at least one Dickensian character, probably more. Ebenezer Scrooge, Oliver Twist, David Copperfield, Little Nell . . . some of them have even found their way into the English language. Dickens was supreme in his ability to create memorable characters, many associated with wonderful one-liners. Scrooge and his "Bah, humbug!"; young Oliver and "Please, sir, I want some more"; Uriah Heep being "ever so 'umble"; Mr Bumble's "The law is a' ass" or Sidney Carton's dramatic "It is a far, far better thing that I do, than I have ever done."

Dickens's characters live beyond the printed page. They are still with us a hundred and fifty years later and we can easily believe that they had a life beyond the novels. After all, what did become of Oliver Twist when he grew up? How did Scrooge cope with his new-found generosity? What other crimes did Inspector Bucket investigate?

Ah, Inspector Bucket. Now we're talking. When Dickens introduced Inspector Bucket in *Bleak House* in 1853 he created the first true fictional detective in England. He was modelled on a real police detective, Inspector Field of the Metropolitan Police Force. Dickens frequently accompanied the police on their duties, betraying a fascination beyond the simple research for his books. Dickens was fascinated by crime and criminals, and we should not overlook the significant role that Dickens played in portraying the police in fiction and thereby helping along the fledgling field of crime fiction. The majority of *Oliver Twist*, for example, is set amongst the criminal underworld. There are many crimes in *Our Mutual Friend* whilst in *Martin Chuzzlewit* Dickens created the first fictional private investigator in England in the shape of the mysterious Mr Nadgett. Most puzzling of all is *The Mystery of Edwin Drood*, which involved either a murder or disappearance but was unsolved because Dickens died before he could complete the novel, thus providing plenty of speculation amongst Dickens devotees.

Which brings us to the purpose of this anthology. It is a celebration of Charles Dickens's fascination with crime. Here you will find stories that either feature Dickens himself involved in a crime connected with people and places that he knew or which feature characters from his books likewise involved in a mystery. For example, we find Mr Pickwick consulted over the disappearance of a young woman. We find Oliver Twist having to help the Artful Dodger who has been accused of murder. We find Ebenezer Scrooge, now a changed man, with a stolen baby. We meet David Copperfield in later life not once, but twice: in one story investigating the fate of Mr Murdstone, whilst in another teamed up again with Mr Micawber. We also meet the real Little Nell, who may not be quite the angel we all thought in *The Old Curiosity Shop*. All of Dickens's major works are represented including *Nicholas Nickleby*, *Martin Chuzzlewit*, *A Christmas Carol*, *Bleak House*, *Hard Times*, *Dombey and Son*, *Little Dorrit*, *Great Expectations*, *Our Mutual Friend* and, of course, *The Mystery of Edwin Drood*. Dickens himself also turns a hand to investigating, and we meet up with Mrs Gaskell, S. Baring Gould, even Edgar Allan Poe. All of the stories here are based either directly on characters or incidents in Dickens's works or on events in his life.

You do not need to know Dickens's work to understand the stories. Each one is complete in itself, with any necessary background explained. And to further help set them in context I have provided an introduction to each story which follows Dickens's life.

Every story has been especially written for this book. I was not expecting every author to attempt a pastiche of Dickens's style, though a few have done so admirably. Rather I was after stories that remained true to Dickens's life and to the characters in his books, with the object of bringing alive the world of Charles Dickens and his fascination for the under-world of crime and mystery. So, without further ado let us answer Inspector Bucket's question, "You don't happen to have heard of a murder?" Indeed we have – quite a few. . . .

– *Mike Ashley*

The Marshalsea Handicap

Gillian Linscott

Charles Dickens was born at Landport, a suburb of Ports-mouth, on 7 February 1812. He was the second of what would eventually be eight children, though two of them died in infancy. His father, John, was a clerk in the pay-office at the dockyard. Through his work John and his family were transferred first to London in 1814 and then Chatham in 1817. For the time John Dickens was mod-erately well paid, his salary of £350 in 1820 the equivalent of about £22,000 today, but with a growing family and a determination to give young Charles a good education, it was not enough. Neither was John sensible with his money; rather, like Mr Micawber, he spent beyond his means. Admiralty reforms led to John Dickens and his family having to return to London in 1822 and settle in Camden Town, in what was one of the less salubrious parts of the suburbs. It was an area that the young Dickens explored thoroughly and features time and again in his books. Debts mounted and in February 1824, on his twelfth birthday, young Charles was sent to work in Warren's Blacking Factory, which made shoe blacking, earning a shilling a day. His job was to tie together the bottles of blacking and stick labels on them. The factory was on the bank of the Thames near Charing Cross. Though welcomed by his father, it was too late. Two weeks after Charles had started work, John Dickens was arrested for debt and cast into the Marshalsea Prison. He was soon joined by the rest of his family, except for Charles, who continued to work and who lived in lodgings, unbearably lonely. Such is the point at which our first story begins.

Gillian Linscott is a former reporter and Parliamentary journalist, and the author of the Nell Bray series of suffragette mysteries that began with Sister Beneath the Sheet *(1991) and includes the award-winning* Blood on the Wood *(2000). Although most of her books are set in the early 20th century,* Murder, I Presume *(1990) takes place in 1874 in the aftermath of the death of Dr Livingstone.*

"Right," I told them. "They're under starter's orders and these are the odds." I showed them the list:

Little Wife – evens.

Geranium – three to one.

Glue Boy – three to one.

The Inventor – ten to one.

Holy Joe – twenty to one.

Fifty to one the field.

"Geranium should be better odds." Watts, moaning as usual.

"Think so? Father Christmas is fond of flowers. Don't you remember he turned up one day with a rose in his button-hole?"

"Carnation," Natty said. "It was a clove carnation. And how you got it narrowed down to those five?"

"Makes no odds whether it was a carnation or a dandelion. Instinct's what I go by and instinct tells me there's only five in the field worth a second look."

Instinct's worth something, true, but inside knowledge is worth a good bit more and that was what I had, though I'd no intention of letting on to Watts and Natty. The thing is, if you've been a customer of a place as often as I have, you're

valued by the management. The top storey but one of
Marshalsea debtors' prison, south of the Thames in Southwark, has probably never had a more regular patron than me
– in and out two or three times a year as my luck goes up or
down – and the governor and I are like old school chums. So
when it came to some tips from the stable on the annual
Marshalsea Father Christmas Handicap Stakes, he put me
right.

"He's got it narrowed down to five and as it happens three
of them are on your floor. You know Mr Perkins?"

"The one with the pretty little wife who brings his dinner
in every afternoon?"

"That's the one. Mr Shipham is very sentimental about
wives. His own died young and he confided that little Mrs
Perkins reminds him of her."

I should mention here that Mr Shipham is the one we call
Father Christmas, for reasons that will become obvious.

"It's a one-horse race, then?" I said.

"No, because he's not quite made up his mind about Mr
Perkins. He thinks he may be responsible for his own mis-
fortunes and perhaps not as thoughtful towards his wife as he
should be. At present he's rather inclining to two of your
other neighbours. One's Mr Peat."

"Who went bankrupt trying to breed a yellow geranium."

"Mr Shipham thinks it shows praiseworthy enterprise.
Then there's Mr Dickens."

"Pretty ordinary case, I'd say. Government clerk spending
beyond his means. A dozen of those on every floor."

"Yes. But Mr Shipham has been impressed by the son. He
saw him when he came to visit his father and said he thought
he'd go far."

I was surprised. I'd seen the boy on his visits, but he'd
struck me as no more than a twelve-year-old streak of misery,
taking it hard.

"Young Charlie the glue boy, you mean?" I said.

"Why do you call him the glue boy?"

"Because he smells of glue. He works in Warren's Blacking
Factory near the Strand, sticking labels on the tins. Boiled

horses' hooves, that's what they make glue from, and that's what he smells of."

We discussed the two from another floor, a failed inventor and a clergyman who'd spent all his money, and some he hadn't got, trying to put a Bible on every beer house counter, and I went away to make up my betting book.

Now, you won't find the Marshalsea Father Christmas Handicap in any racing calendar and you probably won't have heard about it at all unless you've done time in the Marshalsea yourself, but among debtors it's nearly as famous as the Derby. It isn't run at Christmas, either. That's just the name we give it because for one lucky man it's like all the Christmases he ever had rolled into one, thanks to Mr Shipham. What happened was, around forty years ago when Mr Shipham was about the age that Glue Boy is now, his own father died in the Marshalsea. Young master Shipham supports what's left of the family and goes on to make a fortune in the building trade, but how ever much money he makes it preys on his mind that he couldn't save his own dad. So once a year, on his father's birthday, he chooses the most deserving man in the prison and pays off his debts up to the sum of two hundred pounds. Now, since a lot of poor devils end up in here for owing no more than thirty pounds or so, that's the key to the door and a bit over. Mr Shipham starts making up his mind a week or two beforehand, discusses things with the governor a bit but mostly relies on his own judgement. What he does is sit quietly in the common rooms in every part of the place, just watching and listening to what goes on. Now, you might think that would mean he couldn't move for people crowding round him and begging him to choose them, only the Marshalsea Stakes has its rules like any other and the main one is that the debtors and their friends and relations mustn't approach him or even let on they notice him. Well, that's asking a lot, of course, but it helps that he's a quiet old gent, nothing special to look at and his clothes as plain as anybody's, only better quality if you get up close. So he can sit of an evening on a bench by the fire with his pipe and after a while people do get used to him more or less and the drunks start drinking and the swearers start effing and blinding again, all nearly natural. That's the point we were at when I made my final list of the odds with just a few days to go to the big day.

Now, seeing what the governor had said, you might think I was wrong making Perkins and the little wife favourite, but taking my meals in the same common room as them I'd had a good chance to weigh them up and reckoned the governor wasn't allowing enough for her form. To my mind, she had winner's enclosure written all over her. She was as pretty as a doll fresh out of the toy box, big blue eyes, little wisps of fair hair showing underneath her bonnet. She always kept herself neat, even though there couldn't be anything to spend on clothes, her collars and cuffs starched and laundered, little boots clean even after tripping through the muddy streets round the Marshalsea every afternoon carrying her basket. That basket was a winner in its own right. For a start, it was so big and heavy that a man with any warmth in his heart couldn't stop himself from offering to carry it for her. I've seen two of the most hardened sinners in the place practically fighting each other for the privilege of carrying it up the last flight of stairs. Then when she sat down with Perkins at their share of the long common room table and unpacked it, every eye in the room was on it, like kids at a Punch and Judy show. Every day there'd be two clean handkerchiefs for Perkins (who sniffed a good deal), every other day a clean shirt, once a week a clean pillowcase. I daresay King George himself didn't have better care taken of his linen than Perkins in the Marshalsea. Then, bless you, she'd unfold a snowy white napkin, put it down in front of him and take his dinner out of her basket. By then, you could hear a sound like the sea sucking round rocks when the tide goes out. It was all the other men in the room licking their lips. We got to know the menu by heart. Sundays, for a treat, he got big slices of meat off the joint with potatoes tucked up in newspaper to keep them warm, followed by a slice of apple pie. Mondays was cold cuts and pickle, Tuesdays what was left of the cold cuts done in a curry, Wednesdays a lamb cutlet with a neat little pot of mint sauce. She'd sit opposite watching him eat, not taking a morsel herself then, when he was quite done, pack the plate and knife and fork back in her basket and put his dirty linen that she was taking away for washing on top. Then she'd give him a peck on the cheek – always embarrassed at having to do it in front of a roomful of strangers – and slip away, light as a wisp of hay blowing across the paddock. Talking about her round the fire afterwards on the day that I'd worked out the odds, the three of us agreed she'd thrown herself away when she married Perkins. He'd owned a couple of draper's shops before his problems and it could be that she'd been impressed with seeing his name up over the doors. But he was a poor enough creature in himself, blaming all the world for what had happened to him, bearing grudges.

"He doesn't appreciate what he's got," Watts said.

"Picking the poor woman up like that over a pair of gloves," Natty agreed.

Watching her as we did, we'd all noticed that her hands when she packed up her basket were sporting a neat pair of lilac-coloured gloves. So had Perkins.

"Are those new gloves you've bought?"

She'd coloured up.

"Of course not. I found them in the back of a drawer."

"Practically accusing her of going out buying finery when he was locked up for debt," Natty said.

"Even if she had, what difference would a pair of gloves make?" added Watts.

I noticed that Glue Boy was standing not far away, listening to us. Usually he spent his visits talking to his father but his senior's attention was taken up with a couple of the younger brats. It struck me that when he wasn't blubbing Glue Boy's eyes were better than the rest of him, big and wary like a thoroughbred's, noticing things. When Natty and Watts moved off to their card school I patted the bench beside me, inviting him to sit down. He did but a bit gingerly, as if he expected the bench to be dirty.

"So how d'you rate Mrs Perkins?" I asked him.

"She is the very model of a devoted wife."

I could have burst out laughing. Here was this shaver trying to sound like a gentleman three times his age. His voice was clear and carrying, like a child actor's. Then I noticed him glancing towards Mr Shipham, sitting quietly by the fire.

"Oh-ho, my lad, you're not as green as you're grass-looking," I thought. I lowered my voice and moved closer to him, in spite of the whiff. "She's the reason why Perkins is a furlong or two in front of your father."

He nodded. He'd seen that.

"But the race isn't over till it's won," I told him. "Mr Shipham is fairly impressed with you."

I'm not sure why I told him that, only I enjoy a close finish and it seemed to me the great handicapper had dealt a bit too lightly with Perkins. I could see Glue Boy had taken in what I said. He had the sense not to glance towards Mr Shipham again but later, when it was time for Glue Boy to go, he made a great business of saying goodbye to his father and even, gawd help us, kneeled down on the floor for his blessing. Over-egging it a bit, I thought, but from the thoughtful look on Mr Shipham's face, it had played well.

That was on the Monday evening, with only two clear days to go to the finish, the birthday of Mr Shipham's late dad falling on a Thursday that year. On the Tuesday night, Perkins went and got himself poisoned. We didn't know it was poison at first. All the day visitors had left, including Mr Shipham. The outside doors were locked. Inside, some of us were in bed already and a few, including Watts, Natty and me, were dredging the bottom of the punch-bowl round what was left of the fire. Then the shrieking started, coming from the cubbyhole of a room that Perkins shared with another cove. We all looked at each other. Perkins had been complaining of stomach gripes earlier, but then he was always complaining of something so we didn't take any notice. Then the cove he shared with put his head round the door, yelling that Perkins was dying and to fetch the governor quick. The governor came and had him carried to the sick room. Perkins was groaning and shrieking all the time, face grey, so we had to admit that for once he did have something properly wrong with him.

"Twisted gut," Natty said. "A cousin of mine died from it."

"Gallstones," said Watts.

Geranium, who'd been woken up by the noise and reckoned he knew about medicine, said it was a burst appendix. It wasn't worth making a book on it and just as well because by the time the outside doors were unlocked in the morning, all bets would have been off. The word had spread round the Marshalsea that Perkins was dead of rat poison. Now, being hundreds of years old, the Marshalsea's got more than its fair quota of rats, so rat poison's more common than sugar here. Every now and then, some poor blighter who can't settle himself philosophically to being locked up decides to take a few mouthfuls of it as the quickest way out. So if the prison doctor said it was rat poison, rat poison it was, leaving open only the question of how it got inside Perkins.

"For a start, he didn't know he was taking it," Natty said.

No argument about that. A man with a good chance of being out with all his debts paid in two days and a loving little wife waiting for him isn't going to take the boneyard exit of his own free will. Our common room had filled with visitors from outside plus debtors from other floors who wanted to know all about it. No sign of Mr Shipham. The word was that he was closeted with the governor, quite distressed.

"They'll have to send somebody to let his wife know," Watts said.

"That's being seen to," said somebody from the ground floor. "Can't have her tripping in this afternoon with her basket as usual and finding him in his coffin."

Natty took his pipe out of his mouth and gave the man an old-fashioned look.

"How come you lot on the ground floor know about the basket, then?"

Several people spoke at once, saying much the same thing – everyone in the whole Marshalsea knew about Mrs Perkins and the daily visit with her old man's dinner. Truth is, not a lot happens here and we gossip like farm wives on market day. You could feel the atmosphere change. Natty's question, and his tone of voice, had brought into the open the question we were all asking ourselves. If somebody nobbles one of the favourites, who gains?

"Got to be one on your list, hasn't it?" Watts said.

Murmurs of agreement from all round. They all knew the odds and most of them had got bets on.

"Not necessarily," I said. "It doesn't have to be one of the favourites. It could be anybody who thought he was in with a chance."

There was no point in pretending that Perkins' death had nothing to do with the Marshalsea Handicap so we didn't try.

"You wouldn't risk getting your neck stretched if you were only an outside chance," somebody objected.

"That's the whole point about debtors," Watts said. "We always think the outside chance is going to come up."

Couldn't have put it better myself. I looked round, wondering if any of the favourites was listening. None that I could see. Geranium had taken himself off somewhere and Dickens had shut himself in his own room with his wife and young brats. Only I noticed his lad Glue Boy standing on the edge of our group, taking in every word.

"Look at it logically, though," Natty said. "Biggest chance, biggest motive. It makes sense to start with the favourites. Then you ask yourself, who out of them had the best chance of feeding him rat poison without anybody knowing."

"You'd slip it in his dinner," said the man from the ground floor.

Which was true enough, only our little group didn't like it or the way he said it. It meant that he was putting suspicion fair and square on our top-storey-but-one common room.

We were the ones with the opportunity. I pointed out that it
didn't need to be in his dinner, he could have been given
something with poison in it by anyone, any time of the day.
But the argument didn't stand up for long. Rat poison acts
pretty quickly and Perkins was a creature of routine. He'd
eaten his dinner, drunk a glass of water with it and nothing
else. So it had to be in the dinner and if you accepted that our
common room had the best opportunity, well . . .

"It puts Geranium and Dickens right in the frame," said
the man from the ground floor.

My eyes went to Glue Boy. His whole body flinched and
for a moment his eyes screwed up tight as if he wanted to shut
out everything. Next second, they were wide open again, as if
his life depended on taking in every detail of the scene. He
said nothing. I don't think the man from the ground floor had
intended any harm to him, he just didn't know who the lad
was. But there wasn't time to think any more about Glue
Boy, because a new voice spoke up. A slow, preachy kind of
voice.

"If *in the frame* means under greatest suspicion . . ."

Several impatient voices assured him that it did. It was
Holy Joe, the clergyman. Until then, I hadn't known he was
in the room. He was sitting on a bench, some way apart from
the group. A balding, egg-shaped man, very satisfied with
himself in spite of where he'd landed up.

"Then the argument is proceeding on a false premise.
There would have been ample opportunity for a person from
another floor to have introduced a noxious substance into the
unfortunate man's repast."

"How?"

We all spoke at once. He'd probably never caught a
congregation's attention from the pulpit the way he held
ours and you could see him enjoying it.

"The fact of the matter is that Mrs Perkins left the basket
containing her husband's dinner on the landing of the floor
below for some time yesterday when she was paying a visit to
me in our common room."

Noises of incredulity all round. The idea of Mrs Perkins

bothering with Holy Joe when there were plenty of other men in the place to talk to didn't please anybody. Watts expressed the general feeling.

"Why the hell would she want to visit you?"

Holy Joe glared at him.

"Because, unlike some people, Mrs Perkins has a proper Christian spirit. In spite of her adversities, she came to make a small contribution to my Bible fund."

That silenced us for a while. Against all the odds, Holy Joe still cherished this mad scheme of putting Bibles in beer houses. He'd tried to get most of us to stump up for it, with as much chance of success as running a three-legged donkey in the Gold Cup.

"How much?" somebody asked.

"A shilling. Not a great deal, perhaps, but you know the parable of the widow's mite . . ."

"She wasn't a widow then," somebody said.

We were worried that Holy Joe was going to start preaching at us.

"Was she with you long?" I said.

"Ten minutes or more. She asked me about my work and we prayed together."

"And the basket was out on the landing all the time?"

"Yes, indeed. I accompanied her out to the landing and carried it upstairs for her, as far as this landing."

Then, probably judging that he'd made his dramatic effect, he got up and left. Natty, Watts and I moved away from the rest of the group and formed a huddle in the corner to talk it over.

"If he's right, anybody had time to do it," Watts said. "Whoever it is notices her basket on the landing, nips down to the basement for the nearest dish of rat poison and sprinkles it over Perkins' dinner while she's in there praying."

"If he is right," Natty said. "But why make such a point of telling us?"

"Well, it puts suspicion away from him for a start," said

Watts. "He couldn't be inside praying with her and outside with the rat poison at the same time."

"But he's admitted to carrying the basket upstairs for her. He could have put it in then."

"Twenty stairs or so and her walking just in front of him? Don't be daft."

"You're both of you missing the point," I said. "It's not who his story puts suspicion away from, it's who it puts it onto."

Silence for a while as they thought about it.

"The Inventor?" Natty said.

"Yes, he's on the same floor as Holy Joe and they can't stand each other."

The Inventor was a bit of a free-thinker, though he'd been keeping that quiet when Mr Shipham was around so as not to spoil his chances. Men from the floor below were fed up with arguments between him and Holy Joe about miracles.

"So he's implying that the Inventor had a good chance of seeing the basket there on the landing?" Natty said.

"Well, it might be true, mightn't it, even if it is Holy Joe that says so," Watts said. "If it is, then we have to add another one to the list. It's Geranium, or Dickens, or the Inventor."

Watts had spoken quite loudly, certainly loudly enough to reach the ears of Glue Boy who, just by chance, had moved over to look out of the window near us when we started our discussion. I'd noticed, but the other two hadn't. What's more, Glue Boy had noticed that I'd noticed.

I went over, casual like, and stood beside him at the window.

"Taking the day off from the factory, are you?"

He gave me an unfriendly look, too big for a child-sized face.

"They're saying my father killed Perkins?"

"Well, somebody killed him," I said.

"It wasn't my father."

"How do you know? You weren't here last night."

He coloured up.

"I had business somewhere else."

Business, gawd help us. It was this solemnity of his that made me tougher with him than I might have been with an ordinary twelve-year-old brat. If he wanted to play the grown-up, he could have it.

"Just as well, then," I said. "At least nobody could say you slipped the poison in his curry."

I was watching him, wondering whether he was going to take a swing at me or burst into tears. A boy that age could do either. He did neither.

"Curry, yes." He said it quite coolly. "Tuesday night, so it was curry."

He stared at me, and the eyes that met mine weren't a child's. He'd understood something that Natty, Watts and all the rest of them had missed.

"That's the size of it," I said. "Always curry on Tuesdays. Nothing better for hiding the taste of rat poison."

"But not everyone would know that," he said. "They all knew about her bringing him dinner every day, but they wouldn't know what it was."

"Not unless they were in the same room with him when he ate his dinner," I said.

"And you're saying it brings it back to my father or the geranium man?"

"I'm not saying anything," I said.

He looked away.

"You haven't asked me where I was last night," he said.

"I'm not one to pry into a gentleman's private affairs."

"I was at Astley's."

I laughed. "Nothing like the circus for taking your mind off your troubles."

Astley's Amphitheatre in Lambeth, not far upriver. No blame to the lad if he took a night off from attending on dad in the Marshalsea to watch clowns and Cossack riders. But something in the way he said it suggested there was more to it than that.

"A boy from the postroom where I work knows a back way in."

"So you can get in without the formality of passing the pay office? Don't worry, we knew the back way in when I was your age."

"We managed to get to the front of the side part of the gallery. You can see the people in the expensive seats from there."

"Well?"

"I noticed a particular couple because they came in late, halfway through the evening. The woman turned round once or twice and I could see her face quite clearly. She was wearing an Indian shawl and a bonnet with blue and purple feathers."

"Very tasteful, I'm sure."

"The man with her was big and broad shouldered, with black hair, side whiskers and a moustache. When the clowns were on, he had the loudest laugh of all. You could hear it over all the others, like a donkey braying. He had his arm round her most of the time."

He paused and looked at me. The next words came out in a rush.

"She had a bag of whelks on her lap. He kept leaning over and taking one. And once she . . . she took a whelk out of the shell for him and held it out to him in her fingers and he took it between his lips, like feeding a parrot."

"You sure it was whelks, not winkles?"

"It might have been winkles," he admitted.

"And you recognized little Mrs Perkins?" I said.

He jumped back, eyes wide.

"How did you know?"

As well as surprise, there was annoyance at having his story spoiled. I glanced round and signalled to him to keep his voice down.

"I didn't know about Astley's but I guessed there was something going on," I said.

"How?"

He didn't believe me.

"The gloves. You were there that evening. You should have noticed too, since you're so sharp-eyed."

"I did notice. He picked her up about her gloves. Everybody heard."

"That's right. The gloves she said she'd found in the back of a drawer. He didn't say anything at the time, but he knew all right. And she knew she'd given herself away."

"But why shouldn't she have found them in the back of a drawer?"

"You're forgetting what Perkins did for a living before he came in here."

"He was a shopkeeper."

He stared at me as if I weren't playing fair.

"Yes, but what sort of shopkeeper?" I said.

I watched his face as the answer came to him.

"A draper."

"Exactly. A man who'll have been dealing in ladies' gloves six days a week for the past twenty years or so. Do you think he wouldn't be able to tell the difference between a spanking new pair and a pair that had been lying around in the back of a drawer so long he'd forgotten them? He could have done it blindfold by the smell alone. And since he hadn't bought them for her, some other man had or she wouldn't have lied about them."

"And she knew he'd guessed?"

"Yes. So she knew too there'd be hell to pay once he got out of the Marshalsea. That's why she did it."

"And all the time she was talking to the clergyman, her basket was out on the landing with the rat poison already in the curry."

"That's right, prepared by her own loving hands. And she had the cunning to go and get prayed over by Holy Joe so that anybody coming up and down that staircase would come under suspicion and muddy the waters nicely if people started investigating."

"Yes," he said. "I'd worked out that part of it."

Which might even have been true. It sounded like the truth. He said nothing for a while, staring down out of the window.

"You said if people started investigating . . ."

"Which they won't," I said. "What's one debtor, more or less? I daresay they'll go through the motions, but they don't know what we know."

You wouldn't catch me talking to the law and I knew nobody would take any notice of Glue Boy.

"So she'll get away with it?"

"Women usually do," I said.

Watts and Natty were looking in our direction, curious because we'd had our heads together so long.

"But if people think my father did it . . ."

"Don't worry about that. I'll put the word round where it matters."

He blew his cheeks out in a sigh of relief, gone back to being boyish again.

"And what will happen about Mr Shipham and the money?"

"Oh, that." I had inside information again and had intended to hang on to it a bit longer because it hurts me to have to give people their stakes back. Still, he had a right to know.

"That's off, for this year at any rate. He and the governor have decided to declare the race null and void, so the two hundred pounds is going to widows and orphans."

"Oh," he said.

Then he went across to his father's room and that was it.

Not long afterwards his father had a bit of good luck and got out anyway. I didn't expect to set eyes on Glue Boy again, but as it happened I did. It was ten years or so later, Epsom Downs on Derby Day. There he was, walking around with his hat, cane and watch-chain, quite the young dandy. He wasn't taking any notice of the horses, just strolling about looking at people. Then our eyes met and he flinched, as if seeing me had taken him back where he didn't want to go. He recovered quickly. When I reintroduced myself I noticed that the smell coming off him these days was one of Floris's best, with spices and a hint of cedarwood. We talked about the weather and the crowds and didn't mention the Marshalsea. He said he was surprised I'd recognized him from all that time back, only he didn't sound really surprised, as if being recognized was his due. I hardly did, I said, him having turned out so smart. It was the eyes that had it. I'd have recognized them anywhere out of ten thousand.

The Three-legged Cat
of Great Clatterden

Mary Reed and Eric Mayer

John Dickens was able to pay off his debt when he inherited some money following the death of his mother in April 1824. For a while young Charles continued to work at the blacking factory but his father, re-employed by the Admiralty, soon sent his son back to school. Poor health allowed John Dickens to retire on a small pension in January 1825 and he now revealed new skills as a parliamentary reporter. Income improved and the family moved to neighbouring Somers Town living, for a while, in the same house where Mary Shelley (the author of Frankenstein) *had been born.*

Charles left school in 1827 and worked as an office boy at one firm of solicitors and then as a clerk at another, but it was not long before he became a legal reporter, keeping track of events in the old probate courts known collectively as the Doctors' Commons. In March 1832 he followed his father as a parliamentary reporter and, two years later, thanks to his uncle, John Barrow, Dickens secured a job as a political reporter for the Morning Chronicle, *then a close rival to* The Times. *By now Dickens had already sold several short stories, starting with "Dinner at Poplar*

Walk" (Monthly Magazine, *December 1833). This, and others, all appeared anonymously, but proved popular and in order to stake an identity Dickens adopted the alias "Boz" in August 1834. The "sketches" were subsequently collected together as Dickens's first book,* Sketches by Boz, *published in February 1836.*

Soon after, Dickens began work on The Posthumous Papers of the Pickwick Club, *which was issued in monthly parts from April 1836. Reception of the book was cool to begin with, because Dickens was limited to writing episodes around sporting pictures by Robert Seymour, but after Seymour's suicide Dickens had a free hand and the series took off. By its conclusion in November 1837 each monthly instalment was selling 40,000 copies. Dickens was famous.*

The Pickwick Papers *follows the various adventures of members of the Pickwick Club in their sporting and romantic entanglements. Pickwick is often called in to help resolve some romantic problem or another, and that's no different in the following story, a hitherto unreported adventure of the Pickwickians.*

Mary Reed and Eric Mayer are best known for their series featuring John the Eunuch, set at the time of the Emperor Justinian. The series began with One for Sorrow *in 1999 and has now reached* Six for Gold *(2005) with more in the works.*

In Which The Intrepid Mr Pickwick and Mr Tupman Journey To Kent, View An Unusual Antiquity, And Assist Mr Stephen Rooksbee Of That Parish In Solving A Mystery

S amuel Pickwick's merry eyes twinkled behind his moon-shaped spectacles as he applied the great engine of his intellect to deciphering the words spilling in an anguished and passionate torrent from the lips of his rotund friend Tracy Tupman.

As ever, it was a matter to do with one of the fair sex, a preoccupation with whom being both the susceptible Mr Tupman's glory and his bane.

"You say she went to visit her aunt and ran afoul of a three-legged cat," said Mr Pickwick. "Does this ferocious feline belong to the aunt?"

"It's not that sort of cat!" Mr Tupman drew from the pocket of his waistcoat a linen handkerchief, with which he proceeded to mop his brow. The Goswell Street rooms occupied by his companion had grown exceedingly warm, the heat of midsummer being augmented by both the fiery passions of Mr Tupman and the workings of Mr Pickwick's gigantic intellect. "It's a hill figure such as the White Horse of Uffington," he went on.

"Enormous depictions that can be seen for miles? Made by the lifting off the turf to exposure the chalky soil below? They can be thousands of years old!" remarked the learned Mr Pickwick, who could have added considerably more to his description.

"That's so. This one's known as the Three-legged Cat of Great Clatterden. I stayed in the village inn on my journey and told its proprietor I'd bring my learned colleague – you, Mr Pickwick – to investigate this interesting antiquity. But all such thoughts were driven out of my mind when I arose the next morning to find the innkeeper's sister was gone. He told me she'd left to visit her aunt, but then word came on the next coach that she had never arrived. It greatly pains me to think of the tender words his sister and I had exchanged only the day before."

"Try not to distress yourself, my dear Tupman," Mr Pickwick replied. "I admit the hill figure is of enormous scientific interest, but what makes you suppose this cat is involved in her disappearance?"

"Because of what the boy told me. A mercenary little ruffian who answers to the name of Herbie. He seemed to reside in the stable, and was forever wanting to clean my boots or carry my portmanteau or escort me on a tour of the village – which consists of a single street, mark you – and all for a price. Naturally I declined his offer. He had the sort of face suggesting a character that will inevitably lead him to wear a hemp rope for a cravat."

Mr Pickwick tut-tutted at this sad intelligence, and then interjected several sagacious observations concerning the wisdom of frugality, the recounting of which would turn this simple tale into a philosophical treatise, and finally asked his distraught friend to provide as much detail as possible concerning the mysterious event.

"I suspect the boy overheard what passed between myself and the innkeeper," Mr Tupman said. "When I rushed out to catch the London coach, the boy was lounging at the door smirking at me. Naturally I demanded what it was he found so humorous, considering the dire circumstances. He remained silent. 'Has the cat got your tongue?' I remonstrated."

" 'It's not my tongue the cat's got,' he replied. 'It's her tongue, and all the rest of her besides. It must be. Because last night, just when that big fat moon was scratching its belly on the tops of the pine trees, I seen her climbing the hillside all by herself, climbing up to the field where that three-legged cat was lying in wait.' "

Around the gently curving road across undulating countryside the commercial chariot thundered on, the sound of its rumbling wheels punctuated by sharp cracks of the whip. By the time it came to a halt at the inn door, the elderly proprietor was waiting on the step.

Readers, had we been the skylarks about whom Mr Shelley has written so tenderly, and were we wheeling over ripening corn or meadows dotted with placid cows, and in addition were such birds blessed with the power of speech accorded to mankind, we might have formed an avian chorus to announce the coach with as deep a chorus of joy as sang in the bosom of Stephen Rooksbee, landlord of the Trout and Basket Inn, for he knew heat and summer dust worked up a thirst in horse and traveler alike, and he stood ready to slake both.

In a fashion reminiscent of an eager collie, albeit one

grizzled and somewhat rheumatic in the hind legs, Mr Rooksbee herded the new arrivals inside his hostelry. He smiled and nodded at each guest. But did a cloud pass across his face as the two esteemed gentlemen from the Pickwick Club descended from the coach? Surely not, for when had the jolly countenance of Mr Pickwick presaged anything but fair weather?

Mr Rooksbee settled his charges in the bar parlor, a low-beamed room filled by the comforts of settles, round tables, a wide fireplace, and not least, after a long coach journey, the comfort of not being constantly jostled by ruts in the road.

Mr Rooksbee approached the table where sat his visitors from London. "'tis a pleasure to see you again, Mr Tupman," he remarked in a sorrowful tone which revealed to the sensitive perceptions of Mr Pickwick something of the anguish the old man had succeeded in concealing from his less discerning guests. "And your friend . . . certainly it is not that scientific gentleman you told me about?"

"Certainly it is," replied Mr Tupman. "You see before you none other than Mr Samuel Pickwick, an observer of human nature, a scholar of vast knowledge, a living compendium of the most interesting and astonishing facts, and just the man to unravel the mystery of what has befallen your dear sister Alice."

At this Mr Rooksbee took heart and brightened somewhat. "Then he's only come to look for Alice?"

"I know you told me not to trouble myself with the matter," Mr Tupman continued, "but how could a man in whose chest there yet beats a heart abandon a maid so fair? There is no further news of your sister?"

"'Fraid not, sir. I'm fair flummoxed, and that's a fact. We've looked everywhere, we have. I've even had the boy searching around the village and the fields and the hills. Yes, even the hill at the back of my inn, which is too much of a climb to ask of refined gentlemen such as yourselves and especially in this weather. Nor would the thorns respect your tights, sirs."

Mr Pickwick thanked him for his consideration.

"And is Herbie back yet?" inquired Mr Tupman, his hand moving protectively toward the pocket where he kept his purse.

"I haven't seen him since this morning," replied Mr Rooksbee. "He must still be out searching, but if you need your boots polished or any small service of that sort, I'm sure he'll be back soon. Now, if you two gentleman will be staying the night, I suspect I'll be able to find a chop or two for dinner, along with some vegetables and how about a nice bit of goat's milk cheese? I'll have my girl bring you something to eat right away."

The innkeeper bustled off, not neglecting to take orders from his other guests on his way to the kitchen.

"It's most inconvenient the boy not being here, but we must bear it as best we can," remarked Mr Pickwick.

"Yes, indeed. When we see him we can question him further about seeing Alice walking up toward the cat."

"Really I was thinking about how dusty my boots were," said Mr Pickwick, his keen eyes taking in every detail of the crowded room. A man so versed in the wonders of nature could not help but notice how the walls were partially concealed by – for one could not honestly say decorated with – badly executed watercolors depicting horses the like of which were never seen in equine circles, along with formless blobs – perhaps tittlebats, perhaps weasels – and sundry other portraits whose originals, if these were faithfully rendered, would have populated the dreams of anyone unfortunate to see them in the flesh.

"It would be better if they had a painting of the three-legged cat figure, don't you think?"

The speaker was a youngish man seated at the table nearest the corner where the Pickwickians were ensconced. His hair and coat were black, his nose was a sharp point, and he was as thin as a scrivener's pen. He introduced himself as Edward Clarke, tutor to the son of a minor member of the nobility.

"Why do you say that, sir?" wondered Mr Pickwick.

"Because most of our fellow guests are here to see the cat. It's quite the local attraction, particularly among the unlearned and superstitious."

"You are familiar with Great Clatterden?" Mr Pickwick asked.

Mr Clarke admitted that he passed through the village now and then.

The astute Mr Pickwick would not have neglected to inquire further except that they were interrupted by the arrival of the sizzling chops.

It is the sad task of the writers to report that the chops were a disappointment and the vegetables watery and few, although the serving girl, dressed in a shapeless black garment topped with a sacking apron and who could not have brightened more than twenty summers, caught Mr Tupman's romantic eye, even though his heart remained the captive of one who was sadly absent.

The cheese however was excellent and our two adventurers did it full justice. As the parlor began to empty, Mr Tupman leaned forward and whispered to Mr Pickwick, "I am sure you have noticed we were not the only diners to find our victuals lacking. Not a soul has finished his meal."

Mr Pickwick immediately saw that this was true of their neighbor the tutor, who stood up, leaving a small side dish untouched.

The tutor noticed the direction of the learned man's sharp, inquisitive gaze. "That's what they call the cat's bit," he explained. "Nearly everyone buys a bit for the cat. Supposed to be good luck. Certainly it's good luck for those who will eat it when we're gone. There's no end to the tales . . . but I need to be off. When he heard I would be passing through Great Clatterden my employer insisted I toss a penny to the cat as the moon rises. It's reputed to have quite a different effect than pouring a libation at dawn. All humbug, of course. Comes from a lack of education."

As Mr Clarke left, the serving girl returned. She had enlivened her dark outfit by the device of a red kerchief around her neck and simpered as she poured cider from a large stone jug.

"Are you fine gentlemen here for the scouring?" she asked. "'Tis Midsummer's Day tomorrow. Everyone helps to clean our hill figure, you know, pull up any weeds that's sprouted on it. There's a meal afterwards, with a bonfire and dancing far into the night." The saucy lass accompanied this pronouncement with a look at Mr Tupman which caused the poor man's cheeks and every last one of his chins to turn red.

"Alas, if only I had two of those noble organs which pulsate in our breasts," he murmured apologetically.

The serving girl narrowed her eyes. "I seen you talking with Alice, sir. A sly old fox, she is. Her brother keeps a sharp eye out for Cupid and shows him the door the moment he turns up. But young hearts and old ones will find a way. Alice is spoken for." She turned on her heel and departed.

"What did she mean by saying Alice is spoken for?" Mr Tupman expostulated. "I had the impression the dear lady had never known romance in her life. But women, Mr Pickwick, can be very jealous creatures."

Mr Pickwick beamed benignly. "My dear sir, do you suppose I haven't been searching for the dear lady ever since you brought your problem to me? My mind covers the ground faster than my feet could accomplish. Now I intend to continue my urgent work by inviting our host to sit with us for a pipe of tobacco and an hour of conversation."

And having gained Mr Rooksbee's attention that is exactly what he proceeded to do. Ever tactful and mindful of the terrible strain the innkeeper was bearing with the stoicism of his class, Mr Pickwick first steered the conversation to everyday topics such as the unusual warmth of the summer, the virtues of Kentish cider, the watercolours on the walls.

Mr Rooksbee puffed out a cloud of smoke. "The former owner were powerful fond of drawing and painting, he were, and I have left them up due to sentimentality and cracks in the plaster. Sentimentality, sirs, is a curse, and without naming names, there are those whose love is not returned by the object of their affections who might best turn their attention elsewhere."

Having ascertained that Mr Rooksbee had entered a reflective state of mind, Mr Pickwick took out his notebook and invited their host to enlarge their stock of information about the strange cat.

"Well, you may laugh, gentlemen, but that there cat is responsible for half the matches in Kent, for 'tis widely known if a couple walk round it, 'tis as binding as a tenancy paper, and they will marry within the year."

Mr Tupman paled and his chins sank into his cravat. "Is that so?" he quavered.

"Why, certainly, sir. Spinsters visit from miles around to trap a man, and the vicar, he do have queues of couples waiting to be wed most weekends. Every man in the county knows the dangers of that cat."

After some encouragement, Mr Rooksbee went on relating local cat lore. Suddenly he stopped and tipped his head one side. He had risen to his feet in as near an approximation of a leap as his creaking bones would allow before Mr Pickwick was aware of a sound like distant thunder. By the time he identified the sound as that of a coach, Mr Rooksbee had hobbled to the parlour door.

"'Tis the late coach," he exclaimed. The prospect of new customers had kindled a warm glow of friendly greeting in his watery eyes. On this evening, however, the innkeeper was destined for disappointment. Upon throwing open the door of the Trout and Basket he was confronted only by the boy Herbie, who stuck a note into his hand.

"'Ere, Mr Rooksbee. Coach driver left this. Said it's from Miss Alice's old aunt." Having discharged his mission, Herbie screwed up his face at Mr Pickwick, directed a malignant glare at Mr Tupman, and raced off into the night.

The moment the innkeeper read the paper the glow in his eyes went out. He swayed from side to side and began to moan.

The kindly Mr Pickwick rushed to the stricken man's side. "Whatever is the matter, my friend?"

"It's Alice. She's disappeared."

"Yes, yes, we know," said Mr Pickwick, recognizing at once a case of incipient hysteria. "Is there further word then? Nothing terrible has happened?"

Mr Rooksbee shook his head. "No. Her aunt . . . she is just . . . reminding me . . . that she's still . . . missing . . . Ah, my good Mr Pickwick, if you are the wise man your friend makes you out to be you will surely find my sister. You and Mr Tupman must go to Dover at once and look into the matter."

Mr Pickwick assured him firmly that he had nothing to fear and that the missing Alice would soon return to hearth and home.

Mark well, readers, that while a lesser intellect might have attempted to unravel the problem of the woman's disappearance by asking directly after her, Mr Pickwick's more subtle powers of reasoning had revealed to him a better way.

"Don't you see, Mr Rooksbee?" he went on. "The answer lies not with your Alice but with the three-legged cat of Great Clatterden. Once we learn what it has to tell us, we will discover what has become of your sister."

This statement of good intentions elicited from the old innkeeper a howl of despair which only confirmed Mr Pickwick's diagnosis of hysteria.

"Quickly, Mr Tupman," he said, "administer a good dose of cider. Then we are off to bed. There's no point confronting a crisis without a proper night's rest."

"I venture to suggest that the custom we have been hearing about is a clear survival of pagan sacrifice, which is to say offering coins to the cat rather than . . . anything else," Mr Pickwick remarked in an undertone to Mr Tupman as they took a candle set in a precarious wax bed on a saucer and retired to the attic room they had been assigned.

Mr Rooksbee, having been sufficiently sedated by liquid comfort, had been placed in the care of the red kerchiefed serving girl, who sighed and fluttered her eyelids in such a way as to clearly indicate that although the innkeeper might have reason to mourn the absence of his sister, if he chose, Mr Tupman would not.

"It's all very well to say the cat holds the answer to Alice's disappearance," observed Mr Tupman, "but I should think her brother, who claims to have put her on the coach, might know something more as well. Do you suppose Alice came down the hill once she went up? And did you see the way that odious boy looked at us and then ran off? Might he be avoiding us? Does he know more than he told me?"

"Try to remember, Mr Tupman," Mr Pickwick assured him, "that the cat at least can be depended upon to tell us the truth, unlike the people here. I regret to say each and every one of them may be a suspect, for what that chalky feline reveals to us comes from our own close examinations of it and not by way of its own lips."

Mr Tupman let out a mournful sigh, the mention of cat's lips having reminded him of Alice's lips and the sweet words which had emerged from them.

Their room faced the hill behind the Trout and Basket and the two travellers had an excellent view of the famous wonder of Great Clatterden. It was a fine, clear night, a huge moon flooding the landscape with bone-coloured light, outlining every blade of grass and bush and throwing into sharp relief the monstrous shape of a cat carved in the side of the hill.

Mr Pickwick looked out, entranced, for several minutes and then produced his ever present notebook. "Now, Mr Tupman, would you take that figure to be a domestic cat or a leopard or similar wild beast?"

"I would take it to be a crow with an extra leg. Or a cow, or possibly a rather emaciated hedgehog," replied Mr Tupman in a distracted tone. "But as we are informed it is a cat – and I can quite definitely make out an ear or two – I should call it a domestic grimalkin."

"A fine example of observational prowess, sir," Mr Pickwick remarked. "Let me note that down immediately. Do you see also how its tail is curled, posing a perfect likeness to a question mark, and one might say almost serving as a message to seekers after knowledge?"

"Which end is the tail?"

Mr Tupman's gloomy voice drew his friend's attention away from the hillside feline. "You're looking unwell, Mr Tupman," he observed. "Dinner disagree with you?"

The other denied it. "It's just . . . well . . . I have promised to marry the innkeeper's sister."

"My dear sir! Congratulations are in order! But now of course with this tragic—"

"I fear you misunderstand," his friend groaned. "The engagement came about in an unintended fashion. I knew nothing of Cupid's connection with the cat until the innkeeper mentioned it tonight. Before I left, Alice and I strolled right around the monstrous feline!"

Mr Pickwick offered such comfort to his distraught companion as he could, and then retired with his head a whirl of the romantic legends related by their host, including how the figure represented a monstrous cat, companion to a local giant, both of whom preyed on travellers until a passing knight vanquished them by force of arms, and the local belief that if a rustic and his wife reclined upon the cat and bathed in the light of the full moon they would be blessed with a large family. Indeed, he blushed to wonder if the unpleasant little Herbie had been the result of such an unnatural, not to mention uncomfortable, conception.

Yet while Mr Pickwick's slumber was haunted by a monstrous cat chasing him with lethal intent – not to mention accompanied by several other creatures whose portraits adorned the walls of the inn, their shape and menacing aspect suggesting both river rats and wild boars – these nightmares causing him to wake with a yell and disturb the innocent slumbers of Mr Tupman and others sheltered under the roof of the Trout and Basket Inn, we cannot in all honesty deny, dear readers, that in this singular circumstance the goat's milk cheese was entirely blameless.

The Pickwickians were awakened at dawn by the joyous songs of Great Clatterden's countless winged inhabitants who, not being informed of the identity of the gargantuan hillside predator, sworn enemy of their avian race, did not recognize it as anything they should fear.

Mr Tupman gloomily remarked he and Mr Pickwick would at least have an early start on climbing the hill to inspect the figure, adding he hoped to develop a few blisters as such pain in his feet might distract him from the agony in his bosom.

Indeed, to the common mind, it may have appeared the way to inspect a cat is to look at the cat, but Mr Pickwick, that great man, immediately saw a better method. For, as he explained as he and Mr Tupman trudged up the dusty road, in these rustic villages the fount of all knowledge is the vicar.

So it was they presently found themselves in the untidy, book-lined study of the Reverend Clarence Clopton, a gnarled old oak of a man whose hoary head swayed and whose knobby hands waved in the winds of disputation as he challenged every detail of the legends vouchsafed by the innkeeper.

"I fear you were misled, sirs," Mr Clopton said, taking another sip of port. "Mr Rooksbee is known for his, I will not say falsehoods, but rather over-fertile imagination. It runs in the family, sirs. Why, only last year he accused my curate, Mr Philpot, of paying unwanted attentions to Miss Alice. Naturally, I interviewed the man, and was assured all that transpired between them was he wished her a pleasant good morning whenever he saw her."

Mr Pickwick remarked this seemed perfectly reasonable and polite, a charming demonstration that courtesy was not lacking in bucolic surroundings.

"Quite so," replied Mr Clopton. "And I may say I believe him, since Mr Philpot has a good character despite a sad tendency to placing small wagers with my parishioners, though he is endeavoring to overcome that defect."

The vicar's tone grew confidential. "In fact, although we must be charitable, it is Mr Rooksbee, one of the more difficult of my flock, about whom I worry. It is true he provides a home to his sister, although he expects her to work long hours among travellers not always of the best upbringing, begging your pardon and present company excepted, in return for nothing but board and bread. It's my opinion that's why he's kept such a close eye on her all these years. Doesn't want to lose her help, you see, being as close with his pennies as a Kentish oyster."

Mr Tupman dabbed at his eyes, almost overcome by emotion at the thought of the fair Alice being relegated to a life of lonely drudgery. Mr Pickwick kindly changed the subject. "What then is the truth about the hill figure?" he asked.

"I must look out a paper I wrote some time ago, Mr Pickwick. The Antiquarian Society received it with most flattering interest. I was able to place the figure's age precisely at between 2,000 and 30 years – the latter being the number of years since I arrived here to take up my position and first saw the cat with my own eyes. I am told the former proprietor of the Trout and Basket made certain that the figure was maintained regularly and may have been the first to undertake that task in some time. In fact, I owe not a little of my scholarly reputation to that cat."

"Fascinating, sir, fascinating indeed," Mr Pickwick remarked. "And particularly given you are situated in a less travelled location, where local customs and beliefs too often go unrecorded and are ultimately lost to the scholar."

Mr Clopton sighed. "You are quite right, sir. Now, I admit we may not be as well known as Dover or Canterbury, but for the antiquarian we have much of interest. For example, we're not far from that deep valley which I regret to say my parishioners still refer to as the Devil's Kneading Trough. Young villagers often gather there on summer nights, and I may add it is my firm conviction they don't go up there seeking to view the sea."

Mr Pickwick observed that to a man of the cloth such as Mr Clopton such behaviour must be upsetting.

The vicar paused for a moment. "Yes, of course, though not compared to the fact we're still fighting the remnants of heathen customs," he admitted. "My predecessor spent twenty years persuading the villagers to abandon erecting a maypole, and before his time it is said they were still in the habit of casting small animals into the midsummer bonfire. Of course, I have no direct knowledge of that."

"As a hard-headed man of science such as myself, I understand you must confine your speculations to verifiable facts," said Mr Pickwick. "However, for reasons I shall not delve into at this time, I am also interested in legends surrounding this wonderful cat figure."

The vicar's chuckle sounded like the rustle of autumnal leaves. "Stuff and nonsense, all of them! Consider the naive belief it serves as a sort of feline cupid. Why, as a scientific experiment, I myself have escorted more than one young lady to view it, and remain a bachelor to this day!"

Mr Tupman was heard to mutter comments casting aspersions upon the honour of a certain churchman.

"Yet even these superstitions can bring about good, sirs," Mr Clopton – fortunately being hard of hearing and therefore unable to take up Mr Tupman's grievances – continued. "The villagers do quite well catering to visitors who want to walk up there. Take Paynter, the village cobbler and harness maker. Does a roaring trade in stout shoes, if you will believe it, once the curious hear about the titled lady who insisted on climbing the hill in dainty slippers more suited for dancing, slipped, broke her leg, and could not attend a ball for six months. You can be certain that's one of the first things they hear about at the inn."

He paused. "Yet I cannot blame my flock, for these humble services they perform, not to mention the little boys earning an honest penny by taking visitors up the hill to tell them the legends in situ, has helped my parishioners buy comforts they might have otherwise lacked. Indeed, one might say that not only does the cat look out over Great Clatterden from its lofty elevation, but that it looks out for the local residents as well."

"I suspect a considerable number of travellers come to see the cat?" asked Mr Pickwick.

"More pass through here in a month than actually live here," confirmed the vicar.

"Among these strangers, have you noticed any who might, shall we say, have given the impression they were here for some devious purpose?"

Mr Clopton shook his head. "I can't say I have personally, Mr Pickwick, although my curate did mention a man who, so he said, appeared to be paying undue attentions to Miss Alice."

"Not a local man, then?"

"No. A traveller, or so Mr Philpot supposed."

The vicar's two visitors took their leave. They had barely stepped back into the street before Mr Tupman burst out. "Ah, poor Alice! I see it all now. It's that rogue the curate saw with her who's responsible. That explains everything, or would, if we knew who it might be."

Mr Pickwick smiled. "I have an idea about that, but first let us consult the cat."

An hour later the stout figure of Mr Pickwick could have been spotted from the Trout and Basket Inn – where telescopes were available for rental – toiling up the steep hill toward its heights, the still stouter figure of Mr Tupman toiling even more mightily and at an increasing distance behind.

It had turned into another warm day and the pair were happy to finally arrive at their destination and sit down on a stretch of scrubby grass to view, spread out below them, an expanse of rolling meadows amongst which the handful of structures forming Great Clatterden appeared hardly worthy of the prefix of its name. Further up the steep slope behind them, a thick wood murmured in mysterious fashion which, with the somnolent sound of bees busy in the clover and wild flowers forming splashes of colour on the hill, produced a feeling of languor.

However, Mr Pickwick, while resting his legs, refrained from resting his mind, for he could not help but notice below the winding ribbon of the road which should have borne Alice Rooksbee safely to her aunt's house but, for some reason mysteriously related to the cat upon which he now, very nearly, was seated, had not done so. He made notes in a furious manner while Mr Tupman scattered scraps of bread around the grass in a desultory fashion, a sure way to locate a lost love, or so he had been told at the inn.

Finally, Mr Pickwick closed his notebook with a snap,

resettled his glasses on his nose, and climbed to his feet. He began to pace back and forth across the slope, occasionally stopping to peer down at the chalk filled furrows forming the cat's crude outline.

The sun beat down as Mr Pickwick examined the figure and cogitated. He walked between the cat's ears, along its back and down to the tip of its tail, a large perambulating flea in tights, gaiters, and a waistcoat.

Suddenly Mr Pickwick let out a cry of triumph. "Mr Tupman! I have found it!"

"What's that?" exclaimed Mr Tupman, who had fallen into a dreary reverie. "You've found her? Found Alice?"

"Not Alice. The cat's missing leg. Do you note this patch of nettles? I believe the leg must have descended from the body at this exact point but it was allowed to become over-grown. Perhaps someone refused to grasp the nettles last year. Why, this shall only serve to spread the fame of our august society. When I write my paper I shall name it 'The Pickwickian Leg'. What a splendid discovery!"

"Ah, yes," sighed Mr Tupman. "A splendid discovery, but how does it help us find Alice?"

Mr Pickwick was doubtless about to answer when there came from the woods above them a terrible cry of pain, as if the cat had caught a rodent in its merciless jaws.

Before our adventurers could react, the boy Herbie burst from the woods, howling and holding his ear. He raced past the pair and vanished downhill as the stick-thin figure of the tutor with whom Mr Pickwick had spoken the previous evening strolled out of the thicket whence the boy had come.

"Caught the little beggar collecting good luck coins tossed to the cat," he explained. "Tried to get away, but I caught him and gave him a good boxing around the ears. First principle of education. Box around the ears helps open the mind. And what are you doing up here, Pickwick? Come up to see the humbug for yourself, have you? If it's a cat, I'm a goose!"

"Care to elucidate, sir?" Mr Pickwick queried.

"Don't tell me you haven't noticed a certain similarity

between this . . . whatever it is . . . and all those paintings of
. . . whatever they are . . . adorning the walls of the inn?"

Having made this mysterious observation, the tutor sauntered off towards the village.

"What a puzzling remark," Mr Tupman observed. "What
could he mean?"

"Perhaps that the former owner of the inn was inspired by
this ancient work to create his own artistic if primitive
interpretations? What interests me more is what he was
doing up here, or in fact, what he is doing in Great Clatterden
at all. Perhaps it is time for us to seek out the boy Herbie."

An account of the doughty Pickwickians' journey back
down the rugged hill and their stoicism in the face of gorse,
brambles and rocks would make an adventure in itself.
Suffice it to say, when they had regained the level ground,
at great cost to Mr Pickwick's tights, they went immediately
to the inn's stables. Entering them as stealthily as possible,
despite Mr Tupman's laboured breathing and Mr Pickwick's decided limp they surprised the aforementioned
Herbie poking at a pile of straw in a shadowy corner of
an empty stall. Startled, he whirled around and attempted
to bolt past them but Mr Pickwick grabbed him by the arm.
Although, dear readers, truth to tell, the two gentlemen
standing side by side left very little room for passage
between or around them.

"Young man, we wish to have a word with you," said Mr
Pickwick sternly. "You told Mr Tupman you saw Miss Alice
going up the hill alone. Are you certain she was alone?"

Herbie glared his captor and tried, unsuccessfully, to free
his arm.

"Is it possible you did not also see, let us say, a thin man
dressed in black?" persisted Mr Pickwick.

"No, sir. Just Alice, all by herself," came the reply.

"And did you see her come down again?"

"No, I didn't," the lad admitted.

Mr Tupman gasped. "She never came down! Mr Pickwick, this means she cannot have got on the coach and in turn

explains why her brother has been acting in such a strange manner."

"Please don't leap to conclusions, my friend," said Mr Pickwick calmly. "Now, Herbie, what were you doing up there today?"

The boy narrowed his eyes. "I were checking to see whether anyone'd left any coins for the cat. Just checking, see? Wanted to get there before anyone else went to do the same, like."

Mr Pickwick looked thoughtful. Few men would have noticed the way Herbie's gaze slid to the pile of straw in the corner, but Mr Pickwick, that great man, that close observer of humanity, made note of the fact. "What were you hiding in the straw?" he asked. "Mr Tupman, if you would be so good . . .?"

His friend bent with difficulty and when he straightened up, with still more difficulty, he held a large carving knife in his trembling hand.

Now some may suppose a rustic boy can find any number of innocent uses for such an implement, but Mr Pickwick could see the truth of the matter and perhaps Herbie saw Mr Pickwick saw the truth of the matter, which would explain why he blurted out his explanation. "I was just sharpening it, sir, ready like. I'm hoping to find a chicken for the festivities tonight."

Mr Pickwick nodded, gave him a penny, and dismissed him to his duties.

"How terrible to see such an intent in one so young," cried Mr Tupman when they were alone again. "He was going to kill a chicken to roast over that bonfire the serving girl mentioned. But surely he would have to steal the bird?"

"I fear it is far worse than that, Mr Tupman, but his admission is the last piece of the puzzle. I am happy to announce I have constructed a theory to account for the disappearance of Alice."

"Does it have anything to do with the tutor? His continued presence here seems highly suspicious. Why isn't he at home teaching his charge instead of lurking about in woods?" said

Mr Tupman. "On the other hand, that obnoxious boy is always underfoot. With a knife, we now learn. It would not surprise me to learn he might well be up to no good. And the serving girl . . . she didn't seem to like Alice, did she? Not to mention Mr Rooksbee has been acting in a most peculiar manner, although I suppose that is understandable in the circumstances. Or do you suppose the vicar is hiding some pertinent fact?"

Mr Pickwick could not but help suppress a smile as he listened to his friend's innocent musings, but then his expression turned dark, or as dark as was possible for that good-natured gentleman.

"I regret to tell you my theory is nothing to do with any of that," he replied. "It is to do with human nature, but I fear nature of an inhuman nature."

Ticking off points on his plump fingers as he explained, Mr Pickwick continued. "First item of particulars: the cat is undoubtedly a figure of heathen origin and of great age. Second item of particulars: if I may presume to mention a delicate matter, it is widely believed to be connected with matters of heart and hearth, vital to all communities. Third item of particulars: Midsummer Day is tomorrow, the time of the annual scouring. Fourth item of particulars: you've just recalled the serving girl who mentioned those celebrations include a bonfire, not to mention a meal and dancing. Fifth item of particulars: Mr Clopton indicated pagan customs have not completely died out hereabouts."

Mr Tupman observed he was certain the vicar would not be in evidence at such festivities, and doubtless viewed them with horror.

"Undoubtedly, Mr Tupman. But consider all these items taken together. What do they suggest?"

Mr Tupman had to admit they suggested nothing to him. But then he was a creature of the heart, and there were very few who could have put the facts together in the manner Mr Pickwick did, and fewer still of such an intellect as to make the breathtaking leap from these seemingly unconnected matters to his conclusion.

Mr Pickwick paused and gathered himself up, as if he were addressing the entire Pickwick Club rather than a single member. "Mr Tupman, think of what the boy just said. He planned to kill a chicken for these unholy festivities. Do you think he meant to eat it? Do you think that such a large cat could be placated by a small chicken? Be brave, my friend, for I must tell you that it is obvious Alice has been abducted in order to serve as a human sacrifice to the cat."

By the time the moon had escaped the grasping limbs of trees atop the hill and floated free, shedding its spectral glow on the enormous – if poorly rendered – cat and the crowd gathered around the bonfire near it, our intrepid Pickwickians had already spent several hours ensconced in a thick patch of shrubbery at the edge of the woods, watching as villagers scoured the feline and threw weeds and brush on the blaze illuminating the proceedings.

Now the terrible scraping of a fiddle accompanied by an infernal banging on pie tins rose into the night sky and the villagers danced. There was the serving girl stepping out in a sprightly fashion with a man in a cobbler's apron, her red kerchief catching the firelight, while the odious Herbie threw sticks into the flames and cackled with glee at the explosions of sparks thus engendered.

The crowd far exceeded the population of Great Clatterden. There were a great many spectators, and not all were guests at the Trout and Basket Inn. Stationed behind a wooden table, Mr Rooksbee was doing a brisk trade in cider and pork pies.

"Monstrous, monstrous," groaned Mr Tupman.

Mr Pickwick made no reply, entranced as he was by the scene before him. Who would have guessed such savagery still existed in the wilds of Kent? Yet firelight reflecting off his spectacles gave even that amiable gentleman something of the appearance of a red-eyed demon.

"Look there, Mr Pickwick! Isn't that the vicar?" whispered Mr Tupman.

Horribly enough, dear readers, it was true. Mr Clopton

was clearly visible against the leaping flames, which glinted off the keen edge of the carving knife he carried. It was the ever-observant Mr Pickwick, however, who first noticed two other figures moving toward the bonfire.

One was an older woman, not uncomely, dressed in her Sunday best, accompanied by . . . nay, led by . . . nay, pulled by the elbow toward the roaring flames . . . by a strange man in solemn garb.

"Alice!" cried Mr Rooksbee.

"Philpot!" cried the vicar.

"Mr Tupman!" cried Mr Pickwick.

But in vain.

Whatever subtle plan Mr Pickwick had devised to save the innkeeper's sister from a pagan death was superseded by the tender-hearted and impetuous Mr Tupman, who upon spying his love burst from the bushes in an explosion of leaves and twigs.

There issued from Mr Tupman's lips a bone-chilling roar of rage, or as near to one as he could manage. Before anyone knew what was happening, he had thrown himself bodily on the man who grasped Alice's arm, knocking him to the ground by his sheer weight rather than any athletic prowess.

By the time Mr Pickwick reached the fray, his friend was rolling about in the grass with Mr Philpot, while Alice inexplicably beat on Mr Tupman's head with her dainty fists.

A considerable number of loud remonstrations and throat clearings restored order. The curate, released from Mr Tupman's grasp, got to his feet, brushing chalk and grass off his coat.

"What are you doing here, Philpot?" demanded Mr Clopton. "This is no place for a curate!"

"Nor a vicar, I should think," retorted the younger, though hardly young, man to the vicar's consternation.

"Sir! You will attend a meeting with me tomorrow at nine sharp!" the cleric replied. "I do not propose to discuss—"

"Unhand my sister, you swine!" exclaimed Mr Rooksbee somewhat belatedly, although it must be admitted that to Mr Tupman it appeared the innkeeper had just thought to protest, particularly since he had taken no part in assisting Mr Tupman in the unhanding of Alice.

"You may call me Mrs Philpot, if you please," Alice simpered.

"We were married by special licence a few hours ago and have returned to celebrate," explained her curate husband. "When you insisted Alice go off to her aunt, I saw our chance to wed. I thought I had better take it while I could, after observing this gentleman here pouring sugary words into Alice's ears." He nodded toward Mr Tupman.

"So that's the stranger you told me you saw talking to Alice?" put in Mr Clopton.

"Yes, it is. Alice and I met up here to make our arrangements the night. We often met up here," he concluded, with a fond look at his blushing spouse.

Mr Rooksbee gaped in horror. A small sound of anguish escaped from Mr Tupman as he clapped a hand to his chest.

"Oh, poor, dear Mr Tupman," said Alice. "I am so sorry, but what you so ardently desired could never be, for my affections already belonged to another."

"Come now, Mr Tupman," put in Mr Pickwick. "A glass of cider and a nice pork pie will lessen your anguish. Despair always seems worse on an empty stomach. If it lifts your spirits, consider you've played the part of Cupid in all this, because if I'm not mistaken Mr Rooksbee sent his sister away solely to save her from your attentions. However, he didn't realize that she was really missing until he received the aunt's note after dinner yesterday."

"I suspect it's more likely he sent Miss Alice away to dissuade your friend from returning and bringing his scientific colleague to Great Clatterden."

The speaker was Mr Clarke, the thin tutor, who had been hanging back among the spectators. With the toe of his boot he scraped at the chalk furrow at his feet. "You see, if the three-legged cat were to be revealed as nothing but a humbug, drawn – if you can call it that – by the former landlord of the Trout and Basket Inn in order to improve business . . . well . . ."

Mr Pickwick's eyes gleamed with sudden understanding. "Yes, I see what you mean, sir! The cat helps everyone in the village earn a few extra pennies. If one of those scientific impostors who have so vexed the Pickwick Society in the past were to pronounce this remarkable figure to be a fraud, it would do inestimable damage. Luckily, I am not one of those small-minded men lacking in the capacity to appreciate the world's wonders. As soon as I return to London I shall begin work on my next paper, to be entitled 'An Account of the Three-Legged Cat of Great Clatterden, An Investigation Into Its Antiquity and the Discovery of Its Missing Leg'. Indeed, I believe your cat will become so famous there will be an even larger stream of visitors to your fair village."

Mr Tupman, bereft as he felt, nevertheless gazed at his friend with deep admiration. "Again I am amazed by your brilliance, Mr Pickwick. You led us straight to Alice, even if you could not lead her to me. And all that nonsense about sacrifices was nothing more than a ruse, wasn't it?"

Mr Pickwick merely beamed.

Dear readers, thus was the mystery solved, and let no one repeat the calumny that the immense cheer from the assembly greeting Mr Pickwick's announcement drowned out the Trout and Basket serving girl, whose muttered, "But none of that there rubbish about walking round the cat meaning marriage is true! No wonder she was so agreeable about going to Dover! And how did she get her claws into the curate to begin with? Not but what an old bone like her is fit for a scraggy dog like him!" reached only the unwashed ears of the grubby boy Herbie as he stood by, gnawing on a leg carved from the plump corpse of a fowl by the vicar. For as we all know, while we render all honour to the blushing legions of the fairer sex, it's not only cats who go hunting for prey.

Murder in Murray's Court

David Stuart Davies

1836 and 1837 were significant years for Dickens – indeed, for English literature. Not only did they see the book publication of Sketches by Boz, *the start of* The Pickwick Papers *and Dickens take on the role as editor of* Bentley's Miscellany, *they also saw his marriage to Catherine Hogarth on 2 April 1836. Dickens was besotted with Catherine's younger sister, Mary, who died suddenly in May 1837, apparently of heart failure, at the age of only seventeen. Dickens would later enshrine her memory in fiction as the angelic Little Nell. The death of Mary affected Dickens's ability to write far more so than the birth of his first son, Charles Jr, had done in January. By now Dickens was writing two monthly serials –* The Pickwick Papers *and* Oliver Twist. *But in May, the Dickens production-line ceased for Mary's funeral and there were no instalments of either book the following month.*

Oliver Twist *had started as a serial in* Bentley's Miscellany *in February 1837 and would run until April 1839. It was a complete change from his earlier work and his first piece of social commentary. The story of* Oliver Twist *is well known – that of an orphaned baby left in a workhouse and who falls in with the Artful Dodger, one of*

*a gang of street criminals run by Fagin. At the end of the
novel we learn the true nature of Twist's parentage and
how his wicked half-brother, Monks, had conspired with
Fagin to turn Oliver into a criminal so that he would be
disinherited. The novel ends with Oliver adopted by Mr
Brownlow and able to live a comfortable life. But what
happened to him and the Artful Dodger afterwards?
That's what this story explores.*

*David Stuart Davies is the author of a number of
Sherlock Holmes novels, including* Sherlock Holmes
and the Hentzau Affair *(1991) and* The Veiled Detective *(2004), as well as a series featuring his wartime
detective Johnny One-Eye, which includes* Comes the
Dark *(2006).*

It is one of the great failings of human nature that we
cannot escape from our Unpleasant Past. It lies festering
like some graveyard ghoul in those dark regions of the brain
where our cheerful thoughts never care to wander for they
have brisk, cheerful and uplifting business to be about elsewhere. But our Unpleasant Past waits in the gloomy, craggy
corners, in the slimy recesses, patiently humming some little
discordant, self satisfied tune while it bides its time until it is
the moment to strike; the moment to remind us of how it was,
how unpleasant, painful and demoralizing it was. It only
needs an image, a place, a word, a taste, a smell, a touch, a
smile, a laugh, a blow or any of a thousand other trifles to
prompt it into action. It only needs a very little thing.

Or, indeed, a dream.

For it is in dreams that the dark unconscious has full reign.
In that sleeping time of night, our moral protectors are
dormant, wrapped in their own comforting nightgowns
and are at rest. At this time, past midnight, when the stars
are at their fiercest in the heavens, our Unpleasant Past leaves
its secret place and rides forth, unhindered by any restraint,
to feed our minds with those bad memories.

Thus it was with Mr Oliver Twist whose brain, during the

daylight hours, is so full of business and love, optimism and anticipation, care and consideration, jollity and extravagance, enthusiasm and patience that the past, unpleasant though it was, and it was very unpleasant indeed, does not come to bother him. The shield of goodness which surrounds him is too strong for the darts of his Unpleasant Past. In the day-time, that is.

But at night, there is a different story to tell. The good Mr Twist is placed on the rack of bad dreams and lives again in the perspiring dark of his feverish bed the torments of his childhood. Out of the bedroom shadows come figures from his past, animated by imagination and fear, to taunt him. Here the fearful Bill Sikes rises up, apparently alive and just as vicious, his hand grasping for Oliver's neck. Oliver can see him, hear him, can smell and almost touch him. And then comes the dangling form of the hanged Fagin, dancing in sprightly fashion on the gallows as though he were part of a music-hall troupe, his bright avaricious eyes, wide open and sparkling like two puddles caught in the moonlight.

On the occasions of these nocturnal visitations, Oliver Twist would rise from his bed, drenched in perspiration, weak with fatigue and fearful to return to the uncharted regions of sleep in case the nightmare demons finally had their way with him. Thankfully such occasions are not frequent, but when they come they have a dual effect upon the hero of our tale. They make him gloriously thankful to the Lord for the influence, beneficence and love of the recently deceased Mr Brownlow but they also rob him of energy and brightness of mind for a day or two, after which the memory of the night fears fades . . . until the next time.

However, used to encountering the spirits of his past in bad dreams, Oliver Twist had gradually built a fortress around his sensibilities to aid him; but he was not prepared for one such figure, albeit not a fearful one, to pop up before him in the flesh.

This singular occurrence took place early one spring morning, as he was approaching the offices of Gripwind and Biddle, the firm where he was employed as a junior solicitor. (However, as the fulsome and barrel-shaped senior partner Horatio Gripwind was accustomed to observe – "but not junior, for much longer, Master Twist, if I get my little way. A full-blown partner is what you'll be, if I get my little way, Master Twist.")

On this particular morning as Oliver approached the bright blue door with the gold knocker in the shape of a lion's head, he felt a firm tap, tap, tap on his shoulder. Strange as it may seem, he recognized that tap, tap, tap. It was familiar to him as the touch of rain upon his brow or sunshine on his cheek. He swung around and came face to face with the tap, tap, tapper himself.

"Oliver, my dear fellow. How are you?"

Standing before him was none other than John Dawkins, who will be better known to the reader, and indeed to Oliver Twist himself, as "The Artful Dodger", a sobriquet bestowed upon him in his youth because of his ability to "dodge" or steal handkerchiefs, purses, gold watches and other trifles from passing folk without them feeling a thing. It was an art, indeed.

"Dodger." Oliver found himself using the name out loud for the first time in some ten years.

"I am that wery gentleman and am so wery pleased to see you again, my dear Mr Twist. My, you look a fine gentleman. So refined. So elegant."

Oliver wished that he could reciprocate these compliments. Life it seemed had not treated Dodger well in the intervening years since last they had met. He never had been a fresh-faced, smooth-skinned lad with a fine physique but he had a swagger, a penchant for extravagant, eccentric clothing and bright blue eyes which charmed and twinkled. This sad creature before him, attired in dull clothes, frayed at the edges and elsewhere if one were prepared to examine closely, with the sunken cheeks, a sallow complexion and rheumy eyes, looked old before his time. There was some of the old fire in his demeanour; but, like an old fire, the flames died down occasionally, giving the impression that they were about to go out.

After the surprise of encountering Dodger, a wave of sadness crashed down on Oliver to see his old comrade in such a derelict condition. "My dear Dodger, are you well? Should you be out? You look done in."

"Not as done in as I might be, Oliver, my dear, if them what persecutes me gets their way."

"What on earth do you mean?"

"I have little time before I am arrested for a most heinous crime which I swear to you I did not commit."

"A crime. What crime?"

"The capital crime of murder."

"Come into my office and tell me all about it."

Dodger beamed. "That is what I hoped you would say, my dear Oliver, because you are my last hope. You must save me from the gallows."

Once ensconced in his small but comfortable cell in the premises of Gripwind and Biddle, Oliver instructed his clerk, Alfred Murk, to brew the kettle and provide tea for his good self and his guest, Mr Dawkins. Once supplied with the steaming beverage, Oliver approached the matter in a most methodical and professional manner. He drew a neatly bound notebook from his desk and dipped his quill dramatically into the inkpot.

"Now Dodger, give me your story and do not spare me any details."

Dodger clasped his giant hat on his lap, his scrawny fingers appearing either side of the brim like two albino spiders. "I must say at the outset, my dear Oliver, that I cannot fund your services. Coins of the realm and I are strangers at present and have been for some time, as you will soon learn. I came to you to see if I might reclaim a debt of friendship for your assistance."

Oliver took a sip of tea. "Of course. I would not think of charging you for my services. They are the services of an old friend – I just hope they may be efficacious to you."

"Efficacious is a good word and you are a kind gent. Well, to come to the point. I have fallen on bad times of late. My creditors are legion. A king's ransom would not, I fear, rescue me from the pit. Ah, fear not, Oliver. I do not come to you for money. It is just that you should know my condition. I have a wife. Not in the eyes of God, as you might say, but we have lived together for nearly a year. We've got a small gaff down Stepney way in Anderson's Buildings. Annie Pulbright is her name. A sweet thing when she's sober and she is generally good to me. Well, it came to pass last week that my landlord, a toad of a fellow by the name of Joseph Jangles to whom I owe great amounts of money, threatened to throw us out and to damage both myself and my dear Annie if I did not cough up on the rent within forty-eight hours. What was a man to do? I tried dodging for while, but pickin's were slim. It's not like in old Fagin's time when the game was a good 'un. And, to be plain, my old hands ain't as nimble as they were. So what was my last resort? The money lender, of course. King leeches in the good old city of London. I went to Buggs in Murray's Court. I'd heard he was the least wicious of the brood, which is not to say much. Well, Oliver, I was Faust to his Devil. I sold my soul to him for a mere handful of coin. The interest was four hundred percent, payable within a month or his clerk, an ape of a man called Croker, would kill me. As simple as that."

Oliver was no stranger to the notion of how cheap life was in the vilest quarters of the city of London or how the poor devils who dwelt on the edge of the abyss were forced as a matter of course to accept their precarious lot.

"It was arranged that I go around last evening to pick up my money and sign, in blood it would seem, the deed of agreement with Mr Buggs. I goes along at the appointed hour. Everythin' were most quiet, Oliver. I should have been wary of that quiet but I needed the money so I walks into his office. There were no sign of Croker, Buggs's man, who usually stands guard. Buggs is there sitting behind his desk, bolt upright, his pince-nez balanced on his nose . . . and a dirty great dagger sticking into his heart."

Oliver Twist gasped, replicating the sound of a faulty bellows. "He was dead?"

"As the door nail, my dear friend. Murdered."

"What did you do?"

Dodger cocked a disbelieving ironical eyebrow at Oliver. "The obvious. I looked for the cash. I did not have to look far. It was there in a bag before him on the desk. I scooped that up, slipped it in my secret pocket . . . you remember my secret pocket . . ."

Oliver nodded.

". . . and high-tailed it for the door. Only to run smack into Croker who was just acomin' in from the street. He stopped me dead. 'What's your hurry?' he says suspicious-like and drags me back into his master's office. Then there is a scene straight out of one them plays at Drury Lane. Despite his bulk and brutish ways, on seeing old Buggs dead in the chair, Croker throws himself to the floor like a woman, wringing of his hands and wailing and sobbing fit to burst his giant chest. It were as though he'd found his own mother garrotted in bed. While all this is going on, I decide to make myself scarce and I sidles towards the door. But that man must have eyes like an eagle. No sooner had my hand reached for the latch than he was up off his knees and a flying at me, screaming, 'Halt, murderer!' and grabs me round the neck and hauls me into the street.

" 'Police!' he cries. 'Murder has been done!' he cries. 'I've caught the murderer,' he cries.

"I protested my innocence, I even gave him the bag of money back from my secret pocket, but he wouldn't listen to me. Just as two peelers were making their way down the street in response to his yells, I managed to wrench myself away from the brute and sprint off in the opposite direction with wild cries of 'Murderer' burning in my ears. I ran to my place and informs Annie of my plight. Quite rightly she says that it is not safe for me to stay there. I grabbed some bread and cheese and left. I spent the night by the river wonderin' what to do. I reached one big conclusion, I did: what I needs is a friend to help me out of this particular bear pit what I got myself innocently into; a friend who has a particular legal turn of mind."

Oliver gave a wry grin. "You mean me."

Dodger nodded his head so vigorously that it seemed that his pupils were in danger of being propelled from their sockets. "I do. I hurried home to tell Annie of my decision before coming here. It cannot be long before the law gets its clutches on me and throws me in the darkest dungeon. I do not relish dangling on the end of a rope like old Fagin for I am an innocent man."

Sometimes fiction is accused of manipulating fate for dramatic purposes, but if this is true it is only because fiction mirrors true life. This moment in Oliver Twist's chamber is a fine example of the practice. For Dodger had only just uttered the words concerning the law getting its clutches on him when Twist's clerk, Alfred Murk, entered, begging their pardon and stating that there were two gentlemen of the law outside whose business it was to arrest Mr John Dawkins for murder.

At this very moment a young woman entered, pushing past Murk. She was a gaunt, sallow-faced creature, with blonde ringlets and was attired in a blue and white gingham dress. She might have been pretty once, but poverty, malnutrition and hard times had scrubbed the bloom of youth from her features and dimmed the brightness in her eyes.

"Oh, John," she cried as she threw her arms around Dodger. "My John, they are here for you."

This creature, whom Oliver assumed was Dodger's "wife", had hardly uttered these words before two Bow Street Runners entered and disentangled the woman and grasped hold of the craven John Dawkins.

"Fear not, I shall do my best for you," assured Oliver as the careworn and defeated Dodger was hauled off to Newgate Prison with the promise of a swift trial and an even swifter hanging.

With tears forming in Dodger's eyes, he smiled bravely at his old friend. "For the first time in my life, I am innocent."

To note that Murray's Court is one of the vilest alleys in London graces it with no great distinction. There are many vile alleys in London. Indeed, it could be said that alleys of the vile category outweigh the other kind. Nevertheless, as Oliver Twist was able to attest at first hand, by appearance and smell, that Murray's Court had certainly earned a high ranking within the aforementioned "vile category". In one dingy corner stood the premises of "Theobald Buggs, Usurer to the Gentry". Naturally the establishment was in darkness, not so much out of respect for the deceased owner whose corpulent corpse was currently resting in the police morgue but because there was no one there to run the business.

Oliver approached the grubby door and tried the handle. To his delight and surprise it opened and he stepped inside. The place was illuminated by the pale shafts of daylight that struggled in through the grime of the windows, glad to be away from the unpleasant atmosphere outside. In this supernatural half light he saw a figure flitting about the room, a strange squeaky wail issuing from it. If this apparition had not been so small in stature and slight of build, Oliver might have been persuaded that it was the shade of Buggs himself come back to haunt his old quarters. It was in fact Lizzie Dottle, Buggs's maid servant, whose job it was every third Thursday in the month to dust the premises. It was such a Thursday and despite the fact that her employer was no more, she was about her business for she was of the hope and the opinion that if the work was carried out, someone would pay her for it.

Suddenly becoming aware of a dark stranger in the room, she ceased her singing, for that bizarre strangulated noise issuing from her thin lips was her tuneless rendition of one of the popular alehouse songs of the moment, turned and gave a shriek of surprise.

"Lawks a mercy!" she cried, her hands flying to her face.

"I apologise for startling you, madam," said Oliver. "I was wondering if Mr Croker was about the premises."

Lizzie Dottle shook her head. "I ain't seen hide nor hair of him this mornin', sir. He'll most likely be in The Brass Baboon, a whetting of his whistle."

"I see," said Oliver, moving towards the far end of the cramped chamber, to the door which he supposed led to Buggs's inner chamber. On reaching the door he placed his hand upon the doorknob. "Is this where it happened?" he whispered, affecting a ghoulish intonation which he believed would appeal to his companion.

Lizzie Dottle's eyes widened. "It is, sir. A blade right through the heart, sir. He bled like a pig – or so they say. The bloodstains are still there, sir. Want a look?"

Oliver nodded. "I should be most interested."

Lizzie scurried past him and bade him enter. The room was dark, dank and dusty. Oliver raised the blind. If anything the chamber grew darker.

"It was in this werry chair where the foul murderer struck him."

Oliver examined the chair. The leather padding was scored and ripped where the knife had gone through Buggs's chest and out the other side. A large bloodstain in the shape of Italy formed around it. On the corner of the chair there was a scrap of material which had been caught by the rough edge. Oliver extricated the material and examined it. It was unremarkable. A piece of cheap cloth but of a pattern he had seen before. Behind Buggs's chair was a large safe. Oliver glanced at it slyly but his actions were spotted, even in the gloom, by eagle-eyed Lizzie.

"It's empty!" she cackled. "First thing I looked at when I arrived this morning."

"But isn't that where he kept his money, surely?"

"I believe it was. He'd everythin' in there from pennies to big white notes. But not now."

"Where's it all gone? Have the police got it?"

Lizzie shook her head, "No, they have not. It's the murderer what has the lot. He'll have stashed it somewhere. Much good it'll do him on the gallows."

Oliver knew this was impossible; or to be more precise, he knew that Dodger couldn't have the money. He didn't even get away with the bag containing his loan. Someone has been very clever here, thought the young Mr Twist, stroking his chin in a thoughtful manner. Now who could that be? The words formed in his mind but did not emerge in spoken form.

Able Croker was at this time, as Lizzie Dottle had surmised, whetting his whistle at The Brass Baboon. In fact he was making it an urgent mission to enter into the realms of senselessness by the archway of alcohol as soon as possible. He was on his fourth mug of ale already. Able Croker was a bereft man: he had lost his master and his position but he had lost a great deal more if the Truth could be told, but unfortunately for him the Truth could not be told. Not unless he wanted to stand on the gallows alongside, or, indeed, instead of, the Dawkins creature. He had been a fool and getting nothing for your pains is the penalty for being a fool in this world. He drained his mug dry and banged it on the counter to attract the serving wench for a refill.

As he slumped back down in his chair, half in his cups and fully in his depression, he was aware of someone taking a seat by him. It was a slim, young, clean-shaven fellow in a stylish coat and with an odour of soap and water about him. A gentleman in fact.

At first Croker had the idea that this individual might be a representative of the law, but he was too smart, too refined, and too sweet-smelling.

"Have I the pleasure of addressing Able Croker, Mr Buggs's late employee?" he asked quietly, leaning forward in order not to raise his voice much above a whisper.

"I'm Croker, but I can't says as how it's much of a pleasure to converse with such a wretched soul. I was, as you so rightly say, an employee of Mr Buggs. Now he is dead and I have no occupation. But that is half my sorrow. I was expecting to be married before the year was out, but my true love has upped and left me."

"My condolences on your double loss," said the gentleman. "Allow me to buy you a mug of ale to ease your bereavement."

This fellow certainly was a gentleman. Croker's hazy eyes

brightened momentarily and his furry tongue travelled across his blubbery lips in anticipation of a free drink.

"That's very kind of you, sir."

Oliver, for he was the gentleman in question, purchased a beer for Croker and a small porter for himself.

Croker had by now finished his own drink and as soon as Oliver placed the new mug before him, he snatched it up, pressed it to his lips and took a great, noisy gulp.

Wiping his mouth with his sleeve, he grinned at Oliver.

Oliver grinned back. "What have you done with the money?" he said as quietly and as reasonably as he had done before, but there was now a cold, steely glint in his eyes.

Conflicting emotions registered on Croker's face. There was surprise which was quickly elevated to shock, but there was also bewilderment and a tinge of regret playing about the eyes. All these were wiped away after a brief interval to be replaced by a glare of indignation. "I don't know what you be talking about," said Croker, mouthing the words carefully as the alcohol was now starting to take its effect on his brain and more particularly his tongue.

Oliver smiled gently. "Oh, yes you do. I am referring to the contents of Mr Buggs's safe."

For a fleeting moment Croker harboured the thought that he had been wrong about this fine gentleman and he was indeed a policeman of sorts. But no, his cuffs were clean, his manner was too relaxed and he exuded a refinement not found with the officers of the law.

"I know nothing about that. The safe was empty when I got there. The murderer must have it."

"But you apprehended the murderer. He only had one bag of money about his person."

"I know nothing about the safe."

He was lying. Oliver could at least tell that. Fagin had taught him about the wicked ways of men. He may be a novice at solving crime but not at associating with thieves, scoundrels and career liars. Certainly Croker was of the latter breed, if not of the others. It was time for a leap in the dark. Oliver had an imagination and he had been using it as he'd made his way to this gloomy hostelry. He had been inspired by the discovery of the piece of material at the scene of the crime and the fact that he had seen the same material several times as he had passed through the narrow streets as part of a commonly worn cheap dress. This had prompted him to construct several possible scenarios in which such a dress featured.

"And so you have lost your lady friend also, eh?" said Oliver casually, changing the subject, as though he were not making a great point.

Croker nodded absentmindedly, staring deeply into his ale as though the answer to all life's problems lay just beneath the surface froth.

"She has deserted you. Your flaxen-haired sweetheart. You have my sympathies. I know the pain of losing a loved one."

Oliver now was in danger of over-dramatizing the moment, but the words and the theatrical sentiment rang true for Croker and his eyes brimmed with tears.

"I thought she loved me. I trusted her but all she cared about . . . all she cared about . . ."

"Was the money."

Croker nodded vigorously, words failing him in his misery.

"She wooed you and learned all about Mr Buggs's wealth. Is that true?"

Another vigorous nod.

"You were going to rob the old fellow, take his money and run away together."

Croker drained his tankard before replying. He knew this sweet-smelling fellow was just too clever for him. "I loved her. It was her idea so I went along with it. But she did it all without me. I never knew there would be . . . there would be murder involved."

Oliver believed him. Poor old Croker had been a pawn, a dim, sentimental, easily fooled pawn in the game of a very clever woman.

"Where did she live?"

Croker shook his head, his features virtually melting with

despair: the eyes sagged, brimming with tears and the thick lips flopped low in a miserable grimace. "That's the worst of it," he moaned. "I do not know. We always met in here or went back to my place. I now realize that I knew very little about her."

How clever, thought Oliver.

"Now I have lost my sweetheart and my position."

"Never mind," said Oliver rising. "Count your blessings. At least you'll not be hanged for murder." He placed a small coin on the rough table. "Have another mug of ale and think sweet thoughts."

Anderson Buildings in Stepney is one of those over-populated pustules of the face of London: a tenement held together by dirt, penury and squalor. One can smell it before one sees it and when one sees it, one wished one hadn't. The vision stays with you, like some indelible stain, for days. Oliver was sympathetic to the notion that one might do anything – including committing murder – to escape the degrading clutch of Anderson Buildings. The acrid smell of poverty assailed his nostrils, as he stood at the entrance of this grim edifice. In the shadows some way behind him stood two tallish figures watching him carefully. Just at that moment a tiny rat-like creature emerged from the dank interior. He was furry of whisker and furtive of eye, and yet Oliver suspected that he was a member of the human race.

"Excuse me, sir," said Oliver.

The creature looked astounded to be addressed in such a polite manner. However, the expression of surprise soon turned to one of suspicion.

"What d'yer wants?" came the less than civilized reply, escaping over a row of rotten teeth.

"Could you tell me in which of these apartments Mr Dawkins and his lady friend live? I am a friend of theirs."

"A friend, eh? Not a debtor then?" The creature uttered a throaty chuckle, exposing more decrepit teeth.

Oliver shook his head vigorously.

"You'll find them on the second landing. Number 32."

With these words, he scurried off, his coat tails brushing the pavement behind him. Oliver half-expected to see a fine furry tail peeking out from beneath.

Reaching number 32 Anderson Buildings was an unpleasant experience for Oliver, passing as he did foul-smelling debris of an uncertain nature on the stairs, shambling figures that edged by him reeking of drink or despair and hearing the muffled cries and sobs of several children mingled with a chorus of whelps from imprisoned dogs, all housed in the various cells within the building. Standing before the shabby door of number 32, he did not knock, but instead entered without soliciting an invitation.

It was a small, windowless, dimly lighted room – a guttering candle the only source of illumination. There was a rough table, an old chaise lounge which seemed insistent on losing its stuffing and a bed. Standing by the bed, leaning over a small trunk arranging the contents was Annie Pullbright.

"Making good your escape, Annie," said Oliver quietly.

Annie was so occupied in her task that she did not hear Oliver enter. When he spoke and she noticed her visitor for the first time, she screamed and fell back on the bed in surprise.

Oliver took a step forward but she was on her feet instantly. "What d'you want?" she snarled, her eyes flashing in anger.

"I've come for you, Annie. And the money. I know you murdered Mr Buggs and tried to put the blame on your man, poor Dawkins."

Annie's face paled and she emitted an unconvincing laugh. "What nonsense you speak."

Oliver shook his head. "It was a cunning plan and very nearly worked. You sought the attention of Croker, pretending to care for him, persuading the poor infatuated fellow to confide in you the secrets of Mr Buggs's business. Together you planned to rob him and then disappear. But you wanted the money all for yourself, didn't you? And that meant that you needed to get rid of John Dawkins too, so that you would be free of all shackles. You persuaded John to take out a loan from Buggs and when he went to collect it, you made sure Croker was elsewhere, probably in the ale house, dreaming of a life of connubial bliss with you. Then you went to Buggs's office in advance of John and stabbed him to death and emptied the safe – you knew the combination, thanks to Croker's idle tongue. Of course you made sure that the money John had arranged to borrow was left so that he would be implicated in murder – which he was. Then when John told you that he was going to engage my help, you informed the police so that he could be arrested in my offices. How else would they have known where he was?"

Annie sneered. "You must be one of those writer fellows 'cos that's a very fancy story."

"It's the truth and you know it. I'm sure if I pulled back that layer of clothes in the trunk there, I'd find Mr Buggs's fortune."

"You don't touch my trunk," she snapped, taking a step forward and clenching her fists.

Oliver ignored her. "You must have been dreaming of buying yourself all sorts of pretty dresses with the money. Something better than that cheap dress you're wearing now."

Annie looked down at her dress in puzzlement.

"Especially," continued Oliver, "as you've torn that one. Down the side there. See, there's a piece of material missing."

Annie gazed at the tear. "So what? It's nothing."

"It is everything." Oliver held up a fragment of matching sprigged cotton. "You left this behind in Mr Buggs's office. It's from your dress and it is spotted with Buggs's blood."

"You devil," she screamed and rushed at Oliver with her arms outstretched, her long grubby fingernails reaching for his face. He stepped back and pulled a whistle from his pocket.

When the two Bow Street Runners entered the dingy room, they found the young smart gentleman struggling manfully with a fiery hellcat, her talons only inches away from his eyes. "This is the lady, gentlemen," he cried as the policemen pulled Annie off him. "I think you'll find the stolen cash in that trunk there."

Annie Pulbright leaned forward and spat in Oliver's face.

The door of Newgate Prison slammed shut behind John Dawkins. He was on the outside and a free man again. As he stepped forward, exercising his newly found liberty, he found someone by his side, falling in step with him.

"Oliver, my dear," he cried and threw his arms around his old friend. "How can I thank you?"

Oliver laughed. "It is I who should thank you. I've had the most exciting time. It was great fun solving the crime. I'm just sorry that in doing so you have lost someone you cared for."

Dodger shrugged. "She wasn't worth it, was she? I think I knew in my heart she would leave me sooner or later. That's what life is all about, ain't it? Sometimes it's good and sometimes it's rotten."

"Well," said Oliver, with a smile, "I do believe it is time for you to have some of the good. Now the plan is for us to partake of a splendid lunch to celebrate your freedom and then for me to see if I can secure you some kind of position with my firm."

The Dodger beamed. "Why that's wonderful, Oliver. Who could ask for more?"

The Leaping Lover

Kage Baker

Even while *Oliver Twist* was still running in *Bentley's Miscellany*, Dickens began *Nicholas Nickleby*, issued in monthly parts from April 1838. When Nicholas's father dies the family is left destitute and Nicholas ends up taking a teaching job at a remote school in Yorkshire run by the vicious Wackford Squeers. Squeers's daughter, Fanny, believes Nicholas may love her, an infatuation she has for any young man she encounters. Nickleby loathes the entire family and eventually attacks Squeers and escapes, taking with him the young boy Smike who has been left physically and mentally damaged by Squeers's brutality. The paths of Squeers and Nickleby cross again in London where Squeers has come to join forces with Nickleby's evil uncle Ralph to thwart Nicholas's plans. Fanny Squeers's only real friend is Matilda – or Tilda – Price to whom she writes long, vainglorious letters full of her imaginings and idiosyncratic spelling.

It is one of those wonderful coincidences that at the same time that *Nicholas Nickleby* first appeared, London was a-tremble with news of a bizarre criminal whom the press had dubbed Spring-Heel'd Jack. Jack would pounce on his victims from seemingly out of nowhere and escape by leaping high walls, often with the sound of a demonic laugh. The attacks ran between November 1837 and March 1838, and a man, Thomas Milbank, was eventually arrested and claimed he was Jack. But sightings continued and the episode soon passed into folklore. The true nature of Spring-Heel'd Jack was never solved – though if Fanny Squeers had her way . . .

Kage Baker is best known for her series of time-travel novels known collectively as *The Company*, which began with *In the Garden of Iden* (1997). Her interests go beyond science fiction, though, as she has worked as a graphic artist, mural painter and, for many years, as a stage manager and theatre director of Elizabethan and other productions.

12 January 1838, Friday Morning
My Dear Matilda,

My fond regards to all those at Greta Bridge which seems very quaint to me now, as London is so far removed it is as great a diffrence as Heaven above Earth I suppose. You would scarcely believe what a time I am having at Aunt Pyelott's. The glittring Society! The refined Gentlemen, so very solicitors for ones comfort! Such attentions I have received! But you will have to imagine it all as I could not begin to describe it.

I am gazing out as I write at a district known as Lime House, very genteel and of great antikwity. The Pyelotts reside in a gracious mansion in Salmon Lane, kinveniently located above Uncle Pyelott's premises. The Garden is pleasantly rustick and Aunt Pyelott has a hen shed to make it more like the Country as that is the current fashion here, only of course she has a Boy to see to the eggs.

We often promernod through London, perhaps down to the Comercial Road or even as far as the Basin to see the Barges, and I wore my yellow morning gown the other day, the one that John said sets off my eyes so nice, but I was obliged to wear my black boots because of the kindition of the lane rather than the Maroko slippers which I would have much prefered. However I have a new Gown being prepared of exquisitt green stuff for the Ball which is being held Friday next and the sempstress is

French of course and she informs me black slippers are all the Thing now so I shall be fashionably shod.

I almost neglected to mention, Aunt Pyelott's cousin resides here as well, a Poor Relation, Miss Maud Bellman. She is a plain little thing with specktacles but quite agreeable and anxious to make herself useful as indeed she should be. I shall perhaps endevour to make something of her as the Poor if left to themselves often descend to degerdation. Aunt Pyelott has graciously gotten her a ticket to the Ball as well, though I cannot imagine the poor thing will show to her advantage.

I must away – Madame Hector is here for my fitting. Pray write and tell me how you are getting on and my kind regards to all the Prices.

I remain
Yours and cetrer
Fanny Squeers

20 January 1838, Saturday Noon

Dear Tilda,

Perhaps you were expecting some fond account of the Ball which I was at only last night but oh, what a far more terrible tale I have to tell!

Though I will say the Ball was a Triumph. As I suspected I far outshone poor Miss Bellman, who wore only a sort of puce dress more fitting to Tea but then she hadn't any better, and I pity the creature. I condesinded to encourage her a little, and offered her the use of my old violet shawl with the jet beads, but she declined, at which I was secretly a little releeved because really it was too fine considering the other stuff she had on and not her colour at all.

The evening was fine for the season and so we walked there, the Ball being held at the Caledonian Arms up the lane. We had some exitement at the door for I nearly thought I had left my Invitation but at the last moment Miss Bellman found it in the bottom of my reticule for me. She really may make someone a 1st rate ladys maid with a little training and I must speak to Aunt Pyelott about it.

As for the Society at the Ball, well that was a little dissapoint-

ing because most of the men present were in the trade (clerks
and such) and I could see they were somewhat overwelmed by
my carriage. I graciously declined to dance with most of them
although there was one Gentleman who is in Ship Chandlering
or something, quite well to do, Mr Clement I recall is his name,
and he was there with his Partners Mr Tacker and Mr Johnson.
I made sure to dance with all three.

I pitied one tall fellow with black whiskers who gazed at me
with such elockwent longing! Had he mustard enough courage
to speak to me, I declare I might have danced with him; little did
I suspect his Wild Nature! But I am getting ahead of myself.
Miss Bellman, poor creature, danced with one or two fellows of
the lower sort and her face got quite red, which may have been
the affect of the gin punch.

Uncle Pyelott was to have called for us in a Handsom but we
left rather early as I was a little fateeged. Oh, Tilda, what small
twists of Chance decide our Fate! For if I had waited – but you
shall hear what befell next.

I was rather apprinsieve I confess coming away from Bow Common, on account of there was no more than a gibrous moon by
which to see, and no light except the watchmans all the way across
the field at the Cable Manefactry. What ironey! For we were quite
unmolested all that open way, and the attack did not come until we
had once reached the Shelter of houses.

What, I hear you exclaim, attack! Yes, Tilda, attack! For as we were
nearly to the bridge over the canal, on a sudden a Frightful
Aparishen sprung out of an alley! He was quite tall, cloaked in
Inky Black, which he flung back to Reveal a Horrific Counternance. There was a spark of fire at his Bosom and then he breathed
out flames. I naturally screamed in terror and so I need hardly add
did Miss Bellman, the more so when the Monster then seezed me in
his Powerful Arms and tore at my rayment with Fearful Claws!!!!

What his intentions were you can scarcely imagine, as you have
led a sheltered life, but I was fainting and almost unable to
struggle against the Force of his Passion, and what might have
happened if Miss Bellman had not found a half brick in the lane
and struck my Asailant, I dare not imagine. His head rang like a
dinner bell as he was wearing some sort of helment. He used

dreadful langwedge then and released me, and then – to my astonishment – sprang away over a wall and we heard him running into the infathemable shadows of night!

I screamed all the way home though more from Fear and Shock than Injury, as his claws left only a scratch or two and some brooses this morning. I begged Miss Bellman not to tell Uncle Pyelott for reasons which will become plain, which were: that I suspect it was the handsome Clerk with black whiskers who so admired me at the Ball.

How I am certain it was no Unearthly Feind? You may wonder, but his face was at a distance of but inches and I saw plain he wore a mask. Also when he vommited fire there was a strong smell of gin afterward and I have seen gypsys at the Fair do as much, taking a mouthful of spirits and then blowing it across a brand. Miss Bellman found a burnt match in the lane as she was endevring to revive me and I do not doubt that was where the fire come from.

Poor man! Being unable to Approach me by reason of my Exalted Station, he contrived a desprate plan to sasiate his violent thwarted passion. I pity him but cannot somehow bring myself to condem him for it. Yet if my pa were to hear of this he would see him transported or at least hung.

When I contemplait what nearly occurred I fall into swooning. Be glad, Tilda, that you are unlikely to undergo such arrowing ordeals in Greta Bridge.

> I remain
> Yours and cetrer
> Fanny Squeers

25 January 1838, Thursday Morning

Oh Tilda,

I am so dreadfully low. I must unburden myself; though I cannot expect you to comperhend the nature of my woe. I do not think anybody could unless it might be Helen of Troy or King Arthurs wife whose name I cannot recall at the moment but who also was the cause of great suffering because of her fatal beauty.

My secret lover was not discouraged by the half brick, it

seems. For some few nights after the Ball he has been seen several times around Salmon Lane, and in Catherine Street and on Bow Common. He is clearly haunting my path in hopes of beholding me once more. This is the consequence of passions feury denyed I suppose, that drives a man to madness, but of course I am staying in at night – it were worse madness to tempt him further. So all sorts of persons have been making kimplaint to the constables about a tall masked man who leapt out from the gloom of night to surprize them, only to assault them when he discovered they were not me. There has been a blacksmith, a Respectable merchant and two boys so attacked. The children in the Lane have taking to calling him Spring-Heel'd Jack.

All this were misery enough for me to endure, knowing my accurst charms to be the cause of so much trouble. Judge then with what horror I learned the news late this morning that my poor Admirer is now also accused of Murder!

You remember Mr Clement that I told you about, the prosprous gentleman who had a Ship Chandlery warehouse? He was the foremost of those who danced with me at the ball, and very pleasant and agreeable he was too, not so old for a man with so much money. Well he is dead! Stabbed through the heart, and left to waller in his own goar! It happened only last night. He and one of his partners had just left their counting-house in the Comercial Road and walked homeward. The partner (I think it was Mr Tacker) parted from him at Dalglish Street and was going on for he lives hard by St. Anns.

Mr Tacker had not got far when he heard a shout coming out of Dalglish Street. "Here's Spring-Heel'd Jack!" he thought it said. And following on this was a scream that he thought might be Mr Clement. He ran back and turned into Dalglish Street, only to see his friend laying dead there, weltering in blood! He looked all round but it was at a point where two lanes crossed and the Murderer might have run off in any direction. He raised the cry and the Police came but it was too late. They have arrested Mr Tacker as he was seen by the bleeding Corpse and there were no witnesses.

But it is said by everybody that the real Murderer is Spring-Heel'd Jack, because there were two boot-prints in the mud by Mr Clement's Corpse but none leading up to it nor away, and it is supposed only Jack can leap so. Whatever shall I do? Can I think that I am responsibble for this shocking crime by reason of my beauty?

Be grateful, Tilda, that you will never bear such a weight on your conscience.

I remain

Yours and cetrer

Fanny Squeers

18 February 1838, Sunday Afternoon

My dear Matilda,

So much has happened since last I put Pen to Paper, I hardly know where to begin. What news, you will surely ask, of Spring-Heel'd Jack? What of the Infamous Murder? Read on and see for yourself.

You will recall I was sunk in woe at the thought that my dashing Admirer was guilty of so fowl a crime. Miss Bellman heard my tears and was so considerate as to ask what the matter was. Silly Creature! As though it were not too plain. But I must not be unkind as she has no admirers and so no understanding of my grief. When I told her my fear she said it was certainly very queer that everyone said Spring-Heel'd Jack took such prodee-jous leaps, when she had not seen him demonstrate any such Power.

I told her not to be a goose, because I myself had seen him Leap a wall at least ten feet high with but one bound. She replyed, that it wasn't ten feet but only four or five at most. I grew quite cross with her until we went out and looked at the very wall and I saw that she was correct in her asertion. The late hour, the shadows of night and my mortal terror must have affected my apperhension of the scene.

That was when the idea struck me like a Bolt from Heaven! What if some other person had designed to murder poor Mr Clement, perhaps for his money, and seezed the opertunety of all the uproar over Jack's pranks to do it but make it appear as if it was Jack? I was convinced this was what had really happened and knew then that I must go to the Police, even at the risk of my good name, to explane things. If my Admirer were to be captured he would surely hang, unjustly, and my heart should break.

So I took Miss Bellman with me to the Police Station and it was very unsatisfacktry, you would think they would grant some creedence to a gentlemans daughter. So far from listening they were quite rude and positively jokular in their disbelief, but I determined not to leave the Station until I had some satisfaction. At last the Inspector called out a man of his, Constable Trumpiter, and bid him go out with us to look at the scene of the murder.

This Trumpiter is a pleasant youth if rather common and listened very thoughtfully to me as we walked back to Dalglish Street. Miss Bellman would keep interrupting me to explane things I should have thought were perfectly clear, but he heard her out without kimplaint. When we got to the scene of the murder I was in danger of swooning as there was still Blood in the street. Much of the area had been trampled over since the morning but we could still see the two boot prints in the mud by where the Corpse had layed.

I told the Constable what I had seen with my own eyes, vizz that Spring-Heel'd Jack was only a man in a mask and could never have jumped over the houses to either side in the lane, never mind what foolish folk claimed, and that it were much more likely to have been Mr Tacker done him in after all and put the boot prints there a-purpose to deceive. For I do not think I mentioned it before but Mr Tacker is a sallow and ill-favoured sort of fellow, just what you would expect a Murderer to look like.

"Why, Miss Squeers, I am glad you explaned," said Constable Trumpiter. "You are perseptive to be sure. Only we are not certain of Mr Tacker's gilt, because of the matter of the murder weppun." I wanted to know what he meant by that and he told me that the Dagger that made the fatal wound was nowhere to be found at the scene, nor did Mr Tacker have it on him, and he had had no place to hide it before the Police came running into the lane in answer to Mr Tacker's cries.

"Why have you arrested him then?" said Miss Bellman, rather forwardly I thought. To which the Constable made reply that they had to arrest somebody or there would be Outcry, and in any case Mr Tacker might turn out to have done it after all. "But what about the murder weppun then?" she said. "Where is it?"

Poor creature, she has no idea that a true lady is diferdent and unassuming and never speaks up like that. Poor Constable Trumpiter sighed and with a nice show of patience said we should search for it again, if she liked, but the Police had already hunted pretty thoroughly. So we looked up and down Dalglish Street. "What horror," you are perhaps saying, Tilda, "to chance upon a Goary Blade!" And well you might. Thankfully we did not find any such a thing, but I heard Constable Trumpiter and Miss Bellman exclaiming over something and when I run to see, they were looking at some footprints they found in a little lane which serves as a conexion between Dalglish and Magaret Streets.

It was the prints of someone who had stood in his stocking feet hard by the wall. Constable Trumpiter showed me how they came up from the Comercial Road and it was plain where the man had stopped and pulled his boots off and stood a long time by the wall, for his prints was very plain there. Then the stocking prints ran out into Dalglish Street and vanished under all the treading down of the Policemens boots. The two boot prints by the blood was the very same as the ones of the man who was wearing them before he pulled them off to wait in his stockings! And we looked a little more and found the stocking prints running back into the little lane, and out into the Comercial Road again. And I saw there, just at the kerbstone, a tiny drop of Blood!

So I said it was plain the Murderer had been hiding in the lane, took off his boots so as to run quiet, and waited till Mr Clement came along Dalglish Street, whereupon he run out and stabbed him, dropped his boots down so as to make the prints, yelled "Here's Spring-Heel'd Jack!" then run back the same way he came. Constable Trumpiter looked at me with admiration in his eyes and said he supposed it happened just so. He has peticklely fine eyes.

I then said what I thought, which was, that it might have been a Red Indian who slipped into the hold of some ship and traveled to England and crept out at Lime House, for they are supposed to delight in murder when it is least expected. But Miss Bellman said a Red Indian would be unlikely to know about Spring-Heel'd Jack. Which I suppose is true.

Then Miss Bellman spoke up again and said she thought the murderer must have pitched the Bloody Blade in Lime House Basin. And it really seemed likely, because the last we could see of the prints before they dissapeared from being trampled by everyone in the Comercial Road, was that they seemed to be running for the Basin.

Constable Trumpiter was very taken with my prespickiticity, I could see, but he remained silent a while as he walked back and forth, looking time and again on what we had found. At last he said, "It cannot have been a lunatic, for the deed was carefully planned; but who would want to kill Mr Clement?"

And I replyed that it must have been Mr Tacker after all, that he might inherit all the Wealth of their business (for I knew Mr Clement was a bachelor, you may be sure I asked at the Ball before I danced with him).

Miss Bellman said then that we ought to go speak with the prisoner, at which I very nearly swooned again at the mere idea but then thought better of it as he might confess the more readily if confronted by me with what I know. And, you know, Tilda, that though I am sensitive and shrink from unpleasantness, I can steal myself to face even Roaring Savages in matters of the heart.

So Constable Trumpiter took us round to see the Wretch in his tank. He had been weeping, most unmanly. My blood boiled to see him there, and I was all for striking him and demanding the Truth, but Miss Bellman put herself foreward again and asked him to account for himself, rather timidly I thought. Mr Tacker asked the Constable whether he had to reply and the Constable said he had better, for we would not be denied.

Miss Bellman then asked Mr Tacker why he wept so, and he said "I am an innocent man", and called on God to witness he had not murdered Mr Clement. She then asked him what had happened and he said that on Wednesday all had perceded as usual, except that at midday the younger partner Mr Johnson had gotten word that his mother was ill and left to rush to her bedside. So he, Mr Tacker I mean, had shut up the office at 6 o'clock and he and Mr Clement walked together along the Comercial Road as was their dayly custom. They parted at Dalglish Street like they always done and Mr Tacker walked on, suspecting nothing was amiss until he heard the shouting.

I then asked him the question which was burning foremost, which was "Did you see a tall man in a cloak, wearing a mask?" which he replyed that he had not done, indeed he had seen nobody but the deceesed lying there until the first Policeman come running in answer to his cries for help. And Miss Bellman asked had he quarreled with Mr Clement and he said "No, never".

But I could tell he was seezed by some great fear, as I am peticklely good at noticing that, so I said a little roughly that he had better not lie, for Truth Will Out. And the Constable said too that all his affairs would be gone into to veryfy what he said, and Mr Johnson questioned as well.

At which Mr Tacker blubbed again like a baby and, throwing up his hands to Heaven, said "Oh, then it will all be known" and told us that he had borrowed against the business funds but meant to pay it back, and would have done so already but for an enexplicable delay on the part of his corispondent.

Constable Trumpiter looked very grave at that and went and asked his Superior to step in and listen. They made Mr Tacker explane. He said that some six months past he had gotten a letter from a very respectable Widow whose late husband was the Treasurer for a society of Frenchmen who were supposed to be Investers but really had secret plans to Overthrow the French Government. And when her husband had found this out he was horrorfied as well he might be and took the money and hid it in an account in the French Bank, meaning to transfer it to the Bank of England, but then the villains apperhended his plan and had him Asassinated. So his Widow was desprate to transfer the money and a mutual friend had recommended she write to Mr Tacker as an honest man. All he had to do was open a French Bank Account in his name with Six Hundred Pounds and make her his signee on it so she could transfer the villains' horde to his account and thence to an English account, in return for which kindness to a lady she would give him half the sum, which amounted to Ten Thousand Pounds in our money.

Well I would have done the same if I was a gentleman but the Inspector and Constable Trumpiter were pleased to be humerous about the whole thing and thought it a great joke. I was sorry for Mr Tacker then and felt quite sure he had not done it after all. He got down on his knees and swore that the money would be replaced as soon as the French Widow wrote back to him, and that he was guilty of no other irregulerity and certainly not murder. For if Mr Clement had not untimely died it had never come to light. They told him that was for the Coroner to hear out.

Constable Trumpiter asked him where Mr Johnson (that was the young partner) lived, as he must be questioned. He gave us an address in Foxes Lane. Then Constable Trumpiter saw us out and I said we must go round to Foxes Lane at once to speak to Mr Johnson, and Constable Trumpeter said we ladies could not possibly go there by ourselves as it is not in the best neborhood, and so offered to escort us. At which Miss Bellman simpered rather I am afraid. But I graciously thanked him and said we should be glad of the company.

Miss Bellman chattered on as we walked, saying that if so great a booby as Mr Tacker had planned the murder, it had been extrornry. I thought that rather unfeeling of her. But Constable Trumpiter said he did not seem like much of a suspect now, still we would be surprized at the things he had seen in the Police. Whereon Miss Bellman, with rather too much artfulness, asked him to tell us please, whereupon he related several remarkable occurrences of Crime as we walked along. It is pity he is so common for he is rather clever, and very much the gentleman in his manners.

We got to Foxes Lane and it was indeed no place I should care to go alone, very mean and low, and it fell out that Mr Johnson lived in a lodging-house there. Or I should say, had lived: for when we knocked the owner of the Premises came and looked over the railings and said he was Cleared Out, having left Wendesday last. Which, you will remember, Tilda, was the day of the Murder!

Constable Trumpiter looked very grave at that and said he

must be let in to search. To which the owner responded with alacrity and I must say people do respect the Police, they might almost be gentlemen.

We found a bare mean room quite empty but for some few Items of Furnituer that went with the premises, the bed and washstand and a monstrous old Scotch Chest. Miss Bellman went poking about whilst Constable Trumpiter spoke to the owner and found out that Mr Johnson had not run off owing anything, indeed he had paid up and arranged for his trunk to be sent away two days before. And Miss Bellman looked at Constable Trumpiter as much as to say that that was odd since he had got the news about his Mother being ill only afterward on Wendesday. Constable Trumpiter asked where the trunk had been sent and the owner did not recall except it was to the village of H—.

Just then Miss Bellman exclaimed, having been looking in the kimpartments in the Scotch Chest. There was an envelop stuck in the back of one, that had slid down so only a corner was poking out, as perhaps it had been missed in a hasty removal. Constable Trumpiter came and tried to get it out but couldn't pinch it hard enough and in the end I had to do it myself as my arm was siffishently slender enough to get back there and my fingers are quite strong when it comes to pinching.

It was a letter addressed to a Mr Edmund Tollivere of Swan Cottage in H—. I opened it and read it at once and it was only from a servant telling him his grandfather was taking clear broth now and felt much better, and asking whether he wanted his books sent on. I thought it must be from some former lodger but Miss Bellman pointed out that the village was the same as where the trunk was sent. Also it was dated just last month.

I saw plain that Mr Johnson must have been the murderer, or why would he be living under a false name and running off in such haste? I said as much to Constable Trumpiter, who agreed that it was highly suspicious.

By this time it was quite late and so Constable Trumpiter escorted us back to Salmon Lane and we parted, with him promising to bring all this matter to the attention of the

Inspector. I was sure my poor Admirer was out of danger of unjust Persecution.

Alas! I had not reckoned with Jack's foolish persistence. That very night he surprized a carpenter walking home late and blew fire in his face, as well as kicked him pretty hard and trampled on him somewhat. Constable Trumpiter came round to see me next day looking greatly aggreeved, to say that a Degelation of Citizens had been to the Police Station and demanded that Spring-Heel'd Jack must be brought to Justice. In consequence of which the Inspector would not listen to what we had found out about the mysterious Mr Johnson, but ordered all his men to extra duty after dark, and I gather made some insulting remarks to Constable Trumpiter as well. His fine eyes flashed with impatience as he spoke of it.

Whereupon Miss Bellman, who happened to be sewing in the room and heard this, said that we might go to H— ourselves and see what we might find out, as it is only an hours journey out of London. Constable Trumpiter said then that if we ladies were intent on going, he would go with us, since he was not on duty until half past Nine.

I was a little concerned about the perpritey of this but Miss Bellman is all of seven-and-twenty, quite old and plain enough to serve as a suitable Chaperone. So we left a note for Aunt Pyelott, who had taken a glass of cordial for the Headache and was resting, and hired a man to drive us to H—.

H— must be a pretty little town in summer, I was surprized to find such a rustick spot so close to London, with a nice Inn called the Moulders Arms where we had some refreshment for which Constable Trumpiter paid, very much like a gentleman though I suppose a Constable's wages is not very great, and I fear he was showing off a little for my sake which was dear of him. Afterward he advised me to walk about and enjoy the fresh air and pleasant sights while he went round to make some inquiries.

Miss Bellman wanted to see the shops, though of course she has no money either, and there was only the one shop in any case. But nothing would do but she must go in, so we did. It was very like Mr Wealies shop in Greta Bridge only rather bigger with more wares. I diverted myself looking at things but Miss Bellman engaged the shopmistress in continuous chatter and really I could not think what she was at at first.

She began with cumpliments about what a pleasantly situated spot H— is and how nice the air is and asked the shopmistress, did folk live to great age thereabouts? Because she had an Elderly Relation in London who the Doctors advise must quit business for his health, and he wouldn't, but she thought that if she might find a convenient place close by London he might agree. Now I almost said out loud "What stuff" because of course she has no such relation unless it was Uncle Pyelott and he is quite well.

But you see it was an Artful Ruse. For she got the lady to talking about all the old folk in the village, Gammer This and Old Mistress That and Mr Somebody's uncle who was a hundred and two though deaf as a post and blind and had to be kept by the Hob like a baby and couldn't remember a thing past three-quarters of an Hour though when he was clear headed he could tell you all about being at Calcutta with Clive. "So all the old folks are quite hale and sound?" said Miss Bellman.

"Well," quoth the shopmistress, "There is poor old Mr Spool, who has been ailing these three years and is expected to go off any time now; and he is only five-and-seventy I think; but sorrow and temper have shortened his years, which only goes to show that money ain't everything," and of course Miss Bellman asked what did she mean?

Well it seems that this Spool had been given to prudent Industry and built a manefactry somewhere in the north and made his fortune quite young. He came down to H— and built a Mansion and married. Before many years wore out he was blest with a son and then a daughter. But lately he has been greatly dissapointed in the grandson who has been ordered out of the house.

And Miss Bellman said, "Would that be young Mr Tollivere?" which quite amazed me and was the first inkling I had she is a cunning and crafty creature, for one who looks so simple. And the shopmistress said, "Oh, so you heard of him, have you?" and added that he was indeed wild in his ways and she told about how when he was no more than ten years old he came into her shop and made off with two fistsful of sugar sticks to a value of sixpence.

A man came in then to buy limiment for Sheep so we said Good Afternoon and left.

I asked Miss Bellman what she was getting at and she said, "Don't you see? If Mr Johnson is really Mr Tollivere, then we know he is a bad sort. What business did he have going up to London incognitto?"

I said, that I supposed he needed money but was too proud to let it be known he had to go into a business. And supposing he had done the Murder for the money? But Miss Bellman asked why did he leave London then, you would think he had staid and got the benefit of Mr Tacker being arrested, which would leave him in possesssion of their Firm. Which I didn't know. By then it was snowing some so we went back to the Moulders Arms because Miss Bellman is thin blooded and not robust as I am.

We were having a warm by the public room fire when Constable Trumpiter came in looking very handsome, with the cold putting a bloom in his cheeks, and have I mentioned his hair is curly and a nice chesnut color? He swept off his hat and sat down by us and looked at me very direct and said, "Miss Squeers, you danced with Mr Johnson, did you not?" To which I replyed that I did, and he said "If I was to give you a pencil and paper, could you draw his counternance?"

At which I blushed for I never learnt drawing as my pa engaged that drawing-master but he left after a week and took the spoons too. So I demured. Constable Trumpiter said "Perhaps then you might describe him to me?" and he took out a notebook and pencil and licked the pencil point. "Was his face round or long?" So I said long and gave other particulers, with him asking more questions, and in a few minutes he held out the open book and said, "Is that him?"

I declare, Tilda, he had Mr Johnson, or should I say Mr Tollivere, to the life. He tapped the book with his pencil and said that he had found out the way to Swan Cottage by asking, and had gone there and watched, and seen this very gentleman standing at a window of the cottage. I was all for going there direct and having him Arrested, but Constable Trumpiter said we needed more Evidence he had done something wrong.

Miss Bellman then exitedly told him about what we had found out from the shopmistress. The Constable's eyes sparkled something lovely, he was very pleased; he said he'd just go up and see what he could learn from the servants up at The Larch, which was Mr Spool's Mansion. Miss Bellman wanted to go too, which shows a kumplete lack of discretion about what is proper, but Constable Trumpiter very kindly pointed out the snow was falling rather harder now and she ought to remain by the fire.

So we sat in the snug and had muffins and tea, and I am afraid Miss Bellman displaid an unbecoming apptite. She is rather plump, and if she goes on in this way I do not doubt but that her figger will be the worse for it. Still it is unlikely to matter much, as she is certain to make an old maid.

She lowered herself so far as to engage in conversation with the serving-maid who brought the muffins, asking what the news of the day was. The girl replyed, that there was to be a great party come Coronation Day, and Squire H— had put in an order for six barrels of wine to drink the little Queen's health, to be ordered special from France.

Miss Bellman then asked if it was likely Mr Spool would attend, at which the girl made a great show of scorn and said not likely; that he was a quarrelsome old man (only man is not the word she used, but to write the same would pollewt my pen) and hated everyone, and was like to die before summer ever came anyway. Then she coloured and said she was sorry to speak so, if we knew the man.

Of course we didn't, but this was more of Miss Bellman's cunning, for she said, "We only know him by hearsay; but I had heard Mr Spool was recovering and expected to live a while yet."

The saucy girl then put her finger by her nose and said she heard diffrent; and went so far as to sit down across from us and impart the news that her brother who knew the gardner at The Larch had heard that Mr Spool was sending to find his son, that he had quarreled with years agone, so as to make amends, and why should he do that unless he were like to die?

Miss Bellman said she supposed it might be so; and asked whether the old man had had any news of the boy. The girl said he wasn't a boy, if he was still alive; he would be quite old himself now. But from what she had heard, the earth might have swallowed him up for all that any one knew what had become of him, since he walked out of his fathers house declaring he would never see him again, and that was thirty years ago.

Miss Bellman said that was a great pity and the girl asked if there was anything else we wanted. I told her, "No, I thank you" and when she had gone I wished to have a few words with Miss Bellman about her deplorble habit of conversation with any-body.

But she exclaimed, that she'd give a pretty penny to know how much money Mr Spool had to leave to his Heirs. Which was such a common thing to say, I was quite repelled, though I wondered about the money myself. So we sat there, though she did not seem to notice my Mortifyed Silence because she was thinking quite hard, muttering to herself now and again, and her cheeks were so red from the cold and then sitting by the fire that I pitied her, for anyone seeing her must think she had been drinking Liquor.

Presently Constable Trumpiter came running in and said we must rouse our coachman if we were to get back to Lime House before nightfall. When we were back in the coach, Miss Bellman repeated what she had heard from the serving maid, and Constable Trumpiter forbore to rebeuke her, but listened cour-teously.

Then he told us what he had learned, which was that Mr Spool had a great deal of money indeed, and had had someone in to see about rewriting his will. It was supposed he had meant to Disinheirit his Grandson, Mr Tollivere. He had forborn doing this while his daughter was alive, but she had gone to her eternal reward two years since, leaving the Wastrel some little money of her own.

I saw at once that here "Mr Johnson" was caught out in another lie, for had he not said his mother was ill? And here she was dead. Which I said to Constable Trumpiter, who quite agreed. Though I still could not disern why the undoubted villain should kill a complete stranger like poor Mr Clement.

We parted with many respectful remarks and that night I lay in dreadful nightmares, all about Murder and Bloody Blades. Then I was in the shop in H— and it was full of sticks of sugar shaped like little Policemen, and when I turned around there was Spring-Heel'd Jack, who went down on one knee to offer me his heart, which made of metal and ran with blue and white Flames.

Next morning we heard how my poor Admirer had led the Police a merry chase, though they had been out with clubs and nets to catch him, and still had jumped out at an old woman near the Gas Works and pulled her hair. You can imagine that I breathed a sigh of relief to know that he had evaded Capture another night, but I did wish he would ceese this foolish passionate behaviour.

In the afternoon Constable Trumpiter came to the door, looking rather tired but smiling, and asked whether I and Miss Bellman would like to go with him back to H—, for he had just come from making more Inquiries and felt sure he had enough Evidence now to make an Arrest. I said yes with great alacrity and very nearly danced with impatience while Miss Bellman explaned to Aunt Pyelott. Aunt Pyelott was disinclined to let us go at first and the more so when she saw the two stout fellows Constable Trumpiter had with him, but on hearing what we were about she said to be sure and get a share in any fines that might be collected. Which had not even entered my mind I am sure.

In the coach, Constable Trumpiter told us what he had found out by going to the late Mr Clement's house. The Housekeeper had let him go through Mr Clement's papers and he had been specially interested in a packet relating to Mr Clement's late father: Certifiket of Death, debts paid and such. Most interesting of all, he said, were some old letters from a Miss Adeline Spool (later Mrs Adeline Tollivere) at The Larch, H—.

It seemed plain to me that this Mr Clement's father must have had some romantic connexion with Miss Spool, and perhaps there was a Missing Heir. What if Mr Clement had been Mr Johnson's (though I should call him Mr Tollivere) Lost elder

Brother? Except of course he should be ilejitimate, but sometimes great families hush that sort of thing up. Constable
Trumpiter said that all would be revealed in due time.

We were delayed on the Road what with one of the Horses
going lame and had to change for a fresh one at Five Mile House,
so it was twilight when we arrived in H——. We drove straight to
Swan Cottage. Constable Trumpiter said we ladies had perhaps
ought to remain in the Coach as there was likely to be unpleasantness when he arrested Edmund Tollivere. He got out with
the two stout gentlemen, who took a pair of clubs from under
the seat, and they went and knocked at the door of the
cottage. No sooner had they been admitted than Miss Bellman
said she must know what befell, and I agreed, so we got out and
walked round the cottage to see if there was any convenient
window to listen at. I am afraid I tript over and fell in a lettuce-
frame, which dissarrayed my hair rather.

Just round a box-tree on the corner of the house was a
window, and we could see in as well, though by reason of the
falling dark we could not be seen. The two stout gentleman
were standing at either door, and Mr Tollivere stood before his
hearth. Oh, what a change had come over his countenance! For
I had seen him at the Ball the very pictuer of agreeableness, but
now his expression was all compounded of fear, scorn and
wickedness genrally, and it made my blood boil to see him so
and think of his awful designs.

Constable Trumpiter stood before him, very grave, and was
just saying something about the suspicious circumstances attending Mr Tollivere's hasty removal from London, where he
was living under a false name. Mr Tollivere said he'd done no
such thing; he had lived quietly at Swan Cottage these five
years and never traveled. Constable Trumpiter said he had
witnesses to prove otherwise.

Mr Tollivere then sneered and said he had witnesses of his
own who would swear that he'd never gone up to London at all.
Constable Trumpiter, with no show of annoyance, said that
there was also the matter of the murdered man being Mr
Tollivere's cousin, which made the next likely to inherit a sure
suspect in the fowl crime.

"Oh, very likely," said Mr Tollivere, "My Grandfather has had paid men searching for his son for years now; they should have found him if anyone might, if he were still alive."

"But they did not have what you had," said Constable Trumpiter steadily. "Letters from Edgar Spool to his sister, your late mother, letting her know that he was well and had settled in London under the name of Clement." He went on to say that later Mr Spool-Clement must have written that he was married, for his sister wrote back to ask whether he would not reconcile with his father on the happy occasion. But, said Constable Trumpiter, he must have refused; for her next letter was dated some years later, offering consolation to her brothers widow and son.

"And when your mother died," said Constable Trumpiter, "You, going through her papers, found the letters from her brother, and learnt from them that you had a Cousin, and who he was and where he was likely to be. It was then you first planned to murder him." For you see Tilda, the Cousin (that was young Mr Clement, the deceased), should he be found, would stand to inherit all the Fortune.

How I admired Constable Trumpiter! He stood tall and straight and looked so handsome in his uniform as he was laying these charges. Edmund Tollivere said it was all rubbish and Constable Trumpiter said no it wasn't. He then went on to describe how Mr Tollivere had come to London, sought out his cousin, joined the Partnership under an Assumed Name, and watched all his cousins habits so as to learn when he might best do the dreadful deed.

When Spring-Heel'd Jack begun to Frequent Lime House, Mr Tollivere devised his Wicked Plan, to make it look as though my mad Admirer done it. When I heard this I was struck dumb with horror at the wicked cleverness of it all, for though I had been sure he was Guilty I had not understood the Depth of his Cunning. And when I thought of poor Jack, who is only mad for love of me, being drawn into his web of deseet my rath knew no bounds!

Constable Trumpiter said, "Now, sir, will you come with us to London? For you must go before the Magistrait."

Would you believe it Tilda, Mr Tollivere said that he would not; that Constable Trumpiter had no proof of his cock-and-a-bull story, and they were not in London, and if they did not quit his house instant he would see Constable Trumpiter dismissed from the Police for making False Accusations. But his voice was a little shrill and he was sweating.

I was in such a perfect feury I was insensible to danger, and seezed the window and pulled it open, and pointing my finger at him accused him of Murder; whereat all in the room started and Mr Tollivere was so dismayed by the Violent Emotion in my countenance that he screamed and backed into the fender, which put him in mind of Hellfire perhaps, for he fell over howling and begging for mercy, and I realized he thought I was an Aparishen, perhaps of Stern Justice herself.

Anyone would have despised him, to see him so unmanned by womans beauty. And it seemed that while he was Groveling there with his trousers afire he let slip some few words that he had been led astray by bad companions and had only done it because he was in debt, cetrer, which Constable Trumpiter told him was a confession.

Well they put manacles on him strait and now he sits in gaol and will be Tried and Hung, I have no doubt. I am happy and sereen for I have cleared my Admirers name, or at least have ensured that he will not be taken up for Murder. I cannot imagine how anyone could plot the death of his own Flesh and Blood. But then my Family is a very diffrent sort, as we Squeerses are all very fond of ourselves.

Oh, Tilda, how quiet things must be at Greta Bridge, compared to this! I am afraid I shall find it rather dull when I return. My best regards.

I remain
Yours and cetrer
Fanny Squeers

23 February 1838, Friday evening
Oh, Tilda, the Infamy of Men!
But you will not find this letter blotted with my tears. I am full of stern resolution and contempt for these poor creatures.

The news of Mr Tollivere's arrest was scarcely a day old when I had word that Spring-Heel'd Jack had proved false to me. He went to a house in Bow, enticed a Miss Alsop to come out to him in the Lane, and there Took Liberties with her person in a most shocking manner that left no doubt it was the same man who but a fortnight ago was so perockupied with me. It was Romeo and Rosaline played over. And there can be no question about his mistaking her for me because she had a candle by which he must have seen her quite clear.

After all my labours on his behalf to clear him of suspicion! I thought it really past anything for Rank Ingrattitude.

You should know too that Constable Trumpiter has proposed Marriage to Miss Bellman. We were all rather surprized but really it is much the best thing for her, even though he is so very common, as she is not likely ever to get a better offer. It is good for her she has such sharp eyes, she will need them when she must sew buttons on a poor Policemans uniform. And I daresay her plumpness will greatly diminish when she has to live on the sort of victuels a Policemans wage affords. May they be very happy together. I have no doubt they will be. But I had thought him a more discriminating person.

When we had been confronted with this news Uncle Pyelott was very cheerful, as well he might be since now he will be spared the expence of Miss Bellman's keep, and said we should have a bottle of Madeera to celebrate. But there were none in the Sideboard and Aunt Pyelott asked if I might step out to the Wine Merchants which was still open. I was glad of any excuse to get out of the parlour, even on so dark an evening, for it was hard to conceal my Disdain at the imoderit way Miss Bellman was behaving with Constable Trumpiter.

I was coming back and had not got above four or five yards from the Spirits Shop when who should have the effrontary to leap out before me but Spring-Heel'd Jack! My indignation knew no bounds and as you know I am Fearless when once my Temper is up. I brake the bottle of Madeera on a convenient wall and rushed at him with it, and the booby turned as if to run but I caught him and tript him up. The bottle did not cut him very badly because he wore some sort of oilskin, and he knocked it from my hand as I was dragging his helment off, but I took off part of his ear anyway and got my Knees on his Chest and so held him down pretty well as I renched the Mask off.

Imagine my amazement, Tilda, when I tell you it was not the handsome man with the black whiskers at all! I recognised him for a shy dull fellow who had stood mute by the Punch Bowl and wore a vulgar waistcoat that hardly danced with anybody. Which, as I remember because I asked at the time, was because he was only somebody's Clerk and not worth Cultivating the acquaintance of.

At the thought that such as he had dared to assault me, a gentlemans daughter, my very Blood boiled in my vanes. I rained Blows on him with my fists and pulled out his hair until he was screaming and weeping and emploring Mercy. He said it was only a joke and he meant no harm, and promised he would never do it any more. Only the thought that if he were taken by the Police it would all get into the papers made me decyst, and in any case he was making so much Noise someone might have come out to inquire what was the matter.

I did him an Injury he will not soon forget and, rising, pitched the disgusting Mask into the Canal. When I came back with the new bottle of Madeera he was dragging himself away on his hands and knees and begun to whemper when he saw me, but I spurned to notice him and only kicked him once in passing for I had done with him.

When I got back to Aunt Pyelott's I was quite faint at the dreadfulness of everything and was obliged to retire to my Chamber the rest of the evening.

It has all spoilt the City for me rather and I have decided to quit London next week, instead of staying until summer. I return to Dotheboys Hall sadder, Tilda, but ever so much wiser. I shall not again soon – if ever indeed – lose my heart to perfidious Men.

> I remain
> Yours and Cetrer
> Fanny Squeers

The End of Little Nell

Robert Barnard

In 1839 Dickens resigned his editorship of Bentley's Miscellany *and planned to issue a cheaper weekly magazine,* Master Humphrey's Clock, *to be filled almost entirely by his own writings. The magazine appeared in April 1840 and with it the first episode of* The Old Curiosity Shop. *This is the story of Little Nell and her grandfather, who owns an old antique shop. Nell looks after the shop and has no idea where her grandfather, who sleeps by day, goes at night. However, we learn that he has been borrowing money from the villainous Daniel Quilp, who believes the old man is a rich miser, though he had gambled that money away. When Quilp discovers this he takes possession of the shop, and Nell and her grandfather take to the road. Most of the rest of the novel tells of their adventures as they travel through town and country and meet an assortment of Dickensian characters, including Codlin and Short who run a travelling Punch and Judy show. Probably the most memorable scene in the story is when Little Nell dies. Dickens drew upon his own emotions following the death of his wife's sister, Mary, and his description brought the whole of Britain – and much of America – to tears.*

Robert Barnard, who has been called the "Jane Austen of mystery writers", is an expert in English literature, having taught it and written about it in the years before he turned to crime fiction. He is a noted expert in the works of Charles Dickens, having written Imagery and Theme in the Novels of Dickens *(1974). He is equally an expert on the Brontë sisters, having recently co-authored* A Brontë Encyclopedia *(2007). He has written several historical mysteries under the alias Bernard Bastable, including a series in which Mozart lives on into old age, which began with* Dead, Mr Mozart *(1995). Several of Barnard's mysteries focus on children and the dilemmas of childhood and books like* Little Victims *(1983),* Out of the Blackout *(1985),* The Masters of the House *(1994) and* The Bones in the Attic *(2001) explore many of the same issues as Dickens's novels. But Barnard is also a little mischievous at times and in the following story gives us an insight into the true nature of* Little Nell.

They were all poor country people in the church, for the castle in which the old family had died, was an empty ruin, and there were none but humble folks for seven miles around. They would gather round her in the porch, before and after the service; young children would cluster at her skirts; and aged men and women forsake their gossips, to give her a kindly greeting. None of them, young or old, thought of passing the child without a friendly word; the humblest and rudest had good wishes to bestow.

Right! That's enough of that garbage. Though I've a lot more of it up my sleeve before "Little Nell" can be allowed to die. The great British public can't get enough of such sentimental twaddle, and they shall get it a-plenty. When the book is finished I shall offer it to Mrs Norton, or Mrs Gore, and if it's not in their line I'll load it off on to Charles Dickens, who is certainly a low fellow, but he does a nice line in weepies himself. He'll take it on, put his name to it, earn a tidy sum. I have to say I sometimes enjoy writing about Nell myself, but that's probably because I enjoy re-creating myself in a totally false image. I think the image assumed its final perfect form for the pervy schoolmaster we met early in our travels – though I'd done the sweet *ingenue* quite often while serving in the Shop. Oh! that schoolmaster! What a twerp! All one ever got out of him was solicitude, tears and references to his favourite pupil who died back in the old village. You'd think people would have got suspicious of a schoolteacher who built his emotional life around a bright pupil who was dead. Particularly a bright *boy* pupil. But not everyone has my sophistication in these matters.

My re-creation of myself in the syrupy-sweet image of "Little Nell" began when the gaming houses and casinos of London started to get wise to grandad's and my little scam. That scam involving my taking three or four years off my age and being always taken to gambling dens by Kit Nubble – a dim spark if ever I saw one. Grandfather always went on his own, so no one ever associated us, and I could wander round the tables where he was playing and then sign him the details of what was in their hands. When they did get wise to us every establishment in London was circularized with our details, which was mighty unfair, and meant we had to take to the road and find out-of-town establishments where we could ply our trade without detection. We kept moving, because if one person keeps winning the big boys soon get suspicious. Sometimes we tried a bit of begging, but that was mainly for laughs. My grandfather has a great sense of humour.

Mind you, I don't like the road, not as I like London, where I always feel at home. You see some really odd types on the road. Take Mrs (a courtesy title, I wouldn't mind betting) Jarley, her of the waxworks – musty mummies trailed around the country in a procession of carts and caravans, and presenting a very cut-price version of Mme Tussaud's classy show in Baker Street. Mrs Jarley really took a shine to me, and it didn't take me long to guess that she was of the Sapphic persuasion.

"Such a sweet child," she would say, patting me on the

thighs, the arms, and any joint that took her fancy. "She reminds me of the dear young queen."

The dear young queen strikes me as having a mental age of about twelve, and looks like the chinless wonders who inflict their feebleness on the Household Cavalry and any regiment with colourful gear to camp around in. I did not take kindly to the comparison.

"Her Majesty seems very neglectful of her duties as head of the Church of England," I said. "Sad that one so young shuns the proper Sunday observance."

"I had no idea," said Mrs Jarley, stopping her patting.

"Ah – London knows," I said. "And London keeps it to itself."

There's nothing like a bit of Metropolitan insider knowledge to make provincials feel inferior. And if you haven't got any insider knowledge, make it up.

I enjoyed my time with the waxworks display. I enjoyed presenting myself as a child barely into double figures. I enjoyed luring people into the tatty display by highly inflated claims of what it contained. I enjoyed most of all slipping off in the night to various rustic gambling hells to ply our trade and hone our skills. The Jarley routine of moving from one place to another made this last pleasure easier to procure. One or two visits to the local low place and we were on the road to another source of income. Grandfather was over the moon, and kept his winnings about his person. He never knew exactly how much he had won, so when I was putting him to bed drunk in the early hours I could abstract a bit for my own use.

Needless to say I put a rather different gloss on these activities in the manuscript I was preparing to hawk to Mrs Norton or that vulgar, jumped-up newspaper reporter Mr Dickens.

This pleasant life changed when we met up again with Codlin and Short. We had made their acquaintance a few months earlier, somewhere near Birmingham. You won't be surprised to hear they were an odd couple. I had no problem with them because I was used to the phenomenon from our

London circles: the pair of men, usually middle-aged, who squabbled and competed and bad-mouthed each other to outsiders but who really were as close-knit as a nut and a bolt. And Codlin was definitely the nut. He was always insisting that *he* was my real friend, not Short, and I never quite realized what his motives in doing this were – whether he had plans for some scam or other that required a young, virginal, stupendously innocent creature. Or was he hoping to get tips on my grandfather's unrivalled techniques in card-play, the tables, horse-racing and cock-fighting?

We were on the way to Stratford-on-Avon, and Mrs Jarley was stroking my hair and telling me what a wonderful Shakespearean actress I would make in a few years – instancing Cordelia, Miranda and Celia, and I guessed these were innocent, slightly wet creatures, without an ounce of spunk.

"You have an aura," she was saying, "a heavenly atmosphere that envelopes you, so that you would be an ideal embodiment—"

My mind strayed from this fulsome garbage and I saw, further along up the main street of the small town we were passing through, two peak-capped figures gazing into a shop window. Peelers. Members of that elite body of men recruited by Sir Robert Peel when he was Home Secretary, to reduce crime in the cities by their unique combination of brains and brawn. I *don't* think! Just look at how much, or little, they get paid and guess how likely it is that the job will attract the elite.

I was just thinking the set of the two backs bending forward to survey the wares exhibited in the window reminded me of people I knew when they turned round as they heard the approach of hoofs and wheels.

Codlin and Short!

As we passed them by I raised my hand, and was rewarded by a double wave, very enthusiastic, in return. They began walking vigorously along beside us, only slowly getting left behind.

Fortunately we stopped at a public house on the edge of the town. Well, not fortunately – inevitably. We stop in nearly every town, so that Mrs Jarley can lubricate her coster-woman's voice and her travelling hands. When she had steamed off to get her gin and water, grandfather brought me my shrub, with double rum to taste, and he went to mingle with the local mugs while I waited for the precious pair to catch us up.

"Well, you have landed on your feet!" came a voice from the caravan doorway. Actually I was still recumbent on Mrs Jarley's well-padded couch, but I knew what he meant.

"We'd heard about the two new members of the company, and we guessed it had to be you and grandad. Mrs Jarley taken a fancy to you, has she?" asked Short.

"Actually I am extremely useful to the Museum manage-ment," I said demurely. "I've brought hundreds through the door."

"Didn't answer my question, did she, Codlin?" said Short, grinning.

"Don't be so personal, Short. A girl's got a right to her secrets, hasn't she, my darling?"

"And does Grandad get hundreds through the door too?" asked Short. "Or does he suggest a quick game of vingt-et-un, and line his pockets that way? His sort of swindle is not so different from Jarley's kind, when you come down to it."

Codlin nodded.

"Morally speaking I think you've hit the nail on the head, Short."

"I'm not used to hearing you moralize," I said. "I suppose it's the new job, is it?"

"Oh, the new job! No, my darling, Sir Robert's successor doesn't pay us to moralize. He pays us to catch criminals. Or failing that to keep track of them." Short paused. "It's a real police state he's created, but we're the *last* people who can talk about that. We get messages and send messages, and that means some little placeman in Westminster can put pins in his wall-map of England and show where all the big criminals and most of the small ones as well are at any moment."

"Which is why we're happy to have caught up with you again," said Codlin.

"But why? We're not big criminals."

"You're middle-ranking. And the gambling industry has a lot of good friends in this government, thanks to their readiness to grease the right palms. So we're just telling you: there are stories going round linking a widespread gambling scam to a certain travelling display of ageing waxworks. Get me? And if you or your revered grandfather slips us a ten quid note and renews it every time our paths cross, we'll keep you informed and tip you the wink when it's time to move on."

"Wouldn't Sir Robert, or his successor, be angry if he found out?"

"Livid – if he found out. But if he wants to stamp out corruption in the nation's police force he'd better start paying us what we're worth." He wagged a finger in my face. "Until then he'll find that the work never gets done."

"We're public guardians bold and daring," sang Short, in a quavering baritone: "When danger looms we're never there."

"But if we see a helpless woman, or little boys who do no harm," took up Codlin, "we run 'em in, we run 'em in – I say, is that your revered Grandaddy I see coming towards us?"

It was, and when he heard what the pair were offering he stumped up. Always good to have friends in high places. We decamped quietly from the waxworks display that evening, taking a quite different route from them, and leaving Mrs Jarley with nowhere to put her hands.

The places we stopped at, on all of which we left our mark, I will not mention in detail, but we rarely stopped long enough to need a warning from Codlin and Short. We were on to a very good thing. Our lives changed, however, when we happened on the village to which the schoolmaster whom we had encountered early on in our travels had moved. Here he was, large as life and just as dispiriting. He was still mourning the bright young pupil he had had years before, and still polishing the young hypocrite's halo every day of his life. A right little teacher's pet that limb of Satan must have been! It occurred to us that this was the sort of place we could well settle down in.

Well, as soon as the idea occurred to us, we wrote to Codlin and Short. We explained that there were several towns within walking distance, as well as several lucrative hell-holes. We had made a series of nocturnal excursions after the village was asleep (at about 8.30, in order to save candles), and we really felt the place would answer, at least for a year or two. We heard back from them that they could think of no reason why it shouldn't, and they would keep us informed as to anything they heard of that could be construed as a threat. And so things went on for three or four months.

Then I got bored.

I suppose we should have expected that. The night excursions still held a charm, but the daytime was terrible – catching up on sleep and enduring shiver-making visits from the school-teacher or from his equally unappetizing friend The Bachelor – a local notable of similar habits and notions (my impersonation of infantile goodness and sweetness confirmed all his preconceptions about the non-carnal nature of the English female). I was tired of them all. I wanted London, I wanted stir, glamour, rich pickings. I was even nostalgic about Dan Quilp, one of our London friends, who had managed to evict grandfather from the Old Curiosity Shop: beneath his ugly, dwarfish exterior there lurked a diabolical energy, both criminal and sexual. He radiated an indiscriminate hunger and love of wreaking havoc. I understood why women were both repelled and thrilled by him. I wanted to get a share in that electricity, match myself with him. I hadn't been so excited since those lovely years when I was the only girl member of Fagin's gang.

I always remember the ending of Codlin and Short's letter, when we had written to them to broach the problem. It read: "Why doesn't she die?"

When we wrote asking them to elaborate on the question, they sketched in the plan which eventually with slight changes we adopted.

"Have dear little Eleanor sicken, slowly, inexorably. Orchestrate a chorus of village concern as she sinks, passing into a better world. Resist the temptation to open the deathbed scene to the general public at a shilling a time. Do it all tastefully. Have her practise short breathing – getting tiny gulps in in a way that hardly moves the lungs. When she is 'dead' have a simple funeral, though one marked by inconsolable local grief. Take the coffin to the local church and have grandpa mount guard over her all night. Keep a supply of sand in the vestry (NOT rubble, it tends to rattle). Fill (or half fill) the coffin with it. In the morning have the ceremony, bury the sand, and get Nell off to London suitably disguised – as her real self, we would suggest. Hey presto! In the future she can come back to visit her grandad if she wants to – posing as a long-lost cousin."

It was a wonderful idea! It left grandad free to use his great gifts in the country gaming holes, and it left me in London sampling the high life of Mayfair and the low life of Dan Quilp and his haunts. I liked the idea so much that I fell ill the very day we got the letter.

I didn't overdo it, of course. I am nothing if not tasteful. At first I was very brave, denying that I was ill at all. When they commented on my pallid complexion (flea powder) I shook my head bravely, then said there was nothing wrong. Then I thought it must be something I had eaten. Then I lost the use of my legs (they all shook their heads gravely at that). Before ten days were out I was permanently confined to bed, offering my visitors sickening platitudes, and sweetly prophesying I would soon be up again and as busy as ever. Tears flowed like cataracts. Behind their hands everyone started making suggestions for the gravestone.

The end was unutterably poignant. We made it semi-public. The schoolmaster and The Bachelor were there, and a couple of rustics who could be relied on to get everything wrong and then rehash their account to the whole village, over and over again. I was visibly failing, and much whiter than the sheets on my bed. When the little knot of witnesses was assembled I began the tearful climax to my short life.

"Grandad," I said (he was sitting on my bed, and now clutched my hand in his horny one), "I think a change is coming. I think I am getting better. Is the sun shining? How I would love to see the sun again. It is getting light. The whole world is becoming brighter. I feel I am in a new place – better and more lovely than anything I have known before—"

And so on. And on. I managed about ten minutes of this, and then my voice started to fade. Words could be heard – "world", "bright", "sun" and others, but nothing together that made sense until I suddenly said "Grandad, give me the sun" and my head fell back on the pillow, and my grandfather let out an anguished howl.

Artistic, I'm sure you'll agree.

The witnesses clustered round, observing the lifeless corpse and the sobbing frame of that old fraud my grandfather. Then he stood up, still wracked with sobs, and ushered them out of the door.

He drew the heavy curtains, locked the door, and then the pair of us had a good if quiet laugh. After a while grandad slipped out to order a coffin from the village carpenter. He found it was almost ready, as the carpenter with his practised eye had made a note of the likely size and had done most of the work a couple of weeks earlier. We, or he, took delivery that evening.

We made a slight change of plan. The nights were drawing in and the days were nippy. I didn't fancy (as we had planned) a long day in the staircase leading up the church tower while the funeral went ahead and night fell. We agreed to do the substitution in the cottage. We had a showing of me in the coffin next day, when the whole village and rustic dolts from miles around filed past uttering idiocies like "She do seem at peace" and "Oh what a 'eavenly hexpression she do 'ave". When that collection of human rubble had passed through I jumped out of the coffin. Grandfather and I heaved the sack of sand (purloined by him from a building site) into the coffin and he nailed it down extremely tightly. We heaved it on to a trestle and went to bed in Grandad's bed. It will not have passed my sharper readers by that, whatever else he was, Grandad was certainly not my grandfather.

I have, writing now from the Old Curiosity Shop and

awaiting another visit from dear, excitable Mr Quilp, who is finding me a bit of a handful, only one or two details to add. The next day, the funeral, was a big laugh. It was the last day of Little Nell, that brilliant creation the world had come to love. The vicar was in church, and the schoolmaster, the Old Bachelor, the gravedigger and Grandad assembled in our cottage to carry the coffin to the churchyard. As they were heaving it up on to their shoulders the schoolmaster said, in his typically spiritless tone of voice:

"I'm sure Little Nell is already there, at home in Paradise, chanting with the heavenly choir."

"I'd lay you ten pounds at whatever odds you choose to name that she's up there now, singing along with them other angels, lungs fit to bust," said Grandad, winking towards the bedroom door, where I was surveying the delicious scene through the keyhole and barely suppressing my roars of laughter.

I laugh when I think of that now. We made such fools of them all, Grandad and I. Putty in our hands, that's what they were. I long to have Mr Quilp helpless like the yokels, also putty in my hands. Already he is mad with jealousy every time I look at a London swell, which is fairly often, because they're on every street corner. But I must go very slowly. I have so much to learn from Mr Quilp about crime, about gaining the upper hand over the fools around me. I learned a lot from Fagin, but I could not use my sex with him, for obvious reasons. With Quilp I can use my sex to get from him every jot and tittle he knows. I said to him two evening ago I needed above all to learn, and he was my chosen master, the one who would lead me up the path to my being Europe's Queen of Crime. "Wait till I see you next time," said my dear Quilp. "I'll give you a lesson as'll last you a lifetime."

I think that's him. Those are his uneven steps on the stairs. I can't wait to see his delicious deformed body. His hands are on the doorkn—

Here the creator of Little Nell fell silent for ever.

Encounter in the Dark

F. Gwynplaine MacIntyre

Dickens followed The Old Curiosity Shop *with* Barnaby Rudge, *his first historical novel and, though not intended solely as a murder mystery, arguably one of the first historical whodunnits. The contract for the novel had been outstanding for several years and had become a millstone around Dickens's neck. Once it was completed he determined to escape the restriction of monthly serials and decided to explore America – an enthusiasm that was not shared by his wife, Kate. Amongst other things, she dreaded leaving the children – there were four by now, Charles, Mary, Kate and Walter. To help console her, Dickens agreed she could be accompanied by her maid, Anne. The American trip lasted from January to June 1842 and Dickens wrote a detailed travelogue in* American Notes, *which was published at the end of the year. It's not ranked amongst his most interesting books but it remains a useful study of American society at that time, and shows much that disturbed Dickens about America, especially slavery. He also used the tour to promote the need for a copyright agreement between Britain and America to stop the piracy of books and stories. Dickens was incensed that American publishers could grow rich on reprinting his work without paying a penny.*

Dickens's itinerary was exhausting – Boston, Hartford, New Haven, New York, Philadelphia, Baltimore, Washington, Richmond, Harrisburg, Pittsburgh, Cincinnati . . . and on and on. And all the time Dickens was in demand and he could not relax. He was feted and applauded, and long before the journey was over Dickens felt trapped by his own fame. He had discovered how difficult it was to escape his celebrity.

One of the places which Dickens enjoyed was Philadelphia. While there, he was keen to see the vast new Eastern Penitentiary, at the time the largest building in America, and a special visit was arranged for him. One man who must have envied Dickens was Edgar Allan Poe. Three years older than Dickens, Poe was struggling to find anything remotely like the same attention for his stories and poems. He hoped that Dickens might be his ticket to fame and sought to meet the man when he came to Philadelphia. Dickens made no mention of Poe in his Notes, *though the meeting took place, much as described in the following story.*

F. Gwynplaine MacIntyre is the author and co-author of several books, including the science-fiction novels The DNA Disaster *(1991) and* The Woman Between the Worlds *(1994). His non-fiction has been published in* The New York Daily News, Literary Review, Games Magazine *and many British and US publications. In 2003, he was short-listed for the Montblanc/Spectator Award for his arts journalism.*

6 March, 1842

The blood! The unrelenting blood! Its flow cannot be stanched!

The dread pestilence of *tubercular consumption*, so recently christened by Doctor Schönlein of Berlin, is at once both the red death and the *white plague*, the latter so named for the ashen death-pallor it confers on its victims. This pallor haunts my earliest memory: when I was not yet two years old, I recall my mother coughing up consumptive blood and tubercular lesions as she died in the cellar of the Indian Queen tavern, in Richmond. Eleven years ago, in Baltimore, the self-same plague carried off my brother Henry, and I left my posting at West Point scantly in time to reach his bedside before he succumbed.

Now, here in Philadelphia, the white plague has marked its next prey. Three fortnights past, on the twentieth of January – the evening after my thirty-third birthday – I was with my sweet wife, in our rented home at the adjunction of Coats Street and Fairmount on this city's northwestern outskirts. My darling Virginia was at her piano-forte, performing Thomas Moore's "Come Rest in This Bosom". She sweetly sang, in her light and clear soprano . . . when, at midpoint through the third stanza:

> ". . . thine Angel I'll be
> 'mid the horrors of this.
> Through the furnace, unshrinking . . ."

Oh, Judas! I beheld the sudden gushing from her mouth, the swift eruption, as my little wife Virginia incontinently coughed up tubercular blood. In the six weeks since then, her consumption has worsened. There is no cure; there is only grim certainty that this plague, this monstrous red death will eventually devour her.

I have nursed her as best I could. She lies awake with the night sweatings, her thin eyelids so very nearly transparent that I easily perceive the narrow blue veins through her flesh. Her skin has turned as pale as alabaster, in grotesque contrast to her sloe-black eyes. Virginia lies moaning in her narrow bed, with the roof-beam nearly scraping her forehead . . . for our meagre cottage is so small, and its roof inclined so sharply, that the rafter barely affords a passage of three inches above my sick wife as she repines in her agony.

I have fed her Jew's beer, and purchased such medications as I can afford or pledge upon. Her mother Maria, my aunt –

my beloved Muddy, as we call her – renders such assistance as she can. We must take it in turns to fan my wife, and so cool her fevers, else she cannot breathe at all. Even sweet Catterina, our little tortoise-shell cat, gives aid by lying closely with my wife in her narrow bed, and so sharing the tiny warmth of her own body. This past fortnight, Virginia has haemorrhaged thrice. The bright flame of my little wife's existence, so briefly lighted, steadily dwindles into gloom.

We are fortunate, at least, that here in my adopted city Philadelphia I have attained the proudest growth of my literary endeavours. I am situated as editor of *Graham's Magazine*, reaping a yearly wage just above $800. Six days ago, on the end-month, George Graham paid me $58 of my salary: I have already spent nearly all on medicines and repayment of debts, yet this sum is the veritable purse of Fortunatus when contrasted with the pathetic wages I received in New-York and Baltimore.

Here in Philadelphia, this past April witnessed in *Graham's Magazine* the publication of my "Murders in the Rue Morgue", something altogether new and different in literature: a tale of ratiocination and deduction; of a crime committed, clues perceived, and a solution deduced. In spasmodic leaps, my reputation grows . . . and I yearn that my invalid wife may yet live long enough to behold the sacred day when chance and fortune elevate me to the station rightfully my due, as the author and journalist *Edgar A. Poe*.

It maddens me that I remain so little known, so unacclaimed. Recent numbers of the *Philadelphia Public Ledger* have heralded the approach of the English author Charles Dickens, visiting America on a lecture tour. Dickens! The most applauded author in the world! The most beloved . . . and, assuredly, the wealthiest. This man Dickens is three years younger than I; in consequence, he has spent the less time toiling at our mutual craft. Yet fame, wealth, adulation come easily to him, while I labour in unjust obscurity. Last May, I reviewed Mr Dickens's novel *Barnaby Rudge* for the *Saturday Evening Post* . . . and in such wise I glean a few crumbs of the public crust for myself and my writing, as a parasite upon the works of Dickens! Meantime, my own two volumes of *Tales of the Grotesque and Arabesque* were first published nearly two years past by Lea & Blanchard of this city, yet continue to lie fallow in the book-stalls. If justice dwelt in earthly realms, this Charles Dickens would be writing reviews of my tales, while I would be touring the world and harvesting acclaim!

Still, I may yet achieve a portion of my due. The gazettes report that, yester-evening, Mr Dickens arrived in Philadelphia from New-York. He has slipped past me in the night, then: for my small rented hovel in northwestern Philadelphia stands only a few yards north to the tracks of the Columbia Rail Road which conveyed Mr Dickens to this place.

I have sent greetings to Mr Dickens by courier, taking care to refer to the two volumes of my *Tales*. This morning, while my poor wife coughed and vomited, I received a reply from Dickens, vowing that he will deign to meet me in his rooms at the United States Hotel, in tomorrow's forenoon. I mean to urge him to take copies of my stories back to Britain with him, and thus contrive that the combined weight of my literary skill and Mr Dickens's influences will persuade some London publisher to bring forth an edition of my *Tales*. There being no copyright agreement a-twixt our two nations, I can only hope that England's publishers will prove honest enough to midwife my stories without diddling me out of fair payment. The world has cheated me more than enough.

7 March

The United States Hotel, on Chesnut Street between Fourth and Fifth Streets, is at once both familiar ground and yet alien domain to me. Familiar, because my editorial desk in the offices of *Graham's Magazine* is situated on the top storey of Mr Graham's premises at the southwest corner of Chesnut and Third, affording me a splendid view of the roof and façade of the hotel. The *Philadelphia Public Ledger* emits its gazettes from a lower storey of the same building as Graham's offices. At the crossroads of Chesnut and Fourth, adjoining the hotel to its east, stand the mocking portals of Lea & Blanchard: alleged publishers of my *Tales of the Grotesque*, which they refuse to advertise. Within that same block of edifices – Chesnut, between Fourth and Fifth – I am taunted by the eight Doric pillars forming the mocking countenance of the Second Bank of the United States, which failed so ignominiously thirteen months ago. Before that debacle, I had contracted with Mr Graham to finance – and with his colleague J. R. Pollock to publish – what would have been my proudest achievement: *The Penn Magazine*, a journal to be wholly edited and largely written by myself. Had the bank suspensions not queered my prospects for this venture, I would now be a successful editor, with sufficient wealth to house my dear wife and her mother in a far more healthful domicile. When the Second Bank collapsed, it killed my hopes . . . yet the edifice still stands, taunting me. Just farther westward on Chesnut, between Seventh and Eighth Streets, stands the Masonic Hall where – three years past – I glimpsed within its exhibition cage the bestial *Ourang-Outang* that inspired my "Murders in the Rue Morgue". This thoroughfare, indeed, is known to me.

Yet the United States Hotel – the most luxurious guest-house in Philadelphia – is *terra incognita* . . . for I have never previously entered its foyer, owing to the fact that my shabby appearance would at once declaim me as a trespasser in such wealthed environs.

At quarter-past eleven this morning I entered the hotel, dressed in a suit of sombre black – formerly blue, yet dyed the darker colour to conceal its frayings – and a mended pair of gloves . . . for I have nothing better to wear. In the hotel's lobby, lacking a *carte-visite*, I gave my name to a negro pageboy along with Mr Dickens's regards, and I was swiftly ushered into the suite of the distinguished Englishman.

Charles Dickens, I observed, wore a fawn-coloured morning-suit and a chocolate-coloured velvet waistcoat, surmounted with a watch-chain and fob which are – my instincts warrant it – genuine gold. His necktie, of dark green silk, is restrained by a tie-clasp ornamented in diamonds: I am confident as to their authenticity. In this man's mere ornaments, I am confronted by more wealth than I have ever possessed in my lifetime!

Dickens is clean-shaven, with smooth youthful features nearly girlish in tone, framed by auburn hair: a trifle longer than the American fashion, and a more attractive hue than my own dark brown tresses. At five foot nine, he stands an inch taller than myself. I have studied this man's particulars intently enough to know that Charles Dickens's thirtieth birthday occurred precisely one month ago this very day, yet he might easily pass for a man of some seven years younger. If his soul knows aught of hunger or despair, I fail to discern it in his smooth unlined face.

As his first lecture of the day was imminent – in the theatre just west of here: at Sixth Street, below the Arcade – I hastened to my purpose. Giving Mr Dickens the two volumes of my *Tales of the Grotesque and Arabesque*, I made bold to suggest that he might find some London publisher willing to venture them. Hoping to drum up some interest in my poetic achievements, I drew Dickens into a comparison between my own verse "Al Aaraaf" and Emerson's "The Humble Bee", the latter ode being laughable in its ineptitude.

At this point Dickens interrupted me, remarking that he was due upon the lecture stage. I was gratified by the interest he expressed – either genuine, or impressively feigned – in my opinions, and he asked me to meet him again after his *matinée* lecture.

I would gladly have attended Dickens's lecture, but I lacked the price of a ticket and he ventured no hint of arranging my entry on a *gratis* basis. I excused myself, and hastened to the Chesnut Street Theatre. A vast crowd of Philadelphians had assembled, hoping for a glimpse of the famous "Boz". They seemed far more interested in getting a look at him than in hearing anything he had to say.

As I loitered outside the showplace, from within I heard

the shouts and applause of the audience who had assembled to hear Mr Dickens. Between the huzzahs, I occasionally heard a solitary voice raised in tones of eloquence. I could not distinguish its words, yet I marked this instantly by his London accent as the voice of Dickens himself. It is a curious fact that an observant auditor can readily discern a foreign accent, even when the speaker is too distant for his precise words to be rendered coherent.

While I waited at the door, an exceedingly well-dressed and pompous figure strolled up to the theatre's portico. He was short, about thirty years of age, yet heavy-set with the beginnings of stoutness. He wore sleek black side-whiskers, and his back-hair grew longer than is fashionable, compensating for incipient baldness at the front. A black silk necktie was fashioned into an elaborately floppy bow beneath his doubled chin. He bowed obsequiously to me, and he doffed a prosperous-looking high-crowned silk hat.

"Good day to you, sir!" he boomed at me. "Have you come to hear Mister Dickens? I have the honour to be his personal friend of long standing."

"You also have the distinctive accent of a Philadelphian," I told him, ignoring the hand which he proffered. "Your vowels proclaim that you have lived in this metropolis all your life . . . and, since Charles Dickens has only just arrived here last night, you cannot have known him very long."

"Er, ah, true!" the newcomer admitted. "I am indeed a proud *alumnus* of Philadelphia's free-school system. I refer, of course, to knowing Mr Dickens through his novels and essays." The stranger bowed again, more elaborately. "Permit me to introduce myself. I am . . ."

"You are a hatter," I told him.

The man stood thunderstruck. "You have seen my hat-shop in Sixth Street, then."

"No; I have seen the stain on your fingertips." I pointed to his right hand, on the extremities of which was a bright carrot-colored stain. Hatters obtain the felt for their hats by a process known as "carroting": this requires the treatment of fur pelts with a solution of mercuric nitrate, which leaves a vivid orange residue.

The pompous intruder resumed his pomposity. "I am indeed a hatter, sir, among my other talents." He brandished his headgear. "This tile, I make so bold, is one of my own manufacture. I am Colonel Thomas Birch Florence, at your service."

Now I knew this man, for his name had preceded his face into my consciousness. Colonel Florence! He has been prominent in Philadelphia's temperance movement, which explains why our paths have never crossed. As for Tom Florence's colonelcy: his alleged rank was self-awarded, when he formed a regiment of Philadelphia militiamen to fight in the Texas Revolution. His militia's bravados festooned themselves with medals and epaulets, yet ventured no nearer to Texas than the quayside of the Philadelphia Navy Yard.

I had not yet gleaned as much of Charles Dickens's attentions as I'd hoped, and now I feared that this hat-maker intended to usurp those same attentions for himself. "What brings you away from your *chapeaux*?" I carefully inquired of Colonel Florence.

"Why, sir, I mean to persuade the great Boz to take a moment to greet eight or nine of my friends from Philadelphia's political clubs," Florence explained, with no small amount of bluster. "As well, to greet a delegation of businessmen from Smith's Hall, in the Lombard Street district."

At this name, I felt my lip curl in contempt. "The men who congregate in Smith's Hall are all of a colour, and the wrong one at that," I rejoined. "I hardly suppose that the world's most esteemed author will deign to shake hands with a mob of common Africans."

Colonel Florence seemed outraged. "They are Americans, sir! And God's children, as well. Surely, your sympathies lie with the abolitionist cause, sir?"

I did not choose to give answer. Smith's Hall, I am reliably informed, was built as a meeting-place for escaped slaves and their would-be saviours, and the hall's construction was financed by a wealthy negro businessman. The mere thought that a savage blackamoor might prosper, while I lack funds to purchase medicine for my dear wife, provokes me to a phrensy of anger . . .

By the sounds of applause within the Chesnut Street Theatre, I knew that Mr Dickens had nearly terminated his lecture. I hastened back to the United States Hotel, where again I persuaded the coloured pageboy to usher me into the celebrity's presence. This time, when I entered the parlour of Dickens's hotel suite, I found the room unoccupied. Yet a moment later the author emerged, having exchanged his previous morning-suit for a yellow silk dressing-gown with violet facings. I suppressed my revulsion at this *gaucherie*, reminding myself that I needed the gentleman's good favours. Dickens seemed genuinely pleased to see me again, as he seated himself on the chaise-longue while giving sign that I was to make myself comfortable in the suite's second-best chair.

"Mister Poe," he began. "I am greatly impressed with your powers of intuition. You published a review of my serial novel *Barnaby Rudge* while the series was not yet completed, yet you correctly guessed the murderer's identity, as well as several other details."

"That was not intuition," I corrected him. "It is ratiocination, or rational *detection*. My review in the *Saturday Evening Post* correctly foretold several particulars of your novel, and I was wrong in only one prediction. I anticipated that Grip, the talking raven owned by Rudge, would play a major rôle in the plot's *denouement*. Your raven, Mr Dickens, was a powerful symbolic device, yet you ultimately squandered him."

"Did I, quotha!" Charles Dickens held a trace of scorn in his reply, and of a sudden I felt acutely conscious of the shabbiness of my own garments – and the shabbiness of my very life – in contrast to his. "Well, Poe, go ahead with a raven of your own, then, and see if you'll have better success than I did."

"Perhaps I will, sir," I assured him.

"Tell me more of these *detections*," Dickens went on. "I have read your 'Murders in the Rue Morgue'. My dear Poe! This is altogether a new form of literature, deserving a new name. The *puzzle-story*, one might call it: a mystery to be unriddled by the reader, with all the clues in plain sight. You must write more of those . . . *mysteries*."

"I intend to," I said graciously. By way of an example of the science of detection – and hoping to impress Mr Dickens – I now related my encounter with the self-commissioned Colonel Florence, and told of how I had deduced his trade by a stain on his fingers. I saw the Englishman's dark grey eyes taking silent inventory of my hands as I spoke, for I had taken off my shabby gloves.

"A clever trick, sir, to know a hatter by his carroting," said Dickens. "Let me return your trick of deductive observation. You are clearly a man deeply preoccupied: an author who does much of his writing in late hours, by dim lamp-light . . . for I perceive ink-stains between the two major fingers of your right hand, as well as the white flakes of crystallized lamp oil – we call it *paraffin* in England – on your clothes: indeed, there is a general odour of paraffin about you. Further, I mark a peculiar stain on your left shoe: a mingling of both yellow sputum and dark brown tubercular blood. And, pray: what is this amber-coloured stain on your shirt-cuff?"

The sputum and blood had been coughed up by my little dear wife this morning: the amber stain a residue of the Jew's beer which is now her sole nutrient. I felt my face flush with anger, that this well-dressed and wealthy Dickens should call attention to my own shabbied garments and the stains of my preoccupations. At the same moment, I felt an up-welling surge of self-pity at my undeserved penury and its consequences. In that instant, I confessed all to Dickens: my wife's illness, our poverty and hard living conditions . . . even the bank failure which had dashed my hopes of editorial success.

But, hold! This outburst is unseemly. With a manful effort, I derailed myself from my incontinent confession and I swiftly made a change of topic: "In fact, sir, my 'Murders in the Rue Morgue' was entirely fiction," I told Dickens, "but I am now in progress of a sequel, based on the true unsolved mystery of a Manhattan cigar-girl who . . ."

Just this instant, the parlour door swung open and a red-faced man arrived, in extreme agitation. "Mister Dickens!" he panted. "A word with you, sir."

Dickens performed the introductions: this new arrival was William Hoysradt, the hotel's assistant manager. Hoysradt clutched to-day's edition of *The Daily Chronicle*. "Did you place this advertisement without the hotel's consent, Mister Dickens?" he asked.

I stole a glance over Dickens's shoulder as he perused the newspaper. On its third page was a "squib" advertisement, announcing that Mister Charles Dickens of London would appear for one hour on the morning of March eighth – tomorrow – in the lobby of the United States Hotel, and would shake hands with all who chose to meet him. The squib gave assurance that ladies attending the event would be quite safe, as there would be no admittance granted either to negroes or firemen.

"This is disastrous!" said Hoysradt, mopping his forehead with a handkerchief. "The hotel's directors will never approve. The thought of every ruffian and Irishman in Philadelphia, tracking street-dust into our . . ."

"It is preposterous, sir," said Dickens. "I made no such offer, and I am certain that my secretary Putnam made none on my behalf. You may assure your directors, Hoysradt, that I have no intention of . . ."

"Please, Mister Dickens!" The red-faced manager looked as if he were about to burst from syncope. "If only it were that simple. This advertisement, or a variant, is in every Philadelphia paper. Even the *Episcopal Recorder*! The entire city has seen it, I tell you. Already, we have had more than ninety inquiries . . ."

I saw Dickens turn pale. Hoysradt continued gibbering. The gist of his outburst was this: although Charles Dickens did not want to perform this impromptu reception, and the hotel's management held no desire to host it, on the whole it would be better for the event to proceed than otherwise, lest the disappointed hordes foment a riot in the hotel's lobby.

In my private thoughts, I found it galling that thousands of Philadelphians might clamour for a chance to shake Charles Dickens's hand, while I – an author of no less skill than Dickens – must struggle to make myself known, and the only people eager to meet me are bill-collectors. Now I tried to turn the conversation back to the vital topic of Dickens using his influence to speak on my behalf to London publishers. But it was clear that this unsolicited advertisement – and the identity of the unknown advertiser – had altered Dickens's priorities. Urging me towards the door, Dickens swiftly promised that he would indeed advocate my *Tales of the Grotesque and Arabesque* upon his return to England. I found myself out in the corridor, still holding my mended gloves.

8 March

My poor little wife grows more ill by the hour. Aunt Maria, dearest Muddy – in one fell bargain she is at once my father's elder sister, my mother-in-law, and my substitute mother – has done as best she can to cool her daughter's fevers. I find myself thinking of Dickens's gold watch-chain and diamond tie-clasp. With those baubles, I could purchase a dozen pharmacists' dispensaries . . . and all the medications on their shelves, to save my dear little Virginia.

I have not slept this past night. After sitting up through half the dark hours with my sick wife – her mother keeping vigil through the other half – I am resolved to meet Dickens again, and to prevail on him to help us. It is unfair that one *belles-lettreist* enjoys so much wealth and adulation, while another of even greater talents lingers in paupered obscurity.

It is now just past sunrise. In a few hours, the crowd will assemble to greet Charles Dickens at the United States Hotel, while my wife languishes here in ill-health. I confess that I covet Dickens's acclaim, and its material rewards. Still,

I have little desire to witness, and even less urge to chronicle, the assured chaos that will greet him before noon to-day.

Yet I am drawn to his fame, as a moth to the flame.

Before Charles Dickens reached the hotel's carpeted lobby, he was already aware of a bizarre buzzing sound like the wings of thousands of bees. The noise put him in mind of "The Humble Bee", the ridiculous series of couplets by the poet Ralph Waldo Emerson which only yester-morning Dickens had discussed with that shabbily-dressed American . . . what was his name? *Poe?* The thought of yesterday's encounter with the impoverished poet Poe filled Dickens with embarrassment. Did this unfortunate Mr Poe not apprehend that his very name was French slang for "*chamber-pot*"? With an effort, Dickens put yesterday's events out of his mind. Yet now, as he approached the lobby of the United States Hotel, he was aware that the loudening noise before him was not a monstrous *buzzbuzzbuzz* but rather the sound of hundreds of human throats clamouring "*Boz! Boz! Boz!*" Nervously, Dickens adjusted the jewelled tie-pin restraining the Hanover knot in his green silk cravat.

On the stair-landing were Mr Hoysradt and Dickens's assistant George Putnam. The two men positioned themselves at either side of Dickens, as if they were his bodyguards. "That man Poe you met yesterday," Putnam began. "I've made some inquiries, and . . ."

"Not now, George." Charles Dickens put a finger to his lips, then nodded in the direction of the buzzing clamour, which threatened to burst open the intervening door. Putnam nodded in turn. Nearly in unison, all three men took a deep breath, then Hoysradt flung open the door.

In the hotel lobby were crowded the whole populace of Philadelphia . . . or so seeming, at least. Strategically positioned near the front desk, his hands to his lapels, stood the whiskered Colonel Florence. As Dickens arrived, the colonel cheerfully called above the huzzbuzz of the throng: "Charlie Dickens, my friend! I've promised a few dozen of my friends that they might shake hands with you."

Dozens? "The man can't count," Putnam whispered at Dickens's right side. "There are three hundred people in this lobby, easy, and at least twice that number crowded into the streets beyond."

The next hour was agony for Dickens. He found himself pumping hands and swapping bankrupt how-dee-do's with a succession of American strangers, most of whom took alien delight in chewing thick cuds of tobacco, and spitting its liquidities in the vague direction of brass pots: spittoons, provided for that purpose. The one fortunate aspect of this vast crowd was that its very force of numbers discouraged any individual Philadelphian from tarrying more than a few seconds; only Colonel Florence lingered, maintaining the peculiar posture which Dickens had observed exhibited by Yankees in their more prideful moments: that habit of thrusting their thumbs into their armpits while splaying their fingers. Tom Florence maintained a constant presence near Charles Dickens, while all the other Philadelphians were compelled to offer Dickens their tributes of only scant praise and a handshake, before being prodded to give way by the flood of worshippers behind them.

Each member of this vast Philadelphian horde had his own distinctive odour, none of them pleasant to Dickens's nostrils. One man, with a dark brown beard and long side-whiskers – who hastily shook Dickens's hand and moved on – had about himself a strong aroma of paraffin, reminding Dickens of his yesterday encounter with Edgar Poe, and the latter's system of deduction. Wiping an ink-stain from his own hand as this man departed, Dickens felt a sudden stirring of interest as it occurred to him that it ought to be possible for a skilled detective to read the narrative of each man in this crowd – his profession, his vices, his habits – merely by intuiting *the clues to each man*.

For an hour, the only sounds in the hotel lobby were the steady murmur of "Boz! Boz!" and the hurried praises of the individual hand-shakers, as well as an undertone of constant spitting, and the occasional metallic ring of a spittoon when someone's expectoration found its target. On the whole,

Dickens thought, the crowd were extraordinarily well-be-
haved for Americans: few coughed, there was no shouting
except for one brief sudden yelp, and – surprisingly – nobody
spoke an oath more pungent than "*loco-foco!*". At last, the
crowd showed signs of diminishing, and soon only a few
dozen attention-seekers remained.

George Putnam showed Dickens a memorandum-book,
scored with innumerable tally-marks. "I kept count, sir." He
smiled weakly. "To-day you have shaken hands nine hundred and sixty-three times."

Colonel Florence, with one final and unwanted effulgence
to his "friend, Mister Dickens" had left. The lobby was now
uninhabited, except for Dickens and Putnam, Mr Hoysradt,
and a couple of minor hotel employees. No, wait: there was
oddly one straggler. A black-bearded man was asleep on a
horse-hair settee in one corner of the lobby, his head cush-
ioned against the arm-rest. That any man should sleep
through an event such as this was quite laughable to Dickens.
By his posture, the bearded man reminded Dickens of some
elderly clubman in the Beefsteak Club, or White's in Piccadilly, snoozing his afternoon away after a hearty English
luncheon.

As William Hoysradt strode across the lobby to wake this
slumberer, Dickens was suddenly aware that his own cravat
had unaccustomedly undone itself. He put a hand to his
throat. "My tie-pin's gone!"

Putnam was startled. "What? Your diamond clasp, sir?"

"No, not the diamond, Putnam. I chose to wear my . . ."
Dickens was interrupted by a shout from Hoysradt, who had
nudged the sleeping man . . . only to have him tumble out of
the settee and onto the hotel's blue carpet.

"He's *dead!*" shouted Hoysradt.

Although Charles Dickens had often written of death and
the dead, those corpses were fiction whilst this was reality:
Dickens had such a horror of the dead that now he instinctively recoiled from the bearded man on the floor. Yet he
watched from a distance, morbidly fascinated, as George
Putnam knelt and pushed aside one portion of the dead man's

beard, unbuttoning the man's stiff collar while placing two fingers of his right hand against the bared throat.

"There's a pulse. A faint one," said Putnam. "This man's still alive, but just barely. He wants a hospital, quickly." Putnam started to unbutton the man's coat, then shuddered and quickly closed the garment. "Lord God! He's all over blood! The lining of his coat is quite soaked with it."

Dickens suddenly discovered that he had been holding his breath. Now he expelled it, relieved that the dead man was not dead after all. As Putnam held aside the stranger's beard, Dickens observed that there was something about this stranger's face – something out of the common – that made him approach, and take a closer look.

The bearded man looked familiar, and Dickens remembered him as one of the more than nine hundred Philadelphians who – less than an hour earlier – had pressured him for a handshake. It was only this man's unusual and prolific beard – looking as if a beaver had taken up lodgings in his face – which caused him to stand out in Dickens's memory. Now, examining the bearded man again, Dickens noticed something so obviously wrong as to cause him to wonder that he had not noticed it previously.

"Putnam! This beard is *false!*" With a swift movement, Dickens snatched the jet-black beard from the unconscious man's face. It came off easily, leaving behind only some stubble of a darker and more natural hue. In his teenhood years and early twenties, Charles Dickens had participated in amateur theatricals, so he knew of several spirit adhesives suitable for attaching a crepe-hair beard.

Now, Dickens felt a sharp peculiar thrill as he recalled his discussion with Edgar Poe, and Poe's tales of detection. Here was a true mystery: why would a beardless man disguise himself so elaborately? And was his collapsion in this place mere coincidence, or something larger? With mounting excitement, Dickens saw that – by following Poe's rules of observation and deduction – it might well be possible to unwrap this enigma.

A negro pageboy had arrived, in the hotel's livery. Red-faced, Hoysradt gave this youth his instructions: "Lock the door, then fetch a policeman. Tell nothing to anyone."

As the pageboy hurried away, William Hoysradt glanced nervously at the unbearded man, then towards Dickens and Putnam. "Gentlemen, I regret your involvement in this matter. This man before us is no common man of the crowd."

The fastidious Dickens, unaccustomed to having his neck-cloth wander loose from his throat without a tie-clasp, tried to tuck in its ends. "Explain yourself, sir."

Hoysradt gestured towards the unconscious figure. "I know this man. Rather, I have met him twice, and read of him several times. After reading about him, I never expected to see him again. He is Hosea J. Levis, head cashier at the Schuylkill Bank in this city. Last year, he embezzled and diverted more than a million dollars from the bank's funds. It caused a plague of bank failures: the Moyamensing, the Merchants, and most particularly the Second Bank, which stands not twelve yards from this hotel. Mister Dickens, as you are a foreigner, you may not appreciate what every man in America knows: the failure of the Second Bank of the United States thirteen months ago triggered a nation-wide panic, which even now . . ."

At that moment the pageboy returned with a uniformed constable, whom Hoysradt clearly recognized. "Officer Whisner! I'm glad it's you who's come. Good work, lad." This last was addressed to the pageboy.

The policeman Whisner was already examining the unconscious Levis. "Is it syncope, d'you think?" asked Putnam.

"Not unless syncope carries a dagger." The policeman lifted the flap of the unconscious man's coat, pointing to a tiny puncture in his shirtfront, directly above the heart. "This man's been stabbed. And not by accident." Then, as if noticing the victim's face for the first time: "Sam Hill! It's Levis!"

"You know him, I take it?" asked Dickens, moving nearer as his curiosity overcame his aversion for bloodshed.

"You take it wrong," said Officer Whisner. "I never met Levis, but I know his face from the handbills and 'Wanted' posters. Got one here in my tunic."

"Have you any idea who would stab Hosea Levis?" Dickens asked.

The American policeman gave him a sidelong look. "You just blow into town, mister? Would you like a list of every person who'd want to stick a snickersnee into H. J. Levis? Sure! Got a Philadelphia street directory?"

George Putnam, with his customary discretion, drew Dickens aside. "Sir, I've read about this Levis fellow. He caused the wholesale failure of America's national banking system. His embezzlements from the Schuylkill Bank led to the exposure of irregularities at the other banks. One large theft cascaded many more discoveries. The scandal transpired in February 1841. It grew worse a month later, in March, when the Americans inaugurated a new President – Mister William Harrison – who did not enjoy the trust and reliance of the banking establishment. The financial unease grew still worse in April, when President Harrison died abruptly after only thirty days in office. America's gold and silver coinage are sound, but most of the Yankee banknotes are no better than . . . well, sir, pen-wipes."

"I've had an eye out for this here jasper," said Whisner, kneeling over the insensible figure. "I recall there were reports that Levis got arrested in Kentucky last year, but those turned out to be false rumours. If a sawbones can get Levis patched up until he tells us where he's got the shin-plasters salted away, then . . ."

"Shin-plasters?" Dickens was uneasy with American slang. "D'you mean, the stolen funds?"

Whisner nodded. "Just when the banks are starting to calm down, and making specie payments again, this had to happen. A million dollars is a lot of money for one man to spend; I reckon Levis has still got most of it hid."

Charles Dickens felt a prickling of the hairs at the back of his neck. This embezzlement could be the plot of his next serial! His imagination already weaving the threads of his

fictional tapestry, Dickens mentally relocated the embezzlement to a British bank – to be of greater interest to his readers
– and he was translating Hosea Levis into the disowned son
of an English merchant who . . .

"Mister Dickens, sir." George Putnam was gently shaking
his arm. "Please. The last thing we want is to get embroiled
in this crime, which is clearly a strictly local act of revenge.
Need I remind you that to-morrow morning we leave by
steamboat for your speaking engagement in Baltimore?
Further, there is the event which you had asked me to
arrange for you *this afternoon*. The tour of the Penitentiary?"

For a moment, Dickens did not grasp the meaning of his
secretary's words. Then he remembered: yes, he had commitments elsewhere, and no time to linger in this place to
solve a crime which possessed no want of suspects. With a
sigh of regret, Dickens began to excuse himself, when the
flapping ends of his cravat reminded him of another lapse.
"My tie-pin! I say, constable . . ."

"Yes, Mister Boz?"

"My tie-pin appears to have vanished. Perhaps stolen by
one of the nearly one thousand strangers who passed close to
me this morning and shook my hand."

The constable made a low whistling sound. "One thousand! Mister, that sure narrows down your list of suspects."

"Perhaps I *can* narrow it," said Dickens, ignoring the
policeman's sarcasm. "I have observed the criminal mind
closely enough to notice that a man who embezzles a fortune
– as this man Levis has done – all the same has no scruple to
prevent him from committing thefts of a far more petty
nature. If this Levis stole my tie-pin, it might still be on
his person."

"Might be, but it ain't," said the American policeman,
who had already emptied Levis's pockets, and was now
spreading their contents on the hotel's carpet. "According
to these here calling-cards, this Levis jasper has been living
under the name John Riggs. I can put that down in my report
as his name, for now, and sort this out later. Mightn't be a
good idea to put round that Hosea Levis has been stabbed."

The negro pageboy, displaying commendable initiative, had evidently summoned medical assistance without instruction to do so: Dickens had not seen him leave, yet now the liveried boy returned with two stretcher-bearers, who straightaway attended to the body on the carpet.

Dickens felt a plucking at his arm: it was Putnam again. "We really *must* leave, sir!" For a moment, it occurred to Dickens that perhaps the fellow Edgar Poe should be given a chance to solve this crime. His talent for deduction was well up to the task, and Poe had the advantage of being a resident of Philadelphia.

Whereas Dickens was merely passing through, and had other engagements. As Putnam was reminding him, he had an appointment within prison walls . . .

The Eastern State Penitentiary is now, in this year of Our Lord 1842, the largest and most expensive building ever constructed in the United States. It stands in the northwest outskirts of Philadelphia. It is designed, built, and overseen so as to conform to the new method of penal incarceration known as the Pennsylvania System, which condemns every inmate to silence and solitary confinement for the span of his or her sentence. Prisoners in transit through the building – because they are new arrivals, or more rarely because they have been reassigned from one cell to another – are required to wear a tarred burlap hood in the prison's corridors, so as to remain blind and mumchance while under escort.

Charles Dickens – obsessed with prisons, their inmates, and their management – had expressed a desire to visit this wondrous new penitentiary. On the afternoon of March eighth, he was escorted through the prison by its assistant governor Frederick Vaux and a warden, James Brodrigg.

The entrance to the Penitentiary stands in Coats Street. The high outer wall, completely surrounding the prison, is entirely unconnected to any structure housing the inmates. As Dickens stepped through the massive gate, expecting to see dank hallways, he was pleasantly surprised to observe a spacious garden occupying the grounds between the cell-

blocks and the outer walls. Mr Vaux explained that trusted
inmates who had earned the privilege were assigned to tend
this garden, but were forbidden to speak, or to make eye
contact, or in any way to acknowledge one another's existence, while in the open air.

At the far end of the garden, Dickens and his escorts
passed through a wicket into the main building. Here there
was a corridor leading into a large circular chamber. Eight
corridors – including the one by which they had arrived –
radiated from this circular room, at intervals of forty-five
degrees of arc. Finding himself at the nexus where eight radii
converged, Dickens was strangely reminded of an octopus,
with its tentacles splayed forth in eight directions. Then a
more accurate image stirred within his intellect: this prison
was the great *Panopticon* which had been conceived and
designed in England by the liberal reformer Jeremy Ben-
tham. Never constructed in Britain, here was that prison
brought forth to reality in brick and limestone and flesh.

For there were prisoners in these walls. Seven of the
octopoid corridors – all of them save the entranceway – were
flanked on both sides by a long row of low cell doors, with a
number on a brass disc above each. That was the lower tier. A
flight of stairs at the base of each tentacle led to an upper
gallery of cells, nearly identical to the lower.

Mr Vaux and Mr Brodrigg had promised to introduce
Charles Dickens to some of the most unusual and least
violent inhabitants of the prison. Further, these prisoners
– normally required to toil in silence, or silently meditate –
would be privileged to converse with the distinguished
visitor Mr Dickens: to answer his questions, and to question
him in turn if they so wished.

Each cell in the Eastern State Penitentiary has two doors:
the outer of sturdy oak, the inner of iron grate-work; this
inner door has a trap opening through which food and
laundry may be passed. Each inmate upon arrival is issued
a Bible, a slate and a pencil, pen, ink-horn and paper. There
is a small shelf in each cell for the prisoner's washbasin, cup,
plate, soap and razor: prisoners who cannot be entrusted with

a razor are confined elsewhere. Dickens was astounded to discover that each cell had its own water-pump, so that the prisoners could obtain water freely, disposing of excess via a sluice in the floor. Each cell contains one bedstead, designed to turn up against the wall when not occupied, so that the prisoner has more space for his loom, or bench, or wheel, or whatever kit defined his labours.

The first inmate whom Dickens interviewed was two-thirds' through a sentence of nine years for the crime of *translating*: receipt of stolen goods, and their conversion. This man quietly asserted his utter innocence of the charge, yet Mr Vaux had informed Dickens that his current sentence marked this prisoner's second conviction for that offence.

The translator wore a paper hat of his own ingenious design, and was pleased when Dickens complimented him for it. Over the span of many months, this inmate had constructed a sort of Dutch clock out of various discarded objects, with a vinegar flask as its pendulum. He proudly informed Charles Dickens of his hope to modify the clock so that it would chime the hour, by means of a small hammer and a bell made of tin.

The prisoner was not allowed to own paints, owing to the toxic elements in many of the pigments. However, he had hoarded scraps of coloured yarn: he had patiently sorted these by colour, and then soaked them in water to draw out the dyes. With his shaving brush, he had painted a few crude images of women on the walls of his cell. The female likeness above the door, he proudly told his visitor, was a portrait of the Lady of the Lake.

In another cell within another corridor, Charles Dickens encountered a large negro who had been occupied in the outer world as a burglar, yet who within these walls operated a small lathe upon which he fashioned screws and bolts. Consenting to be interviewed, he loudly blessed the day that he had entered this prison, and vowed that he would never commit another theft. But the black footpad recounted the details of his previous crimes with such evident delight that it was clear he had no plans of reformation.

One small and timid little prisoner was allowed, as an indulgence, to keep rabbits. His cell therefore had an unpleasant closeness; in consequence, the men escorting Dickens permitted this convict to step out into the corridor for his interview. He stood blinking in the sunlight from the nearby window, shading his haggard face with one hand while clutching a white rabbit to his chest. As the interview drew to an end, this creature abruptly pulled itself free, tumbled to the floor, and then quickly hopped back into the open cell. The rabbit-breeder, now dismissed, nodded meekly and crept hastily after his pet. Charles Dickens, watching this timorous behaviour, found himself at a loss to find much difference between rabbit and human.

In the female sector of the penitentiary were three young women in adjacent cells, having been sent down for conspiracy to rob a mutual victim. Dickens observed that they were marked from birth with plain coarse features, but that – in the silence and solitude of their imprisonment – they had grown to be quite beautiful. The youngest and prettiest of the trio, not yet twenty years old, occupied a cell with walls whitewashed so thoroughly as to remind Charles Dickens of snow, and winter, and Christmas. Far high up in the outer wall of this maiden's cell was a small chink in the brickwork, through which a narrow strip of sky and sunlight pierced the prison's gloom. In that shaft of sunlight, Dickens watched while Mr Vaux interviewed this penitent: "In a word, you are happy here?"

Her mournful eyes were downcast. She attempted to nod, but left the gesture uncompleted. "I . . . *try* to be," she said at last, and burst into tears. With a shudder, Dickens turned away.

As there seemed to be no imminent threat to his safety, Dickens inquired of his hosts if he might move freely through the prison's corridors, unescorted. Mr Brodrigg reminded him that, under American law, Dickens assumed responsibility for his own safety when he came within this prison's walls. Mr Vaux assured Dickens that the most violent inmates in the Philadelphia prison system were situated else-

where, and that this penitentiary's residents had all demonstrated at least outward signs of sincere penitence. Bidding
temporary farewell to his hosts, then, Dickens returned to the
central hub of the Panopticon, and next chose another radius
at random. He set forth down this long hall, between the
cells. The acoustics of the Panopticon were so perfectly
balanced that Dickens could hear his own footfalls echoing
within each of the other seven radii . . . and now, suddenly,
another set of footfalls came nearer, as if following the sound
of Dickens's steps.

In the darkness, a hooded figure shambled down the
corridor. Charles Dickens knew the prison's rules: an inmate
who earned a place in the penitentiary's honour system was
permitted to perform errands unsupervised, providing he
remained hooded and silent. Dickens stood fascinated, as the
hooded man approached.

The gas-light in the corridor was dim, and the prisoner's
vision hampered further by the tarred burlap encasing his
head. The approaching hooded figure kept close to the wall,
using it for guidance as he crept along the corridor. To give
this man – this fellow human – as much privacy and dignity
as possible in this inhuman place, Dickens cast his eyes
downward as the hooded prisoner reached him. Moving
aside, Dickens endeavoured to give the oncoming stranger
a wide berth . . . yet the hooded man brushed up against him
in the narrow corridor.

There was a sudden tautness in Dickens's coat. He had
experienced this before, among the pickpockets of Bermond-
sey and the East End. Quickly, Dickens thrust his right hand
into his right-side coat pocket, encountering another hand
there already. He tightened his grip on its wrist, drawing this
alien hand forth. The hooded prisoner did not struggle as his
own right hand was extracted by Charles Dickens from
Dickens's own pocket.

The guilty fingers were clutching an object: Dickens's tie-
pin.

His own right hand still holding fast the prisoner's wrist,
Charles Dickens reached out in the dark with his left hand

and seized the prisoner's burlap hood. "You show a great interest in my possessions . . . Mister *Poe*."

Dickens snatched away the hood, revealing the pale sweaty face of Edgar Allan Poe.

"You recognized me," murmured Poe. "*How?*"

Farther down the prison corridor, the sounds emerging from one particular cell made plain that this cell's denizen was engaged in work as a cobbler. Still holding fast to Poe's wrist, Dickens drew him nearer to this cell, so that the steady *tack-tack-tack* of its occupant at his shoemaker's last would supply some cover for their whispered conversation.

"My agent George Putnam made some inquiries about you, after our meeting," Dickens said to Poe. "I was intrigued to learn, sir, that you reside scarcely three city blocks westward of this Eastern State Penitentiary. Nonetheless, I did not expect to meet you actually within this prison's gates."

Poe smiled bitterly, while fingering the eyeholes of his burlap hoodwink. "Then you are in the minority, Mr Dickens, for there are thousands of others who fully expect that Edgar Allan Poe will eventually be found in one prison or another."

"Fair enough." Dickens nodded. "As to how I recognized you . . ." Dickens once again cast his eyes downward, towards both men's feet. His own bespoke shoes, made for him by Gillingham's in Old Bond Street, were naturally crafted to fit him. But the far more penurious Edgar Poe was obliged to own a pair of "straights", the inexpensive working-man's shoes which were made to fit either the left or the right foot equally well, and which therefore fitted equally badly on both. Yesterday, Dickens had remarked a distinctive stain of sputum and blood on Poe's left shoe. Just before unmasking Poe in this prison corridor, Dickens had seen that self-same stain on the hooded prisoner's *right* shoe . . . and known it as both the same stain and the same shoe, now worn by the same man's other foot.

Charles Dickens had sufficient sympathy for his fellow man, and sufficient tact, to know that Poe's pride would be wounded were he to learn that Dickens had recognized him by a stain on his shoe . . . a stain more shameful because Poe clearly lacked the money to buy a proper pair of symmetrics – shoes with a distinct left and right – and because Poe lacked either the time or the diligence to clean his shoes properly. Rather than give a truthful answer to Poe's question, then, Dickens replied: "I recognized you, sir, by . . . the air of authority about you, undisguised even when your head was shrouded in that hood."

Poe preened himself, and almost seemed to purr. "You are a poor sort of pick-thief, though," Dickens went on, "for I noticed your hand in my pocket as soon as it entered. And you are even more a curious exemplar of the cut-purse trade by the fact that your hand within my pocket was making a *deposit*, not a withdrawal."

The purloined object now returned to Charles Dickens's hand was not the precious diamond tie-clasp which he had worn during his first meeting with Edgar Poe. That article was still safe in Dickens's travel-case, packed for his onward journey. This tie-pin in his hand was a *diamanté* counterfeit, of cheap paste: a "prop" memento from Dickens's days as an actor. When dressing himself this morning for the unwanted reception, Dickens had chosen this ornament – rather than the other – to be worn in the confusion of that crowded hotel lobby. The paste tie-pin, if misadventured, would be no real loss.

"You are an honest man, to return this to me," said Dickens, tactfully neglecting to mention that Poe had returned a worthless object, and that Poe had kept the tie-pin long enough to ascertain its worthlessness.

Poe licked his lips nervously before replying: "When you agreed to shake hands with all comers at today's reception in the hotel, Mr Dickens, I joined the receiving line, so as to gaze one more time upon the most famous and popular author alive. However, so as not to seem desperate – seeking an audience with you three times in two days – I saw fit to wear a disguise."

Dickens nodded. "Indeed; while I was shaking hands in the reception line, I noticed a man who . . ." Charles Dickens checked himself abruptly, narrowly avoiding another revelation that might give offence to the pauper Poe. During his ordeal in the hotel lobby this morning, Dickens had suddenly been reminded of Poe when a man approached him emitting the same paraffin stench as this Philadelphia author . . . and whose handshake had transferred inkstains to Dickens's fingers. That man's hair had been dark brown: the same shade as Poe's, but he had a beard and side-whiskers which Poe lacked. The facial adornments had been a disguise, then. "There was a man in the reception line who had . . . the same *air* about himself as you possess," said Dickens diplomatically.

Again, Poe preened himself. "Well, Mister Boz, as I stood in that long line of well-wishers, waiting my turn to greet you, I had much opportunity to examine the man directly in front of me in the receiving line. Comprehend my surprise when I saw that he too was disguised, in a beaver-beard even less convincing than my own. You may guess my astonishment when – plain as day, mind you – this bearded scapegrace briefly greeted you in the hotel lobby . . . and as his right hand clasped yours, I saw his left hand plunge to your waistcoat, and plunder this tie-pin."

Dickens nodded again. The gaudy *diamanté* ornament looked expensive enough to be worth stealing.

Poe resumed his confession: "I was so outraged at this man's . . . *ahem!* I was about to say his *bare-faced* theft, but his false beaver makes that description incorrect. I was so enraged by his theft that, quite without thinking, I took out my letter-opener and . . ."

As Poe uttered these words, his left hand reached within his coat. Charles Dickens, with a rapid movement of his own left hand, seized Poe's wrist and held it fast while Dickens's right hand explored the inner pocket where Poe's fingers had ventured. Dickens's eyes widened in astonishment. "This is your 'letter-opener', Poe?" The Englishman drew the object forth, and the gas-light of the prison corridor gleamed on a narrow steel blade which Charles Dickens now brandished by its wooden handle.

" '*Is this a dagger which I see before me?*' " he declaimed. "If my memory serves, Poe, this is a blade of the sort which Venetian assassins call a *stiletto*."

Poe stared fixedly into Dickens's eyes, neither man blinking.

There was a dark stain on the blade. Charles Dickens had already observed that Poe was untidy in his habits; Dickens felt certain that it was the blood of Hosea Levis which the unkempt Poe had neglected to clean from the stiletto.

"You stabbed Levis with this knife," Dickens accused him. "Quite *without* thinking, Poe? Are you certain?" Dickens released his grasp on Poe, yet retained hold of Poe's dagger. In the dim light of the prison corridor, Charles Dickens's soft grey eyes seemed like gimlets piercing the mind of Edgar Poe. "Again, sir, I have learnt a few things about you. Thirteen months ago, you nearly obtained a position of comfort and respect for yourself."

Edgar Poe sighed heavily. In early 1841 – just over a year past – Poe had drawn up a prospectus for a new periodical titled *The Penn Magazine*, to be edited by himself at a comfortable salary, and published by his colleague George Graham. The Second Bank of the United States had promised to advance sufficient funds to launch the publication . . . then withdrawn that promise when the Schuylkill Bank collapsed.

"Strange, is it not?" said Edgar Allan Poe. "Men's lives are hostage to random elements of chance. My editorial career was extinguished by the diddlings of Levis, an utter stranger. Yet other souls prosper from incidents equally random. Our United States are now governed by John Tyler, better known as 'His Accidency': a man who was never elected President, yet leapfrogged into the office over William Henry Harrison's corpse."

"I wonder, Poe," said Dickens, peering carefully into the eyes of the other man while, nearby, the prison-cobbler steadily continued his *tack-tack-tack*. "During your long wait in the reception line, observing the man in front of you as he occasionally turned in profile and glanced round, did you recognize the face which adorns police handbills throughout Philadelphia? Did you see through his beard, and know him as Hosea Levis . . . the man whose embezzlement doomed your unborn enterprise? I wonder, Edgar Poe: when your blade stabbed Levis, was your hand guided by conscious thought? If it was, sir, then I give you credit for merely wounding the man rather than killing him, and so allowing him to be taken into custody. Answer this at least, Poe: when you infiltrated the horde of Philadelphians who had turned out to shake hands with the famous Charles Dickens, what happenstance prompted you to attend the affair in disguise . . . and equipped with a dagger of murderous design?"

Dickens had noted that Edgar Poe's forehead was unusually high and broad; now, a vein in that forehead began to quiver. "I deserve to be as famous as you are, sir," Poe answered. "I have laboured for acclaim as hard as you have done – harder! – yet it eludes me. I have observed from history, though, that there are two ways to achieve renown: either become a great man, or be the obscure man who kills that great man."

"So, you entered the lobby of the United States Hotel this morning," Dickens asked, "equipped with dagger and disguise, expecting to confront me, and intending to become famous?"

Edgar Allan Poe, already pale and sallow, turned more pale at this moment.

"What I *intended* is a matter known only to my soul and its maker," Poe said carefully. "In the time it took me to venture from my home in Philadelphia's northwest outskirts to the hotel, I recalled that my wife and my aunt are dependent upon me for their welfare. If I were alone in the world, with no dependents, this morning's events might have run otherwise."

For a long moment, each man peered into the other's soul. It was Dickens who looked away first, shuddering. He still held forth the stiletto. Quietly, Poe took this weapon by its haft, and returned the Italian dagger to his own inner pocket.

"Explain this, at least," Dickens prompted him. "How come you to be in this prison, wearing a hood as if you were one of the inmates?"

Poe laughed mirthlessly. "Easy enough, sir. The guards and warders of this penitentiary are notoriously hospitable to bribes. Even someone as paupered as myself can raise enough coin to bribe one of the gatesmen here." Poe held up a new-minted American silver dollar, depicting robed Liberty seated with cap and shield, gazing skyward at an arc of thirteen stars. "I gave a guard one of these dollar coins, plus a three-dollar banknote from the Republic of Texas."

Dickens stared hard at Poe. "You bribed your way *into* prison, sir? Most of the traffic flows in the opposite direction. Well, at least that explains the hood you wore: you did not wish to attract the attentions of prison guards whom you had not bribed, therefore you hooded yourself so that they would assume you were an inmate. But why bribe your way *into* prison, man?"

Edgar Allan Poe sighed once more, then spoke: "Mister Dickens, I will be plain with you. My writings are not so known as they deserve to be. I am nowhere near so rich as I merit. I desperately need both wealth and acclaim: the former, so as to have funds to aid my sickening wife, and the latter to heal my sickened soul. You have so much, sir, and I so very little. I desired to make an impression on you, to make sure you would keep your promise and commend me to the London publishers. When I learnt that you would be visiting this penitentiary – quite near my Coats Street residence – I slipped in here, determined to return this stolen tie-pin to you, and so affix myself in your memory."

Poe's words, with their combination of braggadocio and humility, had the chime of truth. Charles Dickens clasped Poe's hand, and shook it firmly. "I assure you, Poe, that I shan't forget you soon. This morning, while dressing in my hotel suite, I glanced through your *Tales of the Grotesque*. Several of them seemed familiar . . . and then I recalled why. They have already been published in London magazines: without attribution to your name, and I suspect without compense to your pocket. Confound our two nations, then: yours and mine, which share a language but refuse to share a copyright law. Truly, both John Bull and Cousin Jonathan pick each other's pockets."

Edgar Poe bit his lip nervously. For a moment, he reminded Charles Dickens of this prison's timid inmate who kept rabbits. Now Dickens spoke: "I will say one thing more, Poe. I shall not look within your soul, to learn whether or not your stabbing of Hosea Levis was intentional assault. But know this much: you and I, as authors, must repeatedly journey into the darkest regions of men's souls, and describe what we find there. I have read enough of your work, Poe, to see that you are peculiarly qualified to chart the darker paths of humanity. As for your own path, sir: it would better suit your talents if you remain in sunlight, rather than take some dark course of action which might ensure that your next detection story will be penned inside a prison cell."

Perhaps it was the dampness of this penitentiary, but there was perspiration on Poe's forehead. He wiped it, with a grimy handkerchief.

Dickens reached out and clasped both of Poe's stained hands within his own manicured grip. "You have given me a gift, Poe. Your 'Murders in the Rue Morgue', and your discussion of its structure, have taught me the rudiments of your *detection-stories*. I intend to apply your rules within my own fictions, and to write a few mystery tales of my own. For that gift, I thank you." Dickens twisted Poe's hands slightly within his own grasp, and the expression on Poe's countenance changed as he was aware of some intrusion between his palms. "My regards to your ailing wife, sir," Dickens went on. "And . . . may this find her better."

Dickens turned, and strode away down the corridor, eager to rejoin his escorts Vaux and Brodrigg. Edgar Allan Poe, blinking and shuddering in the prison darkness, opened his hands to see what was within them. He beheld a double eagle: a twenty-dollar gold piece. A charity-gift from a wealthy author to a less fortunate one.

Poe's pride urged him to fling the coin into the brick-dust. But necessity overruled his pride. He pocketed the coin, turned, and hurried down the corridor of the nearest dark radius towards the distant sunlight beyond . . . all the while sensing that, in time, it would be the darkness that claimed him evermore.

The Lord No Zoo

Deirdre Counihan

On his return from America it took Dickens some while to summon up the energy or inclination to return to writing fiction. He found the production of American Notes *an onerous chore, but once he had settled down to his next book and decided on the name,* Martin Chuzzlewit, *it all began to flow again. He was happy with the novel, although sales were poor initially until they recovered when the public took the eccentric character of the nurse, Sairey Gamp, to their hearts.*

In Martin Chuzzlewit, *Dickens created one of the first private investigators in English fiction in the shape of Mr Nadgett, who unmasks Jonas Chuzzlewit as the murderer of the swindler Montague Tigg. Jonas Chuzzlewit had married Mercy Pecksniff, the daughter of Seth Pecksniff, an architect who had tried to inveigle himself in with the rich, old Martin Chuzzlewit, in the hope of benefiting in his will. Jonas's cousin, Chevy Slyme, had worked with Tigg, also in the hope of gaining an inheritance, but he subsequently joins the police force. The real hero of the novel is not the younger Martin Chuzzlewit (grandson of the old man) but Tom Pinch, Pecksniff's saintly assistant who sees good in everyone and tries his best to make everyone happy.*

One of the key features of the novel, evident from the opening paragraph, is the matter of ancestry and inheritance. Dickens takes much time explaining the complicated Chuzzlewit family tree and concocting the joke that upon his death bed, one especially obscure member of the family, when asked who his grandfather was, responded "the Lord No Zoo", which thereafter became synonymous with any dubious ancestry.

The following story takes place some years after the end of the novel and is set at the Great Exhibition, held in Hyde Park during the summer of 1851. It was organized at the behest of Prince Albert, husband of Queen Victoria, who wanted to celebrate all that was wonderful about technical and industrial progress throughout the world. It was here that Joseph Paxton created the original Crystal Palace. Dickens visited the Exhibition twice but was not enthused by it, even though it displayed two statues based on his characters, Oliver Twist and Little Nell.

Deirdre Counihan is a specialist in art and art history, particularly archaeological art. Her knowledge is central to her novel The Panther *(2006), an alternate history set on the Silk Road, which she travelled along herself a few years ago. She is also co-editor, with her sister, of the literary magazine* Scheherazade.

I magine a forgotten palace, vast in its dignity, a dark house of a thousand windows. Imagine an edifice so immense that in its heyday guests would be given confetti of different colours to guide them, like Hansel and Gretel, safe back to their allotted rooms.

Imagine what was the longest ornamental façade in Europe, yet everywhere enveloped in a thick morning mist that seeped its way up from the valley below, rancid with the effluent of pits and foundries and furnaces, and coiled its way round even the statues on the topmost pediments. Contemplate the crowd of thousands, all in their drab best, who trudged up the magnificent avenue of three hundred beech-trees, through the dawn rain, to shift and shuffle respectfully on the hundred acres of rolling lawns.

This was The House of Frame. Only five windows flickered with a sickly light in that time just before daybreak. Only one mourner stood beside the coffin of Clarence, The Fifteenth Duke, on its silver bier, ready for the funeral procession, ready for the footmen and the wreaths and the hearse drawn by four black horses which would conduct its occupant, once one of the richest men in Great Britain (but dead now, it was rumoured, in deepest ignominy) to his family's tomb.

Only one mourner had kept a vigil through the night: a dignified lady of advanced years, but dressed in the height of good taste, The Dowager Lady Frame; and beside her stood her lawyer. He was there to tell her of another death, of a most insignificant man, a retired man in a small way of business over two hundred miles away in the south, and she was pleased, grimly delighted.

"I knew it!" she said. "I knew that Clarence could not be my child. Oh Edward, disgusting father of a disgusting son!"

It was a bright, cloud scudding, spring afternoon. Daffodils nodded in the balmy breeze, the wet grass sparkled in the sunlight and small birds hopped and twittered among the froth of jewel green that sought to cover the naked branches. It was the sort of afternoon when lambs should gambol among primrose-scattered meadows: what better day then, for the distinguished clan of Chuzzlewit to dine and frolic "à la begere" at the idyllic setting of Shepherd's Bush?

They were all there, young and old – a little uncertain maybe of the precise costume required for this event, as there was an odd mixture of small shepherdesses with flower-decked bonnets who were racing around with crooks in determined pursuit of little boys resplendent in feathered hats and Lincoln green.

Some of the adults were relaxing among the hampers of broken meats from their excellent repast, and a few of them had retreated to the comfort of the several barouches which were drawn up on the turf, but most of them were gathered in a wide circle around the focus of the day – a large green-striped and flower-bedecked balloon which bobbed on its tethers like an eager pony, the ropes held in place by a burley posse of top-hatted retainers as the blushing, young patrons of the day picked their way across the turf, mounted the neat set of flower swathed steps and were handed down into the balloon basket by the waiting, green-uniformed, elaborately mustachioed balloonist.

The newly–weds, Augustus Moddle and his blushing bride, Mercy Chuzzlewit, née Pecksniff, who had doffed her widow's greys for a delightful ensemble of china blue, smiled and waved shyly as the ropes were loosened and with a friendly creaking from the basket, the balloon started its steady ascent to the dappled sky.

"Oh, what an occasion of joy! Who would have thought it after so many years!" cried a bony matron, dressed in violent and most unbecoming green, who was standing at the very forefront of the guests and dabbing her eyes with a neat lace handkerchief that she had taken from a small basket at her wrist. "Why, this has been so like the days of my youth when Mr Todgers was courting me, and his friend Gus Moddle (that was Augustus's Papa) was courting my dearest girlhood companion, Elfrida Fitz 'F' at The Flora Tea Gardens in Bayswater Road. Everyone would be dressed like Robin Hood and go flitting among the glades – so conducive to romance! There would be concerts and fireworks and everything that you purchased, from the porter to champagne, was of the very apogee of quality. Such happy days! Oh, I am quite overcome."

"But let us hope that today's nuptials prove to be of a more enduring nature than those of our good Mrs 'T', eh, Jinkins!" quipped a somewhat loudly dressed gentleman not far behind her, *sotto voce*, to the man standing at his left

"Don't you even think to mock dear Mrs Todgers or make comments on the potential endurance of the noble institution of matrimony when you were content to abandon that good woman's nurturing haven for the sake of a house full of furniture, Gander!" whispered his lady wife with quiet menace from beside him on the right. By way of emphasizing her statement, Mrs Charity Gander, née Pecksniff, a youngish, sharp-chinned lady in pastel green, gave him a swift and well-aimed dig in the ribs.

"No, no – indeed my love," choked the loudly dressed gentleman. "I was merely venturing to hope that this time young Augustus would conduct himself with a little more commitment than he did of yore. His loss, I assure you, has been entirely to my gain."

Mrs Gander quelled him with a look, which implied that she certainly didn't consider that it had been to hers.

"Come, come now," whispered their friend Jinkins hurriedly. "Bygones should be bygones. There is nothing to condemn in a fellow for being realistic about life. I am sure that poor Augustus has always tried to behave with honour throughout – it is simply that he never had much grasp on reality. Too noble by half."

"Well, he seems grasping enough now!" was Gander's swift riposte – ever the one for a good joke, was Gander, even if it meant bruised ribs. "Which 'Nobility' is it that he is after these days? The Lord Knowzwat? Ha?"

"No, no, The Lord No Zoo!" countered Jinkins with alacrity.

"Allow me!" hissed Charity with a savage flourish of her shawl, "to sweep the cobwebs from such a venerable stab at wit. Augustus presumes to The Lordship of Frame, of The House of Frame of Frame-Adby near Sheffield – as even the smallest street urchin would know since it is everywhere in the news, and he is but one of a hundred who are laying claim to it – completely ridiculous!"

Suddenly this shower of verbal vindictiveness was halted by the spectacular swish of a totally material shower of sand as the balloonist set about attempting to gain serious height by jettisoning the contents of one of the sand bags. The massed Chuzzlewits broke into excited "Oohs" and "Aahs" and a delighted clapping of hands as the brisk west wind peppered a fair dose of it into the crowd and beyond the edges of the mooring circle.

A lachrymose, but beaming, Mrs Todgers turned round to address the threesome, seemingly oblivious to their busy bickering. "Ah Cherry, my love," she exclaimed, "What joy you must be feeling. All that is missing to make this a perfect day is the presence of your dear Papa. How tragic that he should have been advised to go abroad for the good of his health before this happy outcome!"

"Was it his health, then?" laughed Jinkins gently. "Why I understood poor Mr Pecksniff was gone away to Van Dieman's Land to avoid his creditors."

"Not at all!" bridled Charity ferociously. "He is gone to take up the splendid, architectural, business challenges of a new land."

"And we all hope that he will fare rather better than dear Charity's cousin Martin did with the projected town of Eden in America," sniggered her husband Gander loyally.

"Well, he snapped back on his feet swiftly enough, did he not?" responded Charity, with a smart stamp on Gander's unwary foot, by way of emphasis.

There were more cheers as another gout of sand sprayed across the congregation, to fall almost on the easterly edge of the gathering, where the barouches were drawn up in a semicircle. Mr Tom Pinch, youthfully bald as an egg, was sitting on the step of one of these, surrounded by an excited assortment of small relatives who were busy insisting that dear "Uncle Dumpty" should make them all paper birds of various shapes and sizes, so that they could see whose bird would fly best- if at all. Inside the barouche, both of them heavily pregnant and resting, were the mothers of the said children, his sister Ruth Westlock and their closest friend Mary Chuzzlewit, née Graham.

Tom Pinch looked up to the fast dwindling silhouette of the balloon with a worried smile. "Let's hope young Augustus doesn't decide to do jump ship this time; that would be a very long fall," he observed to himself.

High in the rising basket, Augustus had no thought of looking down on the dwindling assembly. He only had eyes for "She who had been Another's" but was now entirely his own. Truly his soul, as well as their bodies, was up among the clouds. Captain Bailey, the green-uniformed balloonist, had placed at their disposal a weighted, linen-backed map, which he deftly unfolded in coordination with their flight path. Merry seemed ecstatic, all excited smiles and delighted pointing out of landmarks below them as the westerly wind steadily took them towards the City of London. Every time she pointed something out, the sunlight glowed and shimmered through the largest opal betrothal ring that any one England had ever seen, even on the hand of the youthful Queen Victoria (and her partiality for large opals was scarcely a secret). Augustus breathed a sigh of unalloyed bliss.

"Oh, do look down there, Augustus, dearest," trilled Merry, almost with the exuberance of the Merry he had first met so long ago. "Look down on the right – that glitter in that piece of parkland! Dear Bailey says that that is Hyde Park and all those struts and girders and cart tracks among the trees are where they are putting up the crystal pavilion that cousin Martin is helping Mr Paxton to make for Prince Albert's Great Exhibition!"

Augustus looked down among the swirls of fluffy cloud and picked out the familiar shapes of the basin in Kensington Gardens and the Serpentine in Hyde Park gleaming like polished steel set in the green sward beneath them. "But the trees! Those wonderful trees – surely they are not to be sacrificed for the sake of a season's entertainment!" he cried, bereft at the thought of any loss of England's verdure. He had seen too much of pink desert in his other life even to pluck a single blade of grass.

The green uniformed balloonist nodded sagely and twirled his ginger moustache in shrewd reassurance.

"No, no, Augustus, dear Bailey tells me that they are going to save all the trees by building the glass pavilion over them. Is that not wonderful?" rejoiced Merry, at what might be her cousin Martin's ingenious solution.

Now the cloud swirled again as they sped along Mayfair, and soon Captain Bailey pointed out Covent Garden Market just visible on their left, The Strand below with the slate grey river on their right, then fast along what must be Fleet Street until the moment Augustus had been hoping for. Indeed, Bailey had surpassed himself in navigation, for there was the massive Dome of St Paul's Cathedral right ahead of them, vast and sanctifying. Joyfully Augustus reached inside his paletot jacket to the place above his heart and drew out a small beribboned package tied in with a single hothouse flower. This time everything must be perfect. He held it out to Merry, his love, his own.

There was a sudden lurch as the wind shifted brusquely round to the North, the bloom was snatched from his hand and spiralled its way down to land on a half completed coffin in Mould the undertaker's yard, just off Cheapside, from whence the bemused workman retrieved it and stuck it in a fold of his paper carpenter's hat.

The new Mrs Mercy Moddle saw her husband's face fall and was quick to react. "Oh, that was so sensitive, so romantic, Augustus, dear." She unwrapped the delicate pink scarf as light as thistledown.

"You wore one like that the night I first saw you."

"Oh, I know I did, and you remembered." She blushed. "The present I have for you is not anything so sweetly thought of, but it was made with all my love." She held out her own small package, where, neatly wrapped in tissue, lay a pair of Gentleman's braces worked by her own hand. "You see, I stitched in an air balloon just above each front fastening – dear Bailey had informed me of this secret surprise just as I was completing them."

"And look where we've just a-come to!" gasped the uniformed balloonist in question wiping back a manly tear. "Now that is what I calls a coincidence!" There among the house tops that stretched away on every side of them, the long familiar path of its shadow stretching away northeast of them, stood the friendly Monument with every hair erect upon his golden head, and somewhere close below it all three of them knew there nestled the elusive place of their first meeting.

"Mrs Todger's Commercial Boarding House!" they laughed in delighted unison.

Tom Pinch and his brother-in-law John Westlock were waiting, by prior appointment, in the cool of the early morning by the small bridge-house next to the Serpentine and were enjoying the antics of the ducks, who even at that primeval hour seemed to be on the alert for the prospect of possible feeding, and had dispatched a quacking scouting party who were fast approaching from the resting place of the main duck-posse, alongside the small, three-masted man-of-war, which, flag bedecked, was becalmed there for the duration of Prince Albert's great exhibition.

"Comical, aren't they?" observed their best friend Martin Chuzzlewit, as he strode towards them both over the bridge. "It is those fifty thousand packed lunches that visitors insist on bringing with them every day. No one likes the food from the Tea Rooms. It reached crisis point with the pigeons inside, you know – bird droppings everywhere, all over the prime exhibits. Her Majesty was desperate; she takes it so personally, every detail." He gave a brief laugh. "But Wellington, The Iron Duke, came to the rescue, of course. Sparrow-hawks, he recommended. Sparrow-hawks. So now we have them swooping around all night and scarce a pigeon in sight. Poor Bailey is very unhappy about it; all his caged birds become nearly hysterical."

"Frustrating for the poor hawks as well, I should imagine," observed Tom as Martin conducted them back over the bridge towards the magnificence of Paxton's crystal extravaganza, which he in his own small way had helped to expedite.

"So he is Bailey, here, not Captain Bailey?" observed John Westlock, who was not quite awake yet, but liked to get things right.

"Yes. He is 'Captain' Bailey when he conducts his 'Flights of Fancy', otherwise he is Bailey of 'Sweedlepipe and Bailey's Bird Emporium'. They have a most charming display of caged song birds which hang along some of the aisles and I find Bailey is here to tend them around this time on most mornings. Would I be right in thinking that Young Tomkin kept your household awake all night again John? You seem a trifle enervated, if I may say so. Martin Minor has a fine pair of lungs too – but at least it gets me up in time. We have to start early here – you never know when the Royals will make visit and they are apt to come here before the crowds flock in at nine – the Queen likes to see any new exhibits that have arrived and things still trickle in every day even now. She, and sometimes the Prince, too, will call by quite informally – no bodyguard at all – though we do have our own police and detectives posted here, including my cousin Chevy Slyme, but they are very underused, there has been no trouble at all so far."

"This is all most kind of you, Chuzzlewit," said John, "since you must be so confoundedly busy all the time."

"Most grateful!" added Tom with great enthusiasm (he seemed to be coping rather better with the restricted sleeping patterns imposed on the burgeoning Westlock family by his small namesake).

"Nonsense fellows, what are friends for – opportunity of a lifetime!" Martin responded, all bonhomie.

The three of them had by now reached the entrance to The Crystal Palace, and the doormen, on seeing Martin, waved them through.

Tom, who had not visited the Great Exhibition before (though John had) was completely awestruck by the sight: it seemed to him that they must be in some palace that had been landed in front of Aladdin by a genie. When he managed to regain his focus on reality, he started to take in the columns painted in vertical stripes of blue, white and yellow, contrasting with a multitude of red, curtains and canopies and painted signs which had an almost overpowering effect when combined with the profusion of flowers and palms and the much-vaunted, protected elm trees which flourished in the hot-house atmosphere – no wonder the pigeons had felt themselves in heaven.

But Martin was bustling them along, determined they

must see everything: the famous glass fountain, the fabled organ – Tom must see the organ but was given hardly a moment to take it in.

There were a great many statues, many of them of young ladies where the skilful carving of their drapery left little of their underlying anatomy to the imagination. The unmarried Tom blushed and was relieved to find, conspicuously displayed, two telling representations of Mr Dickens's popular characters Little Nell and Oliver Twist.

"Ah, by 'Hughes Ball of Boston', what a wonderful name," observed John Westlock, who always tried to read the inscriptions if Martin would give them the time.

"I have no idea what Mr Dickens has to say of them," observed Martin. "I had not heard that he is particularly taken by the exhibition, all told."

Yes, Martin was full of stories – would they believe the near disaster that had been the opening ceremony, when even Lord Granville who was in charge of the Royal Commission was obliged to take up a broom at the last minute to clear detritus from the Royal dais? Not to mention the "Mysterious Chinaman" – now his was the choicest tale of all, Martin averred. China, it seemed, had inscrutably refused to send an exhibit, but some kind of a display was cobbled together with contributions from various private British collections. However, imagine the bewilderment of the organizing committee, not to mention the Queen and Prince Albert, when at the opening ceremony, just as the Hallelujah Chorus rang out, a Chinaman dressed in magnificent robes burst through the crowd and prostrated himself in front of the throne. "A diplomatic nightmare. No one knew what to do with the fellow," laughed Martin. "They ended up placing him between the Archbishop of Canterbury and The Duke of Wellington and he marched right through the whole building in a threesome with them. The crowd were delighted, but here is the jest – he was the captain of a Chinese junk moored out on the river for the tourist trade! Would you believe it? They call him 'The Lord No Zoo', these days, you know."

"How intriguing!" Tom said.

"Most original," said the weary John. "No doubt he has made a mint from it".

They hurried on. Tom made a determined halt for breath in front of the Indian exhibit which was a feast of splendour, from a gold-and-silver throne to a whole stuffed elephant complete with howdah, not to mention the fabled but strangely disappointing Koh-I-Noor diamond, worth a king's ransom, and newly acquired by Britain at the end of the Sikh Wars. It was displayed in a most unprepossessing six-foot-high sort of birdcage. "Yes, they were hoping to make it glitter by using gas jets, you see the nozzles there," explained Martin. "Someone will be along to light them shortly, I expect. It doesn't work very effectively."

"What a shame," said John. "But you even have gas laid on here? Amazing!"

"Yes, indeed. Now I know what I must show you, John. It arrived just the other day, but I expect they will have installed it by now. It is one of those wonders where one is amazed that anyone ever imagined that there could be a need to invent it. The place is full of oddities, particularly from America, but this one is British – from Dundee, I think. It's called 'The Gentleperson's Patented Portable Ablutionary Device'."

"Some sort of hip-bath?" queried Tom.

"Nothing near so simple," laughed the delighted Martin. "Just come and see."

Martin shot away at great speed through the myriad complexities of the exhibition, and had it not been for the basic simplicity of the palace's design and the possibility of looking up through the foliage for glimpses of the roof, poor Tom would have felt himself in danger of getting hopelessly lost in a jungle, never to see his hearth and home again. But he and John just managed to keep in Martin's general direction by dint of listening to his continual stream of repartee on the wonders and drawbacks of the patented marvel that he was about to introduce them to, and his doubts that anyone in their right mind would contemplate having such a thing in their bedchamber.

"That is a most peculiar odour wafting this way," observed Tom breathlessly. "It makes it a little difficult to keep one's breath, quite sickly in fact, like burning bacon."

"Or maybe Monday's wash," added John. "I don't relish this at all – I fear that something must be very wrong."

The two of them finally broke out of a patch of dark shrubbery and into an exhibition area that seemed to display a great many large objects of highly polished brass, only to find their way barred by a determined row of top-hatted, brass-buttoned, police officers. What alarming incident had they stumbled into?

"It's all right Chevy, they are here with me," said a white-faced Martin, standing in the clearing with his constabulary cousin, Chevy Slyme. In the background, beside some substantial and partially overset brass device, stood Mr Bailey of "Sweedlepipe and Bailey's Bird Emporium", the chalkiness of his complexion only made more apparent by the bright orange of his hair and moustache. "Dear God, this is a terrible thing, can't we at least turn those burners off?"

There seemed to be a great deal of sudsy water, with little islands of grease washing around the floor; a powerful group of gas burners, welded onto a ring, was playing onto the dented underside of a large brass hip bath; various crumpled bits of brazen superstructure that might recently have been a showering device, and various taps and handles that could have constituted a hand-pumping system, were all that seemed to be left of the wonderful "Gentleperson's Patented Portable Ablutionary Device".

The horror, however remained – sticking out of the bath-tub, in various uncoordinated and unsuitable directions, were the remains of someone who appeared to have been its occupant at the time of the accident: someone likely fully clothed, for his left foot, complete with elastic-sided boot still occupying the strap of his tastefully checked trousers, was the first thing that one saw. The second thing that one saw was one of the Duke of Wellington's sparrow-hawks perching thoughtfully on the steaming knee. After that it was better to look away rather than take in the unfortunate contents of its beak.

"And, Bailey, for heaven's sake can't you remove that appalling bird?"

"No, Mr Chuzzlewit, I can't, sir," said Bailey firmly. "Falconry is a specialist subject. Song-birds is my chosen field. We have already sent for the Duke's man. He will be along directly – he is always around."

"But supposing Her Majesty . . ."

Too late! Sixth-sensing some contretemps in what was their favourite gallery, the Royal couple had hastened to the scene.

"*Gott in Himmel*!" exclaimed Prince Albert. "Whatever has happened here?"

"Someone seems to have been taking an impromptu morning dip, Your Royal Highness, which has misfired," said Chevy Slyme as levelly as he could.

"An accident, you think?" said Queen Victoria, her voice implying that she was fairly determined that this is what it should be. "But who is it and how can they have got in? Surely they must have been authorized? Albert my dear, I do hope that what I seem to see in that bird's beak is not what one might imagine."

"No, no, my love," said Albert. "Best to look away, I think. Well, Officer, who do you think this unfortunate person might be?"

"We are, naturally, engaged conducting urgent enquiries on that matter, Your Royal Highness and will report back to you as soon as is humanly possible," averred Officer Slyme, with an uncharacteristic hint of desperation in his voice. "As her Majesty has observed, there must have been some authorization."

Mr Bailey, who had at least succeeded in switching off the gas-jets during this confrontation, cleared his throat nervously. "I fear I may know his identity, poor fellow (Your Majesty, Royal Sir). I would know those braces anywhere."

"Well?"

"It's Augustus Moddle – that's newly Sixteenth Duke of Frame."

Martin, John and Tom took a squeamish look over the side of the bath and nodded in horrified, incredulous agreement.

"I fear that would seem to be the case, Your Majesty," Martin stammered, white-lipped.

"You know him sufficiently well?"

"Regrettably, that is the case, Ma'am. He is – was – married to my cousin, Mercy Chuzzlewit."

Prince Albert seemed close to losing his fabled sang-froid. "Not Frame, surely not Frame all over again! Like father, like son, a second time?"

Queen Victoria took on a look of steel. "This will not do," she said. "This simply will not do! Poor dear Dowager Lady Frame, she has endured enough! Now listen to me! This will be tidied up at once, as though it had never happened. I expect a thorough investigation into this unfortunate accident delivered personally to me, and I know, Gentlemen, that I can rely on your loyalty in this matter." With that the Royal pair swept off to happier climes within their cherished crystal wonderland. "Thank heavens none of the children were with us this morning, Albert," were her final words on the subject.

Mr Mould, the undertaker from Cheapside, was not what might be called in his first flush of youth, nor could he be considered, these days, to be in the pink of health, but he still conducted his business to the very highest standards.

For this reason, surrounded by the bosom of his family, his buxom wife, his angelic daughters and their respective loving spouses (now two of his doughtiest assistants) what more could he do than express on behalf of all of them his shock, his shame and total bewilderment at the professional calamity that had just befallen their family undertaking?

"What more could we have done, what better could we have given them – four horses, the best quality ostrich plumes, velvet trimmings and the smartest of walking attendants (young Tacker looked superb), not to mention the expense of your two good spouses, our drivers here, decked out in new cloth cloaks and smart top boots? And Highgate Cemetery too, such a perfect setting, decidedly London's most fashionable necropolis."

"Indeed, indeed, Papa," chimed his seraphic daughters. "That massive Egyptian Avenue, that vast Pharaonic arch! But what went wrong?"

The sons-in-law groaned. "Poor Lady Frame, such a sweet young thing," said one.

"Poor Mercy Pecksniff that she once was, always such a perfect client, how much more should she have to bear?" added the other, contemplating his shining new boots – which pinched.

"But what happened?" cried their exasperated wives in unison.

"There were two widows."

"Impossible!"

"I'm afraid it's true. There was dear young Lady Frame, or the poor widow Chuzzlewit, as it seems she now may be all over again . . ."

"She was so sensitive to have things done as they should be. Nothing but the best, in tribute to a love so newly sanctified. She vowed to be dressed in the profoundest of mourning. We offered her 'Very Poignant', you know," said his elder daughter – the pair of them had extended the family business to include "Mould's Discreet Mourning Warehouse" which they ran between them with distinct success.

"Yes," said the younger, "but she settled for 'Inconsolable' watered silk to match the sentiment you see, newly imported from the Continent."

"And her sister Charity, she chose 'Deeply Afflicted', a black crepe – made up very sombre and interesting."

"All of the highest quality, too," observed the younger daughter worriedly, doing a sharp addition of their possible company losses.

"So who is this supposed 'other' Lady Frame?" snapped their incredulous mother.

"Rich, I'd say," said the elder son-in-law.

"Marmalade heiress from Aberdeen," said the younger.

"No, Dundee, I thought," said their father-in-law morosely.

"She had sailed all the way down to London with half her staff, to congratulate the new Lord Frame, all of them in a steamer and intending to see him at the Crystal Palace – and instead she finds that she is a widow and he was a bigamist."

"Poor soul," said Mrs Mould.

"Like I said, she's not poor – all of them in deepest mourning – and her all tricked out in black velvet – real Genoa. It would take a deal of money to organize that so fast," observed son-in-law senior.

"Surely it's not proper to mourn in velvet, and never in summer," said Mrs Mould, now really shocked

"Oh, no, on the contrary, Mama, it's quite the thing, just coming in."

"Oh, yes, a splendid black," added her younger daughter. "We call it 'Luxury of Woe' . . . it sells at eighteen shillings a yard, superb quality, fit for the handsomest style of domestic calamity. But it's a very proper point – how could she have got all of that set up so swift? – I wonder who she went to?"

"I think you will need to tread with caution, ladies," warned Tom Pinch diffidently. "I am afraid the late Mr Chuzzlewit Senior chose a family solicitor whose office is rather difficult of access." Tom was, indeed quite concerned that three ladies in the current fashions might not be able to squeeze in at all. Tom's work as librarian for The Chuzzlewit Foundation was very flexible, and so he had been able to take the time to escort the sisters Charity and Mercy, née Pecksniff, and the Dowager Lady Frame, for this urgent legal consultation. Gingerly, he conducted them up a flight of steps well hidden at the back of a house in Austin Friars, across some leads, and through a little blear-eyed glass door up in a corner, inscribed with "Mr Fips & Great Nephew" (the "& Great Nephew" letters being much more newly painted, and smaller than the rest). "Take care," said Tom, opening the door for them. "It can be very dark in this passage."

"Well, nowhere near as dark as it used to be!" observed the widowed Mercy, whose delicate situation was now of such particular concern to them all, but who had come there on several occasions in the past, when she was acting as companion to the elderly Mr Martin Chuzzlewit. "No ancient mat to trip over and no wicked old sideboard waiting in the gloom. He is making changes already – maybe there will even be enough chairs for us to sit on!"

The very junior Mr Fips was a slight young man with hazel eyes and the sleek appearance of a dormouse. Not only had he provided enough chairs for èven Tom, but also, it seemed, he had instigated a repainting of the walls and new varnishing of the floor, thereby totally obliterating Tom's favourite stain in the far corner. Here was a new broom that clearly swept clean and as the interview progressed Tom concluded that under that dreamy exterior there lurked someone with all the pouncing power of a cat.

"Now, Your Ladyships, Mrs Gander, Mr Pinch," began young Mr Fips politely, nodding to each member of the group in turn, "Might we first set out all the facts of this matter as you see them, so I can ensure that I have taken in everything that my good great-uncle has already attempted to verify. Then maybe we can begin to shed a little light on the curious circumstances of your recent tragic family bereavement and also try see how this lady from Dundee can possibly suggest that she and the late Augustus Moddle, Sixteenth Duke of Frame, were somehow legally married."

"Or if the couple had even actually met," pronounced the elegant Dowager Lady Frame – with great firmness of purpose. "This whole thing seems completely preposterous to me. Proving the authenticity of Augustus's claim to the dukedom turned out to be a simple matter, in the end, and my legal staff checked every detail with extreme care.

"If you wish me to sum the matter up, my late husband, Edward, the Fourteenth Duke of Frame, was a man much given to his own indulgencies. The family of Frame has always had a venal streak. That there have been little Fitz-Frames scattered all around the British Isles for generations, not to mention the South Seas, was the least of their short-comings.

"My husband was perhaps the very worst of all his noble line, if you do not count the person whom he insisted was our son Clarence, who became the Fifteenth Duke. The level of anxiety that this cuckoo in the nest managed to give, even to the Royal Family, was beyond belief. To clarify what I am saying – I only ever bore the duke one child and I was always sure that my baby was a girl (I distinctly heard the midwife say as much) but when the baby was finally placed in my arms, after it had been taken out to show my husband, lo and behold, it had become a boy!

"I tried, discreetly, for years to uncover what they might have done with my little girl, but with scant success. However the situation became really urgent when Clarence, my putative male offspring, was verified to be in the final throes of his entirely self-induced illness and there was no indication that he had left any issue, male or otherwise, his predilections having been of an unusual nature. Then I felt it was my beholden duty to set about a search for my daughter in real earnest, as there is absolutely no legal bar to female inheritance to the Frame title or estates.

"My suspicions had long rested with a scion of FitzFrame who was one of my husband's half-brothers and a popular member of his entourage. His unlikely marriage to a female entertainer from Astley's Circus took place at just the time when I first learned that I was pregnant, and they moved away from the area of Frame just after the birth of the baby heir. My agents finally tracked this FitzFrame down to the Salisbury area, where he, now a widower, had become a very highly thought of man of business, and where his daughter (whom I believe to have been my own), Elfrida, had been sent to the most expensive ladies' boarding-seminary in the area – my hopes were raised.

"All too soon, however, they were completely dashed again when we learned that the young lady was but recently dead. I was bereft. I knew that I had lost my own child for good. But the local people round Salisbury informed my men that though Elfrida had always remained living with her father, she had a son, Augustus. It was generally considered that she, too, must have been widowed, since the family was so eminently respectable in every way. But my half-brother-in-law FitzFrame would have nothing to do with any of my enquiries. It was not until the funeral morning of my disgusting changeling son, that I was informed that the wretched man had also died, but had left a deathbed confession (and also one from the midwife) which revealed that everything that I had suspected was correct. All that needed to be done was do discover the whereabouts of my grandson Augustus – but he had completely disappeared."

At this point Mercy, offering the elderly duchess a comforting hand, took up the story. "Poor, dear Augustus. When he came to manhood and was ready to earn his living, he was found a suitable post in the city and his Mama, always, like him, a sensitive soul, consigned him to the care of her dearest school friend Mrs Todgers. But alas, at that haven that is her residence, he not only met me, but due entirely to my wicked folly, lost me to another. In spite of all the care and concern of Mrs Todgers, and my sweetest sister here (who was charity itself to him), poor Augustus found himself quite overthrown when this blow was doubled by the death of his beloved mother. It was then even worse compounded by his brute of a grandfather, who took that moment to tell him that, far from having been a widow, she had in fact been abandoned by her young husband, known as 'Gus', who had reputedly run off to Van Dieman's Land rather than live up to the duties of matrimony and parenthood. Augustus, in despair, decided to leave England and go off in search of him."

"And this appears to be the point where the stories would seem to diverge," nodded Mr Fips sagely. "The solicitors of the other Lady Frame, Miss McMielleur of Dundee, assert that Augustus, having roamed the world in desolation for quite some time, met her in Seville, where she was on a short visit to relatives in connection with the orange harvest. On hearing him mention his identity, she amazed him with the news of the search for him, which had been all the rage when she had but recently left these shores. She persuaded him to come back to Britain with her and, romantically, they were married by the ship's captain, on the voyage home. They have all the dates and the testimony of the ship's captain, which, if correct, would fix the marriage to a good six months before Mr Moddle married Mrs Chuzzlewit. Strangely, since then, she avers that Mr Moddle has stayed with her at her parents' house in Dundee, putting together the papers to prove his claims to the Lordship of Frame, and in perfecting the invention of and implementing the patents to his 'Gentleperson's Ablutionary Device' – the expenses of which were covered by her parents. He left her side only very recently to come to London to pick up his completed device from the manufacturers (Josiah Brodworth and Son) and install it at the Great Exhibition. It was at this time that he wrote to tell her that he had succeeded in his claim to the title of Frame and she set off to meet him in London."

"Josiah Brodworth!" exclaimed Tom. "Why, his was the family that employed my sister Ruth to teach their daughter. She will be most gratified to hear that they now have a son!"

"Terrible people, we met them," remarked Mrs Charity Gander with fervour. "So unkind to dear Ruth; we were both appalled, were we not, sister? I could only think the worst of anyone who was professionally connected to them in some way."

"Why, yes, indeed," agreed her sister Mercy, breaking into tears. "This must all be a pack of lies – is that not so, Lady Frame?"

"Indeed, my dear, do try not to fret in your condition. We are here to set this all straight, are we not, Mr Fips? There were a great many young men who came forward claiming to be Augustus and they were all easy to dismiss. There was never one from Dundee. When Augustus did arrive back in Britain, incidentally on the same ship, the Clipper Schooner *Cupid*, as he had departed for Van Dieman's Land, he told a simple story which it was not difficult to verify.

"On arriving at the place that so many people describe as 'The Back of Beyond', Augustus was pleasantly surprised to find himself fairly swiftly reunited with his errant father, 'Gus', who owned a small mining venture and greeted him with open arms. Sadly 'Gus' was killed in a mining accident – we were shown the relevant newspaper cutting – and Augustus decided to make a brief trip to explore the wild deserts of the main continent of Australia.

"Here, in a game of chance, he won a bag of what he suspected might be opals. He headed back to the friends that he had made in Van Dieman's Land, intending to settle there for good, but he was shown the news of my search for him in a newly arrived copy of *The Times*. It seemed the sensible thing was to return to Britain to discover if he really was the missing Duke of Frame, and also have the putative opals properly assayed. He was, of course, successful in both his objectives, since the opals, wherever they originally came from, proved to be of the premier quality. This has all been verified to my complete satisfaction. How would he have had time to be conducting another whole life in Dundee?"

"And yet," said Mr Fips quietly, "the fact remains that 'The Gentleperson's Patented Ablutionary Device' had been registered under the name of Lord Augustus Frame at the Dundee address and was delivered to him at The Great Exhibition, where he was seen to be present during its installation by countless attending staff, often, to everyone's amusement, even covering his clothing with a workman's smock when checking the mechanism, and where as the result of some tragic accident his body was later found (and some of his closest friends and relatives who were there at the time were able to witness that it was indeed that of His Lordship)."

"Yes, and it was simply some horrid accident," averred the putative Lady Mercy, trying to hold back her sobs. "The police surgeon told us that he had hit the back of his head – probably when he slipped on the soap. My dear friend Mrs Gamp who did the laying out – and is a professional nurse – said just the same."

"There will be an answer," said the Dowager Lady Frame severely. "In the meantime I will not have my undoubted

grand-daughter-in-law distressed at a delicate time by some
hoyden from Dundee! Come, my dears. You have had an
exhausting morning. What you both require is a new bonnet,
or maybe a pelisse – where was it you said you had obtained
your present elegant ensembles, a little place in Cheapside?
How quaint! Perhaps we should pay them a visit."

Mould's Discreet Mourning Warehouse was all of a flutter to
find itself visited by not merely one, but two, duchesses. The
Dowager Lady Frame, used to the professional insincerity of
high fashion modistes, found the place somehow very homely
and touching as the two angelic Mould daughters, and, in
honour of this special occasion, their mother also, plied them
with dainty cups of tea in their discreetly curtained-off rooms
immediately adjoining the undertaker's premises. Every so
often, to be sure, one of the three of them would need to sally
forth to "the front of shop" but otherwise it seemed more like
a sympathetic afternoon call than a business transaction.

As Mrs Mould, whose turn it was, rose to answer the
tinkling bell that heralded one such sortie, the amazed voice
of Mr Mould, the proprietor of all their endeavours, could be
distinctly heard without.

"Why, Mr Pecksniff, by all that's wonderful, is it really
you? We heard you were in foreign parts these days!"

"Not Pa, surely!" cried his gentle offspring in the back
room, almost dropping their tea cups in amazement as the
door swung to behind the receding Mould Mama.

The Dowager Lady Frame sat there in bemusement as the
daughters Pecksniff and the daughters Mould gathered in a
silent semicircle by the half open door and peered through
the black velvet curtains.

"No, not any more!" They heard Mr Pecksniff's stentorian tones as if it was only yesterday. "No, I am returned
in honour. I am returned from the back of beyond in
vengeance of my eldest child. I understand it was you
who conducted the funeral of the late, perfidious Augustus
Moddle, Sixteenth Duke of Frame. I come to clamour for
the rights of this good and tragic lady who stands beside

me, Amelia Moddle, his undoubted and only wife. (And she requires mourning raiment for herself and son at an economic price)."

A bronzed and slightly crestfallen Mr Pecksniff sat with his teacup perched upon his knee as he faced the selection of affronted womenfolk gathered in Mrs Todger's crowded parlour.

The Dowager Lady Frame sat with the marriage lines of Amelia, Mrs Moddle, laid out before her, while she perused them with Mercy and Charity née Pecksniff, who were seated on her either side.

Mrs Amelia Moddle looked pale and tired but seemed a nice enough young woman, with smooth brown hair and a firmness of chin almost to compete with that of Mrs Charity Gander (who was apparently the child whose honour Mr Pecksniff had intended to avenge – distance, it seemed having kept him unaware of what fortune had seemed to offer his other daughter, Mercy).

Kind Mrs Todgers, who had of course offered the travellers what accommodation she could, had placed Amelia in a chair beside her while she attempted to feed bread and milk to the exhausted little boy, Paulie, who was curled up on Amelia's lap and whose likeness to Augustus spoke for itself. Mr Gander and Mr Jinkins and Tom Pinch were refilling and handing round the cups and plates.

"But could you not see it, dear Pa?" said Cherry with practised sweetness, "That if these marriage lines of Amelia's are authentic, and no one is saying that they are not, it would have been well nigh impossible for the Augustus that we know to be the Augustus named in this document. Our Augustus would still have been on board the Clipper Schooner *Cupid* on his way to Van Dieman's Land, not already nest-building with her there. Could your husband not perhaps have been Augustus's Papa, Amelia?"

"No, my Gussie was a beautiful young man. I never even met his father; he never said anything about having one."

"Well, I am at a loss for words," said the Dowager Lady

Frame. "How on earth could Augustus have been in two, if not more, places at once?"

The stunned silence which followed the suggestion of this disturbing notion was broken by the hearty ringing of Mrs Todgers' doorbell, the sounds of the door being opened and the tramp of hearty feet.

"Ah," said a voice. "Just as I have dreamed of it. I'd know that wonderful aroma anywhere."

"What," laughed a second voice. "Not cabbage a-boiling, surely?"

"Why, bless you, no, son, the lady's way with gravy!"

The parlour door was thrust open and there stood Bailey, who had once been the doorman and boots to this very establishment, looking, for all the world, like a small golden sunburst. "You're never going to believe who I've just met up with, a-wandering the street like a lost puppy looking for its home.

A darkly grey-haired strangerer – bronzed and muscularer – stood, smiling, in the doorway.

"Todgers!" gasped his lady wife and slumped all of a heap in her chair.

"Ah, she always was such a sweetly pretty thing to me," sighed the prodigal Todgers, gazing at the tiny, bubble of a miniature of Mrs Todgers in her youth that was tacked up over the kettle holder. "No, I may have behaved without honour, but I never could forget her way with gravy, not ever, worth coming all the way home from the back of beyond for that alone. But what is this that Mr Bailey here has been telling me about poor young Augustus? One does not wish to speak ill of the dead, but it doesn't sound to me as though he has been dealing straight with any of us."

"You knew Augustus Moddle?"

"I have been acquainted with three Augustus Moddles. Which one do you wish to know about?"

"Perhaps you would like to tell us about them in order of their age, for want of any other suitable way of sorting them.

I take it they were not triplets?" sighed the Dowager Lady Frame resignedly.

"Why, bless you, no, ma'am," grinned Todgers. "They were father and sons. The first was 'Gus' Moddle, my oldest friend. Together we courted and married. I my dearest Mrs Todgers here, and he her friend from ladies' boarding school, Elfrida FitzFrame. Alas, the foolishness of youth, we deserted them and set off adventuring to Van Dieman's Land, 'Gus' leaving his infant namesake behind him.

"Worse still, once we were on board the clipper that was taking us to our destination, I discovered that 'Gus' was in fact fleeing with his new love and they were 'married' by the captain on board ship. To my shame I acted as best man to him (for a second time) because I knew yet another small Moddle was on its way. He was born in Van Dieman's Land and we always jokingly called him Gussie Fitz Gus. He was always a wayward lad, the very image of his papa. He left home when he was about fifteen, after his poor mother died. I do not know what became of him.

"About six years ago now, I think it would be, the Augustus Moddle that must be known to all of you, arrived from England and put in an appearance at his father's mine – again, a son the very model of my friend. There was an accident, my friend Gus died and young Augustus ran off to Australia for a bit and returned with nothing but a bag of pebbles that he had won in a game of cards. I thought they might be opals. Then we saw a story in *The Times* about the missing Duke of Frame. It was clear to me that this must be Augustus. I lent him the money for his return to Britain so that he could try his luck with the peerage and the opals. I told him of a place to stay – I even gave him the key.

"He promised that he would keep in touch and let me know of what reception I might get if I were to come back home. He wrote to tell me of his happy news and sent me the money to return – and now I hear of all this tragedy."

"So there have been two Augustus Moddles on the loose in Britain, Gussie and Augustus," sighed the Dowager Lady Frame. "Which one did what, and which of them died?"

"And which one did not – and, more importantly, where is he? Strikes me he could be a very loose cannon," said Gander worriedly.

"So I think I must have married the younger one, that I indeed knew as Gussie, who was born out of true wedlock in Van Dieman's Land," said Mrs Amelia Moddle sadly. "And that unfortunate marmalade heiress was heartily duped by him."

"I do not think you need to repine for her too much," observed Mr Bailey with hearty jollity. "Indeed we found her pretty sanguine about her late 'husband's' possible demise when she asked Mr Tom here, and Mr Martin and Mr John and me to tell her all the circumstances of his accident. Did she not, Mr Tom? A very gallant young lady – not the sort who would let herself be cast down by the possibility of having been misused by a wastrel – if that turned out to be the case. She has even suggested that I cheer her by taking her and her secretary on one of my 'Flights of Fancy' over London should her stay here be prolonged."

All the ladies glared at both Bailey and Tom for fraternising with the enemy.

"However, it would seem that she will not need to be detained in these parts for very long," observed Charity Gander with relish. "My sister Mercy has clearly married the Augustus Moddle that was born in Salisbury, and so she really is Lady Frame after all."

"But why ever did Lord Frame help set up 'The Gentleperson's Patented Portable Ablutionary Device' at the Great Exhibition, if he had not invented it?" remarked a bewildered Mr Pecksniff from his cramped position in the chair by the window.

"Well, I should think you would understand, if anyone did!" Tom Pinch was about to say, but then the light suddenly dawned on him and the scales fell from his eyes as they had when he first realised the real truth of his patron, Mr Pecksniff's, perfidious nature all those years ago.

"You know," he said out loud, "I don't think our Augustus, the Sixteenth Duke, did. I think he went to the Crystal Palace to find out what was going on, and who was taking his name in vain. One Lord Frame was Gussie, leaping about in his workman's smock and the other was Augustus, sporting dear Merry's beautiful braces. Was it an accident? Who has survived? Gussie could cover up his deceit and his crime, but equally, there would be nothing to stop a swift swap of dress if our Augustus was finding being a landed lord too great a strain, which would not surprise me in the least, I am afraid. He could jump ship and start all over again somewhere else."

"There always was a violent side to poor Augustus – I know it to my cost!" sighed Jinkins. "If he has lost his marbles, I hope he isn't lurking somewhere around here."

"Well," said Todgers quietly, "I gave him a key to the cellar that's under here. It has always remained my property – used to be my little bolt-hole you know. Maybe you fellows wouldn't mind coming along with me to have a look. I wouldn't like to think of my dear Mrs Todgers living over a powder keg."

The cellarage at Todgers' was approachable only by a little back door and a rusty grating, and the inhabitants of Todgers' had always assumed that it was the freehold property of someone else, and it was reported to be full of untold wealth – though whether in gold or silver, buts of wine or, indeed casks of gunpowder, no one had ever been sure, but in fact when Mr Todgers finally put in his key, the ancient lock turned with an easy click and everyone feared the worst. There was a distinct smell of bruised oranges down in the cellar under Todgers', and also of stale sacking from all the stored knick-knacks of the Todgers' misspent youth that loomed in bales therein.

And something moved in the darkness at the back.

"Augustus – is that you my boy?" said Mr Todgers gently.

"Who sir, me sir? Why no!" came a querulous sing-song voice. "No, I am a lord. The Lord No Zoo. The joke's on everyone's lips these days, you know."

*   *   *

The knowledge of a duty well performed can be satisfying and vengeance can be sweet. Snug in the safety of the dower-house, the elderly Lady Frame can watch and smile as the great mansion on the hill echoes again with life and laughter as droves of impecunious Chuzzlewits throng in to benefit from the industrious refurbishments of their eminent cousin Seth Pecksniff (aided by his wife Amelia), and offer their support to their tiny grandson Harry, The Seventeenth Duke.

Up in the attics of Frame, lovingly contrived with every comfort and security, by the said Seth, there resides the sad figure referred to by those who know of his existence, as "Poor Gussie". Mostly he is a mild, lachrymose being; sometimes he plays the flute. He does not recognise anyone, not kind Lady Mercy, or her sister-in law Amelia who nurses him so gently, nor even Miss McMielleur, the marmalade heiress from Dundee who took the trouble to fly all the way to visit him at Frame in a balloon piloted by the gallant Bailey (whose hair and moustache gleamed as brightly as any of her oranges from Seville).

Poor Gussie is terrified of baths; his greatest fear in life, it seems, is of slipping on the soap. But at other times he is given to wild rages about a long lost brother who tried to steal his heritage away and who deserved all he got.

No, Gussie is not the sort of house guest that Frame would like to admit to harbouring – but Gussie is from being the first of that kind in Frame's long history. No, it seems, that in the era of the young Seventeenth Duke Harry, his charming mother, dear Lady Mercy, must be prepared to extend the bounties of the great heritage of Frame to the Lord knows who.

The Bartered Child

Charles Todd

No sooner had Dickens completed Martin Chuzzlewit *than he was gripped by an idea for a new story, one that had been struggling to be written for some while but the right vehicle had not presented itself. A visit to a new charity school in Saffron Hill in Camden, near to Dickens's childhood haunts and apparently the very site where Dickens had set Fagin's den, filled Dickens with horror at the state and prospects of the wretched children he saw. He believed it was society's duty to help these children and the idea of a benevolent change in heart by those who could help, coalesced into the first of his Christmas books, the immortal* A Christmas Carol. *It was written at white-heat pace in a little under six weeks and published on 19 December 1843. It was rapturously received by the public and has remained arguably Dickens's best-known and most widely read book. With it Dickens effectively created the spirit of Christmas.*

We all know the story of the miserly Ebenezer Scrooge who, one Christmas Eve, is visited by the ghosts of Christmas Past, Present and Future whereby he discovers what impact he can have upon people. At the end he determines to change and make good. So, just what kind of character does he become? The following story looks at Scrooge ten years later.

The story also touches briefly on Dickens's next book, Dombey and Son, *about which more shortly.*

Charles Todd is the alias used by the mother-son writing team Caroline and Charles Todd. They are the authors of the award-winning Inspector Rutledge series, set in England in the aftermath of the First World War, which began with A Test of Wills *(1996).*

He stopped in front of his door, glancing over his shoulder at the man loitering at the corner of the street. When he turned back to lift the latch, he felt his heart turn over. Marley's face glared back at him from the knocker.

And then it was gone.

Scrooge stood there, his eyes closed, remembering. It had been ten years since that dreadful Christmas Eve. He'd done his best to live up to the visitations he'd received. And he'd never told anyone about them. He still wasn't sure where they had come from, but most certainly he knew why they had come. A warning.

Pride had always been his downfall. Never greed. Money was the measure of his worth, and the more he had, the greater his pride. Only Marley had understood that. What had he done – after all this time – for Marley to come again? Where had he taken a wrong turning? What had he neglected? How had he failed?

But of course, there was no reply – Marley was gone.

He went inside and closed his door behind him.

The house was very different now. The hall was tidy, the stairs carpeted, the drawing room respectably set out. A prosperous merchant's dwelling. Neither blatantly fashionable nor in any way ostentatious. A house where he could invite his friends and his family, where he could be at peace with himself, where he could carry on the charities that had needed his guidance and funds.

Had he been wrong? Should he have left this great barn of a place empty of warmth and instead spent the sums where they could have done more good? Had pride, not necessity, coaxed him into breaking his promise?

What had he done that Marley had come again?

The door knocker clanged hard against its plate, and Scrooge jumped at the unexpected sound. He gathered his wits and went to answer the door himself. In spite of what he'd done in the house, he'd not indulged in servants, though from time to time he'd offered a position to someone in need of work and a good reference. At present there was only a cook and a housekeeper. Marley couldn't expect him to cook his own meals or launder his own sheets. Surely?

The man standing on the step was the one he'd seen loitering across the street. A rough sort, his clothes well used and a two day's growth of beard on his chin.

Scrooge said, "What is it you've come for?" And half expected the fellow to answer, "Robbery."

Instead he mumbled, "I was told, if I come here you'd give me five shillings for the message I carry."

Robbery indeed.

"I shan't know the message's worth until I hear it," Scrooge responded.

"And then you'll not pay me," the man retorted stubbornly.

Scrooge took out his purse and found the shillings. Instead of handing them over, he held them in mid air. "The message, if you please."

The man hesitated, eyeing the coins as if he expected them to vanish. Finally, he handed a folded sheet of paper to Scrooge. It was crumpled and smudged with dirt and something else Scrooge preferred not to imagine. Scrooge took it as the man whisked the shillings out of his hand and disappeared down the street.

"Here!" But it was too late; the man had vanished around the corner.

Shutting the door, Scrooge unfolded the message.

I know where Betsy Talman's baby is. Tonight. The Green Dragon.

There was nothing else.

Betsy Talman was a young woman Scrooge had met destitute and begging on the streets some months ago. He'd employed her as housemaid and her husband as a messenger until she gave birth to her son, then found more suitable work for the couple in Dorset. He had put them on the mail coach himself, but it overturned just short of its destination, and the child had died in the wreckage. Betsy had grieved little short of madness, swearing the baby wasn't dead, that she'd held it in her arms, hadn't she, and she herself had not a scratch on her. But she'd had a severe blow to the head and the child had been buried in the village churchyard before she was allowed to leave her bed.

Now here was someone claiming the child was alive. Truth or trick? The Green Dragon was near the docks, and hardly a place for a respectable merchant to be hanging about, waiting for person or persons unknown to come up to him. In hope of payment for producing a baby, any baby of the right age?

Scrooge debated with himself. Was it wise to open old wounds? On the other hand, what if he didn't meet this person or persons, and the baby, by some miracle, *was* hers?

He'd a fondness for Betsy. Something about her reminded him of Martha Cratchit's little Sally, and he'd been touched by her plight. Her husband was a good and loving man. Scrooge had felt responsible for their loss, having put them on that luckless coach for what he'd believed was a better life than London had provided the little family.

Which brought him back to the note in his hand. If he went to the Green Dragon, how was he to know, if he were shown it, that the boy was Betsy's? Babies looked very much alike, didn't they? And what if he took it, and it wasn't hers, and he was left with it? He couldn't very well ask Betsy to come to the Green Dragon and look at it herself, to be sure!

He remembered Marley's face on the knocker. Perhaps it was a different kind of warning, not one disapproving of his expenditures but one telling him to beware? He was a man of business, not a man of action. He could be in danger.

By dusk, still undecided, he had changed to his third-best

suit of clothes and gone out, taking his cane with him. Much good it would do him at the Green Dragon.

He found a cabbie willing to take him there and wait for him, then sat back in the shadows of the cab, thinking about what the night would bring.

There was a mist rising off the water, grey and unpleasant, when he reached the docks and saw the Green Dragon tucked into a space between a mercantile shop with gear for seamen and a doss house whose smell wafted down the stairs and into the street. Stale sheets, stale beer and stale faces at the windows, men for whom life had nothing left to offer except more pain, more disappointment and more poverty.

The Green Dragon was not as picturesque as its name, and had nothing to do with China or the opium trade. Although as Scrooge walked in and found a table to the rear, he thought that he might have taken over a small ship in company with the dozen or so men already into their cups. The scars on their faces spoke of quick use of the knife, and if any of them had seen the inside of a bath house in living memory, he would be surprised. Tobacco smoke, mixed with the odour of cabbage and sweat, was overwhelming in this back corner, but he was here, and here he'd remain, his back to the wall.

He was thinking about Marley's face on the knocker, when a slim man in black edged around the door and stood surveying the drinkers. His gaze stopped at Scrooge and he began to cross to the table in the rear. Someone called out to him, asking about the latest ship in, and he replied that it was the *Anna Maria*, from Portugal.

He nodded to Scrooge and sat down in the chair opposite. A rough man, close to, with cunning eyes.

Scrooge said, "What am I to call you? You know my name, and I must have yours or we do no business here."

"They call me Ned, mostly."

"What's this about a baby?"

"I've told you. I've seen the lad with my own eyes."

"Yes, well, so you say. But how is it he's still alive, and what have you to do with him?"

"Ah, that you will know tomorrow. I don't fancy being

brought up before the magistrates tonight. Eleven o'clock in the morning, Kensington Gardens. And bring a hundred pounds with you."

"To be robbed in the shrubbery? I think not."

"Suit yourself then. The babe's as well off in the river. No one else wants him."

Ned started to rise, eager to be gone now that no profit was in the offing.

Scrooge said quickly, to keep him there, "You'll not see five shillings, until I've seen this boy."

Ned laughed. "Done. He'll be there. Look for Jenny."

"How does this Jenny know who the child is? If she's in hope of a reward for sending it back to his rightful mother, I tell you straight off that the Talmans don't have a penny to rub together. They're in service."

Ned was unabashed. "Ah, but you've helped them quite a bit, haven't you? Jenny thought the child might be your own, and you'd pay handsomely to have it back."

Scrooge felt his face go red as his anger flared. He'd done well with his temper these last ten years, but sometimes it was out of hand before he could prevent it. "*Mine*?"

"Jenny says." Ned moved like a snake, smoothly and quickly, one minute sitting there, the next out the door, leaving Scrooge at the table, his face flushed with his anger.

It was a clever scheme, this one. Tell him that his long lost "son" was found, tell some other bereaved parent that the baby was hers, and let the bidding war begin. No matter who won – and it was almost certain that Betsy would lose – this man and Jenny would prosper.

But who was the mother of this child? He had until eleven in the morning to find out.

A man with his own 'counting house always had sources of information. A good bargain – a bad investment – a bit of gossip that would stand someone in good stead – information was of value, and sometimes meant money in hand.

Scrooge set out early in the morning, going to first one and then another 'counting house, asking questions and listening to the answers. By ten minutes before eleven, he was in

Kensington Gardens, no wiser than he had been the night before. He chose a bench in the open, sat down in the watery sunlight, and watched nursemaids in starched uniforms take their charges out for the air.

He played the game of which one might be Jenny, the dark-haired nursemaid with narrow eyes and pursed lips or the sly, fair-haired woman who glanced his way twice. Instead it was the red-haired girl with a laughing face who sat down beside him, and in her arms was a baby wrapped in blankets, sleeping quietly. It was difficult to say with such a young child who he most resembled.

Scrooge had no experience of babies. What colour were its eyes? Blue, at a guess. But half of Britain had blue eyes, surely. Fair hair, burnished even in the pale sun. Yet it appeared to be the same age as Betsy's might have been.

He said to Jenny, "How can I be sure this isn't a trick?"

Jenny said, "Well, you must take the matter on trust."

"The mother of this boy has grieved and recovered. Why open old wounds?"

"Why then are you here? Betsy was your housemaid, and if the child were truly *hers*, and not yours, you'd have no interest in the boy."

Scrooge said nothing.

After a moment, Jenny said, "I was hoping you would want him."

Ah, Scrooge thought, here's the rub.

"Because if you don't take him, what's to become of him? I got him from a mother who didn't want him any more. He's not really hers, you see, and they had too many mouths to feed as it was. I told her I thought I might make a little money from him—"

"What do you mean, not really hers?"

But Jenny was frightened now, looking over her shoulder as if she half expected Ned to be hiding in the shrubbery, listening.

"You must tell me," Scrooge urged. "Ned promised the child would go into the river if I didn't meet you."

She stared at him. "He's that cruel," she said, touching the child protectively. Scrooge wondered if the boy might be Jenny's.

"All right, if you swear you won't tell Ned. The wet nurse to the child of a man of means forbade her to see her own boy, and it struck her that if she exchanged the babies, she'd have her own son with her day and night. She did that, thinking no harm would come of it. But this man of means found out she'd taken his lad with her when she went to see her family, and he cast her out. The very day she'd made the swap. And it was too late to get her own boy back, wasn't it? Without being taken up by the police."

Scrooge was appalled. "She left her own child in her employer's house, and now that *this* boy's no more use to her, she's ridding herself of him?"

"I told you, there's too many mouths to feed!" Jenny cried, as if Scrooge couldn't understand, with food on the table three times a day, what hunger was.

"How do you know these things?" he asked sharply.

"I don't know how Ned knows, but he does. He knows everything."

He considered the situation for a moment. "This poor child's real mother – the rich man's wife – is dead, isn't she? Otherwise she'd have seen at once that the wet nurse had exchanged the babies."

Jenny shook her head. "Ned didn't say."

But Scrooge was going rapidly through his acquaintance. Who among them had lost a wife within the past few months, after the birth of a child? Paul Dombey for one. Scrooge himself had attended Fanny Dombey's pathetic funeral and noted Dombey's indifference to her obsequies even while he waxed effusive over his son.

It was a place to begin.

"How do I know you've told me the truth?" he demanded. "Jenny, you mustn't let this child suffer through Ned."

"Then buy him," she begged. "He could be yours, couldn't he? Or give him to Betsy to rear. I tell you, he's not *wanted*!"

"I'll give you fifty pounds for him. And if you're wise, you'll take it and go away where Ned can't find you."

Her face looked old with her worry. "I told you, Ned knows everything. He'd find me." She held out her hand. "If you please, I'll tell Ned that you wanted him for your own. He'll be suspicious, else, and give me no peace."

Scrooge gave her the fifty pounds, and Jenny counted it quickly.

Then she stood up quickly and walked away without looking back.

Scrooge sat there, looking down at the sleeping child. Why hadn't it stirred or cried or demanded to be fed? He picked it up gingerly, and as he did, he caught a sweet scent he recognized. An opiate had been given to this child to keep him quiet!

Shocked, Scrooge calculated his next action. If he took the child to Dombey and Son, there would be a fuss. The best solution was to take it to Dombey's home. His sister Louisa Chick would know where to find the discharged nurse, and confront the woman with him.

He hailed a cab and gave directions to Dombey's house. He was received with warmth by Mrs Chick and her shadow, Miss Tox. Mrs Chick asked, "And is that a baby, dear Mr Scrooge, that I see in your arms? I wasn't aware that you . . ."

Miss Tox substituted gently, ". . . were starting a family."

Scrooge grimaced. "Alas, the child is not mine. In fact, I've come on a delicate matter. You have a child the age of this one, do you not?"

"Oh, dearest little Paul, yes."

"The light of our day," Miss Tox murmured.

"Does he resemble his papa or his mama?"

"His papa, without any doubt." Louisa Chick answered serenely.

"Indubitably," Miss Tox assured him, with a nod.

"Would you be so kind as to let me see him? There's a question of this child's paternity. I must advise, and I have no experience of one this young."

They bustled to help him. Miss Tox took the child from

his arms and carried it to the window. Mrs Chick hurried up the stairs to retrieve young Paul from his nursery.

When she came back, flushed with exertion and pleasure, she presented the sleeping Paul as if he were a royal prince. "Here is our dearest treasure, our joy."

Scrooge stared at the bundle in her arms. He could see no difference between the two boys. "Then consider this child I have with me. If you were the parents of one of these lads, would you know your treasure from the other, if they were somehow confused?"

Mrs Chick stared dubiously at the two sleeping faces. "*This* one," she said, "has nothing to distinguish his features – although it pains me to have to say such a thing to you. But our Paul here has his father's eyes, his father's nose. I'd know him if you brought a thousand babies here and spread them about the furniture."

"One has only to look," echoed Miss Tox.

Scrooge did, and could see very little difference between the children. The width of the chin? The shape of the ears? But then he'd spent only a short time in their company. Perhaps day in and day out, one came to know the small divergences.

He put his thought into words. "Then you feel that the mother of the child I brought here will know him on the instant?"

"Of course she will!"

"And I couldn't confuse you with any other child of the same age?"

"Never," Mrs Chick announced stoutly. "Only look at Paul and remember his father. A Dombey if ever there was one."

Scrooge asked, "There is nothing of his poor mother in him?"

"Nothing. A Dombey through and through."

"Beyond any doubt," Miss Tox agreed.

What could he say in the face of their conviction, when there was no proof of anything? Only the word of a girl like Jenny against the family's certainty.

He must find the nursemaid and persuade her to confess to the exchange.

"I have need of a wet nurse for a week. I understand you employ one who has been with young Paul for some time. She might know of someone trustworthy."

Mrs Chick pursed her mouth. "Polly Toodle, that was. She was discharged. You will not want that one for your sweet child."

"No," Miss Tox added. "She was *not* trustworthy at all."

"Toodle? An odd name," he said.

"As odd as she was. Not surprising, coming from where she did." Miss Tox added "Staggs Gardens," in a voice so soft Scrooge had difficulty hearing it, as if she were ashamed of the address.

"Then I must ask my housekeeper to recommend someone." He rose to take his leave

They were curious about the child and plied him with questions, but Scrooge shook his head and said, "Alas, it is a very private matter. I'm not at liberty to discuss his parentage."

He found a carriage to take him as far as Polly Toodle's humble cottage, but he had no need to ask if she had given away a child. She was sitting in the sun nursing one the same age as the baby he had brought with him. He called to the little family group to ask if Mr Toodle was at home, and she told him he was expected later in the day.

"And you are Mrs Toodle?"

"I am."

He beckoned one of the boys at her feet and handed over five shillings, mentally keeping an accounting of his expenditures thus far. "Tell your father I have repaid my debt," he said, then indicated mother and child on the doorstep. "The little one. Is he a part of your family?"

"Yes, sir."

"And a handsome lad he is. Who do you think he favours, his papa or his mama?"

"His mama, sir. He has her eyes."

*   *   *

Scrooge tapped the roof of his carriage with his cane, and the driver said, "Where to, sir?"

A very good question, one he couldn't answer. Jenny, it appeared, had lied twice. The boy wasn't Betsy's and it wasn't Paul Dombey's. Who then did it belong to? Was it Jenny's, after all? And he'd been lulled into parting with fifty pounds through a tissue of lies? Had she been afraid that Ned, overwhelmed with jealousy, would indeed rid himself of what might well be another man's child? And so this scheme had been hatched, with Ned promised fifty pounds in return for the child's life . . .

Afraid for the drugged child, he ordered the cabbie to take him home. It had been quiet far too long, and Scrooge had no idea when it had last been given nourishment.

Mrs Nelson, his housekeeper, was aghast to see Scrooge walk through his door with an infant in his arms. It was rousing from its sleep, the little mouth working and one arm struggling to free itself from the swaddling blankets. She peered at it short-sightedly.

"What's this, then?"

"A foundling, in need of food and care. You must find a wet nurse at once, if you please, and see that he has whatever he needs to survive."

"But Mr Scrooge—"

He said only, "And keep him safe. If anyone comes to ask for him, you know nothing of him. Do you understand me?"

She was on the point of questioning him, but Scrooge ignored her and went back to the waiting cab. This time he traveled to the police station nearest Kensington Gardens, on the theory that Jenny had known the area where they had met, and must at some time worked nearby. He went inside to find the sergeant at the desk in a heated argument with a chimney sweep.

Scrooge waited with ill-concealed impatience, and when the sweep had finally been satisfied and sent on his way, he said to the sergeant, "Ebenezer Scrooge. I'm here on a matter of some urgency, entrusted to me by a client. Can you tell me if there has been a report of a missing child?"

"You say a child is missing?"

"No. I ask you if one has been reported missing."

"We've not heard of any such thing. I'd be the first to know. Here, what's this about?"

"I'm also attempting to trace a certain young person—" Scrooge described Jenny and that conspicuous red hair, the saucy face, but the sergeant shook his head.

"She's not known to us. What's she done?" He reached for pen and paper. "We'll keep an eye out, if you like."

The last thing Scrooge wanted was anyone looking for Jenny. Not yet, at least.

He extricated himself with some difficulty and a number of lies, and went back to the cab. The driver was sunning himself, eyes closed, face lifted. Scrooge tapped on his knee and said, "If a child went missing, one too young to be useful to a beggar or a tradesman, who would know of it?"

The cabbie eyed him suspiciously. Scrooge, again reckoning his costs, reached for his purse and offered the cabbie half a crown.

The cabbie said reluctantly, "There's Mrs Brown, if you like. She deals in second-hand clothes, but there's not much happens she doesn't hear about. Where there's gossip, there's money to be made."

Half London seemed to thrive on gossip about the other half. He himself had profited more than once from a chance word dropped into a conversation.

"Then by all means, find me this Mrs Brown."

The cabbie was dubious, but Scrooge said harshly as he climbed into the cab, "Get on with it, man, I've had nothing to eat since the morning, and I'm in no mood to argue."

The horse set off at a trot, and Scrooge soon found himself no more than an hour's walk from Staggs Gardens, where Polly Toodle lived. The neighborhood was not to his liking, and he found himself with his hand on his purse, protecting it. The cab drew up before a small, inconspicuous house in a street that appeared to be deserted.

But he was in luck. Mrs Brown herself answered his knock, and he waved five pounds in front of her ugly nose and said,

"I'm in a hurry. There's a child missing, and I'm told you can tell me what I need to know."

She stared at him, a fierce frown on her face. "Who sent you to Good Mother Brown?" she asked suspiciously.

"Jenny," Scrooge answered. "She's afraid Ned will harm the child, and I've agreed to buy it. She promised to meet me at Kensington Gardens, but she wasn't there."

"Ned's a nasty piece of work," she agreed. "I haven't seen Jenny this fortnight. I told her she'd regret ever setting eyes on him. But she told me he'd be rich soon." She looked Scrooge up and down. "Why would the likes of you want to buy a child?"

"That's my business and not yours. If you don't know where to find Jenny, tell me how I can find Ned. It may not be too late!"

The urgency in his voice wasn't pretence. And she seemed to sense it. A gleam of avarice stirred in her eyes, and she said, "Here, he was doing a bit of work for the one they call Samuel Dancy. Don't tell me Ned's gone and cheated him! There's no child, is there? Dancy has paid you to bring him Ned. How much for me if find Ned for you?"

Scrooge said, "I'll find him myself and keep what I've earned." He turned away, expecting her to follow him. And she did.

"If there's money to be made, I'll sell Ned to you. Dancy's not one to cross, and I'd as soon have him owing *me* a favour."

"I don't know any Dancy."

"Yes, you do. He's half-brother to the late Lord Wenhill—"

But Scrooge had got what he wanted, and he swung himself into the cab, leaving her in the road. She ran after him, crying, "I'll have my five pound. I've earned it!"

He tossed the money toward her and left her scrabbling in the dust for it as the cabbie spoke to his horse.

Dancy. Scrooge knew that name. The late Lord Wenhill's father had taken an actress as his second wife, and gossip had it that the family was relieved when she died young of consumption. But their son had become the black sheep of the family.

But what had Dancy to do with this bartered child? He had never married, and if the child was his bastard, he'd rid himself of it without the help of a man like Ned. His reputation in business was one of ruthlessness. There was nothing for it but to go to Lady Wenhill and beg for her help.

Scrooge was forced to return to the police sergeant in Kensington to ask the direction. The man was thoroughly suspicious now.

"What's your business with her ladyship?" he demanded.

Scrooge, lying through his teeth, answered, "There's a question about her late husband's estate."

"Oh, yes. First a missing child, and then a will."

Scrooge smiled. "The child was a separate matter. That was charity. This is money."

He left the sergeant grinning at his back and gave the cabbie directions.

The house fronted a large square, and like most of its neighbors spoke of wealth and pomp. Scrooge walked up the shallow steps to the door and lifted the knocker. A maid in a starched cap opened the door and stared at him.

"Ebenezer Scrooge to see Lady Wenhill."

"She's not in to callers today."

"I think she'll see me. Tell her I've come about Samuel Dancy, her brother-in-law."

The maid went away and came back quickly with a young woman in severe mourning at her heels. The woman's face was drawn, dark shadows under her eyes and lines of grief around her mouth.

She dismissed the maid and said in a low voice, "What is it? Haven't I suffered enough? I've done as I was told, and he promised – *promised*! – to leave me alone!"

"Lady Wenhill," Scrooge answered gently, "I haven't come to distress you. But there's a matter of a baby—"

He thought she was going to faint on the spot. She caught

his arm and dragged him with her to the sitting room over-looking the back garden, shutting the door behind them.

"Is he well? You haven't come to tell me he's dead? Oh, please God, *not that!*"

Scrooge stared at her. "My lady, I don't understand."

"If Samuel sent you, you understand very well! My son – *is he alive or dead?*"

Her hand, still clutching his sleeve, was trembling, and he thought only fear was holding her upright.

"Lady Wenhill, I assure you, I haven't come from Samuel Dancy. I'm trying to find him. But you speak of a child?"

"My son—" she broke off, turning away. "You know nothing of this? Is it true?"

"It is true."

She sat down in a chair by the window and began to cry, sobs racking her body.

"You said something about a child, Lady Wenhill. And it's about a child that I've come." He didn't think she was listening. "I was approached by a young person only this morning, offering me a child. She told me it was the son of a woman who had worked for me until recently. I knew it couldn't be true, but Jenny was afraid that Ned—"

He stopped. Lady Wenhill turned on him with such a violent expression on her face that he stepped back against the door.

"Ned? Ned Paling?"

"I don't know his full name—"

"Describe him to me!"

Scrooge did, and watched the woman before him flush with fury.

"*It was Ned Paling who took my son!*"

"I don't understand, my lady—"

"I retired to our country estate after my husband's death. I was seven months with child, and for my husband's sake I wanted it to be born in Gloucestershire. All the Wenhills for generations have been born there, you see. But when I arrived, I found the servants had been dismissed, new servants in their place. Ned Paling was there, and he became my jailer. There was nothing I could do. No one I could send for help. When I was delivered of a son, Samuel Dancy came into my bedchamber and told me that I had borne a daughter. But I knew I hadn't, I'd seen the child. Still, they brought me a baby and put it in my arms, and insisted that *this* was my child, and so it would be registered, as my daughter."

"Why should he do such a terrible thing?"

"Because of the will – if my child was a son, everything went to him, the title, the property, the family's wealth. If it was a girl, the estate was divided into thirds – for her, for myself, and for Dancy, who would also claim the title."

"And if you hadn't survived? For certainly it would have been easier if you had been reported to have died in child-birth, with your son."

"No, I was safe enough. If neither of us had survived, Dancy got nothing but the title. Every penny would have been put into a trust fund for scholars at Harrow."

Scrooge was beginning to see. "And so he took your child, told you that if you accepted a daughter in its place, your son would live. If you told the world what had been done, the boy would die. But surely there was a doctor in attendance?"

"No, only a midwife."

"And where did this girl come from, so handy to be exchanged for your boy?"

"I don't know. The midwife must have known of some such."

"And that girl is now upstairs, in your nursery?"

"Yes. I can't bear to look at her, but she has every care. Servants, a wet nurse. Everything but my love."

"And has her birth been registered?"

"No. I – I couldn't bear to do it. Not so soon. It made everything final, you see. And once that last step was taken, how could I protect my son?"

Scrooge felt a sudden surge of fear. "Why have you told me this? When you were warned not to tell?"

"Because I'm so terribly afraid something *will* happen to my child, and I'll never be told. You said there was a boy—"

"I must go to him straightaway. Before someone realizes he's in my house and I'm here."

"I'll go with you!"

"No, you mustn't, it isn't safe—"

But she would not hear of staying behind. He took her out to the cab and to his house, where Mrs Nelson had found a woman on the next street willing to suckle a strange child for money. Scrooge thought once more about the accounting for this child, and sighed.

Lady Wenhill was taken to him straightaway, and she touched her son's face with tentative fingers, then asked that he be taken out of the blanket wrapped around him.

"There's a port wine stain on his shoulder. I saw it as the midwife lifted him from my body. My husband had the same—" She stopped, looking down at the tiny shoulder where there was a birthmark, and then she began to cry, reaching for him and holding him to her.

Scrooge said urgently, "Lady Wenhill, we are not safe here. Can you trust your servants here in London?"

She shook her head. "I don't know. They are not the servants we had when my husband was alive."

"Then I'll find a safe haven for you and the boy until we can put an end to this."

He took her to one of his friends, an older man named Henley who had known Marley as well as Scrooge, and whose reputation for honesty and uprightness was unquestioned.

Scrooge spoke to him briefly, asking questions but refusing to answer Henley's. "You must guard this woman and her child," he said again as he prepared to leave, "and if anything should happen to me, you will take them to a place of safety."

Henley protested, but Scrooge clapped him on the shoulder, adding, "Old friend, you must trust me for now."

And then he was out the door and into the waiting cab.

He sat there thinking for several minutes. Ned had spoken of the Portuguese ship, the *Anna Maria,* as if he knew the docks. And according to what Nicholas Henley had told him just now, Samuel Dancy had been a partner in more than one lucrative merchant venture.

Scrooge gave the cabbie the address in the City of one Solomon Gills, and sat back.

Gills was a man of few words, but his workmanship spoke for him. Every ship's captain and merchant in London had come to him at one time or another, and the gossip of the City and the docks flowed in and out his door while he kept his own counsel.

Scrooge found him working on a chronometer. Sol looked up and nodded as he saw who had come in his door.

"What takes you away from your 'counting house, Mr Scrooge? I've not laid eyes on you these six months or more."

"I've come for information, Sol, if you have it."

"I'll give it gladly, if I do."

"I'm looking for one Ned Paling. He works sometimes for Samuel Dancy."

"Ah, the Honourable Samuel Dancy Wenhill. He seldom uses his father's name, I can't think why. Except that his father cut him off without a penny and rumour says his brother did the same."

"There was a will."

"Indeed, and not to Samuel Dancy's liking, they say."

Scrooge said, "Where will I find Ned Paling?"

"He's not been showing himself about of late. It seems he's done well enough for himself that he's avoiding trouble. There's a public house called The Red Slipper that he fancies. Try there."

Scrooge thanked him and went on his way. The Red Slipper was between St Paul's and the river, tucked in a narrow corner. Only the garish red slipper on its sign drew attention to it. Scrooge sent the cab around the corner and settled himself in the shadows of a building down the street from the pub, prepared to wait.

Some two hours later, he saw Ned Paling step out of the pub and walk toward the water. Scrooge followed him. He was no match for a Ned Paling. But he thought perhaps there was a way to solve many problems with one small lie. God knew, he'd told enough that day.

Ned Paling turned around smartly, and caught Scrooge creeping along behind him.

"Old man," he warned, "it isn't safe to meddle with Ned Paling."

Scrooge said, "I've no need to meddle. I've come to tell you I've decided to keep the child for my heir. But Samuel Dancy is not best pleased. He told you to deal with the lad, not sell him. I wouldn't be surprised if Dancy was more than a match for you. A friendly word, that's all. You've done me a good turn, and I've done you one. We're quits." Scrooge made a move to go back the way he'd come.

"Here – how did he find out anything of the sort? Was it you told him the brat was still alive?"

"No, nor was it Jenny. He'd set a watch on you, Ned. That's what Dancy did. I'd watch my back, if I were you."

"How did you know about Dancy? Was it Jenny? I'd have sworn she knew nothing!"

"No, I told you, she didn't betray you. I recognized the man watching you. I knew who his master was. A friendly warning, Ned, that's all this is. Dancy is more powerful than you. You'll turn up floating in the river, and none the wiser. He's got eyes everywhere. Did you think he'd trust you when it came to that boy? That was foolish of you. Consider what befell the midwife and that little girl's mother. Did he leave *them* alive to tell their tale?" He watched as something changed in Ned's face, that shot in the dark striking home. "Take Jenny and your fifty pounds and go as far as you can as quickly as you can!"

Ned said, "It's Dancy's afraid of *me*, not the other way around." But the words were bluster. "I know too much about his affairs."

Scrooge said, "A knife in the back on a dark street, that's all it takes. No courage required there. He could hire any number of men who would kill you for a pittance. You know that as well as I do. Well, I've said what I came to say."

Scrooge walked away, and behind him Ned said again, "He's more afraid of *me*, is Dancy. I know too *much*."

"The river is a quiet grave. You'll tell no one anything when the tide takes you. Goodbye, Ned."

When Scrooge turned the corner, he glanced back. Ned Paling was nowhere to be seen.

His conscience pricked him. But there was no way to prove what Dancy had done. The servants hired by Dancy in place of the Wenhill retainers would have been told nothing – it was too dangerous to trust so many. And any who saw their mistress in distress would have been persuaded that she was half mad with grief to bear a daughter in place of the son she desired to carry on her late husband's name. Indeed, having seen a girl from the start, they would wonder how she now came by a boy. Dancy might even use their concerns to have her committed to an asylum for the incurably insane. As it was, the truth was going to be difficult enough to establish.

There was no safety for Lady Wenhill and the lad now, nor would there be, as long as Dancy walked the streets. There would be other Ned Palings to do his dirty work.

Scrooge's conscience reminded him that the courts should settle the matter. But a trial was uncertain at best. Would a jury believe Lady Wenhill's story – or Dancy's? A good barrister could make twelve men think she was greedy for all the money herself. That it was she who wished to be rid of Dancy because he knew that she had borne a daughter, not a son. And there was no way under the sun to test or prove whether the boy with that stain on his shoulder or the nameless little girl was truly the late Lord Wenhill's heir.

Dancy's word against Lady Wenhill's . . . And he would lose more than a fortune if the truth came out. He would stop at nothing to prevent that. Not one to cross, Mrs Brown had said. Ruthless and vindictive.

As he climbed into the cab for the last time and turned toward his house, Scrooge found himself thinking about that little girl asleep in a crib not her own. Cared for, but not loved. Lady Wenhill would do right by her. But it would be a cold love, not a warm one. And Betsy still grieved for her own boy. How could a foundling, and a girl at that, assuage her loss? Besides, she would have other children in God's good time, and perhaps come to see this adopted daughter as a constant reminder of the dead, not the living.

Martha Cratchit could be persuaded to take the lass, to grow up with young Sally. It would be a kindness – and she was kind. He knew how much she loved children, and once she heard this one's story, her heart would overflow.

Scrooge was tired. And still worried. There were new and trusted servants to be found for the Wenhill houses, the boy's birth to be registered, and guards set to forestall further mischief. Dancy was a formidable opponent, and Ned Paling might be persuaded to set upon Scrooge some evening as he walked home from his 'counting house or from a good dinner with his nephew.

It was not finished yet. But the question was, how *would* it be finished?

He thought again about going to a magistrate, and again dismissed it as chancy at best. There was no *proof*.

Tired as he was, Scrooge slept poorly, dreaming of Marley's face on the door knocker, expecting to see the bed curtains thrust aside in the dark of the night and Ned standing there, the knife in his hand raised high, ready to strike. If Dancy was as clever as everyone felt he was, he'd send Ned on one last errand before murdering him. Scrooge knew too much, had too much of a reputation for honesty and fair worth. Two birds with one stone, as it were.

The next morning a tearful Jenny was at his door, searching for Ned.

"For he's nowhere to be found, and I'm afraid!"

Scrooge thought, "My foreboding wasn't wrong. Dancy has seen to Ned." But aloud he said to Jenny, "You are well out of this business. Take the fifty pounds I've paid you for the child and go away. As far as you can."

"I can't. Ned's looked after me, you see. And he'd find me if I left him. I must wait."

"What do you know of this business with the child?"

"Nothing, I swear to you. Only that Ned came home a fortnight ago with a baby, and said he was to wait until the river was running high. I told him he couldn't do that with a child – that we'd be better off finding a way to make money from him. And so we did."

Her voice was triumphant, as if Ned had proved her right. She added, "He never said where the child had come from.

But he has his ear to the ground. He'd read about Betsy Tallman in the newspapers. A few questions here and there, and he found you. He'd heard about the accident the day Polly Toodle was discharged, but we were afraid to try Dombey. He's a cold man. Ned's clever, he takes the gossip and turns it into money every time. He reads and listens in pubs and pays *attention*. Only, there's a bad streak in him sometimes, and then I'm afraid of what he'll do. He wouldn't have thought twice about the river. I knew that to be true."

Jenny left soon after, forlorn and afraid.

Fearful of being followed, Scrooge waited another day before returning for Lady Wenhill and her baby. He was preparing now to take her to the police, having convinced himself, if only barely, that a trial might succeed after all. There was no other choice, really. He had been foolish to think there was. Honest men seldom prospered in the world of Samuel Dancy. But when he arrived at Nicolas Henley's house in late afternoon, his host came to him in something of a dither.

"This poor woman! I've been afraid to tell her—"

"The child—"

"No, no, not the child! Haven't you heard? Her brother-in-law was found in the river only this morning. Someone had tried to rob him, they fought, and both drowned. They were locked in a terrible embrace, the two of them. The police think they must have gone into the Thames near the Red Slipper, but there's no way to be sure." He tut-tutted with concern. "First her husband, now her brother-in-law. Two funerals in a matter of months. It will be more than a lady of her sensibilities can endure. I've not dared to break the news – you must find a way!"

"Do they know who it was who tried to rob Dancy?"

"The story I heard claimed it was Ned Paling. But I find that hard to believe. A nasty piece of work, Ned was, you'll hear everyone saying it. But murdering *Dancy*? No, there must be a mistake. The two were said to be as thick as thieves."

Scrooge, digesting the news, said, "We are all capable of

more than we know. There are dark places in every soul."
His own included. He had paid his own heavy price for this
venture, and it had nothing to do with shillings and pounds
paid out.

"No, no, I refuse to believe that. You and I would never
knife a man for the sake of his purse."

Scrooge answered him. "I doubt we'll ever know what
transpired. A pity, surely? And now I must see to an entirely
new staff for Lady Wenhill. Any recommendations, old
friend?"

"You never told me why you brought her here."

"Did I not?" Scrooge said. "There were rumours of a
kidnapping. As it turned out, they were false. But better safe
than sorry, I always say."

"I see the need for new servants, then. As you say, better
safe than sorry. And that's a lively boy she has. It would be a
shame if anything happened to him. She dotes on him."

Scrooge could see Lady Wenhill, her face glowing with joy,
coming down the stairs. "Leave us while I break the news."

Henley discreetly withdrew.

Scrooge drew Lady Wenhill into the parlour and told her
what had happened. He expected her to be appalled, but she
said, "That man would have murdered my son. I feel no
sympathy. I'll put on a public face of mourning, but it goes
no deeper." She looked away and then said, "What will
become of the little girl in my house?"

"I have considered a likely home for her. She'll be well
taken care of."

"Is it possible, do you think, to find her mother?"

"I doubt it. I can try; but if you want the truth, I expect
both the midwife and this child's mother are dead. The
mother, because she might some day ask what had become
of her daughter, and the midwife because she couldn't be
trusted with such dangerous information as switching new-
borns. Dancy would have been foolish to leave them alive for
you to discover and persuade to give evidence against him."

"I'll settle a dowry on her, when she marries. I can do no
less."

"It would be kind."

Lady Wenhill nodded. Then she asked, "Why did Ned Paling kill Samuel Dancy? I thought they were in this business together."

Scrooge said only, "Thieves sometimes fall out."

The Little Christian

Rebecca Tope

Although it would be over two years before Dickens commenced another full-length novel, the period 1844 to 1846 was amongst the busiest of his life. He travelled through Italy which led to the volume Pictures from Italy *(1846). He continued with his annual Christmas books, following the success of* A Christmas Carol *with* The Chimes *(1844) and* The Cricket on the Hearth *(1845). He established his own amateur theatrical company and, most time consuming of all, in January 1846 he became the editor of a daily newspaper,* The Daily News. *It is during this chaotic period that the following story is set.*

There is no record that Dickens met the young Sabine Baring-Gould, who would be only eleven at the time of this story but, Rebecca Tope told me, "It is possible that an encounter such as this did take place. Sabine Baring-Gould and Charles Dickens were both in London during the autumn of 1845, as described." If his name is not familiar, his most famous work, the hymn "Onward Christian Soldiers" (1864), will be instantly recognizable. Baring-Gould came from a rich Devonshire family. For much of his life he served as a clergyman and, after his father's death in 1872, became the local squire. He was a dedicated antiquarian with a fascination for all things and wrote prodigiously, having a remarkably long writing career from 1865 until his death in 1924.

Rebecca Tope, who is researching Baring-Gould's biography, is the author of three separate mystery series as well as producing the spin-off books from the Rosemary & Thyme *TV series.*

Autumn 1845

I t was the shiver that first drew him to my attention. On a fine morning in early October, he had no business being cold. No – this was the shivering of misery and loneliness; a boy too young to be away from his mother, not much older than my own Charley. But it was not Charley that this child called to mind as he stood gazing down on the malodorous Thames from the western side of Waterloo Bridge, looking as he had been there for quite a while. There, like a wrinkle in time, stood my own sorry young self.

I approached him delicately, positioning myself at his side, following his line of gaze. He showed no signs of apprehension, but turned a glance of sweet amiability towards me, before giving vent to a sigh.

"Have you ever been to the Italian Alps, sir? Or perhaps to Austria?" came his astonishing words.

I laughed, not quite comfortably, suspecting this lad somehow knew who I was. "I have indeed," I confessed. "In fact, I am only returned from Italy these few months. Pray, what might there be in this vista to recall the mountains to your mind?"

"Not one thing, sir," came the sorrowful reply. "Nothing clean or fresh. The very air is sickening here."

"You are pining for crystal streams and carpets of flowers and smiling singing people," I offered.

"Perhaps so, sir. And . . . the *food*," he burst out. "Good milk and fruit and cheese." His earnest eyes met mine. "Why is the food so dreadful in London?"

I did not attempt an explication of the mechanisms for supplying thousands of city dwellers with wholesome food. Indeed, I barely understood it myself. The child's evident hunger, spiritual as much as bodily, plucked painfully at my heartstrings, not least because I too had gone in want of food in my boyhood. And yet this was no pauper child. His clothes were of good quality, his shoes new and polished. His cap suggested attendance at an educational establishment of some pretension.

"I know a pie shop on the Strand," I said, "where a fellow can find a decent meal. Would you have an hour or so spare to accompany me there and give me the pleasure of your conversation?"

His frown conveyed anxiety on an epic scale. "No, sir, thank you. I ought not to be outside at all." He cast a glance across the bridge to the monstrous building that was Somerset House. "I am meant to be in school. Classes will have begun without me."

A chill hand fingered my insides. "You attend school in Somerset House?"

He nodded. "Kings College, sir. In the basement. I am not permitted to be out into the street alone. It was just—" He sighed again. "The new term began not long ago, you see, sir. I am not yet accustomed to the different masters, and the changes in our work. And the games," he added with a shudder. "I cannot reconcile myself to the games."

"So you made a bid for freedom," I smiled. "Brave man! Would you be interested to know that my poor father worked in that same edifice when I was just a little younger than you are now? A very grim time he had of it, too, or so I believe."

His interest in my words was polite but forced. "Is that so?" he murmured. The sigh that followed was accompanied by another shiver and I was minded to put a comforting arm across his narrow shoulders. But I restrained myself, limiting my solicitude to the taking of both his hands in mine and giving them a warm shake.

"Come," I urged. "If it will help, I could pen a short note to your masters, explaining away your absence without their leave. We need not be long, and I feel sure you have a story you could tell me."

He stiffened beneath my touch, pulling back. "Story, sir?" With a worried frown he glanced again at the river. "You accuse me of telling stories?"

I released my gentle grip, opening my arms as if to let a bird fly free. "I make no accusations, my friend," I assured him. "You may do and go as you wish. But in my very humble opinion, I believe I can offer you some entertainment as well as a good meat pie. Perhaps, too, solace in your exile from home." I cocked my head and waggled my eyebrows, making a face I well knew was irresistible to any child, no matter how solemn.

It worked, and the chuckle thereby elicited brought a thawing of the frost encasing him. "Thank you, sir," he said. "May I introduce myself? I am Sabine Baring-Gould, son of Edward Baring-Gould Esquire of Devonshire."

"I am honoured to make your acquaintance," I bowed. "You might call me Boz." This last I added on a whim, harking back to my young days, once more. The response was dramatic.

"Boz! The same as Mr Charles Dickens?" His eyes sparkled. "My father is a very great admirer of Mr Dickens's books." He hurriedly recounted a description of a journey to the Continent at the time when *Nicholas Nickleby* was being produced and episodes difficult to obtain during their travels. The childish chatter reassured me that he was recovering from his fit of despair – an improvement I awarded myself some credit for.

I smiled and said nothing in response to his unwitting mention of my name, tempted though I may have been to reveal myself. The pleasure at finding my name, as well as my early pseudonym, common currency even with children, was hard to suppress despite having by then enjoyed some years of celebrity.

Then the boy's face fell again and the shiver recurred. "But, sir, I *must* tell you what I have seen, this hour or so past." The words came with whispered urgency and a glance

around at the streets behind us. I raised my brows encoura-
gingly. "A lady, sir, down by the water—" he tipped his chin
at the murk beneath us. "She came from a house along there,
dragging another lady – who appeared to be insensible. She
was heavy, sir, and awkward to move. And she threw her into
the river, sir. She did indeed!"

I gave him the same penetrating gaze I used on my Charley
when his word was in doubt. "Indeed?" I pronounced
sonorously. "And what transpired next?"

"Nothing, sir," came the worried whisper.

"Nothing!"

"The first lady went back the same way and the other one –
the one in the water, sank from sight. It must have been
murder, sir! One lady murdering another." His tone was
more of wonderment than horror – but I did not forget
his strange shivering that now seemed to be explained.

There was no denying the Thames received its share of
corpses, human and animal, though never had I heard an eye
witness report of one being cast in by a respectable female
person.

"All the more need for a pie," I pronounced heartily. "We
should proceed apace, young sir, and feed ourselves while we
consider your experience from every side."

"Am I to be chastized, sir, would you expect? I should not
be here. But the door at Mr Hayes's house was unlocked and
the sky was so blue and clear – I could not help myself. And
the lady, sir – what is to be done about the lady?"

"Think no more of her," I counselled him. "There is
naught to be done for the moment. If we raise a hue and cry
about it, you will be required to stand witness, with your
name in the court annals, and all manner of complications.
Your father would not like that, I'll be bound."

He managed a thin smile. "My father would wish me to do
my duty," he said stiffly. "And my mother, too."

I respected his loyalty, while quite certain that he could not
sustain a formal enquiry into what he thought he had seen. I
stayed with the subject of his parents. "You say they are in
Devonshire? How came they to send you to school in this

noisome spot? Did they not think what they were doing, making you attend classes in a miasmic London basement?"

He shook his head, half reproachful, half amused. "They are in Warwick at present. I am boarding with Mr Hayes. He is one of the masters, and he resides in Queens Square." The look of lost abandonment in his eyes plucked again at my sensitivities, and I threw an arm around his shoulders, in spite of myself. His resistance was fleeting and I sensed the needful child within the layers of clothing.

"Well, we must move along now. For an hour we can forget our troubles together, over a hot pie." The pie had, I confess, begun to lose its appeal for me, the more I mentioned it. Despite young Sabine's evident hunger, and my own powerful views on the treatment of children throughout the land, I did have larger things on my mind. The play I had produced with several friends in Dean Street was over, just a few days since, and my next venture was tugging at me for attention. My wife was demanding my presence, too, for some trifling appointment with some female friends of hers, for which I was already inevitably late. She was awaiting the imminent arrival of our sixth child, her temper uncertain as a result.

The tale of the lady pitching somebody into the Thames acquired larger significance as the boy and I strolled along the Strand in a westerly direction. There were other respectable strollers on the sidewalk, and plenty of traffic passing along, with the general noise and bustle of an ordinary day. The idea of a barefaced murder taking place in the full light of a Thursday morning was sticking firmly in my craw. And yet the boy was no liar, I could see that from his open face. Unless he was deranged – and that struck me as highly improbable – he believed his own story implicitly.

"Murder is a rare event," I remarked, as we entered the pie shop. The smell of hot meat and gravy seemed to intoxicate the lad, and I could see him swallowing the saliva it gave rise to in his mouth. "The only danger in the streets of London today is from pickpockets, for a young gentleman such as yourself."

His response was rueful. "Not a deal in my pockets for the Artful Dodger," he smiled. Again, the casual reference to one of my own creations gave me a thrill. Regularly as it occurred amongst my peers and acquaintances, when it came from the lips of an unknown child, how could I refrain from preening?

The pies purchased, we took them outside and returned to the waterfront, where the boy seemed ill at ease at such public consumption of victuals, despite being so obviously famished. His self-control was almost painful to witness, as he nibbled delicate morsels, glancing around furtively for any observers. I wolfed mine in a deliberate display of uncouth gusto, with the intention of giving him permission to do the same.

Traffic on the river was heavy, with steamers and rowing boats dangerously adjacent. I scanned the water where the boy had described the dumping of a body, thinking that it would surely float to the surface in the constant stirrings from passing vessels, if it indeed existed. I wondered a little about the quality of his eyesight, affected as it might be by long hours in the dim light of his basement school. Had he emerged dazzled into the slanting dawn rays of the sun and seen a kind of mirage, which had been nothing more than a woman emptying slops?

Our conversation flowed jerkily around the meat and pastry. I quizzed him on his experiences of Italy and Austria, and found to my surprise that he was familiar with many other Continental countries too. His father, it seemed, was a convinced traveller, taking the family hither and yon as the whim seized him. I disclosed a few details of my own, not least my recent journey down to Italy, with wife and five children, discovering in the process a great many shared adventures with the Baring-Gould entourage. Their current sojourn in England had already lasted over a year, it seemed, and young Sabine was pining badly for Alpine air.

He was also increasingly agitated about his unauthorized absence from his classes. Mischievously, I suggested to him that he was a pupil at Dotheboys Hall, and could expect a thrashing from a second Wackford Squeers. His amusement was all too fleeting, and I recalled my assurances in the first moments of our encounter that I could render him a service by interceding with his masters.

This I proceeded to do. Detaching a page from my pocket notebook, I penned a brief missive in flowery phrases, to the effect that young Master Baring-Gould had been unavoidably detained by myself, a distant cousin who had unexpectedly found himself in the metropolis, and wished for some company for an hour. Profuse apologies for my failure to make approaches through the proper channels, and – a last thought – the same uncle would enormously appreciate a second engagement in a few days' time, if such could be arranged. I signed it with an illegible scrawl, bearing no resemblance to my actual nomenclature. For reasons I could not immediately perceive, I wished to conceal my identity from the boy for a while longer.

"Will that do?" I asked him, letting him examine the note.

He frowned. "They might believe that I wrote it myself," he said.

"Surely not? An honourable young gentleman such as yourself would never stoop to such dishonest behaviour."

He cocked his head as if suspecting a tease. Then he took the paper, bowed politely and trudged his reluctant way back to his gloomy imprisonment.

For the next few days I was fully engaged by a host of demands on my time. Primary amongst them was my new venture – the establishment of a newspaper, with myself in position as editor. I had urgent messages from my publisher wishing to know the gist of my next Christmas Story, and my father was an ever-present figure in my life at that time, with his refusal ever to take a thing seriously. Small wonder, then, that I was in poor health, from the worry of it all.

But I did not forget my new young friend. The fact that the boy was incarcerated in Somerset House connected him with my father's past, and I mentioned it to him one evening.

"Poor child," he sighed. "The place still haunts my nightmares, to this day. He is in the basement, you say?"

"He describes it with some bitterness," I nodded. "I must make a few moments for a visit, if I can persuade his gaolers to release him to me."

My father gave a sudden chuckle. "I can show you a way in – if it has not been blocked up by this time. I was privy to a secret entrance, in my time there."

He began a tortuous explication of passages and flights of dank steps and a loose stone beneath one of the lower windows which would have graced one of Poe's stories, if it had been told in a less tedious fashion. I laughed and shook my head. "I believe a simple note requesting the boy's company might suffice," I said.

The following day I met with Fanny Kelly and my friend Jerrold, and enjoyed a session in a sedan where we reminisced about the play we had presented. Fanny was full of a scandal she had got from a friend of hers about a certain Mr Heron, with a house on the Strand and a rising career in banking. Fanny had once met the fellow and his wife near the Simplon Pass, of all places. It seemed the wife – a shrewish creature, by all accounts – had failed to fulfil an engagement at a society dinner in Mayfair the previous evening and, when enquiries had been made subsequently, there appeared to be a mysterious absence of the lady in question. Her husband had brusquely dismissed the manservant sent with a solicitous note, saying his wife had gone to visit her sister, who was indisposed. Here Fanny narrowed her eyes, and lowered her voice, "But the truth is, as my friend believes, that there has been a falling-out between husband and wife. She has heard a whisper of a *liaison* between Mr Heron and a certain young lady from Chelsea."

Poor Fanny had a most unsatisfactory audience for her tale. Jerrold and I were considerably more interested in gossiping about Maclise and the way he had disappointed us on the eve of our play rehearsals. But I took enough note of the Herons to keep them at the back of my mind over the next day or so, if only as an example of the kind of story that my own newly established newspaper would not lower itself to publish. It would instead focus on the more cultured aspects of society. At least, that was my ambition. With my father managing to inveigle himself a post on the staff, I could already see that the tone might sink lower than I hoped.

It occurred to me that my new young friend might be legally free on a Saturday afternoon, and be permitted an outing with a relative with little difficulty. Indeed, regarded from the perspective of the accommodating Mr Hayes, it might be seen as a boon to have the child removed for a few hours. Accordingly, I despatched a note to the school requesting that Master Baring-Gould be released into my care from two to four pm that Saturday. My own motives remained obscure to me, but there was a nagging curiosity about his supposed sighting of a body being pitched into the river, from a point not more than a hundred yards from the residence of the politician and his mislaid wife.

And the truth was that I felt sorry for the lad. There was more than a little of myself in him, but he had his own pale looks and lanky growth. I must have been three or four inches smaller at the same age. And, besides my pity, I wished to discover more of him and his family, which from what I had heard thus far seemed a little out of the ordinary. The idle father, journeying across the Continent in search of sunshine and cheap lodging, was of a class and breed I knew too little of. When I had ventured on a similar jaunt, earlier that same year, my wife had vowed never to undertake such an expedition again. What did Mrs B-G think of it, I wondered?

He emerged from a flight of steps onto Lancaster Place, and glanced back at the building with such loathing that it shocked me to see it. He approached me tentatively, as if afraid I might evaporate before his eyes. "Is it not the ugliest building in the whole wide world, sir?" he demanded.

"Not quite," I demurred. "But I concede that it has few pretensions to beauty. My father detested it about as much as you appear to do."

The view from our vantage point presented a motley unfinished appearance, grimed with the smoke of London and the droppings of birds, a sorry vision by any standards. The construction of the Waterloo Bridge was largely to blame – previously no one could have seen the full horrors of the western side of the building.

"Have you not viewed it from the opposite bank of the river?" I asked him. "From there, it appears almost handsome."

He was not persuaded. "It is infinitely worse within," he insisted. "So dark and malodorous. We are more like moles than human beings, down beneath the ground."

"How long are you expecting to be here?"

He shook his head. "I know not, sir. My father's plans are never entirely reliable. My mother wrote to me saying she believes they will be in Warwick for many more months, and she is a little surprised to find herself in England for a second winter in succession. My father dislikes an English winter."

"You do not look altogether well," I noted. As if to endorse my diagnosis, he coughed briefly. I myself had woken that day with some of my familiar malady upon me – a sense of giddiness behind my eyes and pressure in the middle of my head. But this child struck me as weak-chested and vulnerable to the noxious air of London. What were his parents thinking of, consigning him to this purgatory? Surely they must know how unwholesome it was for him?

We wandered eastwards in an unspoken pact to revisit the pie shop on the Strand. An idea was forming of hiring a carriage and taking the air in Regents Park, for both our sakes. But my plan was quickly thwarted when the boy at my side gave a sudden start, and pressed himself close to me.

"What is it?" I demanded.

"That lady, sir." He indicated a tall person in a magenta gown and bonnet walking on the opposite side of the street with an air of great purpose. "It is the same . . . the one I told you of . . ." he stammered incoherently, and it was a few moments before I grasped his drift.

"Not the one you suspected of murder? How can you be sure?"

"I remember her, sir," he said simply. "I am in no doubt."

It seemed improbable to me, on several counts. I attempted to observe the person closely. She was walking in the same direction as ourselves, but it was not easy to keep pace hampered as I was by the shuddering lad hanging back, pulling at my arm. And constant passing traffic obscured my view.

"Will we follow her, sir?" the lad quavered.

Before I could reply, our quarry plunged into an alleyway leading to Covent Garden, and the approach of two carriages speeding dangerously towards us deterred me from attempting to cross the street. "We have lost her," I said.

"I am glad, sir," said the boy. "She causes me great alarm." He put a hand to his narrow chest as if already breathless.

"It occurs to me that I should hear your tale again, in greater detail," I said. "If you persist in its veracity, then I owe you the courtesy of listening more closely. Have you disclosed it to anyone else since we last met?"

He smiled thinly and shook his head. "I have no one I could talk to of such things," he confessed. "The other boys regard me as a curiosity and a weakling. I find them abhorrent." He shuddered expressively, and I had a momentary glimpse of this pale young gentleman standing on the sidelines of the rough and tumble of school life.

"We will find a place to sit quietly and talk," I suggested, finding the idea immensely appealing, after the hurly-burly of the past few weeks, with a great deal more still in prospect.

"If this were Austria or Italy, I should suggest we find a pretty little church," he said, with a sudden lift in his tone that took me by surprise. I had never before encountered a young boy with a feeling for church aesthetics. "There are so many there," he added wistfully. "But in London they are dark and ugly and ungodly."

"Not all of them," I protested mildly, having scant fondness for churches myself in any general way. "Let me show you a favourite of mine." I led him to St Clement Dane's, to the east of where we were standing by barely a quarter of a mile. "You must surely know of this example of Wren's work, being within a few yards of your school," I said.

He blinked in some confusion. "We attend church close to Mr Hayes' home in Queen's Square," he said. He was gazing up at the church steeple as if he had never seen it before.

We went inside, where the light was the first thing that struck us. Plain glass in the windows and a circular apse made it a delightful place to be on a fine day. The boy breathed deeply for the first time since I had met him, and spread his arms in an unconscious gesture indicative of an expanding spirit in a spot that he found safe and welcoming. Then he pressed his hands together, and bowed his head in a silent prayer. Watching him closely, I thought I observed something very rare: an individual of genuine religious spirit. I was momentarily awed by this glimpse and stood well back from him. I felt fear, too – fear that he would not survive to manhood, if his parents continued to neglect him so cruelly and his chest succumbed to further onslaught. I saw before me, I believed, one of those children so often characterized as being "too good for this world". Too sensitive to the callous violence of society, too early cast out from the sheltering arms of his family.

And yet, there was a steely thread in him that gave me cause for hope. Intelligence burned in his eyes, and precocious opinions forged a powerful connection with the world around him. Young Sabine, it seemed, was eager to live and to learn.

"The story," I prompted him. "Sit here and tell me every detail. You'll find me an attentive listener."

We sat side by side, but he turned to face me, his blue eyes frequently on mine, but also flickering from one area of the church to another, as if drawing sustenance from the calm beauty of the place.

"Can you say precisely where the incident took place?" I asked, in the manner of a police officer, tucking in my chin and stroking an invisible moustache. I still missed the whiskers I had grown in Genoa and shaved off on my return to England. In my part as Captain Bombadil in the play I and my friends performed only a few days before the encounter with Master Baring-Gould, I wore false beard and moustache, regretting fiercely the authentic variety that had been so much less itchy.

"On the pavement above the river," he said with deplorable imprecision. "There is a house, and a—" he demonstrated with his hand, drawing a flat jetty in the air, "a place where a boat can be moored. I saw that tall lady come down to that place, dragging another lady, who was insensible. Or—" His face tightened "She could have been *dead*," he whispered.

I held up a finger. "Now, my boy, the part that most puzzles me is how this could occur in the full light of day with so many people present to observe the events. How could it be possible for a body to be cast into the river without apprehension by some public spirited individual?"

"There was only me, sir," he said softly. "I looked around for somebody to call to for assistance. There was no one."

"No one on the bridge? Or the Strand? No one passing on the river in a boat? Come now, this is not possible. What hour of the clock was it?"

"It was not long past dawn, sir."

I stared at him. "Dawn? What in the world were you doing here at dawn? Had Mr Hayes not something to say to your leaving your lodgings so early?" I recalled that it had been not long past eight o'clock when I had first seen him.

He winced. "I let myself out and walked from Queens Square, at first light. I left a message with the maidservant that Mr Hayes was not to worry about me, but that I had an urgent errand."

I saw the scene in my mind's eye – a young lad on the deserted streets, enjoying the clear new day. True, there might be a handful of the more disreputable members of society lodged in doorways and gutters, but they would offer little threat after their night-time debauches. Again, I saw my own young self, on similar strolls in the first light of day. But I also saw my own young Charley, alone in the London streets and a cold hand closed around my heart. This boy must have remained on the bridge for over an hour, if his story were to be credited, simply staring at the swirling water into which he believed a human body had been thrown.

"You must promise me you will never do such a thing again," I abjured him. "What would your mother have to say about it?"

He shook his head miserably. "She would be distressed," he sighed.

"And so you arrived here, and waited for the school doors to be opened. You stood and watched the sun rising over the water, and you dreamed of Alps and spicy meats and cheeses that fill you with a sense of riches. You conjured your dear Mama's features, and wondered how it was they had placed you here so carelessly."

"Exactly, sir," he said, with no sign of surprise at my accurate thought-reading.

"And you witnessed the commission of a murder, and knew not what to do about it."

"I thought perhaps it was all right, sir. That there are practices here that I do not understand. It was a *lady*, sir. Not a servant or a common person."

"Can you say which house she came from?"

He shrugged helplessly. The houses on the south side of the Strand were a hotch potch, indeed, with their backs to the muddy shallows of the river, many of them grimed with London filth and the ordure of gulls.

"Was the tide high or low?"

"High, sir. Very high. The lady sank into the water until she disappeared."

"The dead lady, that is?"

He nodded, his face twisted with worry. "What should I have done, sir?" he asked pathetically. "I doubt me that anyone would have believed my story." He tilted his head. "Do *you* believe me, sir?"

I felt a powerful urge to be kind, even protective. "I will tell you what I think you saw," I said. "It occurs to me that the lady you imagined to be dead was in fact a dummy – a model used by an artist perhaps, or a dressmaker . . ." I found myself inventing wildly. "You will perhaps have noted the way the people of London use their river as a sewer? A place to throw all their unwanted dross. Well, is it not the most probable elucidation, that this is what you saw? Murder, as I said before, is a rare event – especially of one lady by another."

His frown deepened as he examined my words. He was eleven or twelve, a boy utterly innocent of the ways of the city. As I watched his face, he seemed to change. No longer was he the small C. D., forced to find his own way in the streets, perpetually cold and afraid. Starved young Sabine might be, and in sore need of a mother's consoling arms, but his strategies for survival were in no way similar to those I had adopted. This lad, I fancied, put his trust in God, when everything else had failed.

"A dummy would droop lifelessly," he mused. "And it would avowedly sink into the water, and not float. And yet – I did think it was a real lady, sir. I did indeed."

"I understand that you did," I assured him. "I might very well have thought the same thing myself. But we must apply reason to the experience, to find the most fitting explanation for what you saw. And my reason assures me that nothing is less likely than that you witnessed the aftermath of a violent killing."

He meditated for a few moments more. "Mr Boz," he began, startling me slightly until I recalled the name I had given him, "I would greatly prefer to believe there was no murder. It comes to me, you see, in the night, that people should not commit such terrible acts, one upon the other."

How sheltered he must have been, until now. Touring the beauty spots of Europe in a carriage full of his close relatives, exposed to the quaint old towns and cities of Bavaria and southern France, he had been spared the presence of cruelty and wickedness. My adult instinct was to ensure that his innocence continued yet a while.

"I am quite sure of it," I said. "Put it out of your mind, and tell me more of your journeyings. Which of the many places you have seen was your most preferred?"

"Salzburg," he said promptly, with a spark in his eye.

I would have quizzed him longer, but I felt my other obligations pressing on me, and in truth my interest in the lad began to wane as rapidly as it had flared. The church was pleasant enough, but I felt myself a false worshipper, in contrast to the little Christian at my side.

"We should leave," I said. "Such respites are rare and I am grateful to you. But I have to attend some important gentlemen presently."

He glanced up at me with a look of such panic and reproach that I had to defend myself. In a tone most unwarrantably harsh, I repeated my words. "I cannot spare the whole day, young sir. You must forgive me." I was momentarily tempted to add, "Are you really not aware of who I am? What great man has accorded you some moments of his precious time?" But I bit my tongue. I had played with the lad's affections too much as it was.

"I see, sir," he submitted. "I thank you for your company. And for introducing me to this church, which I hope I will be able to visit again." He coughed a little, more from emotion, I thought, than congestion.

I bowed my head close to his. "Do what you can to have yourself reunited with your family," I said urgently. "There is no better place to be. Make no attempt to conceal any illness that might afflict you. I warrant your mother will quickly take you away if she believes you to be severely sick."

"Oh, yes, sir, she would," he assured me. "And I am very often ill." He disclosed to me an incident in the high Alps where his chest had been so badly affected that he was bound with poultices that removed much of his skin. "It worries my Mama considerably."

"Then that is your escape route," I told him, with a wink.

I delivered him back to his lodgings in Queen Square, where a soft-skinned gentleman was glimpsed through the front window, as the maidservant admitted the boy. Mr Hayes, the careless schoolmaster, I assumed. I remain confident to this day that the boy never guessed the identity of the man who was briefly kind to him.

*   *   *

The matter of the woman's body nagged at me as I walked away, facing west. Ahead of me was Bow Street, home to the new police force. On a whim, I entered the building and rapped on the desk. Without revealing my identity I suggested there could be a female cadaver fished from the Thames somewhere adjacent to the Strand who had died in suspicious circumstances. It was a useless spasm of social conscience, and yet it seemed wrong to simply do nothing. The constable made a note of the day and time I gave him and asked laconically what led me to beget such a suspicion. Had I personally witnessed a felonious act? With a sinking sensation in my bowels, I indicated to the contrary. "A whisper," I said with a shrug. "A rumour picked up in a sedan."

He looked down his narrow nose at me. "We cannot proceed on a rumour, sir. Hard evidence – that's the thing. What exactly would you have us do?"

I grimaced and took a step backwards. I could not take the risk of mentioning the name of Mrs Heron as the possible victim, her husband's lover her killer. It was too fanciful an interpretation without giving the name and status of the one and only witness. And that I had no intention of doing – no more than I had of revealing my own details.

"I concede the point," I said. "And yet – perhaps a morsel of extra vigilance in that part of the river might not come amiss."

His long neck seemed to wilt like a thirsty plant and he emitted a soft snort of impatience. "Thank you, sir. Very public-spirited of you."

I left with every intention of casting the entire episode from my mind.

Remembering that I had urgent claims on my attention awaiting me in Fleet Street, I turned back the way I had come, my route lying through Covent Garden and back onto the Strand. Those few months of my life, before young Ally was born, and after the thrills and spills of the play that I performed with my friends, were largely spent in that part of London. The smells and sounds of the river were ever present, along with the constant clatter and swirl of traffic. I recall meetings with other great men of intellect in rooms just above the mass of humanity swarming through their daily dealings on the street below. I was not working on a book in those months, but in hindsight I can see that the ghost of little Paul Dombey was riding upon my shoulder.

For reasons not apparent to my conscious mind, I took the same alleyway from the market to the Strand as the one young Baring-Gould and I had seen the lady in magenta use an hour or so previously. The alley was thronged with people intent on catching the afternoon reductions at the market, the bruised fruit and stale meat dropping hourly in price. I had to dodge and weave my way between them, annoyed at myself for selecting such a narrow thoroughfare. Already my thoughts had turned to my plans for the coming weeks and the discussions I should have to take part in. When the same magenta figure filled my vision, it was some moments before I collected myself. It was a back view, but I recognized the purposeful stride and the hue of the gown. She was returning from a considerable bout of spending, to judge from the bulging bags she carried. Perhaps it was remorse at my dismissal of the boy, or perhaps something struck my unconscious mind as awry, but I resolved to follow the lady and glean something more of her. When she turned to the right at the end of the alley I could not prevent myself from doing likewise, instead of pursuing my intended route to the left.

But then I spotted Mr Chapman, of all people, a few yards ahead of me. Here was a man I most assuredly did not wish to meet, after our falling-out the year before. In great haste, I spun on my heel and positively cantered back towards Somerset House. There I hailed a cab and returned home for the rest of the day.

But there was a restless maggot squirming in my brain, as I reviewed recent events. The lady in magenta had cut such a striking figure that the tale told by the Baring-Gould boy began to seem increasingly convincing to me. It would, I concluded, be lacking in responsibility on my part if I did not attempt to elucidate what might have happened that early morning a few days previously.

I made a point of calling on Fanny that evening, knowing she would be pleased to have a ready ear for her gossip. She was at home to friends, and already there were three or four gathered. "Any fresh news of your Mr Heron?" I invited quietly, after a few moments of social chit-chat.

Her eyes widened. "It seems not," she said. "The talk is all over Town that he has not been seen for several days now. The suspicion is that he has come to some harm, perhaps at the hands of the father of the young lady from Chelsea, who is known to be a decided curmudgeon. The father, that is, not the young lady."

I mused for a second or two. "And Mrs Heron? What of her?"

"No news," said Fanny succinctly. "But she has a sister in Essex, who has probably taken her in."

I frowned at this. "Why would she need taking in, pray?"

Fanny sighed. "Because she would doubtless wish to teach her husband a lesson by leaving him for a while. It is what injured wives do, Mr Dickens." She chuckled mockingly. "As a man of such wisdom and insight, you might have understood that."

"Meanwhile, rumour suggests that the errant husband has fallen foul of an irate father, and learned an even harsher, possibly even fatal, lesson in the process? Are we acquainted with Mrs Heron's likely response to such an eventuality?"

Fanny smirked. "She might find it less than devastating," she acknowledged. "Although the circumstances, once discovered, could prove embarrassing."

"Indeed," I agreed. The story refused to fit with what my young friend had witnessed, and I began to think my own suggestion of a discarded dummy might well be the truth of the matter after all.

But the next day, a Sunday, saw me yet again on Waterloo Bridge, examining the river and puzzling further over the strange events of the past few days. Had Mrs Heron lured the young rival for her affections to her home in the Strand and then slaughtered her and cast the body into the high tide of the Thames? Or had the Essex sister been the perpetrator, defending Mrs Heron's honour in a most extreme act? My over-active imagination toyed with these many ideas while at the same time more than half convinced that no murder had been committed at all, and if it had, then the Herons were not part of it. I walked slowly towards the Aldwych, thinking I honestly could not spare any more attention to this small but intriguing mystery.

And then, for the third time, I sighted the magenta figure, emerging from the largest house on the south side of the Strand and coming directly towards me. It was as if the clouds had parted and a Divine Finger had pointed right at me. I dodged quickly down a flight of steps, which took me into a dingy lowered courtyard adjacent to Somerset House. Peering cautiously over the stonework, I found the woman to be scarcely six yards away. Ducking down, I pressed against a wall beside a grimy window, and recalled on an instant my father's long description of the secret entrance to the building behind me. With a boyish sense of mischief, I tried the stones around two of the windows, but nothing gave to my touch. There was, however, a loose catch and one window readily opened as I pushed at it.

Another time, I promised myself, I might return and explore further. But it would not avail my sleuthing now to climb into the bowels of Somerset House, however strong my curiosity might be.

My next reconnoitre of the street above me revealed the magenta skirts swirling quickly around the corner, and I rushed up the steps in order to follow. The top step was grimed with dog mess, my foot slid sideways and I fell heavily onto the cast iron post alongside the steps.

My shoulder was bruised and my ankle twisted. I leaned my weight on the post and assessed my situation. Although it was not common for my face to be recognized as I walked the London streets, there was a great risk that if I raised a commotion, my identity might be discovered, and the ensuing stories certain to give me much chagrin. I therefore

limped stoically to the pavement's edge, and waved down a
passing cab, very much as I had done the day before. My wife
clumsily bound the ankle and applied liniment to the
shoulder, and gave me scant sympathy.

But I had to know more of the magenta lady. Fate had
placed her in my path too often for me to let the quest drop
now. I knew the house from whence she had emerged, and
could check with Fanny whether or not it was the home of the
Herons. She might also give sufficient of a description to
confirm whether or not it was Mrs Heron herself that I had
seen.

Fanny made a witticism about my repeated visits, but
readily enough provided a verbal portrait of Margaret Heron
as a short fair woman, with a halting gait due to some
degeneration of her joints. Not, I was convinced, the person
in magenta, despite the house being confirmed as her residence. Furthermore, Fanny informed me that the object of
Mr Heron's dalliance had been glimpsed in the custody of
her father, looking pale and defeated. "So much for that little
escapade," said my friend. "The wretched girl will be
married off to the first clerk with a hundred pounds a year
that can be found."

I ought to have let it lie, allowed time to erase the worm of
curiosity gnawing at the depths of my mind. But I was like a
terrier with a rat, and could not relinquish my researches
until I had found a plausible exegesis to fit the known facts.

And so I went to lie in wait, thinking that if there had
indeed been a murder, the villain would long ago have flown
the scene and be in hiding somewhere inconspicuous, and not
in the centre of bustling London. My vantage point was a
doorway on the northern side of the Strand, from which I
could keep a close eye on the building opposite. I had little
expectation of success, and was thinking I could really not
spare the time to act as investigator in this way, when my
pessimism was confounded. Once more, the magenta gown,
now beginning to look a little dusty, came into view, stepping
briskly down from the house into the street. Did this woman
only possess one garment, I asked myself? If she lived in that

house, she ought to have funds for a better wardrobe. I immediately fell into step behind her, as she strode eastwards along the Strand.

There was something unusual about the gait, which caused me much puzzlement. Fanny had referred to a limp, caused by a faulty hip. This was quite different from any such affliction. I watched closely, until it came to me that I had myself adopted the same manner of walking when acting the part of a female in a piece of amateur dramatics. I had studied the differences in the ways men and women move, and with the aid of a cumbersome skirt had taught myself a new mode of perambulation. The person ahead of me was experiencing the same difficulty that I had at first – kicking out the fabric with every step, giving a jerky awkward impression to any onlooker. Unless I was much mistaken, the person I was tailing was no lady.

We proceeded thus in single file all the way to Trafalgar Square, where the crowds gathered daily to admire the new fountains surrounding Nelson on his towering granite column. My quarry made for the nearest fountain, where a slim young woman stood clutching a valise that looked too heavy for her. She had light brown curls escaping from a cream-coloured bonnet, and a turned-up nose. Her cheeks were the very shade of dog rose petals. She glanced perpetually to all sides, and made every effort to shrink from view. The magenta-clad impostor approached her, took the valise and laid a hand briefly on the girl's shoulder. I saw their eyes meet as I circled them cautiously. I saw the man's face beneath his ridiculous bonnet as he gazed down at his lady love. I saw her trusting adoration shine naked from her eyes – and I could do nothing to interrupt such passion. The truth of the matter struck me on an instant. Young Sabine's tall lady was in reality Mr Heron, the victim his hapless wife. My own persistence had won through, and I preened gently at the idea of myself in the role of detective. I, and I alone, had resolved the matter. I took a step towards the couple, intending to apply my hand to the collar of the wife-killer and drag him to Bow Street.

But he had no collar, and the crowds on every side might well take a vast interest in the sight of a man seizing hold of a gentlewoman and accusing her of murder. The young paramour might scream or faint, the business attract all manner of notoriety. I looked again at the lovers before me. What purpose could it serve, I demanded of myself, to send them to the gallows, with the shrewish Mrs Heron already dead and gone? The devoted damsel must have escaped the enraged father, doubtless lulling him by waiting a while before achieving her elopement. How cruel, then, to intercede and consign her to the ungentle chastisement that must surely be her due!

Side by side, with a valise and two bags of meagre necessities between them, the couple, presenting themselves to the world as two women out for a jaunt, made towards Westminster and doubtless a boat to Harwich or similar, escaping to the Continent and a new life together.

The story of the Herons died away quickly, eclipsed by fresher scandals. I mentioned it once more to Fanny, a few weeks later, idly enquiring as to whether they had ever turned up. She shook her head indifferently and shrugged.

"But the house . . .?" I persisted. "And his money. What will happen if neither one of them returns?"

She cocked her head at me. "Why such an interest, Mr Dickens? But I will tell you – I understand the house was on a tenancy, and there is money on deposit somewhere abroad. There is no scandal, Charles, after all. The wife has seen sense and forced her man to escort her on a long migration to take the waters at Wiesbaden, or sip Chablis on the shores of Lake Como, until he forgets all about his little peccadillo."

I accepted her interpretation as if entirely persuaded, and abandoned my faint intention of giving an anonymous report to the police. If Mrs Heron's body ever did wash up from the river, it must by that time be too far gone for identification. Amongst the suicides and the victims of drunken accidents, she simply disappeared from view.

As for young Baring-Gould, his name lodged in a recess of

my mind and less than five years later, it flashed before me in the pages of the *Illustrated London News*. Curiously, after many adventures, I was once again presenting the same play as the one I had been involved in when I met Sabine. This time we were at Knebworth, and I discovered the paper in a rack while idly seeking some easy reading matter. It was four or five months out of date, but appeared never to have been opened. It seems the boy had been doing some excavating in Pau, in the Pyrenees, and his excellent sketches of some mosaics were reproduced in the paper. "A young Englishman," I read, "of sixteen years of age, Mr Baring-Gould, who, having a taste for archaeology, discovered a Roman villa . . ."

Good for him, I rejoiced. He had escaped his gaol and got back to his beloved mountains. Inevitably I connected him to the fortunes of the errant Mr Heron and I wished them both every joy of the sunny mountain heights that all right-thinking persons so admire.

The Fiery Devil

Peter Tremayne

Dickens did not remain for long as editor of the Daily
News. *He embarked on the role with his customary enthusiasm, writing leader articles on various subjects of
social reform, but rapidly tired of the demands and within
eighteen days had resigned and handed the editorship over
to his friend John Forster. Dickens escaped to Switzerland
and at last returned to novel writing with* Dombey and
Son. *It was to be the start of Dickens's most exciting period
as a novelist, producing some of his best and most critically
acclaimed works.*

    Dombey and Son *is the story of Paul Dombey, despe-
rate to have a son to inherit his firm. His first-born is a
daughter, Florence, whom he despises. His wife dies giving
birth to their second child, a son whom he calls Paul, but
the young boy is weak and sickly and dies when still a child,
leaving his father bereft and alone. Paul remarries but it is
a loveless partnership and his new wife, Edith, leaves him
for James Carker, the manager of Dombey's business. A
strong feature in the novel is the growth of the railways in
Britain and it is Carker's death, when he is hit by a train,
that is the basis for the following story.*

    *Peter Tremayne is a renowned expert on all matters
Celtic and has written many studies of the Celtic world*

under his real name of Peter Berresford Ellis. As Tremayne
he is probably best known for his series of mysteries featuring
Sister Fidelma, set in the Celtic world of the 7th century,
which began with Absolution by Murder *(1994)*.

A curse upon the fiery devil, thundering along so smoothly
. . . He loitered about the station, waiting until one should
stay to call there; and when one did, and was detached for water,
he stood parallel with it, watching its huge wheels and brazen
front and thinking what a cruel power and might it held. Ugh!
To see the great wheels slowly turning and to think of being run
down and crushed!
                    Chapter 55, *Dombey and Son*, Charles Dickens, 1848

"Captain Ryder?"

Mr Josiah Plankton peered myopically at the business card
that the young man had offered and glanced up with a quick
bird-like motion of his head. Then he adjusted his gold-
rimmed pince-nez and turned his gaze back to the card.

"Captain Ryder of the Detective Department of the Metropolitan Police?" There was a slight inflection of incredulity in his tone.

"Exactly so, sir," nodded the young man who stood before
him with a pleasant smile on his tanned features.

"You'll excuse my momentary consternation, sir," Mr
Plankton said as he motioned his visitor to a seat in front
of the large ornate desk he occupied. "I was unaware that the
members of the Detective Department of the London Metropolitan Police held military rank."

The young man appeared unabashed as he seated himself
in the chair.

"My captaincy was in the 16th Lancers, sir. I was . . ." He
shifted his weight slightly to adjust his position to one of
greater comfort. "I was wounded last year at the Battle of
Mudki during the Sutlej Campaign and thus, being unable to
serve the colours further, I was persuaded by Colonel Rowan

to join the Metropolitan force in the newly established Detective Department. The colonel considered that I had a talent in that direction."

Mr Plankton laid the young man's card on the ink blotter before him and glanced quizzically at the detective.

"Commissioner Sir Charles Rowan, eh? I have had the pleasure of his acquaintance, for he helped some years ago with the framing of the Solicitors' Act in Parliament. I then represented the Incorporated Law Society of England and Wales. So, do I presume that you are here in an official capacity on behalf of the Commissioner?"

"Your presumption is correct, sir, in that I am here representing the Metropolitan Police."

"Then how may the firm of Scratch, Nellbody and Plankton assist you?"

"I am given to understand that you are solicitors acting for Dombey and Son, the shipping company?"

Mr Plankton gave a sad smile. "I am not sure that such a state of affairs will last many days longer. You have doubtless heard the news from Threadneedle Street?"

Captain Ryder made a faint motion of his hand.

"Then there is truth in the story that the company may soon go into liquidation? Or at least Mister Paul Dombey is to be declared a bankrupt?"

Mr Plankton was serious.

"In any other circumstances, Captain Ryder, I would have replied to you that I am bound by my client's confidence, but the news is all about the town. Dombey and Son will soon cease to trade. Mister Dombey may well be able to call on some reserves but if the firm lasts out a twelve-month, I will be surprised."

"As Dombey and Son are a considerable trading company that, surely – and if I may be so bold to say so – will impinge on the business connection with your own firm, sir?"

Mr Plankton smiled wryly and gestured to his office with an encompassing sweep of his hand. Captain Ryder became aware of several boxes and cases in various stages of being packed. Even some pictures had been taken off their wall hanging in preparation to be crated.

"I am about to retire. The few remaining accounts that exist are being placed elsewhere by my chief clerk, who is also moving to another practice."

"But Messrs Scratch and Nellbody . . .?"

"Have been deceased these last ten years, sir. I am sole partner and now it is time for me to have some peaceful retirement. My intention is to move to France. I think the sun and wine of Provence will be conducive to my constitution after the smog of the City. London is no place for retirement."

"I see, sir," nodded the young man. He paused and then cleared his throat. "I am, sir, placed in a delicate position for my duty persuades me that I need to trespass into what you may deem as the confidential matters of your client."

Mr Plankton replied with a thin smile.

"In which case, sir, I shall decline to answer your questions. However, if you place those questions before me, I will be better able to judge to what extent you may trespass or not."

Captain Ryder gave an apologetic grimace.

"Speaking for the Metropolitan force, our jurisdiction scarcely reaches to Woolwich. We have only recently been requested to extend our policing to that area of the Arsenal. Therefore it is as a special matter of government intervention that we have been asked to pursue some inquiries pursuant to an incident that took place further abroad."

Mr Plankton looked bewildered.

"Government intervention, sir? I am not sure that I am following you."

"We have been asked to intercede in a matter following a request by no less a person than Mister Cudworth of South Eastern Railways who has the ear of . . . of certain government officials."

Mr Plankton spread his hands, still mystified.

"I am at a loss sir. South Eastern Railways? I know of no business dealings between Dombey and Son and South Eastern Railways and . . ."

The solicitor suddenly paused and looked thoughtful.

"Just so, sir," the young man smiled briefly, noting the change of expression. "Two weeks ago today there was an incident at the railway station of Paddock Wood. It used to be called Maidstone Road Halt until a few years ago. It is, as you doubtless know, a station on the main railway line running from London Bridge to Dover. A man was killed at that station. South Eastern Railways, of course, own that line."

A look of understanding began to form on Mr Plankton's features.

"Your client, Mister Paul Dombey, was a witness to this incident," added Captain Ryder as if to clarify matters.

"The incident being when a former employee of Mister Dombey fell in front of the express train from Dover to London," sighed Mr Plankton, shaking his head as though it was distasteful to be reminded of the unpleasantness.

"You are correct in that particular, sir. Except that this was no mere employee but a certain James Carker who had been manager of Dombey and Son and who had recently run away with Mrs Edith Dombey, the wife of his employer."

Mr Plankton made a disapproving sound by clicking his tongue against the roof of his mouth.

"I am aware of these unhappy circumstances, sir, but I hardly see the relevance of any inquiry . . ."

"Furthermore," went on Captain Ryder, interrupting, "certain charges had been laid against James Carker as a suspect in embezzling large sums of money from the company. It is that embezzlement that, in my understanding, has brought the company to the verge of ruin."

"I fail to see in what capacity Mr Cudworth of South Eastern Railways has asked for the inter . . . the intervention of the Detective Department of the Metropolitan force in this matter? Surely the local coroner has dealt with the matter?"

Captain Ryder shook his head in admonishment.

"The inquest is delayed, sir. The running over and killing of a man at a railway station by an express train is not a matter to be dismissed without consequence, sir. South Eastern Railways can be charged with felonious homicide. Naturally, they wish to clear the name of their company and employees.

There are many matters to consider. There are those who would like to see South Eastern Railways suffer misfortune. Considerable wealth has changed hands with that company now attracting a near monopoly on the transportation of goods. Until the line opened four years ago, shipping companies had sent goods by barge along the Medway. Those who invested in such waterway transport would like nothing better than to see this railway forced to close. So this is why we must ask, did the man stumble accidentally under the wheels? Was his death as a result of some negligence by an employee of the railway? Or . . .?" The young man shrugged and left the question hanging in the air. "I have already made initial enquiries and certain sinister facts emerge."

Mr Plankton looked startled, his body more erect in the chair.

"Pray, what manner of sinister facts?" he demanded.

"That the late James Carker was a former manager of Dombey and Son, that he had apparently been accused of embezzlement from the firm for not inconsiderable sums, and that he had run away with Mrs Edith Dombey, the wife of his employer." Captain Ryder ticked the points off on the fingers of his right hand. "These facts lend a certain – shall we say? – interest to his sudden demise. What lends the sinister element is the fact that no less a person than Mr Paul Dombey himself was on the railway platform at the time. The coincidence is singular, to say the least. And there was another, as yet unidentified, person there with him at the precise moment that Carker fell to his death."

"Are you implying that Mister Dombey . . .?"

"It is not my task to imply, sir. I merely state the facts."

"Yet from the facts you seem to speculate . . ."

"Speculation, sir, is a fruitless task. Facts must breed more facts, sir. And it is facts that I come in search of."

"I will say nothing that may harm my client," replied Mr Plankton firmly, folding his hands on the desk before him. "Mister Paul Dombey is a worthy gentleman and already faced with shame and ruin by the deeds of this man Carker and, may God forgive me, but I must say that it is a just recompense for his evil deeds that he has departed life in this manner."

"It is not in the brief of my official capacity to indulge myself in moral judgements," murmured Captain Ryder, "but simply to gather the facts for presentation to be assessed by judge and jury."

Mr Plankton shook his head.

"What I meant . . ." He paused.

"Precisely what did you mean?"

"Simply, that in the demise of James Carker, the world has no cause to grieve. However, his death is little compensation for the financial and emotional loss that Mister Dombey has suffered."

"Again, you express a moral judgement, sir, which I am not at liberty to comment on."

There was an uncomfortable pause.

"What is it that you want from me?" asked the solicitor, finally breaking the silence.

"I believe that you knew James Carker?"

"He was, as you have correctly stated, the manager of Dombey and Son and so we knew each other in a business capacity."

"And in a social capacity?"

"Certainly not," snapped Mr Plankton. "He was sharp of tooth, sly of manner with a watchful eye, soft of foot and oily of tongue. He was, to sum up, sir, a most disagreeable creature. A thorough-going scoundrel. I did not trust him, sir, and certainly would not include him among my social acquaintances."

"Did you ever mention your views to Mister Dombey?"

"It was not my place to question Mister Dombey's judge-ment of the men that he employed. Mr Dombey was a man not to be trifled with so far as his business dealings were concerned."

"Yet you were his legal adviser?"

"And legal advice I gave him when he requested it."

"Did you also know Mrs Dombey?" the young man asked so abruptly that Mr Plankton blinked.

"I have, on occasion, met her." The reply was more guarded.

"I am given to understand that she was formerly the widow of a Colonel Granger before she became Paul Dombey's second wife. Were you aware of that?"

"I was. Mister Dombey's first wife had died in childbirth when his son was born. The son was a weak child and eventually died, leaving Mister Dombey a widower with a daughter who he neglected. He decided to marry again and, as you say, Mrs Granger was thought a suitable match. Again, should you seek a personal opinion, I did not share that view. I once represented her mother, the late Mrs Cleopatra Skewton, over a matter of a small land purchase some years ago. It was not an experience that provided me with esteem for her or her daughter."

"So you knew Mrs Granger before she married Mister Dombey?"

"Briefly, sir, briefly. Never more than a nod, an exchange of polite pleasantry."

"She eloped, if I might apply the word to this matter, with James Carker and they both fled to France?"

"That is so. The facts are not unknown to me as well as to several others in the City. Alas, sir, such scandals are never kept secret for long."

"Indeed. The facts are given in a statement made by Mister Dombey taken down by the superintendent of police at Maidstone. The parish constable at Paddock Wood felt he needed more expert guidance after the incident when the basic facts were known."

Mr Plankton coughed delicately.

"As I say, the facts are not unknown to me. You will have seen from the statement that I was attending on Mister Dombey at the time that he gave his statement to the superintendent. I acted in the capacity of his legal adviser, of course."

"Of course, sir. Which begs the question. How was it that you were on hand when the statement was made? The accident happened at four o'clock in the morning when the Dover to London Express was passing through Paddock Wood station. The same day at precisely noon, you were with Mister Dombey at Paddock Wood. Mister Dombey had passed the night at the Forester's Arms, the inn there, indeed, as had the victim of the accident, James Carker. How were you alerted to the incident and able to travel down to Kent so quickly? The accident prevented any train running on that line until midday. You'll forgive me, sir, but I do so dislike a question unresolved."

Mister Plankton smiled thinly, an almost habitual expression before answering a question.

"Then pray do not trouble yourself, for the resolution is simple. I was already staying at Maidstone where I had proceeded to settle some legal business with an old client preparatory to my retirement."

"Indeed?" Captain Ryder sighed reflectively. "That places you within eight miles of Paddock Wood. How did you . . .?"

"I had booked into the hotel in King Street on the afternoon before the accident. On the morning . . . I left the hotel for a walk, it being my custom to take a stroll every morning. As you may know, sir, the Maidstone police station is also situated in King Street, and at that time I encountered the superintendent of police, with whom I had a passing acquaintance. He told me that a James Carker had fallen under a train at Paddock Wood and the local parish constable was troubled by the circumstances. He had sent to the superintendent to interview a Mister Dombey who had witnessed the incident. I was astonished and felt obliged to point out my connection with Mister Paul Dombey. The superintendent suggested that I should accompany him in his horse and fly to Paddock Wood."

The young detective sat nodding slowly.

Then he said quickly: "So, we have Mister Paul Dombey and James Carker, both having stayed at the Forester's Arms in Paddock Wood. How did they come there on that precise night? Both had just returned from France and separately, with Mister Dombey a few hours behind James Carker."

Mister Plankton sat back, toying for a moment with a silver letter opener that he had picked up from his desk.

"You make it sound extremely sinister, sir. Do you imply that Mister Dombey was following Carker?"

The young man shook his head as if suddenly bewildered.

"Mister Dombey admits to travelling to Dijon in France to confront his wife and Carker after they had eloped together. He had discovered where they were staying on the intelligence of a Mrs Brown. Mister Dombey admits that a confrontation took place but that he left Carker and his wife unharmed and returned via Paris. The fact is that Mister Dombey did board a ferry sailing from Calais only a few hours after the ferry on which Carker had sailed. That both men wound up at the same railway halt to which they were strangers when both might have logically proceeded directly to London is rather singular, is it not? What conclusion would you draw from these facts?"

Mr Plankton's brows drew together.

"Implications do lead to speculation, sir, and I thought that you denied the habit?" he observed dryly.

When Captain Ryder did not respond, the solicitor added defensively: "I have said that I will not say anything which impugns the good name of Mister Dombey."

"You do not have to, sir. However, Mister Dombey admitted during my subsequent inquiry that these were the facts. Therefore I was able to ask my colleague Monsieur Caissidière, at the Préfet de Police in Paris, to contact a police officer in Dijon to take a statement from Mrs Dombey. She confirms the essentials; that she had run off with Carker on a whim to spite her husband whom she thought little of. But she thought even less of Carker. Dombey came to see them in the apartment she had taken in Dijon. There was an altercation but not of a violent kind. Verbal blows were all that were struck. Dombey then left to return to England, leaving his wife to her chosen path. Mrs Dombey then told Carker what she really thought of him and he, in a rage, also took his baggage and left. She further alleged that, while doing so, he had muttered something about settling with someone in

London with whom he had business. His parting taunt to her was that she would be sorry, for he was a rich man."

There was a silence while Mr Plankton studied the face of the young officer before offering a comment.

"You will have read Mister Dombey's statement that he spent a day or two in Paris and so we must conclude that it was purely by chance that he arrived at Dover soon after Carker had landed."

"And a further coincidence that Mister Dombey took a local train and decided to alight at Paddock Wood, the very place where Carker had also alighted," responded the young man sceptically. "Another coincidence that both men stayed the night at the Forester's Arms? Come, sir, one coincidence might be acceptable but surely . . .?"

Mr Plankton shrugged.

"I represent to you the facts as told to me by Mister Dombey and which he placed in his statement. I do not comment on them. All I say is that I have never known Mister Dombey to add dishonesty to the fault of poor judgment of character."

Captain Ryder smiled a trifle sadly.

"If that is so, sir, then we must believe there is a logical explanation for these coincidences. Let us proceed with what we know. I can add that my friend Monsieur Caissidière was thorough on my behalf. He checked Mister Dombey's movements in Paris and found that he had paid a visit to the Havas Agence."

Mr Plankton raised an eyebrow slightly.

Captain Ryder leaned forward in his chair.

"Ah, sir, are you acquainted with the Havas Agence?"

The solicitor shook his head at once.

"The Havas Agence is known even in London, Captain. It is what is called a news agency; a place for the dissemination of news. Monsieur Havas formed it some ten years ago. He has what are called correspondents in each capital who send news items to him in Paris; items from the newspapers that are translated and passed on by the Havas Agence. By use of carrier pigeons they are able to get stories from London morning newspapers so that they can be published in the Paris afternoon editions. It is, indeed, amazing how small the world is growing."

"Exactly so."

"The fact is interesting, sir. But I fail to see . . .?"

"But what would Mister Dombey have to do with a news agency?" smiled Captain Ryder. "Did he not mention his visit to you?"

"Not at all."

"Strange that he did not. Do you know Monsieur Solliec, the Havas Agence correspondent in London?"

Mr Plankton frowned.

"I do not, sir. Oh, I have met him a few times in the coffee house I frequent at luncheon but I cannot say I know him."

"Then have you had any business dealings with a Mister Morfin?"

There was a moment's hesitation before Mr Plankton replied.

"Naturally. Mister Morfin was the assistant manager of Dombey and Son and, since Mister Carker went to France, Mister Morfin has acted as manager. A worthy young man, but he shares the fault with Mister Dombey of not being the best judge of character."

"Perhaps you could elucidate?" Captain Ryder raised an eyebrow.

"He is enamoured of Miss Harriette Carker."

"Ah, you speak of James Carker's sister?"

"Just so, sir. Just so. There is bad blood in that family, sir. Bad blood."

The young man looked thoughtfully at the solicitor.

"I presume that you refer not only to James but to his older brother, John Carker, who also is employed by Mister Dombey?"

"You have carried out a thorough investigation, sir," Mr Plankton observed, nodding quickly. "Do you know of the background of John Carker?"

"I know from my inquiries that he admitted to embezzling money from the firm when he was a young man but claims he immediately reformed and paid it back. However, his younger brother, the late James Carker, never let him forget the matter and mistreated him badly."

Mister Plankton sniffed.

"Reforms do occur, sir. Paul on the road to Damascus and all that. Personally, I place no faith in reformed characters nor in reformers."

"Did you know that Mister Morfin sent John Carker to Dover to meet Mister Dombey from the boat?"

Mr Plankton frowned.

"How did he know when Mister Dombey was arriving?"

"As I have said, Mister Dombey called in at the Havas Agence in Paris. He paid a clerk there to send one of the carrier pigeons that the agency uses to keep in touch with its correspondents in each of the European capitals to Monsieur Solliec in London. The intelligence was that Mister Dombey aimed to arrive in Dover at a particular time. Monsieur Solliec was acquainted with Mister Morfin and was able to pass this on. John Carker was therefore despatched to Dover to meet Mister Dombey. This step was taken because Mister Morfin wanted to give news of the extent of the embezzlement, which had then been fully uncovered. Now, sir, here we have another mystery. There is no mention of John Carker in the statement given by Mister Dombey and which you were witness to."

Mr Plankton was looking astonished.

"I, also, had no knowledge of him at the scene," he replied quietly. "Mister Dombey did not mention him."

"Yet John Carker met Paul Dombey at Dover and they both caught a local train to Paddock Wood, there being no direct trains to London. Unable to further their journey, they stayed at the Forester's Arms, presumably with the intention of remaining there until the first London train the next morning. Now, sir, it seems a coincidence that they both stayed in the same inn as James Carker."

"How do you learn that John Carker was actually with Mister Dombey at the inn, sir?"

"The landlord, naturally."

"But when I went to Paddock Wood . . ."

"Yes, sir? Tell me what transpired?"

"The superintendent from Maidstone and I found Mister Dombey in the inn, fortified by the solicitations of the landlord with some whisky, but was very shaken and horrified by the incident."

"And there was no sign of John Carker?"

"None at all, sir."

"And Mister Dombey's account?"

"As I said, he did not mention John Carker to me. It could be the shock had momentary caused a lapse in memory. As he put in his statement, he had left the inn to await the arrival of the London train. The express train came through first. It was, of course, dark and he could see little. He was aware of someone entering the station after him and moving to one end of the platform. He took no further notice. The express came through and it was only when he heard a terrifying scream and the train came to a stop a little further along the line that he was aware of the tragedy. It was only some while later that the station master and parish constable identified the person who had been killed, a name recognized by Mister Dombey who fainted in shock. But, surely, Captain Ryder, all this you have already read in Mister Dombey's statement, which I witnessed?"

"I have, indeed, sir. It is the things that are not in the statement that concern me. We know from Mister Morfin that John Carker was sent to meet Mister Dombey at Dover and we know from the innkeeper that two men alighted at Paddock Wood from the Dover train to await the London connection the next morning. Why did they alight there and go to the inn where James Carker was? How is it, sir, that John Carker seems to have disappeared from an account of these events?"

Mister Plankton sat back and his fingers drummed a tattoo on his desk top.

"I should think, sir, that even I – who am not a detective – might postulate a probability."

"Which is?" pressed the young man.

"I have already said, there is bad blood in the Carker family. Both brothers have embezzled. But James Carker has embezzled such sums as will bring the firm of Dombey and Son into bankruptcy and liquidation. Consider this, sir . . . who are the beneficiaries from Carker's demise?"

Captain Ryder examined him carefully.

"John and Harriette Carker?"

"Exactly so, sir."

The young man nodded.

"Indeed, indeed. They stand to inherit whatever funds stood to the credit of their brother at his death. But we have already examined his accounts and, do you know the strangest thing? James Carker certainly left a small sum of money but nowhere near the sums that Mister Morfin and the firm's accountants show that he embezzled during his period as manager."

Mr Plankton thought for a moment and then he smiled grimly.

"I have already mentioned that Mr Morfin is devotedly attached to Miss Harriette Carker. Have you checked his accounts? Perhaps . . .?"

Captain Ryder sighed.

"You suggest a conspiracy, sir."

Mr Plankton bent forward intently.

"Have you questioned Mister Dombey about John Carker?"

"We would be poor detectives had we not tried to do so. He claimed he did not think it of pertinence at the time and that he was, in any case, in a state of agitation. But he tells a story that brings forward other questions."

"I do not follow."

"Mister Dombey confirms that John Carker met him at Dover. John Carker then revealed the extent of his brother's embezzlement. Furthermore, he told Dombey that before he had left his lodgings in London a boy delivered a note from Mr Morfin informing him that he should break his return journey at Maidstone, where he should repair to a certain warehouse. There, the note said, John Carker would find goods and materials that were the property of Dombey and Son. He was to ensure their safe transportation to the London warehouse. Dombey himself was unaware of such matters but agreed that the two men should travel from Dover to Paddock Wood, where, a few years prior, the branch line to Maidstone had been opened. However, on arrival, there were no trains continuing to Maidstone until a local train at a quarter to four o'clock the next day. Seeing no reason to spend a further lengthy period at Maidstone, Mister Dombey decided to await the London train at Paddock Wood while his companion, John Carker, went on to Maidstone to deal with the business matters. John Carker left Paddock Wood at a quarter to four, leaving Dombey to await the London slow train at a quarter past the hour. In the intervening time, at precisely four o'clock, came the express, at which time James Carker emerged on the platform and met his death."

Mr Plankton was shaking his head.

"An amazing coincidence of circumstance, sir."

"Even more amazing in a singular manner was the fact that when John Carker reached the warehouse to which he had been directed, no one had heard of any goods or materials for Dombey and Son. Nor did Mister Morfin later admit to sending any such note to John Carker."

"A curious convenience, sir," commented Mr Plankton dryly.

"Convenient, indeed. Leaving Mister Dombey alone on the railway platform with James Carker."

"I refuse to believe the implication. I would presume there is now a warrant out for John Carker? It is clear that there was some base deception here of which Mister Dombey is wholly innocent. As I suggested, the Carkers are a bad lot and I would remind you that Mister Morfin wishes to marry into that family. Conspiracy, sir. It smacks of conspiracy."

Captain Ryder grimaced.

"We have now recovered the note sent to John Carker." He touched his breast pocket lightly. "Which brings me to other matters that worries me. From the start, the facts that have brought me to conclusions of a sinister nature seemed to point to the fact that James Carker's life was taken in unnatural fashion. The evidence now confirms it. His death was brought about by contrivance and terrifying premeditation. He was pushed under the express train but not for reasons of revenge but for gain. You, yourself, have suggested the motive. He had embezzled such a large sum from Dombey and Son that would be an attractive enough proposition. The person who committed the heinous crime of pushing James Carker in front of the express train was clearly a confederate . . . a partner in crime. He was the banker, if you like, of the monies embezzled over the years."

Mr Plankton pulled a face expressing his scepticism.

"But there are several problems with this story. Firstly, you have explained how it was known when Dombey was arriving at Dover. But how did the murderer know James Carker was returning to London and that the arrivals would be close together? If not coincidence, then by wizardry. How did the murderer know James Carker would be at Paddock Wood? It would be an impossible crime without such knowledge."

Captain Ryder sat back, nodding slowly.

"In fact, the murderer knew the movement of James Carker a few days before he knew those of Paul Dombey. The entire set of events was manipulated from the first. The murderer knew both Dombey and Carker would be at Paddock Wood at the same time and his plot was to involve them in his gruesome plan."

Mr Plankton sniffed.

"I don't see how . . . unless we return to suspecting Mister Dombey himself."

"Perhaps we don't have to go that far. The mail system between Dijon and here is remarkably good. We tend to think of France as back in the days of the *poste aux chevaux* but such is not the case. Indeed, sir, they are in advance of us. It is known that three years ago the French introduced a designated wagon on their trains from city to city in which the mail is sorted after it is collected. It saves an entire day in transportation. Mail is collected and delivered every second day in every municipality in France. Before he left Dijon, James Carker wrote a short letter to his confederate telling him that he was *en route* to London. He told him when he was expected to arrive and that he would call on his confederate for his share of the money."

Mr Plankton leaned back with a frown. "Do you say so, sir? Do you have the note?"

"I do say so," confirmed Captain Ryder without responding to the second question. "The confederate did not want to share the riches he had hidden in his accounts with Carker. What is more, the confederate in London wrote care of the harbour master at Dover asking that the note be delivered into the hands of Carker when he arrived. That note suggested that Carker break his journey at the Forester's Arms where he would be met and the matter sorted. Paddock Wood was a quiet spot outside of London and suitable for such a transaction as the murderer had in mind. James Carker obeyed without suspicion."

Captain Ryder paused for a moment before continuing.

"Then came the news from Paris by carrier pigeon as to when Paul Dombey was arriving and – this is the only coincidence – it was to be that same night as James Carker. It so happened that the correspondent of the Havas Agence, Monsieur Solliec, met the murderer, whom he knew by means of the fact that they sometimes frequented the same coffee house. Having discovered that John Carker was being sent to Dover, it was then easy to send a messenger with a note purporting to be from Mister Morfin to John Carker's lodging before he left, a message knowing that it would bring him and Paul Dombey to the inn at Paddock Wood."

"As a solicitor, I see several problems with the story," declared Mr Plankton.

"Let me continue, first. James Carker did not find his confederate at the inn. The landlord said Carker drank a lot of wine with his dinner and displayed various signs of impatience. He then went to his room and fell asleep, having asked to be roused in time to get the early morning train to

London, due at four fifteen in the morning. A short time after, Dombey and John Carker arrived. The murderer had arrived in the darkness of the night and was awaiting his opportunity. We know how the opportunity came about. By the way, the note making the rendezvous was found on the bloody remains of James Carker."

"Amazing, sir. Simply, amazing. By whom was the note signed?"

Captain Ryder shook his head.

"Alas, the hand that penned the note added no signature. One thing, however, was apparent – it was the same hand that penned the note to John Carker instructing him to break the journey at Paddock Wood."

Mr Plankton raised his eyebrows. "By my soul, sir. What a fascinating story you tell. So it was all a plot. A plot to incriminate John Carker in the murder of his brother?"

"It would seem so, sir. A very ingenious plot, if I may say so."

"No one could deny you saying so, sir. Yet I still see some questions that need resolution, sir. If the murderer's plot was to meet with James Carker in the inn and kill him, why wait hidden away until early morning, when John Carker had left for Maidstone on the milk train, and when he had to follow James Carker to the station and hope there were no witnesses to watch him being pushed under the train? It seems a messy plot to me, sir."

"An improvized plot is sometimes a messy one, Mister Plankton."

"Improvized?"

"But the murderer had neglected the fact that an early train would leave Paddock Wood for Maidstone bearing John Carker away from the scene. However, it left Mister Dombey on the platform both as suspect and witness."

"Mister Dombey? Indeed, there is only one person in this tale that would then be the culprit other than John Carker . . . no, no . . . I cannot believe it. It means that it could only be Paul Dombey himself who pushed James Carker to his death."

Captain Ryder leant back with narrowed eyes.

"On the contrary, sir. There was one other person who had the opportunity. Who arranged this entire charade, who actually helped James Carker embezzle and bank the money, using his business connection with Dombey and Son? Indeed, that person's connection with Monsieur Solliec, the correspondent of Havas Agence, allowed him to pick up the intelligence as to the fact that John Carker was meeting the boat at Dover. There was only one person here in London who had access to the information and who James Carker had mailed that he was coming to settle with him and this person was able to stage the meeting at Paddock Wood. I do not have to tell you who that person is, sir."

Mr Josiah Plankton was sitting back with a dreamy look on his face, nodding slightly. He was smiling but there was an expression of vindictive passion on his features.

"You had gone to Maidstone because, for obvious reasons, you did not want to be identified at Paddock Wood," went on Captain Ryder grimly. "You probably waited until well after midnight and perhaps walked or more likely rode the ten miles to the Forester's Arms. You had not realised that John Carker would take the first morning train to Maidstone, a local milk delivery train. And when you reached the inn, you observed some movement. There was Paul Dombey on the station platform. Then came James Carker. You took your opportunity and after the deed was done you vanished into the darkness. You return to Maidstone and arriving there in time for breakfast as if out for an early morning walk. And when you emerged from the hotel . . . that was then you fell in with the superintendent of police. Perhaps that had not been part of your plan, to be forced to go as Paul Dombey's lawyer to the scene of your crime. Yet it was all quite clever. Too clever. But there were too many coincidences to make it believable."

Mr Josiah Plankton did not answer.

In his mind's eye he saw the onrushing black engine with its red warning lights, the shriek of its whistle and pounding roar of its wheels; saw the figure in front of him, soundlessly shrieking against the noise of the great engine, as, like some rag doll, the body was caught up, whirled away upon a jagged mill, struck limb from limb and cast into mutilated fragments in the air. He smiled as he remembered the blood soaked ashes spread across the tracks. How he hated the idea of having to share the wealth with a man like James Carker. But now he was rich. Now he did not have to share those riches with anyone.

He was still smiling absently when Captain Ryder rose, moved to the door and beckoned in the two uniform constables who had been waiting patiently outside.

The Divine Nature

Kate Ellis

A few months after the completion of Dombey and Son, *Dickens's elder sister, Fanny, died, at the age of only 38. It affected Dickens deeply and caused him to think again about his childhood and life's vicissitudes. This manifested itself in his next (and last) Christmas book,* The Haunted Man and the Ghost's Bargain *(1848), and in his efforts to write an autobiography, "My Early Times", which remained unpublished until used by John Forster in writing his biography of Dickens. But these reflections also produced one of Dickens's greatest books and his own favourite,* David Copperfield. *This began to appear in monthly instalments in May 1849 and Dickens was seldom more content than in its production.*

It tells the story of young David whose father had died before he was born. His mother comes under the spell of the stern Edward Murdstone, whom she marries, only to die giving birth to his son. Murdstone and his sister Jane make young David's childhood a misery and David eventually rebels and bites Murdstone. David is sent away, first to a strict, oppressive school and then to work in Murdstone's bottling warehouse – just as Dickens had in the blacking factory. Copperfield lodges with the Micawber family, where the ever-optimistic Mr Micawber, based on Dick-

ens's father, struggles with his finances. The novel traces Copperfield's trials and tribulations as he seeks to make good and to help his friends and his aunt, Betsy Trotwood, who has fallen foul of the calculating Uriah Heep. Copperfield also gets married in error, to the vacuous Dora Spenlow, who dies young, but eventually, after many problems, all comes good. Thanks to Micawber, Uriah Heep's machinations are unveiled, Betsy Trotwood recovers her wealth and finances the Micawber family finding a new life in Australia. And Copperfield finds success as an author and marries his childhood friend, Agnes Wickfield, whom he realizes he has loved all along.

This novel has inspired two stories. Kate Ellis is the author of the Wesley Peterson series of police procedural novels which also have an archaeological element and which began with The Merchant's House *(1998).*

I am a fortunate man. My dear wife, Agnes, has given me much joy, and all England now knows me as David Copperfield, the renowned author. Being a thoughtful man, in idle moments I still think upon my youth and the painful events that formed my nature. However, I was quite unprepared for the unexpected visitor who arrived at our happy home almost a year ago to the day, to resurrect the dark shadows of my past.

Miss Jane Murdstone with her dark brooding eyebrows, hard as metal and forbidding as the iron gate of a prison, had blighted my childhood. And now she was in my house, standing in my hall like a nervous tradesman.

"This lady wishes to see you, Mr Copperfield." My maidservant bobbed a curtsey. She was a small thin child whom my wife, Agnes, had lately taken pity on and employed in our household.

I smiled to put the girl at her ease. Agnes always observed that I was indulgent with the servants – perhaps it was because Peggotty, who had been my mother's servant, was at one time my dearest and only friend. I have no time for those who do not recognise the humanity of those who serve them. "Thank you, Mary," I said.

The girl scurried away like a small frightened creature and I looked Miss Murdstone in the eye. Her black looks had once filled me with terror and now, it seemed, little Mary had sensed the iron coldness that had always surrounded my stepfather's sister.

I had been a young child when I had first made the woman's acquaintance. She had come to the Rookery at the invitation of her brother, Edward, who had inveigled my poor, gentle mother into marriage. Miss Murdstone, with the encouragement of her brother, had taken control of the household, breaking the spirit of my unfortunate mother and taking away all the love and comfort I had ever known. How I had hated the Murdstones then. And now I was a man, the sight of Jane Murdstone still filled my heart with dread and I wondered what ill fortune had brought her here to disturb the peace of my house.

I looked at Miss Murdstone enquiringly, for I had no idea what could have brought about such a visitation. She made no attempt to ask after my health or my family; rather she came straight to the purpose of her visit.

"I have no friends, Mr Copperfield, and no relations neither. But, as you are now a man of some consequence and we are related by marriage, I . . ."

"Related, ma'am?" The remark surprised me. She had never acknowledged kinship of any kind in all the years of our mutual acquaintance.

"In short, sir, I have nobody else to turn to. Will you hear me out?" Her looks belied the desperation of her words. The bushy black eyebrows came together in a frown but her expression remained impassive, as if she was about to comment upon the weather.

I showed her into my study and invited her to sit, sensing this was a conversation best held in private.

"My brother is gone without a word, Mr Copperfield, and I fear some harm had befallen him."

The face of Edward Murdstone emerged, unbidden from

my memory. I saw him as he was when he had courted my
mother with his abundant coal-black hair and whiskers. I saw
his handsome face twisted with hatred as he beat me for what
he called my stubborn disobedience and set in a mask of
hypocrisy as he chided my poor, sweet mother for some
imagined failing or weakness. Then I saw the shock on that
face as I sank my teeth into the hand that had wielded the
cane, and I shuddered, remembering how Murdstone had
ordered me like a dog in those far off days . . . and how I was
forced to obey like one.

She looked up at me, a reproachful glitter in her small,
dark eyes and I turned away, lest she should see the pain on
my face. "What were the circumstances of your brother's
disappearance?" I asked, glancing out of the window at the
garden, full of cheerful colour. Jane Murdstone had brought
winter into the house where warmth and love ruled supreme.
And I hated her for it.

"My brother, as I believe you know, married again – a poor
weak thing close to madness."

How strange, I thought, that both Edward Murdstone's
wives should be "poor weak things". At least he had not
driven my mother to madness. But then she had not lived
long enough for that. Perhaps her untimely death had spared
her a worse fate.

"My brother," she continued, "is a pious and religious
man. He gives public addresses and . . ."

"Your neighbour, Mr Chillip, the doctor, told me some
time ago of your brother's . . . er . . . gift for oratory."

Jane Murdstone pressed her lips together. Mr Chillip, it
seemed, was not a recipient of the Murdstones' approval.

I looked her in the eye. "I heard that your brother has
driven his wife quite mad. I was also informed that your
brother has set up an image of himself which he calls 'The
Divine Nature' and that he is in the habit of consigning
everyone around him to perdition." I watched her, unable to
keep the amusement from my lips. The idea of Murdstone as
a ranting, megalomaniac who mistakes himself for the Almighty was rather sweet to me. But I checked myself. I, who

have had such good fortune, must show some Christian charity.

Jane Murdstone bit her thin lip. "You wished to know the circumstances of his disappearance."

I made my apology, insincere though it was, and she continued. "There is nothing to tell. He went out for a walk one evening and he never returned. That is all."

"Is he in the habit of taking a walk in the evening?"

"My brother takes much exercise. The body is a temple and the Lord wills that we must not let it fall to ruin," she said with a cloying piety that made me sick to my stomach. "In truth, Mr Copperfield, I am exceedingly worried for Edward. I fear that . . ."

"You fear he has met with some accident?"

"In short, sir, yes. And as my only relative, I implore you to aid me in my quest for the truth about . . ."

"I do not see what I can do," I said with uncharacteristic brutality. "I am working on a book at present and my family commitments . . ."

Miss Murdstone, her face hard and impassive as metal, thanked me for my time and swept out with a swish of her bat-black skirts. And as she left I found myself hoping that I would never see her again.

But I should have known that the Murdstones – that name my aunt Betsey Trotwood had once mistaken for "murderer" – would cling to me like seaweed to a drowned corpse.

I received a letter from Mr Chillip the very next day. I was rather surprised that my old friend – the doctor who attended at my birth – should make contact so soon after his name had been mentioned by Jane Murdstone, for I had not heard from him for more than a year. But it is ever thus in such matters.

It was Mr Chillip who had told me how the Murdstones were disliked in the district of Bury St Edmunds, where they resided, and how Murdstone's wealthy young wife – who had only just been of age when they married – was reputed to be quite mad and kept as a prisoner by her husband and his sister. Chillip had also informed me about Murdstone's religious activities – the public talks and the image he had made of himself as The Divine Nature – and his handful of gullible followers. Murdstone, I knew, was possessed of dark good looks and could charm the female sex when it suited him. As he had once charmed my dearest mother, that charm masking his true nature which was far from "divine".

The previous night I had lain awake thinking of Jane Murdstone's visit. Because of the history between us, I had been ready to dismiss her plea for help without sympathy. However, on reflection in the small hours of the morning, listening to my dear Agnes breathing softly beside me, my curiosity grew.

I had been reluctant to aid Miss Murdstone in any way, but the receipt of Mr Chillip's letter rather changed my mind in this respect. "My dearest David," he began and after expressing his good wishes concerning my family's well being and assuring me that his dear wife and his daughter were in the best of health, he came to the matter that most concerned him.

"I must tell you, David, that your step-father Mr Murdstone is vanished – disappeared without trace – and it is the talk of the neighbourhood. I spoke with his sister and she said she was most anxious to consult you as, with your present fame which has indeed spread to our part of the country, she feels you may be in a position to help her. I told her you were busy with your work and family but she was most insistent so I am writing to warn you that you may receive a visit from the lady Mrs Chillip (and Mrs Chillip is a great observer) describes as ferocious. If you should be intrigued by Miss Murdstone's little problem and should decide that a visit to Suffolk would satisfy your curiosity, Mrs Chillip and I would be delighted and honoured if you would stay with us. Mr M's disappearance is, I must say, a most puzzling mystery."

Chillip went on to list Murdstone's recent activities and when I had finished reading the letter, I went to my study and perused my manuscript. Perhaps a short rest from writing would do me good. I could spend a few days in Suffolk – provided I had Agnes's blessing – and return refreshed, perhaps with new ideas. Besides, I was rather flattered at being thought a worthy detective . . . even by the ferocious Miss Jane Murdstone.

And so it was that three days later, I arrived at the house of that trusted doctor and steadfast friend, Mr Chillip and his good wife. But I had no inkling then of the danger I would face.

After spending a congenial hour in the company of Mr and Mrs Chillip, I walked the half mile to the Murdstones' house which was a large, forbidding place shaded by tall laurels, with a black front door and dark curtains at the gloomy windows, giving a house a look of permanent mourning.

An elderly servant with a watchful face opened the door and when Jane Murdstone greeted me I was led into a drawing room of unremitting darkness – a room whose furnishings appeared to absorb any weak sunlight that dared to creep in through the tall windows.

Without further pleasantries, she began her narrative. Edward Murdstone, it seemed, had set out for his usual walk at seven o'clock precisely on the evening of Wednesday 9 May. He usually came back an hour later but that night she waited in vain for his return. When I enquired about Murdstone's wife, Miss Murdstone said that she kept to her room, shut in for her own safety. She spoke of Edward's wife's confinement as though it was something quite ordinary and when I asked to speak to the woman, whose name was Dorothea, I was told that she was sick in mind and body and was not fit to receive visitors or answer questions. I offered to call Mr Chillip to examine her but was informed with icy formality that bothering the doctor was quite unnecessary. Dear Dorothea was quite beyond the help of doctors. It was only because of Edward's devotion and his sense of Christian duty that she hadn't been committed to an asylum. The words filled me with foreboding for the unfortunate woman.

However, I managed to ascertain the basic facts of the case. On the day of his disappearance Edward had received a visit

from a Mr Passnidge – an old business acquaintance. They
were closeted in the study for over an hour before Passnidge
left, saying farewell to Jane Murdstone in the most amiable
manner. Ten minutes after that, Edward Murdstone had left
to take his customary walk, without a word to his sister or to
the servant whose name, I learned, was Dawkins. Murdstone
was never seen again after that and neither, it seemed, was
Mr Passnidge. Passnidge was known to live in Lowestoft and
Jane had sent Dawkins to enquire at his address, only to be
told that Passnidge too had not been seen since the night he
had called on Murdstone.

The name Passnidge was familiar to me but it took me
some time to recall the circumstances of my encounter with
the gentleman. Eventually, I remembered: it was in those
distant days when Murdstone was courting my mother.
Anxious to impress her, that man with the ill-omened black
eyes had taken my young self to an hotel by the sea where we
met with two gentlemen. They were, I think, business
acquaintances rather than friends for they seemed nervous
in his presence – I was a watchful child and I sensed these
things. One of them, I later learned, was his business partner,
Mr Quinion. The other was a Mr Passnidge, although I
never knew anything of his dealings with my stepfather. I
remembered little of Passnidge except that he had seemed an
amiable sort of man. And now he too was missing. Passnidge
had left the house and vanished. Ten minutes later Murdstone had done likewise and it seemed implausible that the
two events should be unconnected. Did somebody lie in wait
for both men, perhaps mistaking Passnidge for the hated
Murdstone? Or had one killed the other and fled? I resolved
to set my mind to the problem.

There was no sign of Dorothea Murdstone at the house. I
saw her in my mind's eye, locked in some far off attic,
wearing rags and fed on scraps. She had been little more
than a child when Murdstone had used his charm to persuade
her to marriage. And she had been an heiress. As I left the
house I looked back, hoping to catch a glimpse of the
unfortunate woman at an upstairs window but there was

nothing and I imagined that her spirit was so broken that even the rare arrival of a visitor elicited no curiosity.

I walked back to the house of Mr Chillip with a heavy heart but upon my arrival, I was distracted from my melancholy by Mrs Chillip, who rushed out to greet me. A body had been found in the river by some schoolboys who'd been fishing, she told me, her pale eyes sparkling.

A drowned man. Mr Murdstone, without a shadow of a doubt.

Mrs Chillip had been mistaken. When Jane Murdstone identified the bloated body she stated quite clearly that it was not her brother who had become hooked on a schoolboy's line like some grim, gigantic fish. She did, however, know the dead man's identity. His name was Passnidge and he had been with her brother the evening he disappeared.

The local constable, it seemed, had concluded that the man, a stranger in the district, had lost his footing and slipped into the water. But I suspected this was idleness on the constable's part. The body was too damaged by its time in the water to yield any clues as to the manner of death but I was certain, given Murdstone's disappearance, that it had been no accident. Murdstone, I was sure, had followed the unfortunate victim and killed him, in spite of his sister's insistence that they had parted on the best of terms. However, I needed to prove it and when I succeeded, my old tormentor would swing from the gallows as a common murderer. Once again, I chided myself for my lack of forgiveness. I should count my blessings and not dwell on past wrongs.

I decided to call upon Miss Murdstone to ask some questions. I also hoped for a glimpse of Dorothea, for this elusive, unhappy woman was beginning to haunt my dreams. Her fate reminded me so much of my own dear mother and perhaps it was this that made me so keen to make the woman's acquaintance.

Jane Murdstone received me with cold politeness and I sensed a new wariness in her manner. It seemed she had

convinced herself that her brother had caught up with Mr
Passnidge on the evening of his disappearance and both had
been attacked by ruffians. She feared that Edward had lost
his memory and was wandering somewhere, perhaps unaware of who he was. He must be found, she said, before he
came to further harm. She looked drawn and anxious. Anxious perhaps that when her brother was found, he might be
brought to justice for Passnidge's murder, although she
adhered steadfastly to her version of events.

While she was in a co-operative frame of mind, I seized the
opportunity to question her further about her brother's life.
He still had business interests in London, it transpired, but
of late his energies were concentrated on his Calling, as she
named it. As we talked I probed with gentle questions and
discovered that the Chapel of the Divine Nature lay in the
grounds of the house and that, on a good Sunday, Mr
Murdstone attracted an enthusiastic and dedicated congregation of ten or twelve, mostly ladies. The sister went on to
praise her brother's eloquence and spiritual gifts – gifts I had
never witnessed during my childhood, unless cruelty and
coldness are gifts of the spirit. I suspected the ladies of his
congregation were swayed by his charismatic charm and his
dark good looks and wondered if one of their brothers,
husbands or fathers had sought revenge for some reason.
But I am an author and by nature imaginative. I ordered
myself to consider only facts.

When I asked to see the chapel, my request was granted
and Miss Murdstone led me across the gardens, notable by
the absence of any colour other than green – flowers not
being favoured in the Murdstone household. The small
chapel itself looked fairly new and had been built, I was
told with the generous contributions of the congregation.
"Such is his triumph against his enemies who will be consigned to perdition," she added with a sly gleam in her black
eyes. I said nothing. Edward Murdstone had always been
adept at extracting money from women and this thought
made me even more eager to set eyes on the present Mrs
Murdstone.

The chapel was painted a deep blue with gold painted stars on the ceiling and furnished with fine oak pews. At the front was what looked like an altar, covered in dark blue velvet and upon the altar stood a likeness of Mr Murdstone, a little smaller than life sized, a benign expression on the carved face, arms raised in benediction. I stared for a while at this blasphemy in stone.

"My brother, the Divine Nature," Miss Murdstone said proudly in an awestruck whisper. I did not reply for I was lost for suitable words.

As we were leaving the chapel, I asked the question that was at the forefront of my mind. "May I speak with Mrs Murdstone? She may know something of your brother's whereabouts."

Jane Murdstone snorted like a pig. "She knows nothing. At the time of his disappearance she was asleep. She cannot help you."

"Nevertheless," I said firmly, "I should like to see her."

"That is impossible. I should be most grateful, Mr Copperfield, if you would make enquiries in the town for my brother. It may be that someone has seen him."

This was doubtful, I thought. If he was at large, somebody would have reported it. I had another idea.

"As I am in the district, I may visit my childhood home at Blunderstone," I said after a few moments. "It was once your brother's home so there is a chance he might have returned there if his memory is lost. Besides, I should like to visit my parents' grave."

"There is nothing at Blunderstone," Miss Murdstone said sharply. "Some old man – little more than a lunatic – was living there but now he is dead and the place has quite fallen to ruin." Suddenly her expression softened. "Perhaps my sister-in-law will be well enough to see you tomorrow," she said.

I made a small bow, sensing the sudden promise of a meeting with Dorothea might be intended to divert me from my visit to Blunderstone. I told her I would call again and when I walked off down the drive, I turned to look at the house. This time I saw a woman at an upstairs window. She possessed a pale beauty and she was dressed all in white – a nightgown perhaps. She stared down at me for a few moments before stepping back from the window. And in those few seconds I saw fear in her large, pleading eyes.

"Oh what news and gossip we have." Mr Chillip beamed all over his face. "What a great observer Mrs Chillip is to be sure." The little man capered into the house and I followed, anxious to learn what Mrs Chillip had observed.

"Oh, Mr Copperfield," Mrs Chillip greeted me as I entered. "The brother of my friend Mrs Dumpleford is a lawyer in Lowestoft and it seems he is acquainted with the late Mr Passnidge. He is visiting his sister presently and when I called on her, I heard all."

"Mrs Chillip is a great observer," Mr Chillip repeated gleefully.

I urged the lady to continue.

She leaned forward and looked around, as though she were afraid of being overheard. "It seems Mr Passnidge has rather a reputation for dishonest dealing and honest folk decline to trust him with their affairs." She paused, a look of triumph on her face. "And there is something more. Daisy, our maid, was talking to the carter and he says Mrs Pipkin's son was walking near the river on the night Mr Murdstone disappeared and he saw a ghost."

"A ghost?"

"Hideous, it was. He said it seemed to float on the water, its garments billowing."

"Was it the ghost of a man or a woman?"

The question seemed to silence Mrs Chillip. She gave the matter some thought before she spoke again. "He couldn't say," she said slowly. "And, in truth, Mrs Pipkin's son is a simple soul. But he saw something that night – no mistake about that."

An hour later I was face to face with Lemuel Pipkin, a great pudding of a boy not yet in his sixteenth year. Mrs Chillip had been truthful when she called him a simple soul but he

kept to his story. On the night Mr Murdstone had vanished,
he had been walking on the river bank when he'd seen a
figure he had taken for a ghost. It had seemed to be floating
on the water or, perhaps, on the bank. On closer questioning
I surmised that the phantom was probably running and that
Pipkin had heard a splash and a cry before he caught sight of
it. He thought it was a man in a voluminous cloak but he
could have been mistaken.

Satisfied that he had told me all he knew, I left Pipkin. I
had a journey to make. And I had Passnidge's Lowestoft
address safely in my pocket.

I had always loved sea air, ever since those happy days of my
childhood staying with Peggotty at Yarmouth. As I walked
the streets of Lowestoft in search of Passnidge's lodgings, I
breathed in deeply and my spirits were lifted by the salty tang
in the breeze.

With the aid of a gentleman who furnished me with
detailed directions, I found the lodgings down a small side
street, little more than an alleyway, and up some rickety
stairs. The landlord, I discovered, lived downstairs and, for
the price of a coin, this thin, hungry-looking man was
willing to admit me. It seemed Mr Passnidge used the
premises for his business as well as his residence and, as
the landlord let me in, I saw that the rooms were shabby
and uncared for, the only sign of prosperity being a large
oak desk beneath the window of the type seen in the more
respectable kind of lawyer's office. The landlord left and I
began my search for anything that connected this man to
Edward Murdstone.

As I sorted through the pile of documents on the desk, my
attention was caught by Murdstone's name on a set of deeds.
I read the papers more closely and discovered that the said
Murdstone was the owner of a house in Blunderstone known
as the Rookery. My heart beat faster. This house was my
birthplace and had passed into Murdstone's ownership on
my dear mother's death, but I had thought it sold long ago. I
then discovered a cryptic letter signed by Murdstone refer-

ring to a Mr B at the R needing extra care and dated a year ago.

After this, my search produced nothing of interest so I left, slipping the landlord another coin for his trouble. I had an uneasy feeling that the answer to all my questions would lie at Blunderstone, where I had first seen the light of day.

Blunderstone was much as I remembered it and I visited my parents' grave beneath the tree in the churchyard, bowing my head as I recalled my dear mother's face. I then walked to the Rookery. Last time I had seen the house the rooks had gone, the tall trees had been lopped and the garden had been left to run to wilderness. Now the garden was more overgrown and there was no sign of life in the house. On my last visit I had observed the old lunatic gentleman sitting at my little window looking out on the churchyard, but now every window was shut up.

Suddenly I heard a deep growling and saw a dog of considerable size bounding towards me. As I began to run, a harsh voice called the dog off and two roughly dressed men hurtled out of the house onto what used to be the lawn. I hurried away. The dog was baring its teeth and I had no wish to encounter the beast at close quarters.

I was walking to the vicarage to make enquiries about my former home when I met a boy, a large lad with ginger hair and abundant freckles who had the alert look of one who knows what is going on in the neighbourhood.

"Good day," I said and the boy returned my greeting. "I see my old home, the Rookery, has been left to decay. Do you know the house?"

"I do indeed, sir," the boy replied. "You lived there, you say?"

"I was born there," I replied and the boy nodded earnestly. "Who lives there now?"

The boy's face clouded. "In truth, I do not know, sir. There was an old gentleman but I have not seen him for many months and I am afraid to go near for fear of the dog, sir."

"Tell me about the old gentleman." My interest was captured and I wondered if this could be the elderly lunatic I had heard of many years before.

"His name was old Barty, sir. Folk called him a lunatic but I talked with him when the people left him at the bottom of the garden. It is true that his mind was befuddled, sir but he said when he didn't take the drinks they gave him he could think quite clearly."

The boy's words alarmed me, although I doubted if he realized the significance of what he had said. He put his hand into his pocket and produced a small silver box which he held out for me to take.

"He gave me this, sir. He said I should keep it always."

I took the box and examined it. It was the sort used for snuff, very handsome and embossed with flowers. I opened it carefully and saw a name inscribed upon the inside of the lid – Bartholomew Barton – and a date, 1836. I thanked the lad for showing me his treasure and asked him where Bartholomew Barton was now. With an expression of great solemnity on his cheerful face he told me he did not know. But as he had not seen the gentleman for a long time, he feared that he was dead.

I pressed a coin into my new friend's hand and took my leave. I would call at the church to seek out Bartholomew Barton's grave. If such a thing existed.

The old man was dead but the Vicar of Blunderstone had not been called upon to conduct the funeral ceremony. He knew of Mr Murdstone and his ownership of the Rookery but, as Murdstone only paid occasional visits – and none of them recent – he did not know the man well. He had learned of Mr Barton's death some weeks after the event and had heard that the burial had taken place in a neighbouring parish. I could tell he thought this a little strange but, as he pointed out, there was probably some simple explanation such as some strong family tie with the other parish.

I thanked him and took my leave before walking to the next village where I found many fine monuments bearing the

name of Barton but none for a Bartholomew. It was my good
fortune to meet the Rector there, who was new to his post but
was pleased to let me peruse the registers. I found no mention
of Bartholomew Barton in the burial register. But I found his
marriage and the birth of his only child. A daughter named
Dorothea.

I stayed at the inn in Blunderstone and returned to Bury St
Edmunds the next day, setting off early. I had to ensure that
what I suspected was true so I visited a church in the town to
peruse the marriage register and then, armed with my new
knowledge, I called upon the Chillips to inform them of my
plans. The good little doctor was eager to accompany me and
I considered his offer for some time before concluding that
the presence of a doctor might be beneficial. We arrived at
the Murdstones' house just before dark and found the place
still and silent. I suddenly felt afraid and I was glad of my
friend's company even though, at his age and stature, he
would hardly strike fear into the heart of an enemy.

I was about to knock upon the door when I spotted a shape
flitting across the garden, making for the chapel. It fluttered
across the grass, white like a ghost, and I abandoned my
knocking in order to follow it.

"What is it?" Mr Chillip asked as he fought to keep up
with me.

"I suspect that's our river bank ghost," I replied.

We were closing on the figure. I could see now that it was a
woman in a voluminous nightgown, her long fair hair stream-
ing behind her. In the twilight she looked ethereal, like a
creature from another world, lighter than air. But as I drew
nearer, I could see that she was thin with the pallor of one
who had been confined for years in some dark prison.

I called out. "Dorothea. Have no fear. We are friends. I
wish to speak with you."

She turned and I saw her face for the first time. She looked
very young and she must once have been beautiful but her
lack of flesh and the dark circles around her wide eyes gave
her face the look of a skull.

I approached her slowly as I would approach some shy, wild creature. "My name is David Copperfield and this is my good friend Mr Chillip. Mr Chillip is a doctor. There is no need to fear. We wish to help you."

She stared for a few moments, ready for flight. Then suddenly she collapsed to the ground in a faint and I rushed forward to scoop her up in my arms. She was as light as a bird as I carried her towards the house. If Miss Murdstone was there, she would not dare to defy me now that I knew the truth about her brother's evil dealings with the Barton family.

Miss Murdstone, however, was absent. The servant, Dawkins, now fearful, said that she was visiting some member of her brother's congregation who claimed to have had a vision that Edward Murdstone, the Divine Nature, had been taken up bodily to Heaven. The man's face was impassive as he said the words and I wondered if he, like me, was thinking that Hell was a more appropriate destination for his master.

Dorothea said little, except that in her sister-in-law's absence, she had not taken the usual drink that Jane always brought for her in the early evening and had thus been able to escape her prison and walk in the grounds. She was weak and confused and Mr Chillip surmised that the Murdstones had dosed her with laudanum to ensure her compliance. The good little doctor insisted that she be taken to his house where Mrs Chillip could nurse her back to health. I readily agreed and the Chillips' carriage was sent for.

We did not press Dorothea for her story that night and she slept like the dead until late the next morning. Mrs Chillip bustled around finding suitable clothes for the young woman and by midday she was seated in the parlour, looking pale but well on the road to recovery from her ordeal which, I surmised, had begun soon after her marriage. For over twelve years she had been kept by the Murdstones, locked in her chamber and subdued with laudanum. It would take her some time to recover from such an existence and I could see that she was nervous, glancing at the window as though she expected her husband or her sister-in-law to arrive any moment to claim her and return her to her prison. I began to wonder whether Edward Murdstone was truly dead or whether he was hiding somewhere, biding his time. I thought of the Rookery with its guard dog and shuddered. If he was hiding there, keeping his sister in ignorance of his whereabouts, it would be up to me to flush him out.

The next day I set off in the carriage with Mr Chillip and a couple of burly manservants for Blunderstone.

We had taken the precaution of bringing some meat along to pacify the dog and the beast availed itself readily of our bounty as we marched past it to the back door.

Fortune was on our side, for the rough men were nowhere to be seen and the only answer to our knock was a distant cry from somewhere deep within the house, like the voice of a ghost. The windows were all shuttered and, if I had not known otherwise, I would have supposed the house to be unoccupied. However, somebody was at home and I felt that I would soon be face to face with Edward Murdstone, the man who had married Dorothea Barton when she was little more than a child and kept her prisoner, as he had her elderly father. I had no doubt his motive was to gain her inheritance. He had, I was sure, killed the old man and had him buried somewhere far away where no questions would be asked. My aunt Betsey Trotwood had unwittingly hit upon the truth when she observed that the name Murdstone sounded like "murderer", for surely that was exactly what he was.

At my signal Mr Chillip's manservants began to break the door. The rotten wood splintered easily and we were soon inside. As I walked through the rooms, undecorated since my childhood, I relived the pains and pleasures of my youth. There were marks on the wallpaper where my mother's pictures had hung and there was the old chair where Peggotty had sat sewing. I could feel tears prick my eyes as I made my way upstairs. There was no sound now and I knew Murdstone had heard us.

I stood silent on the landing and, after a few moments, I heard a scratching sound coming from my old bedroom. Mr

Chillip and the servants were climbing the stairs behind me, but when I held my finger to my lips they froze like statues.

I crept across the landing and flung open the bedroom door. Then I stepped inside the dark, shuttered room and looked around. In this place I had been beaten and had bitten Murdstone's hand until it bled before being imprisoned there for my crime. As my eyes adjusted to the gloom, I saw a figure crouched in the corner – just as I had crouched in terror all those years ago. "Murdstone," I said, my voice trembling.

The figure looked up but it wasn't Murdstone's dark, handsome eyes that met mine. This was a very old man with long white locks and a bent body. I saw something in his face that looked like hope.

"Mr Bartholomew Barton, I presume," I said as I helped him painfully to his feet.

Mr Barton was forgetful and confused but in body, according to Mr Chillip, he was well. We took him from the Rookery where he had been held prisoner for many years by Murdstone and his associates, his property purloined with the aid of the wretched lawyer, Mr Passnidge, kept alive only for his signature on various documents.

I found his reunion with his daughter Dorothea in the Chillips' parlour particularly touching. Neither at first could believe their good fortune. Dorothea had long ago been told her father was dead and Murdstone had told Bartholomew that his daughter had no wish to see him as he was mad – a lunatic. I hated Murdstone then with all the strength of my childhood loathing for the man. Then I remembered that he might be out there somewhere, biding his time. I would not let him win.

With Chillip in attendance, I called upon Miss Murdstone, only to be told by her servant, Dawkins, that she had returned home from her visit to her brother's devoted follower and, on discovering Mrs Murdstone's absence, had driven off in the carriage, presumably in search of her errant sister-in-law.

I wondered afresh where Edward Murdstone could have gone. Had he had an inkling that his perfidy was about to be discovered and left without a word to his sister, a precaution lest she betray him by some accidental word or look? My own guess was that he had gone to London. He had had business dealings there in the past and it is easy for a man to lose himself in that great city.

There was nothing more we could do. We returned to the Chillip residence to find Dorothea with colour in her cheeks and a glow of contentment in her eyes as she sat with her father in the parlour, her white fingers touching his brown mottled hand. She looked up and gave me a nervous smile.

"There is still no word of your husband," I said. "And your sister-in-law is not at home."

She released her father's hand gently and stood up. "Mr Copperfield, I must speak with you," she said softly and led the way into the garden.

As we stood there beneath a tall oak tree, I saw that she was shaking. "Have no fear," I said. "Now that the truth of his dealings is known, he will not dare come back to torment you further. I have no doubt that he killed his associate, Mr Passnidge, so if he returns, he will be arrested for murder and hang for it. You and your father are safe now." I did not know if this was true but I was anxious to reassure her.

She put her hand on my sleeve. "I know where my husband is, Mr Copperfield." She gazed beyond me into the middle distance. "He is the Divine Nature and the Divine Nature would never leave his followers. He always made this promise and I can assure you he has not broken it."

I took hold of her hand. The poor woman was indeed deluded. "If you know where he is, please tell me. I would speak with him," I said, humouring her. For I had no wish to see the man I had always suspected of bringing about my mother's death unless it was to bring him to justice.

"Very well," she whispered. "I will take you to him."

We stood and faced the Divine Nature and the statue seemed to stare back at us, defiant. I glanced at Chillip and saw that he looked mildly alarmed. This was his first visit to the chapel.

Dorothea knelt with her eyes closed as if in prayer. I touched her shoulder and she flinched. "Where is he?" I asked as gently as I could.

She stood up and approached the Divine Nature, her eyes fixed on the image. She put both hands on the altar and knelt again, as though she was worshipping her husband. Then, to my surprise, she slowly raised the blue velvet cloth that covered the altar to reveal something beneath. An oilcloth enveloping a shape the size of a man. An unpleasant odour suddenly filled the chapel, wafting from the direction of the altar. I had smelt something like it before. The odour of death.

It was Mr Chillip who moved first. He rushed to the altar and ushered Dorothea away gently, placing her into my care before putting a handkerchief to his face and unfolding the oilcloth. I knew what he would find there but it still shocked me to look upon the dead face of Edward Murdstone.

Dorothea's body was shaking as I led her outside and we walked until we reached a stone bench beneath a willow tree. "Please tell me all." I sensed she wished to make a confession. That was why she'd led us there.

She sat there, her pale hand clutching mine, her eyes cast downwards as she spoke. "I was driven beyond endurance. A wife is the property of her husband but I had no inkling of . . ." A tear ran down her cheek. "And when he took my father into his power . . ."

"How did he . . .?

"When my father became ill, my husband took him to a house he owned, claiming he would be cared for there until he recovered. But instead he kept him as a prisoner and pacified him with laudanum, as he did me. I was told he was dead but all the time he was a prisoner. Edward had this . . . creature – a lawyer from Lowestoft. Of late I have pretended to take my medicine and poured it away. On the night the lawyer came I crept downstairs and listened at the door. I heard them talking of my father, the old man at the Rookery. When the lawyer left I followed him."

"With a cloak over your nightgown. You were mistaken for a ghost."

She continued as though she hadn't heard me. "I challenged him, pleaded with him to tell me if there was hope that my father wasn't dead, but he refused to answer. He backed away from me in fright and fell into the water and drowned. I was frightened so I returned to the house. I didn't know what else to do."

"And your husband?"

"He had discovered my absence and he was waiting for me. He took me to the chapel . . . said I should be punished for defying The Divine Nature. He forced me to kneel and he . . . he raised his stick to strike me. Then something miraculous happened. He fell to the ground as though God had struck him down. A judgment."

"A seizure, perhaps."

"A judgment. I dragged his body beneath the altar and covered him in an oilcloth I found there. It took all my strength."

"Why didn't you tell your sister-in-law he was dead?"

She thought for a few moments. "I confess I enjoyed seeing her distress. She and her brother had brought me such misery and I wished her to have a taste of it." She looked away. "I am very wicked to have such unholy thoughts."

I put my hand on hers. "I too suffered under the Murdstones in my youth. Murdstone beat me once and I bit him for his pains."

She gave a weak smile.

"As his widow, the house is now yours. You have come into your rightful inheritance. You can care for your father and . . ."

I was interrupted by a shout from Mr Chillip. He stood some way off and beckoned me. I begged Dorothea to excuse me and joined my old friend in the chapel, covering my nose with my sleeve.

He uncovered Murdstone's body. His dead eyes stared at me and his lips were drawn up into a familiar snarl – one I had seen so many years before when he had beaten my young body to break me like a dog.

The good doctor was about to point something out to me but, at that moment, I heard the sound of galloping hooves. As I ran outside I saw a carriage clattering up the drive. It was Miss Murdstone, returned to receive the grim news she had been dreading.

When she saw me running towards her, she stopped the carriage. And as soon as I'd acquainted her with the truth, she dashed to the chapel and cradled her brother's dead, stinking body in her arms, howling like an animal in pain.

Edward Murdstone's funeral was a colourful event. A dozen women – followers of the Divine Nature, deprived of their master – were sobbing and wailing in a most unseemly manner. Jane Murdstone, black-veiled like some great crow, was dignified in comparison. I was the only mourner who had not been a devotee. I felt out of place in such a gathering.

The widow was absent from the proceedings. She had returned to the house with her father and, with new-found boldness, she had ordered her sister-in-law to pack her bags and move to the Rookery – a neglected and miserable establishment.

Jane Murdstone made no move at the funeral to thank me for my efforts. Perhaps she had forgotten that I had come there at her behest. I put her omission down to grief.

I longed to return to Agnes and my work but Mr and Mrs Chillip begged me to stay the night after the funeral and travel back the next day. I accepted their kind invitation, for Mr Chillip had always been a favourite companion of mine in my youth and one of the few people who remembered my dear dead parents in life.

"David," he said as we sat together after our evening meal. "There is a matter that concerns me."

"What is that?" I asked the doctor as I sipped a warming glass of port.

He hesitated, a worried frown on his face. "As a doctor, I examined the body of Edward Murdstone and I observed

marks which . . . which were not consistent with Mrs Murdstone's story. The flesh was broken on his skull and there was
. . . There was a mark on his arm that looked like the bite of
some animal . . . or a human being. I fear I have done wrong
to stay silent.''

There was a long silence. Then I spoke. "You suspect that
it was not the Almighty who struck Murdstone down? You
think that Mrs Murdstone took her own revenge for the
wrongs done to her?" I thought for a few moments. "We
never found the stick she claims he was about to use to beat
her, did we?"

"No indeed, David. The point is, what do we do about our
suspicions?"

I did not answer. My mind was filled with remembrances
of my childhood, of the beatings I had received at the dead
man's hands, of his cold brutality and hypocrisy, of the time
when I too had stopped my suffering with a hearty bite to his
threatening hand. Edward Murdstone was dead and buried
and in my heart I wished him to stay that way. The suffering
had to end.

The next day I returned to Agnes and my home, praying,
as I do now, that I would never hear the name Murdstone
again.

I Encounter an Old Friend
and a New Mystery

Derek Wilson

This is the second of our stories inspired by David Copperfield. *Derek Wilson is a noted historian and biographer who has written books about Henry VIII, Charles I, Francis Drake and the Earl of Leicester. His mystery novels include the Tim Lacy series of art thrillers, starting with* The Triarchs (1994), *plus several historical mysteries, including a series about George Keene, who served as a spy for William Pitt at the time of the wars with France, and another about Nathaniel Gye, a Cambridge don with an interest in the supernatural.*

Over the years I have come to regard the forenoon hours as those most conducive to work. Every morning after breakfast it has been my custom – religiously adhered to – to repair to my desk and to write until midday. The servants are under strict instructions not to disturb me. It was, therefore, with not a little annoyance that one February morning I heard a diffident tap at my study door. It opened to admit our maid bearing a silver salver.

"Begging your pardon, Sir," said she, "but there is a

gentleman called who says you'll want to see him. I told him you don't see no-one of a morning but he was most persistent and as mistress is out I didn't know what I should do, so I put him in the drawing room and said I'd bring his card." She proffered the tray and I picked up the visiting card.

The next instant I sprang to my feet in astonishment. There, elaborately engraved, I read the name Wilkins Micawber JP. Scarcely believing that our unannounced visitor could really be our old friend who, a dozen years previously had departed for the colonies vowing never to return, I rushed across the hallway and threw open the drawing-room door. And there he was – a little more rotund, his face of a duskier hue, his frame enclosed in a topcoat of elegant cut – but without doubt the same affable, ebullient Micawber whose fortunes had been so intimately linked with my own all those years ago. I took him warmly by the hand scarcely finding words to express my delight at seeing him.

"My dear Copperfield," he responded, "dull would he be of soul who was not stirred to the very depths of his being by the warmth of that greeting. The cognizance that, years and oceans have not dimmed the esteem and – dare I say – the affection in which you were once so good as to hold your former indebted servant, instantly banishes from the memory the cruel wave and savage tempest through which it has been my lot to pass on my pilgrimage to these familiar haunts . . ."

"Never doubt it, Mr Micawber. Never doubt it," I rejoined. "Why, to see you again – and looking so . . . prosperous – is a joy I never expected to experience in this world."

At that moment Agnes entered, followed by the maid bearing a tray with glasses and a steaming jug of punch. As the liquid was poured my wife echoed my greeting and it was she who broached the questions which were uppermost in both our minds.

"What brings you back to England, dear Mr Micawber? Are your family with you?"

A look of deep melancholy pervaded his features. "I can report that all the Micawber offspring are so well settled in their various avocations that it would have been no kindness to inflict upon them the long return journey to Albion. However," he added, his voice assuming a sombre tone, "I have also to report that their mother, she who has been the architect of our domestic happiness and the buttress of my life, has preceded us all to a better world."

I commiserated with him and indicated, what was no less than the truth, that I could not conceive of Mr Micawber without Mrs Micawber. I, who was no stranger to grief, yet found it difficult to understand the degree of loss this stalwart gentleman must be experiencing. She whose unshakeable faith had been his only support through so many ordeals was no more. It occurred to me that this return to the scenes of those trials might be some attempt to recapture associations and revivify memories. I was soon to discover that this was but part of Micawber's motivation.

We, of course, pressed our old friend to stay under our roof for just as long as he had a mind to do so, an offer he accepted with his accustomed effusive display of gratitude. It was as he and I sat before a blazing hearth that evening with glasses of mulled wine after dinner, Agnes having made the excuse of domestic responsibilities in order to leave us alone, that Micawber sat forward in his chair and announced in almost conspiratorial tones, "My dear Copperfield, you were kind enough earlier to enquire as to the reason for my return to Albion's wave-tossed shore. I fear that my response was less than candid – No, I will not say that I lacked candour, for transparency, I like to feel, has always been a mark of Wilkins Micawber Esquire. If my narrative was lacking in some particulars it was delicacy that placed a turnkey on my lips. There are certain events which I forbear to broach within the hearing of Mrs Copperfield."

I was instantly alarmed, fearing that Mr Micawber had not entirely shaken off the Micawber of old with his propensity for getting into difficulties. "My dear friend," said I, "If some trouble has befallen you . . ."

He held up his hand. "No, indeed. Indeed no, Mr Copperfield. Ever since those friends, than which no man ever had better, set our feet upon the broad path of opportunity these twelve years since the clan Micawber has prospered." He paused, staring into the fire's crimson heart. "There are, sadly, those who do not share such good fortune even in that land where fortune so abundantly suckles her eager brood." He took out his notecase and from it extracted a small square of card, with dog-eared corners. He passed it across and I found myself looking at a studio portrait of a lady seated on a chaise longue with her husband and three small children ranged around her. The sitters projected an air of serene domestic contentment.

"A handsome family," I observed. "Who are they?"

Micawber took the photograph and gazed upon it for several moments with an expression of mingled sadness and anger. "Handsome, indeed, and happy and industrious and deserving of the good fortune that domiciled with them for many years before the shadow of a great evil fell across their path."

"What evil?" I enquired.

"Murder most foul," Micawber replied in a voice little above a whisper. He sat back in the chair, eyes raised towards the glow of the gas lamp.

"Jed Gringlade – that is the name of this paterfamilias – was a hard-working, honest, conscientious, young man, employed by a firm of chandlers at West India Dock. To the noble enterprise of a highly esteemed proprietor Gringlade brought the dedication and vigour of youth. He rose steadily in the estimation of his employer and was, within a few years, that employer's right-hand-man of business. He had also captured the affections of the estimable merchant's daughter, Emily. In due time the two were united in that blessed state of which you and I, Mr Copperfield, have received ample proof. All this was some seven years ago and, for five of those years, no one, I venture to suggest, could have been happier than Mr and Mrs Gringlade and the three little Gringlades with which their union was blessed."

He paused and a long sigh emanated from deep within him. "Alas for 'domestic happiness, thou only bliss of Paradise that has survived the Fall'. The cup was destined to be dashed from their lips. Wormwood and gall became their appointed portion."

At this point I interrupted my old friend's narrative. Some faint memory stirred in my brain. "This firm of chandlers," I enquired, "was it, by any chance, Avebury and Sons?"

"The very same," Micawber rejoined. "You are acquainted with the lamentable tale?"

"I recall reading something of it. The newspapers at the time made much of the gruesome details. Old Mr Avebury was done to death in his quayside office, was he not?"

Micawber nodded mournfully.

"And suspicion fell upon his junior partner. Would that have been Gringlade?"

"It was, indeed, that unfortunate gentleman."

"But how did you come by the story and the photograph, Mr Micawber? Such a tale is surely of no interest in the distant colonies."

"The full details of that tragedy – at least insofar as he had been unable to unravel them were vouchsafed to me by Jed Gringlade, himself."

My eyes opened wide at that news. "But surely," I expostulated, "that is impossible. The City reporter of *The Times* indicated that Gringlade, full of remorse, had put an end to his life – drowned within yards of where his father-in-law had been struck down."

Micawber nodded sagely. "So Gringlade intended the world to believe, and whether it was tenderness or folly or mere self-preservation that drove him to so desperate a deception Wilkins Micawber will not be the judge of." He paused. "It all fell out upon this wise. Gringlade was beset by the police with question upon question. At a time when all his energies should have been devoted to comforting his distraught wife he was shocked to discover that he was under the necessity of having to defend himself from the guardians of the law who became fixed in their minds that he was their man. Rather than add to the distress of his family by subjecting them to the humiliation a public trial would have occasioned he contrived to disappear. His professional calling brought Gringlade into contact with numerous men who ply their business in great waters and, being of a sociable disposition, he counted not a few of them as friends. He assured me that captains who knew him well were convinced of his innocence. One such readily offered him a berth aboard his clipper and permitted him to work his passage."

"And Mrs Gringlade knew nothing of this?" I enquired. "The double loss must have been unbearable."

"Poor Gringlade acted in haste and desperation. On the long journey he had time in plenty for reflection. He asked one more kindness of the captain who conveyed him to colonial safety. It was he who brought Mrs Gringlade a message informing her of his safety and his determination to send for the family as soon as he had established himself in a strange land."

"And I suppose," said I, "that that is the commission you have now undertaken."

Micawber's glass being now empty, he applied a red-hot poker to the jug and poured himself a fresh draught. This proceeding occupied a full minute during which he offered no response to my observation. At length he said, "There's a deal of injustice in this world, Copperfield, a deal of injustice, as you and I have good cause to know. Gringlade settled in our little community as an industrious man in a modest way of life. He was of a solitary disposition and seldom could he be prevailed upon to join in our communal revels. I was gratified, then, when he singled me out as one worthy of his confidence. Having learned of my intended visit here he confessed all, calculating that I who had the authority to order his arrest and repatriation, was a man of sensibility and independent mind."

"He made an excellent choice," I rejoined.

"Having satisfied myself of Gringlade's veracity," continued Micawber, "I could not but be incensed at the vile injustice of his situation – a family divided and condemned to years of misery by the actions of some blackguard, doubtless still at liberty. 'Wilkins Micawber,' says I to myself, 'these things may not be.' I induced Gringlade to convey to me every known detail of the crime that had led to his ruin."

"To what end?" I asked, for I was truly mystified as to my old friend's intentions.

"You will readily imagine that no day has elapsed these two years past on which poor Gringlade has not brooded on the circumstance surrounding his father-in-law's death. Some of those circumstances were so singular as to persuade him that the villain was someone well known to old Mr Avebury and his family. Gringlade was, of course, in no position to convey his suspicions to the authorities. And there's the injustice of it, Copperfield. There's the injustice that must be addressed. I gave my assurance to Jed Gringlade that I would not only convey his message to Mrs Gringlade but employ my best endeavours in the attempt to clear his name."

"But, surely," I protested, "after all this time it will be difficult to ascertain the truth."

"Perhaps not as difficult as you might imagine, Copperfield." Micawber paused to take a long draught of his beverage. "With every passing month since the perpetration of the vile deed the perpetrator's assurance will have grown. By now, he will believe himself perfectly secure and that very conviction may lead him into betraying himself."

My face must have given ample evidence of my reservation, for Micawber hastened to justify his belief in the success of his mission.

"Gringlade has reached the conclusion," he said, "that there are only three people likely to have had any reason to attack Mr Avebury and the opportunity to do so at the time and place of the crime."

What Micawber described as the "evidential details" were briefly as follows:

On an evening in February Jed Gringlade had received at his home a message from Mr Avebury to go immediately to his father-in-law's office. He had not hesitated but had taken a lantern and ventured forth alone into the wet and wintry darkness. Arrived at the warehouse he let himself in with his key. A lamp was burning in the office situated on the first floor. As he ascended the staircase he noticed wet footprints which indicated that someone else had recently come the same way. On entering the office he beheld the appalling spectacle of his benefactor, his employer and the father of his beloved wife sprawled on his back with blood glistening around a wound in his chest which cannot but have proved instantly fatal. Despite his shock, he had carried out an immediate search of the premises and satisfied himself that the assassin was not lurking there. He first assumed that Avebury must have interrupted a burglar but nothing in the office had been disturbed and a sum of money in Avebury's desk drawer was intact. At this point there came a loud knocking at the outer door. On opening it Gringlade had discovered a constable come to investigate the anonymous report of a disturbance in the warehouse. He led the guardian of the law to the office and revealed his awful discovery. His mind was in such a whirl that he was unable to see the significance of the sequence of events – Avebury's note, the mysterious nocturnal visitor, the equally mysterious summoning of the police. It was only days later that he examined his father-in-law's missive, thrust hurriedly into a pocket, and discovered it to be a forgery. By that time he had already embarked on his course of deception. Though he was not immediately detained by the police, it was obvious that they suspected him of the murder and that his arrest was imminent. In his panic he could discern no means of establishing his innocence and had, therefore, organized his apparent suicide. Telling Emily, that he was going for a walk, he had hidden himself until nightfall, then, leaving some of his clothes at the water's edge, secretly gone on shipboard. The vessel sailed on the morning tide.

At this point in his narrative Micawber produced the closely written sheet of paper. "I prevailed upon Gringlade to set down in detail his own reflections on the crime and his suspicions as to its possible agent," he explained.

At that moment Agnes re-entered the drawing room. We talked for a further hour and were very far from exhausting our store of shared reminiscences when our guest's head began to nod. It was time to retire to our chambers. Lamps were fetched and goodnights said.

Of recent years I had fallen into the habit of personally checking all our ground floor doors and windows before settling for the night. It was when, observing this ritual, that I returned to the drawing room that I noticed that Micawber had left Gringlade's report upon the mantelpiece. I realized that he must have placed it there when rising on my wife's entrance. Since it was obviously a document of great importance to our friend, I picked it up for safe keeping. I had advanced as far as the library, my last port of call, when curiosity got the better of me. Sitting at the table, I laid Gringlade's document on the table and smoothed it out.

The hand was clear, the letters well formed. Obviously they had been inscribed by someone accustomed to writing accurate records or accounts. The text was a model of conciseness and matched the penmanship. It read:

"For more than two years I have pondered the appalling crime inflicted upon my family and considered who might be responsible. At the behest of Mr Wilkins Micawber, Magistrate, I here set down every detail I can recall which might be of help in discovering the truth.

Item: Since robbery was not the motive, I deduce that the murderer may have been someone with a grudge against the late Mr Avebury.

Item: Since it was intended that I should be discovered in close proximity to the deceased I deduce that the murderer was someone with cause to wish me harm.

Item: I further deduce that the murderer was someone who might have thought to gain some advantage from the liquidation of Avebury and Son.

Item: Our business had only one serious rival, an enterprise under the proprietorship of Joseph Stickle, as unscrupulous a man as it would be possible to meet. He would gladly have seen Avebury and Son close their doors and resorted to several underhand tactics to bring that about.

>It was only days before my employer's melancholy demise that I discovered one of Stickle's men loosening a wheel on one of our wagons. Yet I find it hard to believe that even Stickle would resort to deliberate murder in cold blood.
>
>Item: A more likely . . .

I was able to read no further, for, at that instant, our hall clock chimed midnight and I knew that Agnes must be growing anxious and wondering why I had not come to bed. Sleep did not readily visit me that night, for I was much affected by the tragedy Micawber had related and considerably exercised as to whether his optimism regarding his ability to right an old wrong might not be misplaced. As we sat at breakfast the following morning I ventured to ask whether he might value some assistance on his quest. His response was unhesitating.

"My dear Copperfield. My dear, dear Copperfield," he enthused. "What a capital idea and what a good-hearted gentleman you are, to be sure."

Our simple arrangements were soon made, the carriage was ordered and at ten o'clock we set off for the docks. As we travelled I invited Micawber to explain the tactics he proposed to employ in pursuing his enquiry.

He sat back against the padded leather and expatiated. "We of the magistracy," he said, "distinguish between the criminal mind and the non-criminal mind. The former, I regret to say, are hardened by the cruelties of their chosen profession. The shafts of human feeling or remorse seldom penetrate their iron-like carapace. Fortunately, the offender we seek is a man with a non-criminal mind. He has become possessed of a demon. It may be greed or rage or jealousy but, whatever the name of his particular *diabolus*, it will continue to torment him. It will give him no rest. It will whisper in his nocturnal ear that his sin is discovered and fear will be the companion of his waking hours."

"Well," said I, "that may be so but how will it help us to unmask the villain?"

"We have but to suggest," Micawber replied "that we know all and observe his reaction. Watch the eyes, Copperfield. Watch the eyes. However loud and fervent may be his protestations of innocence, his eyes will betray his alarm and his guilt."

"Gringlade ruminated three suspects," I observed. "One was a business rival, by name Joseph Stickle. Who were the others?"

Micawber needed no recourse to his notes in proffering his reply. "Shortly before the doleful event leading to Gringlade's precipitate flight he had dismissed a certain George Narbig for pilfering. The rogue loudly asserted his innocence and swore he would be revenged on the man he called his 'persecutor'. The only other person who bore him ill will was a young fellow employee by the name of Jethro Mallerby."

"What was the cause of his disaffection?" I enquired.

"The pangs of disprized love. He competed for the hand of Emily Avebury but was bested by Gringlade."

"And since Emily was Avebury's only child, whoever won her would also inherit the business," I observed. "That would be motive enough to remove Avebury and his anointed successor."

Our conveyance described a sinuous path through the narrow, congested streets of London's dockland with its babel sounds and competing, pungent odours and emerged, none too soon, on the broad quay front of West India Dock. We enquired our way to the premises of Messrs Avebury and Son. We had abandoned the carriage and were concluding our journey on foot between the piled rows of crates, bales and barrels waiting to be loaded on the ships whose masts and spare reared upwards to our right when my companion drew my attention to a building we were passing. Blackened timbers and the sky visible through its glassless casements eloquently told the tale of recent disaster, but what was of especial interest to Micawber and me was the name board still legible above the boarded entrance: 'Stickles Ships: Chandler'.

"Alas for Joseph Stickle," I said. "It appears that

fate has taken a hand in the rivalry between him and Aveburys."

Arrived at our journey's end, we enquired after the proprietor. It had been agreed that we should pose as gentlemen fitting out a schooner for a pleasure cruise to the coasts and islands and the Caribbean. This imposing subterfuge would, we hoped, gain us an introduction to whoever had stepped into Avebury's shoes as the master of this emporium and provide us with a starting point for our enquiries. We were, accordingly, led through the warehouse to a flight of stairs at the top of which was a door bearing the legend "Office". We entered a large room in which it seemed that every horizontal surface – shelf, table, cabinet and even chair carried its own burden of ledgers, files and loose papers. Three desks were arranged in a row facing the door. Two were occupied by clerks but behind the centre desk, frowningly immersed in checking entries in a large, leather-bound volume, sat a lady dressed in black. We had scarcely recovered our surprise, when the lady in question looked up momentarily from her labour to offer us a cursory greeting. "Good morning, gentlemen," she said, "if it's victualling you require, I'm afraid we are not currently taking on new business."

Recognition was immediate. Micawber was unable to contain his astonishment. "Why, bless my soul, it is Mrs Gringlade, is it not?" At that, she looked up sharply and I noticed that the clerks also stared at us in sudden interest. After a long pause the lady replied, "You are mistaken Sir. My name is Mallerby."

It was some moments before I could think of a suitable response. Then, "You must forgive, my friend, Madam," I said. "You bear a striking resemblance to someone with whom we are slightly acquainted."

The lady could not conceal her alarm. She instantly clapped her hands. It was a signal her clerks obviously understood, for they rose on the instant and hurried from the room. When the door had closed behind them their mistress invited us to be seated and, taking the only two chairs unencumbered by business documents, we complied.

"It is I who must crave forgiveness, Sir," she said. "The name of Gringlade brings back painful memories. Jedediah Gringlade was the name of my first husband. Our marriage was of short duration and, regrettably, not happy. It was a business arrangement, entered into at my father's behest. You will understand, therefore, if I try to close my mind to painful memories." She scrutinized us with eyes that were dark and searching. "May I enquire how you recognized me? I think I have never had the pleasure of acquaintance with you. Who are you? Whence came you?"

We introduced ourselves in brief terms, then Micawber said, "Madam, I come as an emissary from your husband, Mr Gringlade, as fine and upstanding a gentleman as it has ever been my pleasure to encounter, and one, dare I say it, who would be mortified to hear himself described in the terms you have employed to us."

Mrs Mallerby uttered a light laugh but I fancied that there was about it a suggestion of hysteria. "You are very much mistaken, Mr Micawber. I fear you have been the victim of some strange masquerade. Mr Gringlade has been dead these two years past – drowned in the very river that flows past these premises."

"Did you see his body?" I enquired.

Abruptly the lady stood up, her body a-tremble. "This is monstrous behaviour, gentlemen!" she expostulated. "I know not why you should want to distress a poor widow so. It is cruel. Cruel! Please leave." She took up a little bell from the desk and rang it vigorously. Her two acolytes re-entered. "Mr Walsh, show these gentlemen out," she ordered.

The clerk led our way down the staircase. At its foot we passed a man talking agitatedly with a companion and waiting to ascend. There was something about him that compelled attention. I can only describe him as a ruffian dressed as a gentleman. His face was thin, verging on gaunt and disfigured by a scar across one cheek. His coat was of an expert cut with velvet collar and gilt buttons. It covered a frame that was slightly bent forward, as though he were perpetually endeavouring with difficulty to hear what others said to him. He looked equally hard at us, then climbed swiftly to the office we had just left.

"Well, Micawber," said I, as we walked back along the quay, "here's a strange turn of events. Mrs Gringlade, it seems, believes in her husband's guilt and also his suicide. Who's to be believed?"

My friend turned upon me a face lined with such indignation as I did not recall ever having observed even in the days of his own severe trials. "Wilkins Micawber has ever held the gentle sex in high esteem," he said, "but may I observe – yes, I believe in this instance I may truthfully observe – that that *person* it has just been our ill-fortune to encounter is a disgrace to womankind."

"You do not suppose that it might be Gringlade who is the villain? May he not have taken advantage of your good nature to discover whether the coast was now clear for him to return to England?"

"I will stake my life on his honesty, Copperfield," Micawber averred. "My confidence is buttressed by the untruths that lady who calls herself by the name of Mallerby has just uttered."

"But we are in no position to judge the accuracy of her testimony," I protested.

Micawber's agitated stride came to a full halt. Turning to face me, he said. "The lady claimed to believe her husband dead. Wilkins Micawber knows to the contrary. Gringlade sent a message back to his wife informing her of his safe arrival in the colonies. It was entrusted to a certain Mr Llewelyn, master of *Elizabeth Shaw*, a fine clipper ship. The chosen courier is a man of excellent character whom I am privileged to count among my acquaintances. Llewelyn vouched for the safe delivery of the missive. If George Llewelyn asserts that something is so, it is so."

We resumed our walk but had not advanced more than a dozen paces before three men emerged from a side alley and placed themselves squarely in our path. The leader of this little gang was instantly recognizable as the scar-faced man whom we had briefly encountered not five minutes since. It was he who spoke. "Not so fast, you two," he shouted. "We don't like strangers who come here asking questions." He spoke with a heavy continental accent. "Come and discuss your business with us."

"I think not," I replied, with as much calm as I could muster.

At that the trio took a pace forward and Scarface's companions brandished truncheons. I looked around for possible assistance, but the only nearby occupants of the dockside were studiously attending to their own affairs. I reflected that gangs of armed thugs were not uncommon along the waterfront and that prudent bystanders were unlikely to interfere with them. Our carriage was some fifty yards beyond the human barrier. There was no possibility of our regaining it in safety.

Scarface addressed us again with a smile. "I said, 'Come with us'," he repeated. "This way." He gestured towards the alley from which he and his friends had just emerged. It took little imagination to envisage what our fate would be if we accompanied our assailants into that dark, overhung passageway.

"And I replied, 'I think not",' I said. From the pocket of my topcoat I withdrew the small pistol I am accustomed to carrying on those occasions when my affairs take me to the less salubrious areas of the city. I pointed it at the chest of the scar-faced man. "We do, indeed, have business to discuss," I said. "You will accompany us."

For several seconds the rogue glared at us. Then he muttered something to his companions. One of them took a step towards us but when I pointed my weapon at him he stopped. "Our business is with Mr Narbig," I said. "If either of you other gentlemen is here by the time I count to five I will shoot him. One!"

I had only reached three when Scarface's companions concluded that discretion was the better part of valour. They slunk away towards the murky hinterland of the docks.

"Now, Mr Narbig, be so good as to precede us and

remember that my pistol is pointed at the small of your back."

Moments later we were seated in the carriage, Micawber and I on either side of our unwilling guest and my gun prodded into his ribs. I was gratified to see that the ruffian was now perspiring. I gave instructions to the coachman to take us out of this overcrowded region and into the more secluded suburbs.

"Who are you? What you want? Why you come here? How you know my name?" he demanded.

"My friend here will ask the questions," I said. "You will answer them and you would be well advised to answer them truthfully, for be sure that we shall know if you are lying."

Micawber cleared his throat and addressed our prisoner in what I assumed to be his well-practised, stern magisterial manner. "We are here to investigate the murder of Mr Solomon Avebury. I adjure you most solemnly to tell us all you know on that mournful subject."

He shrugged. "I know nothing," he averred.

I thrust the pistol's barrel more firmly into his side. "It is the truth. I was not here when it happened," he insisted.

"You had a grudge against your ex-employer and his assistant, Mr Gringlade," Micawber persisted.

"I was angry. Yes," he admitted. "They dismissed me without cause. It was unjust."

"Where do you claim that you were?" Micawber demanded.

"I was in Liverpool, looking for work," Narbig explained. "Avebury and Gringlade, they had blackened my name here. No one would employ me."

"And yet I see that you have prospered," said I, feeling the cloth of his coat. "Dock workers cannot afford such apparel."

"A rich aunt died and left me some money," replied he truculently.

"So, we are to infer from your silence that you have nothing to tell us," Micawber suggested. "Well, we have testimony to the contrary."

"Pooh," Narbig scoffed. "Testimony from who?"

"Mr Jedediah Gringlade," Micawber replied.

"Nonsense! Gringlade is dead," our prisoner expostulated.

"On the contrary," Micawber rejoined. "He is very much alive and has gathered the evidence that will clear his name."

Narbig shook his head. "No, it's not possible! She told me . . ." He stopped abruptly.

"She? I take it you refer to Mrs Mallerby. And what was it that that good lady told you?" I asked.

Narbig pursed his lips.

"Well, Micawber," I said. "It seems this fellow is determined to carry his silence to the grave. I suggest we waste no more time with him. Another twenty minutes and we shall be in a quiet stretch of woodland. That will suit our purpose very well. Let us enjoy the ride in peace."

"What you mean? Who are you people? Who set you onto me?" Narbig demanded, now very agitated.

By way of reply I put my finger to my lips and sat back against the cushions.

"I tell you I was not there!" the wretched man persisted. "I do not know what happened."

"Of course you were not there. How could you have been? But you most certainly do know what happened and I think you have done very well for yourself by that knowledge," I said. "But no matter. Since you choose not to cooperate, you are of no further use to us."

We had entered a belt of open country near Hackney and I signalled the coachman to stop. "Mr Micawber," I said, "would you be good enough to step down and scout out the land. A quiet lane, perhaps, through those woods up yonder should suit our purposes. I'll keep an eye on this fellow."

Micawber stepped into the roadway, leaving the carriage door open. With a sudden movement Narbig lurched for the opening, stumbled onto the highway, picked himself up, scrambled over a five-barred gate and set off across the fields as fast as his legs would carry him. Micawber's alarmed visage appeared in the doorway. "Copperfield, quick, man," he shouted, "after him. The blackguard is getting away!"

I laughed aloud. "My dear Micawber, you didn't suppose I was going to shoot the fellow, did you? I believe we would have discovered little more by further questioning and we must return to town quickly."

Micawber clambered back into the carriage and flopped onto the seat opposite. I gave instructions to the coachman who whipped up his horses and turned once more towards London. As we jolted along at a lively trot Micawber gazed at me in bewilderment. "My dear Copperfield," he uttered, "much disturbed as I have been by the alarming events of this morning, I experience a greater turbulence of spirit as a result of your actions. We had apprehended the murderer and were in train, as I supposed, to deliver him up to justice. Yet you have allowed him to escape and I dare opine that I am not sanguine of the likelihood of his recapture by the authorities."

"Oh, Narbig is not our man," I said. "I am sure of it. He has an intelligence somewhat above that of the usual international flotsam which drifts into every port in the world, but he lacks the wit to plan an elaborate crime. You have more acquaintance than I with men who live beyond the law. Would you not concur with me that our friend Narbig is a mere opportunist felon, a ruffian good for nothing but waylaying honest citizens or breaking into their houses? He will end up in a prison cell or on the gallows without any assistance from us."

Micawber nodded gravely. Then, laying his top hat beside him on the seat, he passed a hand over his bald dome and asked, "However did you know that Narbig was the miscreant referred to by Gringlade in his letter? Surely you cannot have decided that from the briefest of observations you were able to make on first encountering him."

"I own, dear friend, that that was fortuitous. It had always seemed to me that 'Narbig' was an unusual name, probably foreign. When we saw at Avebury's an uncouth fellow speaking with a heavy accent and facially disfigured – well the pieces of the puzzle came together."

Micawber frowned. "Your reasoning still eludes me," he protested.

"It is simple if one has a slight acquaintance with foreign languages. I have gained a smattering of German on my travels and in the Germanic tongue the word 'narbig' means 'scarred'. I imagine our friend had come to regard his facial wound – doubtless acquired in some tavern brawl or gang fracas – as a badge of honour and so elected to be known as 'Georg' or 'George, the Scarred'."

"And, yet, you still acquit this villain of the murder of the venerable Solomon Avebury?" he demanded.

"I do," said I, "though with the greatest reluctance, for it forces upon me a conclusion so horrible that I shrink from embracing it." As we travelled back to the scene of our earlier adventure I explained to Micawber the line of logic which offered a solution to the mysterious death of Solomon Avebury. His mournful visage was expressive of his unwillingness to concur with my conclusions and he raised several objections, most of which I was able to discount.

"Mallerby, then, must be our man," Micawber suggested, "for he seems to have won Mrs Gringlade and the business. Doubtless he prevailed upon the hapless and defenceless lady to accede to his importunities, even though she knew her husband still lived. What a double-dyed villain! Where do you suppose that we shall locate him?"

"That is a question we must put to his wife," I replied grimly.

When we reached Avebury's warehouse once more and enquired for Mrs Mallerby we were advised that, soon after our earlier visit, she had departed hurriedly for her own home. We obtained directions and hastened in pursuit. Our brief journey took us to a square of elegant houses arranged around an area of greensward and trees. A large carriage and four was drawn up outside the Mallerby residence, into which servants were loading boxes and valises. I jumped down to the cobbles and assisted my friend's descent. "Come, Micawber," said I. "I had feared we might be too late but it seems that we are arrived in the very nick of time."

We hurried into the house, making short work of a burly footman who sought to bar our entry. A quick investigation of the ground floor rooms yielded nothing and we hurried up a grand staircase. There, in a wide chamber containing an imposing, curtained bed and other rich furnishings, we discovered Mrs Mallerby. She stood by an elaborate *coiffeuse* in the midst of a sea of strewn garments which her maid was trying to pack into a large trunk. Mrs Mallerby was in the highest degree distracted. At the sight of us she uttered a little cry and sank upon the bed.

Micawber advanced into the room. "Madam," said he, in a tone at once grave and diffident, "we regret the necessity of imposing on you in this brusque and unannounced manner, but it is of the highest imperativeness that we speak with your husband. Please be so good as to inform us where he may be found."

"My dear friend," I interposed, "we shall not, I fear, locate Jethro Mallerby in this world. This lady, I feel sure, does not wear widow's weeds for her first husband. I am correct, am I not, madam?"

Mrs Mallerby nodded her drooped head and pressed a handkerchief to her eyes.

"What was the manner of his departure?" I demanded sternly.

"A sudden fever," she muttered. "Typhus, our physician diagnosed."

"Brought on, perhaps, by some noxious substance in his food," I suggested.

At that Micawber protested loudly. "My dear Copperfield," said he, "whatever can be your meaning. Surely, you do not suggest . . ."

I motioned him to silence and, at the same time indicated that Mrs Mallerby's maid should leave us. When we were alone and the lady had somewhat composed herself I admonished that flight was useless. "If you will unburden yourself to my friend and me we will undertake whatever lies in our power to help you," I promised.

When she looked up at us it was with a visage remarkably transformed. All feminine softness was departed from her features. Her voice when she replied was sharp.

"What help have I ever had from men?" she demanded scornfully. "Weak, ineffective creatures! My father was an incompetent businessman. Under his control the family concern was sliding steadily towards insolvency. Our rivals, especially Joseph Stickle, were taking trade away from us. I had no desire to end my days in the workhouse, yet that appeared to be the destination to which my father was steering us."

"Surely matters improved when you married Jedediah Gringlade," Micawber suggested. "I can vouch for the fact that he has a good business head on his shoulders."

"Oh, he was clever enough," Mrs Mallerby said, "but weak, *weak!* He would not stand up to my father. Our affairs progressed from bad to worse."

"I imagine," said I, "that Jethro Mallerby was a horse of a different colour."

"Jethro knew what he wanted and knew how to attain it," she agreed.

"So you selected him as your Macbeth to dispose of Duncan."

She glared at us. "I suppose Mr Gringlade has worked out some version of what happened on the night of my father's death. It was entirely Mallerby's plan."

"It was a diabolical plan and one with which you obviously concurred," I rejoined. "No one could have gained access to your father's office on that fateful night without a key and you can have been the only person, apart from your father and your husband, who had access to one. Doubtless you promised yourself to the murderer once your husband should have been hanged for a crime of which he was innocent."

"You must believe me when I say that I rejoice that he avoided that fate," the lady responded. "By his apparent death, Jedediah inadvertently completed the plan for the recovery of Avebury and Son. Under Mallerby's direction business boomed once more."

"I suppose," said Micawber, "that he brought to commercial affairs the same ruthlessness that fired his personal ambition. The combustion that engulfed the premises of your closest rival was, I dare suggest, no accident."

She shrugged. "Commerce is a battlefield, Mr Micawber," she said. "Jethro was an effective general and he soon acquired a lieutenant who was even more devoid of principle than himself."

"I take it you refer to George Narbig," Micawber suggested.

"Detestable, twisted, vile, little German!' Mrs Mallerby cried. "I curse the day he reappeared in our offices and pressed his services upon my husband. It was obvious to me that the man was trouble but I could not persuade Jethro. He believed Narbig and his thugs were worth employing on those nefarious enterprises which were necessary for our business success."

"But the servant rapidly became the master," I suggested.

She nodded miserably. "The wretch possessed himself of our business and family secrets and demanded ever larger sums for his silence. Now that I am obliged to take the helm and manage unaided, that scar-faced monster battens upon the business and takes whatever he wills for himself and his cronies."

The lady's demeanour had changed once again. Gone was the truculently out-thrust jaw and the eyes that glowed with defiance. Now the kerchief was frequently applied to her tear-stained cheeks. "You see, gentlemen, how a poor woman can be ill-used and preyed upon by wicked men," she sobbed.

"I see clearly how greed and ambition can corrupt people of either sex," I responded, "though it grieves us severely that you should have become a party to patricide and mariticide in order to maintain an appearance of gentility."

At that the creature threw herself at our feet. "No, no, gentlemen," she pleaded. "You must not believe me capable of such wickedness."

"What we believe is immaterial, Madam," I replied. "You may save your histrionics for a jury. And now we bid you good day."

From the Mallerby house we drove directly to the nearest police station and made our report. Darkness was spreading across the land before we were at liberty to set out for the familiar comforts of home. For much of our journey Micawber remained silent. I imagined that he was contemplating how he would report to Gringlade on the outcome of his mission. "Well, Copperfield," he remarked at last, "what a day of melancholy revelations we have had and whether or not one should welcome them I confess I am at a loss to comprehend. When truth comes calling one must open the door but he is sometimes an unwelcome guest. I am most grateful for your deliberations; I will not say your assistance for I am cognizant of the fact that I have contributed nothing to the events of this extraordinary day. Left to myself I should have reached entirely erroneous conclusions."

"My dear friend, you wrong yourself abysmally," I rejoined. 'Why, any success we enjoyed was entirely the result of following your methods. 'Watch the eyes,' you counselled and that is precisely what I did. As soon as we confronted Emily Mallerby there flickered in those dark eyes precisely those emotions of guilt and fear which you had counselled me to be alert for. Once it was clear that he lady had much to hide everything else fell into place. Her mourning apparel bespoke a woman not once but twice widowed. When Narbig accosted us so soon after our interview with Mrs Mallerby it was obvious that he had received a warning from her and that they were both anxious to discover exactly what we knew."

"What will happen to Mrs Mallerby, do you suppose?"

"Well," said I, "she has been an accessory to at last one murder and your friend's name can only be cleared if a guilty verdict is brought in against her. Whether or not she was complicit in the death of Mallerby is a matter for conjecture. I suspect the coroner may well authorize an exhumation."

"Poor Gringlade," Micawber sighed, "I cannot doubt that he will forever regret seeking the assistance of Wilkins Micawber."

"Not so, my dear friend," I protested. "Are you not forgetting three people who are more important to him that life itself and on whose behalf we must now expend our energies?"

It was three weeks later that I underwent a most extraordinary experience of *déjà vu*. Agnes and I found ourselves upon the deck of a merchant vessel in the river off Gravesend. Before us stood the substantial figure of Wilkins Micawber and his three charges. Jed Gringlade's six-year-old twin sons each held firmly a hand of their younger sister and each stared wide-eyed at the bustle of a crew preparing to set sail. Twelve intervening years dissolved away like Thames mist and I was once again watching Mr and Mrs Micawber and their children leave as emigrants to begin a new life. Yet the circumstances of this departure differed greatly from that earlier farewell. Micawber now travelled not as a steerage passenger to be crammed and jostled with scores of others quitting their homeland with mixed emotions for some alien shore, but as a respected, first-class voyager resuming his life as a prosperous member of colonial society. I could only hope that the little family which now accompanied him would discover with their loving father the security and fulfilment which had been the happy fate of their temporary guardian.

The bell sounded for visitors to depart. We all said our goodbyes and never did I embrace fellow man more warmly than in those few seconds of farewell to great-hearted Wilkins Micawber. We descended to our boat and stood away from the graceful ship as its sails unfurled. With a crack they bellied out in the stiff evening breeze. We waved and called "Goodbye! God speed!' across the water, then took our seats as the boatmen plied their oars.

Agnes looked at me curiously as we approached the shore. "My dear," she said, "why are you smiling so?"

"Oh," said I, "I am just envisaging the embellished version of this latest adventure with which Mr Wilkins Micawber, Magistrate, will be regaling all his friends – over and over again."

Awaiting the Dawn

Marilyn Todd

Dickens was strongly opposed to capital punishment and wrote several pieces about the subject for the Daily News. *Perhaps the most notable hanging he witnessed, following a notorious trial, was that of Frederick Manning and his wife Maria in November 1849 for the murder of Patrick O'Connor. Like all executions at the time, the hanging was in public, held at Horsemonger Gaol, and Dickens witnessed it from the roof of a neighbouring house. He also mingled with the crowds, gaining an impression of the public's reaction and wrote a letter to* The Times *condemning public executions. He regarded the whole spectacle as "inconceivably awful" and called for its abolition. He believed that rather than be a warning to people, executions attracted the criminal element and served to encourage them. Whether or not his voice had an effect is difficult to say, but it may have been a spark, though it was twenty years before public executions ceased.*

The Manning case and Dickens's reaction were the inspiration for the following story which is set twenty years later, just when public executions had been abolished. Marilyn Todd is best known for her series featuring that cunning vixen of ancient Rome, Claudia Seferus, starting with I, Claudia *(1995).*

She sat with her back straight, hands clasped in her lap. Had it not been for the cold, or perhaps something else, you would have called her handsome, with her dark hair tied back in a bun and her black satin dress pinched in at the waist.

Midnight came. One o'clock. Two.

As the cold intensified, the young woman seemed to draw strength from its cruelty, and through the tiny aperture that passed for a window, a solitary star shone in the blackness. Brighter than a turnkey's stare. Elizabeth watched until it moved out of sight, then shifted position ever so slightly. An economy of movement that attracted attention almost as much as the murder itself.

CENTRAL CRIMINAL COURT, Oct. 2.

Throughout the proceedings, the prisoner sat, as was her custom, as motionless as a statue, looking neither to the left nor the right, and was never once seen to turn her eyes towards her husband.

The Times. 3 Oct., 1868.

Elizabeth fixed on the point where the dawn would eventually brighten. At eight, the prison bell would toll. The chaplain, the governor, the attending surgeon and no less than two turnkeys would accompany the miserable procession towards what yesterday's editorial referred to as "*the awful change*". Her knuckles whitened. Is that what they thought? That placing a cap over someone's head, tightening a rope round their neck, then having the floor drop away equated to nothing more than a shift in personal circumstances?

Her gaze fell to the book lying open beside her. For these past twenty-four days – three clear Sundays being the stipulated interval between sentence being delivered and execution carried out – Elizabeth had had little to do except wait and read, read and wait, wait and read. In the end, she discovered, it was surprisingly easy to overpower reality with a good story, and in this case the book's author was Charles Dickens, its title *Great Expectations*.

The irony of neither was lost.

Subsequent to the hanging he witnessed of another couple who hit the headlines for cold-blooded murder, Mr Dickens launched a campaign for the abolition of capital punishment. And whilst he was not entirely successful in his endeavours, he was not entirely unsuccessful, either. After nineteen years, Parliament finally compromised by decreeing it should at least be a solemn and intimate affair, business to be carried out within the prison, and away from public jeering and scrutiny. And since this law had only just come into being, newspapermen were apparently obliged to find new ways to fire their readers' interest. Without doubt, a phrase as emotive as "*the awful change*" would generate debate. Debate, of course, would keep the paper's profile high. More and more copies would be sold.

And there was no denying that William Lacey's violent and untimely end was proving exceedingly profitable for the broadsheets. Love, lust, money, betrayal, this crime contained every ingredient necessary to keep the presses rolling, especially since so many questions remained unanswered.

THE LEXINGTON-PLACE MURDER.
EXAMINATION OF MR AND MRS MARKHAM.

The proceedings of the case of Mr John Albert Markham, remanded on Tuesday 14th, and of Elizabeth Markham, his wife, remanded Friday, 17th, resumed yesterday at the Southwark Police-court.

Inspector Haywood stated, in reply to a question from the bench, that the prisoners had been permitted an interview. Markham was on record as stating, "I have nothing to say to my wife." Mrs Markham said, "I do not wish to say anything to him, not one word." The interview lasted under two minutes.

At 11 o'clock the prisoners, who have both denied the charge laid against them, were then placed at the bar. Markham, who was first introduced, was elevated on a chair on the right-hand side. In contrast, Mrs Markham was careful to position her chair as far away from her husband as was humanly possible, and did not pass him a look or a token of recognition throughout the day.

The Times. 20 Aug., 1868.

All the world loves a mystery, it makes the front page.

All the world, that is, except for Inspector Haywood, who preferred his solved.

"Until your marriage in June of this year, Mrs Markham, you were employed in the household of Sir Henry James Wilton, who—" he consulted his notes "—who is in coal, I see."

Who sucks money from the north so he can wallow in luxury in the south, she thought, and where more food is thrown out in a week than any one of his miners earns in a month.

"That is correct."

Inspector Haywood. The name conjured up images of a policeman of stature, lean perhaps to the point of bony, even, with unruly dark hair and gimlet eyes. In practice, his fringe was thinning, his waistline thickening, he was shorter than Elizabeth and reeked of carbolic soap. Only the gimlet eyes matched her expectations.

"Where you served as a governess to Sir Henry's daughter?"

"Prudence." A less suitable name for an overindulged, under-exercised brat Elizabeth could not imagine. Even at twelve, she was so fat that it was impossible to tell where face finished and shoulders commenced, and what paradox. Calling her after the virtue of restraint in an environment where moderation was a creature of legend.

Haywood turned a fresh page in his notebook. "Now before we come to how a property owner, landlord and money-lender from Stretford, came to be buried in quick-

lime under your scullery floor, Mrs Markham, perhaps
you would be kind enough to explain how a governess to
the landed gentry came to be acquainted with such a
character."

Elizabeth's gaze travelled round the small, dingy, basement room that served as the inspector's office. Through the
window high up beside the ceiling, mud-splattered hems
scurried past, spats clicked on the pavement, occasionally a
dog would stop to sniff at the glass.

"Mr Lacey gets his boots hand-made at Norton's," she
explained. "The establishment supplies Sir Henry and his
family with their footwear."

He snorted. "Wish I could afford to have my corns and
calluses shod there."

"As, I am sure, do the pit-men of Durham."

"Hmm."

That "hmm", she decided, was of a man looking to make
Chief Inspector, even Superintendent: heights unlikely to be
scaled fretting about social concerns. Whereas securing a
firm case for the prosecution offered a distinctly promising
springboard –

"So it was while ordering a pair of boots for yourself that
you encountered William Lacey?"

Elizabeth flashed him a smile that fell midway between
sympathetic and wry. "Like policemen, Inspector, govern-
esses cannot afford bespoke footwear."

Not only poorly paid, they were neither fish nor fowl in the
world that they lived in. With a position too elevated to allow
them to mix with the servants but too low to join the family,
was there ever a colder, lonelier, more miserable existence?
For the moment, youth was on Elizabeth's side. But unless
she was careful, spinsterhood and poverty were all she had to
look forward to in her old age.

"It was while I was collecting a pair of riding boots for
Prudence that I first made Mr Lacey's acquaintance."

Ordinarily, Norton's delivered. But it just so happened
that Prudence's little fat feet were outstripping their cas-
ings faster than you can say knife, to the point where the

day dawned where she had a pony saddled and waiting downstairs in the yard, but no boots she could squeeze into.

Now in theory, this being Saturday, it should have been Elizabeth's day off. A day normally spent shoring up contacts, putting out feelers, and generally testing the market for husbands. However, she calculated that if she collected the boots in person, Prudence's tantrums could be calmed in a third of the time, and apart from the pleasure of riding in Sir Henry's carriage, which was not to be sniffed at, with its plumed horses and gold crest on the doors, she would also have an opportunity to gaze into the many shop windows that fronted Bond-street.

That was back in February, of course, and to be frank, very little about that first meeting stood out. She'd been too busy picturing herself swirling around dance floors in the various ball gowns or floating in one of the furs to pay much attention to the portly, rather gingerish, customer with gold-rimmed spectacles perched on the end of his nose. For though his tailoring was impeccable, albeit a tad loud, and his pocket-watch worth a small fortune, Elizabeth was eager to escape her governess life. Not desperate.

The inspector licked the tip of his pencil. "Yet a friendship between William Lacey and yourself did develop?"

"No impropriety occurred, if that's what you're suggesting."

"My apologies, Mrs Markham, for implying anything of the sort." All the same, he looked disappointed. "Mr Lacey may have been no stranger to the law, but his housekeeper vouches most vehemently that she found no, uh, traces of improper conduct on the premises. Indeed, even your husband, who himself seems to be of a passionate and sometimes violent nature, has cast no aspersions on your fidelity." The gimlet eyes flickered. "I am simply curious as to what a respectable married woman and an unscrupulous money-lender might have in common."

Of course he was. The press, too. In fact, the whole world had its tongue hanging out, panting.

For one thing, there had been no disguising William Lacey's fascination for Elizabeth. In fact, from the moment he stepped aside to allow her to be served before him, he confided to friends how he had been struck by her poise. By the time they were engaged, in conversation while Prudence's boots were being attended to, he confessed that her wit and intelligence had him enthralled. Indeed, the instant Elizabeth vacated the premises, Lacey was badgering Mr Norton about her and then, having discovered where she worked, boasted many times in the weeks that followed of the various "coincidental" meetings that he engineered.

But the police, the public and the jury were no fools. If his attentions had been unwelcome, Elizabeth was more than capable of quashing them. It was obvious as the nose on their face that she had strung him along, but all she would say on the matter was that Mr Lacey was not husband material.

While making no effort to explain why a renowned drinker and gambler who could not hold a job was.

She shrugged. "Who can say what binds friendship together, Inspector?"

"Obviously not confidences," Haywood snapped back. "Right up until his death, William Lacey remained ignorant in the matter of your marriage, so perhaps you could enlighten me as to why you kept it a secret? Was it that you were ashamed of John Markham?"

"On the contrary." She smiled demurely. "I found my husband exciting."

So did the press. Impoverished spinster living a sheltered life on the one hand. A handsome, cocky, ladies'-man on the other. The fact that he was seven years younger than his bride only added to the piquancy of the pairing, and the newspapers left little doubt in their readership's mind that the new Mrs Markham found her wifely duties less than onerous.

"Then why not tell your 'good friend' about your marriage?"

"How cruel you are, Inspector. When I was only too

keenly aware of Mr Lacey's tenderness towards me, why should I desire to hurt his feelings?"

"And this had nothing to do with the fact that Mr Lacey was of the Roman Catholic persuasion, and that although his wife left him many years previously, he was still legally married?"

"I see absolutely no relevance in the matter."

Haywood's fist slammed down on the table. "Mrs Markham. For broadsheet editors, your composure and beauty might be a front-page dream, but a man is dead. Lured to your lodgings in Lexington-place, shot and then buried like litter beneath your kitchen floor, and quicklime thrown over his body. On the very same morning, if you please, that he transferred five thousand pounds' worth of securities into cash, every penny of which has gone missing, while your own husband accuses you of sending him out to purchase an air pistol, a shovel, a bag of quicklime and two train tickets to Brighton. All this, while you yourself were engaged in giving notice to quit your lodgings and selling the bulk of your furniture to a broker, if you please! Oh, yes, your husband is also on record as stating that, when he returned home from his walk, he found you in the scullery with blood on your dress, the gun in your hand and the victim dead at your feet."

His notebook snapped shut.

"Premeditated murder, Mrs Markham. Now, I grant society has few reasons to mourn William Lacey's passing, but please spare me any pleas about hurting his feelings. The man was killed for a motive as base and pitiless as money, and I have every intention of bringing the perpetrators of this vile crime to justice. So is there anything you wish to say in your defence?" His eyes narrowed at her continued silence. "Nothing? No questions at all that you wish to ask? Not—" he paused "—not even why the young man who promised so ardently to love, cherish and honour you just three short months ago sold you out?"

Elizabeth drew a deep breath. "Maybe there is one thing, Inspector."

"Oh?" He leaned towards her. "And what might that be?"

"I was wondering if I might have a cup of tea, please? With just half a teaspoonful of sugar?"

If her approach infuriated the police, then the public was thrilled. So many questions. So few answers.

What happened to the five thousand pounds? There was no trace of it at Lexington-place and, with the house next to a main thoroughfare, half a dozen witnesses were able to confirm that William Lacey was carrying no baggage when he entered the house.

Which begged another question. Where did William Lacey go between cashing in his securities and calling on the Markhams?

And why, if Elizabeth was truly after his fortune, would a woman of such obvious intelligence kill the golden goose before it had laid any eggs?

The prosecution maintained that William Lacey had confided his intentions to liquidate a large amount of capital and that she set out to relieve him of it in the most brutal and callous way. And then, when William Lacey turned up at the house without it, it was claimed that she shot him out of pique – a point the defence were quick to seize on.

Did Mrs Markham look like a woman who acted out of spite?

The apprehension of the newlyweds at different times and in different locations was also a source of interest and intrigue in the press. They loved the idea of John Markham being run to ground in an hotel in Brighton, then denying all knowledge of the crime. But suddenly switching his story and laying the blame squarely on his wife, once he discovered that she had been apprehended three days afterwards, about to board the boat to Boulogne.

Both prosecution and defence made much of this, as well. Especially since Mrs Markham openly admitted that she had agreed to meet her husband in Brighton, yet had no intentions of fulfilling that arrangement.

The Crown suggested this was a deliberate attempt on her part to make John the scapegoat for cold-blooded murder.

Her defence counsel quite naturally rejected the allegation, asking the jury whether John Markham struck them as the type who could be bullied into buying shovels, air pistols, quicklime, or indeed any other devices that would obviously lead to murder. He bought these items, they insisted, in order to eliminate the only other contender for his wife's affections. For, while Markham did not imagine Elizabeth would violate her marriage vows, he was astute enough to realize that William Lacey was a rich and unrelenting suitor. The motive, they argued, was jealousy, not money. For if, as the Crown alleged, money was at the root of this crime, where was it? Every trunk, suitcase and piece of baggage on the ferry boat had been accounted for, and not one of them contained bulging wads of bank notes.

And of course, all these uncertainties were played out on the front pages of the papers.

What excuse did Elizabeth give William Lacey for leaving her post as a governess?

Was it insecurity on the part of John Albert Markham that eventually drove him to murder?

Was Elizabeth still so besotted with her new and "exciting" husband that she was prepared to cover up the killing of her friend, but not so foolish as to continue to tie herself to the man who had committed such a hideous crime?

Or was it Markham himself who had resolved to kill two birds with one stone, both depriving William Lacey of his money and at the same time securing his wife's affections?

Only two people knew the truth, the editorials contended, and their stories were in conflict. Who was to be believed? The calm and lovely bride, or the arrogant, posturing husband? Perhaps the truth lay somewhere in between, they suggested, and this was nothing more than a classic case of thieves (or in this case, killers) falling out.

Either way, their reporting was utterly without bias, and yet somehow it seemed to reflect public empathy with the lonely spinster approaching her thirtieth birthday, torn between the coarse charisma of John Albert Markham and the steadfast courtship of a wealthy property owner. Strangely, they also reserved some sympathy for Markham, shrewd enough to see that his intelligence did not equal that of either his rival or his wife, that his prospects for work were growing slimmer by the day, and that his animal magnetism was not going to blind Elizabeth to him for ever.

Even William Lacey, for all that he had been shot and buried in an unmarked grave then left to rot, came over as more villain than victim. The press played up his unscrupulous business deals, reported in salacious detail his reputation for evicting widows and orphans, and listed every one of his past brushes with the law, in which only the intervention of smart, expensive lawyers appeared to have kept him out of gaol. The cashing of the securities seemed to simply be a case of bad timing. It wasn't unknown for William Lacey to pay off any persons who had leverage on him, or else use cash to fund business enterprises that could not be traced back to him. Opium trafficking, extortion, vice, protection rackets? These were not unusual trades in Stretford.

Then suddenly everything changed –

CENTRAL CRIMINAL COURT, 5 Oct.

Shortly before 10 o'clock, the jury were brought from the London Coffee house, where they had once again spent the night. The judges, Chief Baron Pettigrew and Mr Justice Cornwell, accompanied by the Lord Mayor and Aldermen Keach, Haines and Webster took their customary seats on the bench and the prisoners were duly placed at the bar.

However, before the first witness of the day could be summoned, an event occurred which caused an animation around the whole of the courtroom.

The Crown produced trial transcripts dating back nineteen years, which showed that the murder of William Lacey was identical in almost every respect to the murder of one Patrick O'Connor, a gauger in the Customs at the London Docks, who was in possession of 4,000*l.* in foreign railway bonds at the time.

The Times. 6, Oct. 1868.

Indeed, the court could only be silenced with cries of "Order, Order!" from the stentorian voice of the usher, when it was shown how Mr O'Connor's remains were discovered beneath the back-kitchen floor of a house belonging to Frederick and Maria Manning.

Born in Switzerland, they learned how Maria Manning emigrated to Britain, where she worked as a lady's maid to the daughter of the Duchess of Sutherland – and apparently developed a taste for her employer's lifestyle. Indeed, it was while working for Lady Blantyre that she encountered the 50-year-old Irishman, a somewhat unsavoury character by all accounts, who amassed much of his fortune through criminal activities. Maria was attracted to O'Connor, but at the time was also involved with Frederick Manning, a railway guard who almost certainly stole property while employed by the railway, which O'Connor was suspected of fencing. Convinced that Frederick was poised to inherit a large sum of money, Maria chose him as her husband, but when she realized this was nothing but a falsehood, she determined to leave him – taking O'Connor's money with her.

Inviting Patrick O'Connor to dinner, the court heard how she drugged him with laudanum, only to find that he'd invited a friend along that night. Undaunted, she invited him round the following evening with promises of sexual favours, and, when he went to wash his hands, shot him twice in the head. When both bullets failed to kill him, Frederick finished him off with a crowbar, and it appears that Patrick O'Connor's last words as he crossed the kitchen floor to wash his hands were, "Haven't you finished digging this drain yet?"

Little realizing it was his own grave he was stepping over.

CENTRAL CRIMINAL COURT, Cont'd.

The court then heard how Mrs Manning paid a visit to the deceased's lodgings and calmly removed everything of value, including his scrip of foreign railway bonds.

She then took a train to Edinburgh, where she was later arrested trying to sell Mr O'Connor's stolen stock.

Frederick was apprehended one week afterwards in Jersey, at first denying any involvement in the crime, but later admitting that he had never liked O'Connor, so he "battered his head in with a ripping-chisel".

The Times. 6 Oct., 1868.

"This was a cold and calculated crime," boomed the rich baritone of Mr Lockhearte, KC, for the Crown.

Tall, distinguished, and with a long pointed nose, his eau-de-cologne carried almost as far as his perfect pronunciation.

"One in which the principal player was equally cold and calculating, and I can offer no better example of Mrs Manning's character than when the jury returned from their deliberations, which, I might add, was in under forty-five minutes."

He paused, as all good actors do.

"While delivering their verdict of guilty, Maria Manning began screaming that they had hounded her worse than a wild animal in the forest, and then proceeded to rant at the judge, as he attempted to pass the death sentence."

Mr Lockhearte turned slowly towards Elizabeth and made a flourish with his wrist.

"As she was led away to the cells, however, Mrs Manning straightened her sleeves and was heard, quite distinctly, to enquire of the turnkeys accompanying her how pleasing they had found her performance."

Seated in her customary corner of the bar, hands folded as was her habit, Elizabeth could feel the hostility of the entire courtroom burning into her. But her face remained expressionless as Mr Lockhearte continued to address his astonished jury.

"There is no suggestion, gentlemen, that Mrs Markham was involved in any way in the murder of Patrick O'Connor, since she was merely a child when the incident took place. However!"

Another flourish, this time with papers.

"The Crown is able to furnish proof that she was a resident in the orphanage not one hundred yards from the gaol where the Mannings were hanged, and I submit this newspaper archive in evidence that she cannot possibly claim to have no knowledge of the event."

THE BERMONDSEY MURDER
EXECUTION OF THE MANNINGS.

For five days past, Horsemonger-lane and its immediate neighbourhood had presented the appearance of a great fair, so large were the crowds collected there, and so intense the state of excitement in which all present appeared to be. The surrounding beer-shops were crowded. Windows commanding a view of the scaffold rose to a Californian price.

Above all, there was a force of 500 police in position on the ground, and though it is not easy to estimate the number of persons who were present at the dreadful spectacle, they probably exceeded 30,000.

The Times. 14 Nov., 1849.

"Can it be coincidence," demanded the faultless vowels of the prosecution, "that, nineteen years later, Elizabeth Markham née Clarke also conspires to befriend a wealthy, disreputable scoundrel? And that while dangling William Lacey on a string of affection, she sets out to marry a man less intelligent than herself, a drinker in the mould of Frederick Manning, whose greed she, too, can manipulate? Good heavens, how are we to tell one crime apart from the other?

Even the escape Mrs Markham planned for herself is identical. Sending her husband to one destination, while she decamps to another, in exactly the same fashion that Maria Manning intended Frederick to carry the can for the murder of Patrick O'Connor."

No sympathy in the courtroom. Not an ounce. Not even for John Albert Markham, the cocky young waster now portrayed as a gull. For, fool or not, he nevertheless conspired to commit cold-blooded murder – and murder was a capital crime.

"Can there be any doubt," Mr Lockhearte demanded of his spellbound audience, "that Elizabeth Markham spent her intervening years as a governess contemplating the circumstances that surrounded that earlier trial, then set about replicating them to her own ends?"

He ran a finger down the length of his patrician nose, then tapped his lower lip.

"Unfortunately for her, the plan rebounded when Mr Lacey failed to turn up with the cash as expected. And whilst we will probably never know to what felonious purpose this money has been put, I suggest to you, gentlemen of the jury, that it was greed pure and simple that lay at the heart of this crime."

You could have heard the proverbial pin drop.

"Mr Lacey's character has not been portrayed in a good light during this trial. He was a ruthless landlord, who had no qualms about evicting any tenant who did not pay their rent, no matter how desperate or temporary their circumstances, and employed even less patience with those to whom he lent money. His rates of interest have proven to be extortionate, his methods of collection questionable in the extreme, but I must ask you to push these points from your mind."

No need, they already had.

"Just like the Mannings twenty years earlier, Elizabeth and John Markham have both attempted to pin responsibility for the crime on the other, but it is the Crown's belief, gentlemen, that although Mrs Markham was the brains behind this scheme, her husband was an all-too-willing partner. Neither, you notice, have uttered a single word of repentance, and it is the Crown's contention that when Mr Lacey turned up at Lexington-place that fateful morning, he was already aware of Mrs Markham's plan to rob him. Perhaps he went there to gloat how he had foiled her, perhaps to denounce her, having discovered the truth of her marriage, perhaps even to expose her to the police in a sudden upsurge of Christian spirit."

Only Lockhearte himself smiled at the joke.

"But I put it to you, gentlemen of the jury, that whatever Mr Lacey may have said or done that fateful morning, it was compelling enough to motivate the Markhams to silence him once and for all."

Looking towards the jury, Elizabeth saw the repugnance in their eyes.

And satisfaction in Inspector Haywood's.

CENTRAL CRIMINAL COURT, 4 Oct.

As Mr Lockhearte, KC, finished summing up the case for the Crown, Mrs Markham stood up, walked across to where her husband was sitting and whispered something in his ear.

Instantly, the constables rushed forward, but there appeared to be no need for intervention. By the time they arrived, the female prisoner was seated facing the bench with her usual composure, while Markham himself was staring at her with a shocked expression and his face white.

The Times. 5 Oct., 1868.

And now, twenty-four days after the jury delivered their guilty verdict, Elizabeth sat alone in the dark and the cold, straining for signs of the approaching dawn. Her thoughts fluttered back to when she was nine years old, squashed among the tatterdemalions of London, who had gathered outside Horsemonger-lane gaol – or rather, Surrey County

Gaol, as it was called now. Not that the name changed anything. It remained the same bleak, dismal hole, where the ghosts of dead convicts howled on the stairs and the souls of the innocent wept silent tears. And the condemned cells as cold as the grave.

But nineteen years ago, as the night had progressed, the assemblage outside the prison grew denser and more raucous. Elizabeth was able to picture the scene as though it were yesterday. The gaunt outline of the gibbet, dark against even the darkness of the night. The ladder leading up to it. The smoke from the prison's chimneys, even, from fires lit inside to keep the November damp at bay. Long before the sky brightened, she remembered, the windows overlooking the scaffold along Horsemonger-lane were crammed with the gentry. Charles John Huffam Dickens unquestionably among them.

With an imperceptible sigh, she reached for the book at her side and ran the flat of her hand across its open pages. Would Pip ever marry the hideous Estelle—? Softly, very softly, she closed the book and replaced it on the bench.

Great Expectations, indeed . . .

How curious that her path crossed with Mr Dickens' all those years ago, neither, of course, having the slightest notion of the impact his influence would have in later years. Yet, as a result of his tireless efforts, only a small group of people would be on hand this morning to witness – to witness—

Elizabeth swallowed. At the time, of course, the spectacle of a husband and wife at the gallows was almost unprecedented, and she couldn't help but wonder what was going through her husband's mind at this dreadful moment. Fourteen years spent in an orphanage, eight as a governess, not to mention watching both parents drown in a boating accident, had left Elizabeth adept at hiding her feelings. No amount of trickery could persuade her to reveal more than she wanted to, but John? For him, too, the seconds would be lumbering past on shackled feet, and he would not be sitting quietly, hands clasped in his lap. Not John. Was he scared, she wondered? Was he down on his knees, praying to his God? Accepting of what the papers referred to the "*awful change*"?

She remembered when Frederick Manning went to the gallows. He wore his best suit, probably his only suit, but what chilled her the most, as she stood there that morning, was the way his shirt-collar had been turned over and loosened, that the rope might be more easily adjusted. She remembered, too, that he'd been shaking so badly that he was unable to mount the scaffold unaided. It had needed a man either side to support him – whereas Maria Manning caused a public sensation. Tying her own black silk handkerchief over her eyes and dressed in a black satin gown, she approached the noose with a firm and unfaltering step. In fact, right up to the end, she remained the consummate performer, and such was the scandal she created, even appealing to Queen Victoria from the condemned cell, that black satin instantly fell out of fashion and had remained that way ever since.

Yet it was neither Frederick's frailty nor Maria's dramatics that inspired Mr Dickens' campaign.

TO THE EDITOR OF *THE TIMES*

When I came upon the scene at midnight, the shrillness of the cries and howls that were raised made my blood run cold. As the night went on, screeching, and laughing, and parodies on Negro melodies, with substitutions of "Mrs Manning" for "Susannah" were added.

When the day dawned, thieves, low prostitutes, ruffians and vagabonds flocked to the ground, with every variety of offensive and foul behaviour.

Fightings, faintings, whistlings, imitations of Punch, brutal jokes, tumultuous demonstrations of indecent delight when swooning women were dragged out of the crowd by the police with their dresses disordered, gave a new zest to the general entertainment.

When the sun rose brightly – as it did – it gilded thousands upon thousands of upturned faces, so inex-

pressibly odious in their brutal mirth that a man had
cause to feel ashamed of the shape he wore, and to
shrink from himself, as fashioned in the image of the
Devil.

When the two miserable creatures who attracted all
this ghastly sight were turned quivering into the air,
there was no more emotion, no more pity, no more
thought that two immortal souls had gone to judgment, than if the name of Christ had never been
heard in this world.

Charles Dickens.
Devonshire-Terrace.,
Tuesday, 13 Nov.

The prosecution was quite correct in its supposition.
Elizabeth's had indeed been one of those gilded upturned
faces, and long after Frederick and Maria Manning were cut
down and the crowd dispersed, she had remained transfixed
beneath the prison gates.

After first denying any knowledge of Patrick O'Connor's
body beneath his kitchen floor, then blaming his wife for
everything, Frederick finally made his confession to his
brother. Even to admitting that he had dug the grave one
month in advance of O'Connor's death.

Maria, on the other hand, demonstrated the same firmness
of character that she had shown from the beginning and
indeed right throughout her trial. She went to her grave,
taking all her secrets with her.

As Elizabeth herself would.

"Why, Mr Lacey, what a coincidence. This must be the third
weekend running that we have bumped into one other!"

Coincidence be damned, and it also was the fourth time
that she had encountered him. The first occasion, of course,
she'd dismissed as pure chance. Then she noticed the glint in
his eye. The same glint Sir Henry Wilton used to get when a
rare Eastern treasure came on the antiquities market, which

meant he wouldn't rest until he had added it to his collection. Like all collectors, Sir Henry was obsessive and Elizabeth recognized the trait in William Lacey at once.

"Upon my soul, Mr Lacey, I do believe you have grown a set of mandy whiskers since last I saw you."

He made an expansive gesture with his hands. "I cannot deny it."

Elizabeth stepped back to admire what was still little more than stubble. "I do declare, whiskers make you quite handsome, Mr Lacey."

He gave her that sly, sideways smile from beneath his ginger lashes that somehow made her skin crawl.

"Not handsome, Miss Clarke."

With a body that had grown pudgy from too much rich food and too little exercise and skin that was waxy from too much time spent indoors, William Lacey was fully aware of his physical shortcomings. Just as he was conscious of his assets.

"Never handsome, I think."

He wound his ridiculously expensive timepiece, to prove the point.

Elizabeth's smile was wry. "Distinguished, then."

He adjusted his gold-rimmed spectacles. "Might I buy you a cream tea, Miss Clarke?"

And so it was, over scones and jam and clotted cream, that the dance began. Elizabeth was no fool. In certain circles, for a woman to remain unmarried when she was approaching thirty was the ultimate humiliation. But a governess, being neither fish nor fowl, fell into no such category, and she, too, knew her worth. She had no money, no prospects, and although she made the most of her appearance and lacked neither wit nor intelligence, there were plenty with more to offer.

Except men are men.

They all want to melt the Ice Queen . . .

"It is unfortunate, Miss Clarke, that I was forced to evict a widow, a toddler and her baby from that very house on Wednesday."

Cream teas had grown into long walks, dinners, picnics, carriage rides. He particularly liked to show her the properties he owned in Shoreditch, Mile End, Stretford, Stepney, and would always let drop the amount he raked in from rents and what he liked to describe as "other enterprises".

"Number 19, at the end there, is currently leased at three times the customary rate." His tongue flickered over his thick, pink lips. "The gentleman in question is being sought by the police, although he assures me it is a misunderstanding and that he is completely innocent. Naturally, I would not rent to him otherwise."

"Naturally."

And so the dance moved on, with both partners keeping smoothly in step with William Lacey continuing to promote his wealth and Elizabeth remaining out of reach. It was exactly as she told Inspector Haywood in her statement. No impropriety took place. But the situation could not continue for ever, and it came to a head at the end of September.

"The orphans you threw in the street, Mr Lacey. Do you not fear for their future?"

More tea, more cakes. Elizabeth did not think she would eat another scone again.

"It is a very different future I am preparing, Miss Clarke." He shot her his strange, sideways glance. "The increase I will be able to obtain from the next tenant will add towards a very comfortable retirement."

Elizabeth folded her hands on the table. "You are a long way from retirement age, I think, Mr Lacey."

Another sly glance. "With the right financial background, a man can retire to the country earlier than one might otherwise have expected." He cleared his throat. "I'm told two can live as cheaply as one there."

At long last the dance was at an end –

"You seem to forget that you are still married, Mr Lacey."

"Technically speaking, Miss Clarke. But in the, uh, country, folk may not always be privy to the full details of a person's marital status. If you take my meaning."

A bogus marriage? And what would she get out of it, if he died? He could change his will at any moment without her knowing, and she wouldn't have a leg to stand on and Elizabeth knew all about collectors. It wasn't that they didn't cherish what they had. But the pleasure of ownership didn't compare with the excitement of chasing after something new.

Elizabeth leaned across the table and smiled from under lowered lashes.

"I have always enjoyed the country, Mr Lacey."

And before he could say anything in reply, the bell in the tea-shop was tinkling at her departure, and by the time he had settled the bill, she was out of sight.

A week passed, a week in which she did not reply to any of his notes. Notes which arrived every day, sometimes twice, and which she burned immediately. Especially since the address was still Sir Henry's.

"Thank you."

She gave the boy who intercepted them his usual farthing, and ten days after their last meeting, set off for Stretford, knowing full well that William Lacey would be at home, going through his accounts, as he did every Thursday afternoon.

"Miss Clarke! Elizabeth!" His surprise was unambiguous, his delight genuine. "Come in."

As he poured them both a glass of sherry, there was no reference to his recent blizzard of letters, no mention of the proposition made across a plate of Eccles cakes. Instead, he tried to kiss her.

She pushed him away with a firmness that surprised him. And a new dance began.

"You do not find me attractive, do you?" he asked at length.

"No, sir, I do not."

"No." He nodded slowly. Sipped the remainder of his sherry. Then stood up, walked across the room and unlocked the top drawer of his bureau. "But you find these attractive, I suspect. Securities, madam. Five thousand pounds in this sheaf alone." He pursed his lips. "Now don't tell me you don't find *that* attractive."

As she stared at the bundle of papers tied up with red string, Elizabeth knew there could be no more beating around the bush. For either of them.

She drew a deep breath. Looked him squarely in the eye. "The honest truth, Mr Lacey? The honest truth is that those things mean nothing to me, nothing at all."

She paused, then walked across to stand so close to him that her breath misted up the lenses of his spectacles.

"But if you were to turn those securities into twenty-pound notes and spread them over the bed in the honeymoon suite of the Claybourne Hotel in the name of Mr & Mrs John Smith—" She blew softly in his ear. "Why, William, I would be yours to command."

Breezing out without a backward glance, she tried to dispel the notion of his oily little body pounding up and down on hers. Surely that was the most repugnant prospect in the world but, after five months, Elizabeth knew William Lacey inside out. She knew he would not hesitate to cash in those securities. Just as she knew he would not hesitate to buy them back the following day!

But one step at a time . . .

For not once, since standing beneath that gaunt, dark gibbet in Horsemonger-lane, had she forgotten Maria Manning. Maria Manning had also grown used to a life in which the beds were soft, the rooms were warm, there was sufficient money to pay for both food and fuel. Maria the lady's maid wanted that for the rest of her life, as did Elizabeth the governess, and hearing about the widows and orphans who were thrown into the street only hardened her resolve against being in thrall to landlords like William Lacey.

The trouble was, Maria Manning was greedy. If she hadn't tried to sell Patrick O'Connor's railway stocks so soon afterwards, if she hadn't kept his valuables to sell on later, indeed if she hadn't tried to have her cake and eat it, in all probability she would have got away with it. And Elizabeth had had twenty years to learn from Maria's mistakes . . .

Drawing on all those Saturdays spent shoring up contacts, putting out feelers and generally testing the market for husbands, she decided John Albert Markham was the best man to take that long walk down the aisle. He drank, he gambled, he bragged and he was lazy, but equally he was handsome, strong and funny, and the marriage bed was hardly an ordeal. Crucially, John Albert Markham was infatuated. He, too, had a passionate desire to melt the Ice Queen and was young enough, and not quite bright enough, to believe that the attraction of opposites would last. Most importantly, however, John was no collector. He was a simple soul who lived on debt in rented lodgings, yet saw a future in which he and Elizabeth raised children, grand-children, lived and died together. And because he was a gambling man, he had no realistic vision of what financial threads might sew this miracle together.

But understood exactly what five thousands pounds could do –

Taking her cue from Maria, Elizabeth brought her hus-band into her plan. And like Frederick Manning twenty years before him, John was a willing partner.

"You're sure he'll bring the money to the house?"

"Absolutely certain," she assured him, with a kiss. "Trust me."

And so, just like Maria Manning, Elizabeth lured William Lacey to Lexington-place (she claimed it was a friend's house), shot him in the same manner as the Mannings had killed O'Connor, with an air pistol (although thankfully, the first bullet killed him outright, the second was simply a precaution) and together she and John buried William Lacey in the quicklime purchased by her husband, just like the Mannings had before them. In fact, so famous was the trial that the prosecution couldn't fail to pick up on the simila-rities, but if Maria could so easily have escaped arrest, how was it that Elizabeth got caught?

"No matter how intelligent murderers think they are," thundered Mr Lockhearte for the Crown, "they always make that one mistake."

He had turned and stared directly to where Elizabeth Markham was sitting, and she saw the triumph in his eyes.

"That one mistake that allows us to claim justice for the victim."

With a jolt of surprise, Elizabeth saw that the sky was changing colour. The dawn, which had been so long in coming, had suddenly arrived, pink, and streaked with grey. With a deep, shuddering breath she adjusted the fringe of black lace that almost, but not quite, covered her eyes. In her mind she had lived this moment a thousand, two thousand times. The chaplain's pious murmurs. The pinioning of the hands. The long walk down the passageways fenced in with gates and side rails. Stepping over the condemned prisoner's own gaping grave.

From somewhere a male voice intruded on the horror. "It's time now, Miss."

Time. What did time mean, when a white cap was about to be placed over one's head and a noose fitted round one's neck? "Thankfully, I shall never know," she whispered to herself, collecting her gloves and reticule.

Through the tiny aperture that passed for a window on this little ferry boat, the lights of the ocean-going liner that would carry her across the Atlantic loomed into view.

New York. New World. New life . . .

CENTRAL CRIMINAL COURT, 4. Oct.

It was not the fact that Mrs Markham suddenly got up and whispered to her husband, however, that caused excitement round the courtroom.

It was because, shortly after she had re-seated herself, Markham jumped out of his own chair and shouted "Very well, I confess! It *was* me! I shot William Lacey with the pistol that I procured for the purpose. My wife is as innocent of this crime as she claims!"

The Times. 5, Oct. 1868.

Do they, Mr Lockhearte? Do all murderers make that one mistake? To be caught waiting to board that boat to Boulogne had been part of Elizabeth's plan. Standing trial was key to it, as well. For, once acquitted, no person may be tried twice for murder. Double jeopardy is not recognized in law.

She picked up the book, whose ending she would never know. Or rather would never care to know. In these past twenty-four days, when all she'd had to do was read and wait and wait and read, she'd had enough Dickens to last her for a lifetime. But what else could she do? It was always possible that John Albert Markham might receive a pardon, or that the truth would somehow come tumbling out.

But now, at the time the prison bell would be tolling and the public executioner positioning her husband over the trapdoor, Elizabeth saw that Mr Lockhearte was quite wrong. With twenty years to learn from Maria Manning's mistakes, she had learned her lessons well.

"Mr & Mrs John Smith?" William Lacey had murmured.

"If I am to give myself to you on a bed of twenty-pound notes, I would prefer to retain at least some small modicum of pride," she replied, with eyes oh-so-demurely downcast.

And there it was. At ten o'clock precisely, William Lacey liquidated five thousand pounds of securities into cash at his bank in Bloomsbury and carried the suitcase . . . straight across the road to the Claybourne Hotel. He obviously made no connection between his bank and the hotel she had chosen. It was, after all, second only to the Ritz. But Elizabeth needed to be sure there was no trail for the police to follow. And who would suspect William Lacey would simply carry his cash over the road?

She watched him leave the hotel after twenty minutes or so. She already had a hackney standing, so that even as the doorman was hailing him a cab, she was already on her way, ahead of him. Having spun her tale of running out on Sir Henry and using her friend's house as a hiding place, she waited. And then, once the body was buried and John on the train to Brighton, a rather tarty-looking Mrs Smith checked into the Bridal Suite, gathered up the bank notes spread across the bed, packed them back in the suitcase, settled the account and deposited the trunk in the Left Luggage Office at Victoria Station.

As Mrs Markham once again, she booked a passage to Boulogne and calmly waited while the alarm was raised and the body found. And what foresight, to send a note to his house after he had left that fateful morning, to make sure the interval would not be long! Then, it was simply a question of waiting.

Waiting to be arrested.

Waiting to be tried.

Waiting for John Albert Markham to bear full responsibility for the crime.

Waiting to claim the trunk of money.

Waiting for this dawn, when the only other person who knew the truth would now be dead . . .

For days after her acquittal, the newspapers had been brimming with speculation about this astonishing reversal of events. What, they goggled, had Mrs Markham whispered to her husband? What could *possibly* be of such great importance that he instantly changed his plea to guilty?

Oh, what fools men are!

"I'm pregnant, John." She patted the black satin gown that had also attracted so much attention in the press. "I'm carrying your child."

It was all the spur he'd needed. The thought of his name, his very bloodline, dying out, when all he had ever wanted was a family was too much for John to bear. He would rather go to his death shouldering the blame than kill his only child.

As Elizabeth knew he would.

And poor, simple, trusting John. Did no one tell him that they don't hang pregnant women?

Ascending the gangplank, dwarfed by the giant liner overhead, Elizabeth dropped her copy of *Great Expectations* into waters turned scarlet with the breaking sky. Never mind Pip's chances of marriage to the vile Estelle. Once in America, and with five thousand pounds behind her, Elizabeth did not think it long before she became a wife again herself.

Or a widow, come to that.

The Letter

Joan Lock

Even before David Copperfield *was completed Dickens had started new commitments. He launched and edited a weekly magazine,* Household Words, *which appeared in March 1850, and to which Dickens contributed copiously, mostly with articles or short stories and his next book,* A Child's History of England, *which was serialized during 1851. He employed as his assistant on the magazine his former secretary at the* Daily News, *William H. Wills, who was a godsend in helping an ever-ambitious Dickens. During all this, Dickens also planned to move house but during 1851 he was struck by three cruel blows. First his wife Catherine was taken seriously ill, shortly after the birth of their ninth child, Dora. Secondly his father died and two weeks later, baby Dora also died, aged barely eight months. Dickens was grief-stricken by Dora's death. As for his father, the two had not been on the best of terms in recent years, but they had become reconciled at the end and the old man's passing clearly closed a chapter in Dickens's mind. After moving house Dickens began his next novel,* Bleak House.

Of particular relevance is the fate of Lady Dedlock and the role played by the cunning lawyer Tulkinghorn to find the truth about her ladyship and the mysterious stranger Nemo, who dies early in the book. Tulkinghorn engages the

help of police detective, Inspector Bucket, who subse-
quently has to investigate the murder of Tulkinghorn.
Thus, in Bleak House, *we have Dickens's first genuine*
"whodunnit", incorporated within and crucial to the
denouement of the novel.

The Detective Branch of Scotland Yard had been
formed in 1842. Starting in 1850, Dickens wrote a series
of pieces for Household Words, *looking at the work of the*
police force. Two of them, under the common heading "A
Detective Police Party" (27 July and 10 August 1850),
feature Inspector Wield and tell how he and his colleagues
tracked down and arrested a horse thief. Wield was a
transparent disguise for a real detective, Inspector Charles
Field, who had headed the Detective Branch since 1849.
Dickens wrote about Field's work in "On Duty with
Inspector Field" (14 June 1851) and it is clear from
Dickens's description of Inspector Bucket that he was also
based on Field. Field retired from the Police Force in
December 1852 though continued to operate as a private
detective. Dickens was the first popular writer to take an
interest in the police force and the matter of crime and its
detection continued to fascinate him.

Joan Lock served as a policewoman in the sixties and
wrote of her experiences (and problems) in Lady Policeman *(1968), plus a more detailed study in* The British
Policewoman *(1978). She has since become renowned for*
her books about the early days of the British police force,
most notably Dreadful Deeds and Awful Murders
(1990), about Scotland Yard's first detectives. She has
also written her own series about Victorian police detective
Sergeant Best, which began with Dead Image *(2000).*
Her detailed knowledge of the period made her a natural to
create a new story about Inspector Bucket.

Inspector Bucket did not hold with letters. He had as little
to do with correspondence as possible, either as a sender
or receiver. In his opinion, not only were they too simple and

direct a way to conduct delicate business, but they could be
dangerous.

He preferred a more roundabout approach. One which
exercised, he would hesitate to say more guile, but at least
more sociability and subtlety. That was it. Subtlety. To
look a person in the eye while pleasantries and information
were exchanged. That was the civilized way to conduct
affairs. Furthermore, he had seen the damage these
thoughts made firm could do when produced as evidence
in a court of law.

No, letters were things to be avoided. Yet here he was
contemplating a pile of them as he sat in the Inspector's office
in Scotland Yard. All, he had no doubt, would be telling him
how to do his job and how to solve this terrible crime which
the newspapers had already dubbed the Chelsea Art Murder.

All notable crimes brought this influx of letters to the
Detective Branch and the Commissioner insisted they were
taken notice of just in case they might hold important
information. In Bucket's experience they never did and
the time he was obliged to waste on them only increased
his dislike and distrust of letters.

He gazed out of the window at the fog which always
seemed to hang low and become trapped in the Yard,
persisting when it had dispersed elsewhere. He sighed,
thoughtfully rubbed the side of his nose with his fat forefinger, and began.

The first three were clearly nonsense born of ignorance of
both the case and the progress of their investigation. The
fourth was from a Mr Billings of Ware who was clearly
deranged. Bucket realized that even before he read the
content. All the tell-tale signs were there: overlarge wild
handwriting punctuated with a great many giant exclamation
marks which gave the impression that the sender was shouting at the recipient – which he probably intended.

By contrast, the fifth letter was written in a small, delicate,
feminine hand on pale blue paper and was controlled both in
execution and content. It said simply,

Dear Mr Bucket,
   With reference to the Praxton House murder I suggest you ask the
butler what he was doing in the garden at midnight on Thursday.
                                    Abigail Sutton (Miss)

That gave Bucket a start but also puzzled him. A butler in the
garden at midnight was certainly an oddity. But what could
he be doing that was sinister? They already had the weapon
and had arrived at a motive. The crime was obviously a
burglary gone wrong.

An awful possibility occurred to the Detective Inspector.
Was there another body out there in the garden? He soon
dismissed that idea as fanciful. Not fitting in with his
conclusions about the crime. He looked again at the pale
blue fine quality notepaper and it occurred to him that the
idea of a butler lurking in the garden at midnight had a
melodramatic tinge to it – such as that found in cheap
novels read by impressionable young ladies with little better
to do.

What was certain was that he must go to see Miss Abigail
Sutton. Even the sociable Bucket usually ignored the insistence of letter writers who demanded that a detective should
call on them – or he sent a sergeant in his stead.

Miss Sutton had not made such a demand. But she had
appended her address: 5, Lilac Villas, Chelsea. These villas
were in the adjacent street to Praxton House, the scene of the
murder. Depending on how sane and sensible Miss Sutton
seemed to be, he would decide whether to put her question to
Sligh, the butler. And, perhaps, he would commence digging
up Praxton House garden.

Number five, Lilac Villas, proved, as he had expected, to
be small, white and feminine in its décor. Miss Abigail
Sutton likewise. Although no longer a young woman she
had a youthful and amused sparkle in her eyes. Dainty would
be the description he would use if pressed. She wore a soft,
cream-coloured gown with a prodigious cascade of lace
ruffles at the wrist, as was the mode among wealthy ladies.

"A detective!" she exclaimed when he was shown in to the

drawing room. "How very exciting! But what could you want with me?"

A disconcerting start perhaps but Bucket was a philosophical man accustomed to disappointment.

"You have doubtless heard about the murder of one of your neighbours, Miss Sutton? That of the artist, Mr Augustus Bellingham?"

"Oh, of course, of course!" She threw her hands in the air and shook her head causing her ruffles and her tight little ringlets to shake and flutter. "No one speaks of anything else. So sad. Such a talented man."

"Indeed. Indeed." Bucket glanced around the room appreciatively. "Judging by your own pictures, madam, if I may be so bold, you would have particular appreciation of art." His eyes lit on one. "Isn't that . . ." he waved his forefinger in the air then brought it to his forehead which he tapped before exclaiming. "I know! Isn't that one of Mr Benchley's fine etchings?"

Miss Sutton smiled. "Absolutely, Inspector."

"And that one." He pointed to a small oil landscape rendered in indeterminate greens and paused. "May I look?"

"Of course." The bemused Miss Sutton nodded. Clearly this was not the sharp, penetrating questioning she had expected from one of the Metropolitan Police's finest. But rather than such personal attentions appearing impertinent on such a short acquaintance Bucket's very enthusiasm and interest were endearing.

She smiled indulgently as he got up to look closely at the painting. His glance also, quite incidentally, included the view from the nearby window and the objects resting on the adjacent side table.

"Fine. Very fine. With such taste I wonder if you are an artist yourself?" He glanced around for evidence of her skills.

She shook her head sadly. "Only an admirer."

"Myself also. My sculptor friend, Alfonso, swears that my artistic talents are merely waiting to be drawn out but," he shook head in concert with his finger. "In that his otherwise excellent judgement fails him."

"You doubtless have other talents," said Miss Sutton consolingly. "For detection, for example."

But he was not to be deflected from the subject of art. "I wonder whether you have any of the late Mr Bellingham's paintings?" He stopped aghast. "Oh, how tactless of me. Living so near and you being an art lover, you may have known him?"

"Oh, no," she smiled. "I don't get about so much in society these days. My health, you know." Her dainty hand fluttered above her chest.

"Ah. A pity, but . . ." He suddenly sat forward as though dragged back involuntarily, "to more serious matters. The death of Mr Bellingham and your letter."

Miss Sutton sat back, perplexed.

"My letter, Mr Bucket? I'm afraid you have the advantage of me there."

He fished about in his pocket and retrieved a large black pocketbook which he ungirdled to reveal the blue notepaper. She frowned at the sight.

"This letter you wrote to Scotland Yard." He held it up but did not offer it for inspection. "The contents refer to the murder of Mr Bellingham and offer us some helpful advice with regard to our investigation."

Miss Sutton gasped then sat up straighter and more stiffly as people of small stature tend to do when attempting to add dignity and gravitas to their pronouncements. "I can assure you, Mr Bucket," she said slowly, "that I wrote no such letter."

"Oh."

His substantial shoulders drooped and his forefinger crept to his upper lip and began to stroke it thoughtfully.

"That is a grave disappointment." He paused. "But it does have your signature and this address is appended."

He held it forward, his meaty fingers obscuring the body of the letter.

Her eyes had lost their amused sparkle and grown icy. "Well, I can assure you, Mr Bucket, I did *not* write that letter."

"Oh, dear, Oh, dear," said Bucket looking defeated. He paused, then said, "But I sense you may recognize the paper?" Not giving her the chance to disagree, he continued, "Might you also recognize the hand?" He held up the letter once more.

Her mouth tightened.

"It is meant, I assume, to imitate my own," she said then held her right palm outwards to ward off any further questions. "If you would leave this with me, Inspector, I will enquire further. I can only say that I have my suspicions."

Bucket had a healthy regard for women's suspicions. Indeed, those of the estimable Mrs Bucket had been of great assistance to him on more than one occasion. In his opinion she was a natural detective.

"Very well. I will return later and we will confer," he told her, then picked up his hat and withdrew.

On his way to Praxton House, Bucket reflected on why, if Miss Sutton *had* written that letter, she now disowned it? Had someone, perhaps the butler, threatened her? But why had she accused him in the first place? How did she know that he was in the garden at midnight? Was it merely servants' gossip? A clue had rested on that table by the window: a pair of opera glasses. But surely they would not be powerful enough to see over into that garden, at midnight *and* enable her to identify the butler? Had she imagined it then? She seemed sane enough and convinced she knew *who* had sent it.

Of course, disclaiming letters sent to Scotland Yard was not unusual. Members of the public, excited by the mystery puffed up by the newspapers, wrote off making wild accusations which they withdrew when they realized the mischief they could cause. (The introduction of the Penny Post had much to answer for in Bucket's estimation.) One officer had been obliged to go all the way to Bristol to see a man who declared himself to be in possession of vital information which could only be disclosed to the ears of a Scotland Yard detective, only for the man to tell him angrily that he had made no such communication.

*   *   *

The murder which had encouraged the latest influx of letters had been that of Mr Augustus Bellingham, successful painter to the gentry. He had been found dead early one morning on the kitchen floor of his Chelsea home, his head crushed by a rounded heavy instrument, which soon proved to be the bloodied kitchen poker left at the scene.

Several valuable items including silver plate were found lying just inside the kitchen door, as was a candle stuck in a flat bar of yellow soap – all of which indicated an aborted burglary. Burglars were obliged to carry their means of illumination with them. Sometimes a darkie – a lantern adjusted to issue only sufficient light to see a keyhole. For better light, once inside, some brought a candle stuck in a bar of soap which could be placed on a flat surface while the burglar rummaged for loot. The candle's whereabouts by the door signalled that the crime had been committed by an outsider, although some wily servants aiming to rob their masters soon became alerted to the candle factor and acted accordingly.

The fact that the Praxton House kitchen door had been jemmied open also pointed to an outside job. Unfortunately, there had been a hard frost that night so there had been no footprints inside nor outside in the soil from which to take a plaster caste. The two women servants and the under butler all lived in slept at the top of the house and so heard nothing. Sligh, the butler in question, had been given the night off to visit his ailing father in Hampshire.

All in all, it looked as though Mr Bellingham, a poor sleeper in the habit of going down to his studio during the night, had heard a noise in the kitchen, gone to investigate and been struck down.

Bucket had had his suspicions about the butler but could find no evidence against him. The other servants, if they knew anything, were not saying. A not unusual occurrence. Servants were usually aware of what was going on below the tranquil surface of an establishment but if their livelihood depended on the goodwill of a suspect their memories could prove faulty.

It had been the butler, however, who had pointed out that some valuables were still missing: gold rings, coins, fob watches and seals. Pawnbrokers were alerted and informants questioned as to what thieves' tattle was saying – which wasn't much – and the house itself was searched including the butlers' pantry. All to no avail although a couple of Chelsea's habitual burglars were being sought. And that had been that. Until the arrival of the letter.

As butlers go the slim, elegant, James Sligh, was a very superior specimen. In his own eyes at least but not in those of Mr Bucket who had been looked down upon by far more impressive examples of the breed. Neither they nor Mr Sligh had dented his confidence in the least.

"Here again, Inspector?"

He stood aside, ushering Bucket through as though this was his very own house, which caused the Inspector to wonder anew about the terms of the victim's will which were not yet revealed.

By the time Lizzy the parlour maid had accepted Bucket's top hat and gloves and he turned back to Sligh, the man's face had assumed an ingratiating smile. He is thinking better of antagonizing the law, thought Bucket, no matter how lowly its representative.

"What can I do for you, Inspector?"

"Answer a few more questions," said Bucket.

Sligh raised his right eyebrow, wrinkling the small diagonal scar that ran through it enhancing rather than detracting from the man's sleek and saturnine appearance.

"As you can see," he gestured towards the hall window at the household carriage in the process of acquiring a funereal aspect, "we imagined the investigation was done with and are getting on with organizing the proper conclusions to this sad business."

Done with and no culprit identified, apart from an unknown burglar, was the unspoken slight. The butler wafted his slim hand towards the drawing room and made as if to guide the Detective Inspector through its door. But Bucket stopped abruptly, held up his pudgy forefinger and smiled in a benign fashion.

"Before the questions I wish to speak to your gardener."

Sligh frowned. "Why would . . . I mean, I assure you old Jeremiah Hardacre knows nothing about . . ."

Bucket waved the said forefinger. "It's purely a personal matter, Mr Sligh, if you would indulge me. You see," he added confidingly, "I'm having problems with my petunias. They are small and puny and apt to expire without warning. On my way here I suddenly thought to myself, Bucket, you're in luck. Praxton House has a splendid garden, doubtless due to your own excellent supervision, Mr Sligh, and surely, I thought, the man responsible for such splendour will be able to help me with my horticultural problems."

Sligh was caught off guard. Before he could respond, he was following Bucket as he made his way towards the rear of the house and into the kitchen.

"This is most generous of you," he said, without halting step. "Mrs Bucket is very particular about her garden, don't you know, and it upsets her if it ain't right."

"He's not here," interposed Sligh, attempting to get ahead of the portly Scotland Yard detective, who was sailing like a stately galleon towards the door which led into the garden.

"I think you're mistaken," Bucket exclaimed, pointing through the kitchen window. "There he is!" He opened the door. "You keep them at it, I see. Admirable. Admirable."

Sligh smiled weakly at this compliment as Bucket exited the kitchen, closing the door firmly behind him.

When Bucket asked his question Hardacre the gardener looked shocked.

"Should be under glass now if you wants to keep 'em!" he exclaimed as though the Inspector had been guilty of some wanton evil act. "Frost kills 'em!"

"Oh yes, yes," said Bucket who scarcely knew a petunia from a Michaelmas daisy. "That's done. That's done. It's when they're coming on they don't seem to thrive like those next door." He shook his head. "And that upsets Mrs Bucket!"

Hardacre leaned back, pushing his gnarled thumbs over the top of his blue canvas apron. "Cut back the straggly roots and dead-head regular. That's what they need!" He paused. "Not too heavy shade neither or they'll pine."

Pine, would they? Plants and flowers were living beings to this man, Bucket noted with approval. He liked an enthusiast.

The gardener, advice duly given, bent down to lift the handles of his barrow ready to go on his way. Bucket stayed him with the finger.

"Just one more horticultural matter I need your expert advice on."

He walked forward among the lawns and flowerbeds, obliging Hardacre to follow. As he went, he expressed wonder at the beauty of the late autumnal display and gave compliments regarding the skills that had produced them. On his heels, a bemused Hardacre muttered about soils and the nurturing required for each plant while Bucket nodded sagely, tapping his forehead as if to ensure that the knowledge had been duly absorbed.

Once well away from the prying ears in the house he suddenly asked, "Has anyone been tampering with your garden?"

"Tampering?" Hardacre looked confused.

Bucket came to his aid. "I'm just tidying up loose ends," he explained, patting the air in a comforting fashion, "and it occurred to me, somewhat late, I admit, that when the murderer made his escape he might have buried some of the tools of his trade here – in case he was waylaid by a vigilant member of the force once outside."

Hardacre nodded, comprehension dawning.

"You'd notice if there had been any fresh digging?"

"Oh, aye," said the gardener, "specially at this time of year – and," he added firmly, "there ain't been none."

As usual Bucket's attention was everywhere. Particularly in the area visible from Miss Sutton's drawing room window.

But he could see no sign of newly disturbed earth or suspiciously bumpy mounds.

"Could even be *recent*, the disturbance," he confided. "Who knows, the thief and murderer could have come back in the dead of night to rescue his jemmy, his wedges, or his ring of skeleton keys."

"I'd 'ave knowed right orff," announced Hardacre adamantly. "Right orff."

Bucket believed him.

So, what else might Sligh have been doing in the garden at midnight, apart from burying something? He glanced over to the apple and pear trees in the kitchen garden. Had Sligh put something among the branches or in the potting shed? But the kitchen garden was not visible from Miss Sutton's window. Of course, he might have just been passing through when she saw him, possibly carrying something sinister? Yes, often the simplest answers were the most likely.

He turned his attention back to Hardacre, who was idly absorbed in dead-heading. Holding up the fat forefinger, he begged just one more indulgence.

"I need the name of a decent hostelry around here. Nothing fancy, just spit and sawdust and a friendly landlord. You see, I'm coming back this way later to see someone and I'll be needing a spot of refreshment to help me on my way."

By good fortune, Hardacre did know such a place and was happy to recommend it: The Cock, just off the King's Road.

Bucket left it late but not too late to enter the long, winding passageway leading to the swing door of the bar of The Cock.

By then, the room had been well warmed and the air thickened by smoke from the roaring fire and the customers' innumerable clay pipes, steam from the huge kettle awaiting hot toddy duty on the hob and fumes from the oil lamps which lit and blackened the walls and windows.

He felt at home with the sawdust and flagstones under his feet. His father had been a publican and it was in such a place that his fondness for society had developed.

Although it was a chilly night one of the two snug corner

seats by the fire was still vacant. But he did not take it. He just stood by the bar, holding his glass of Fine Old East India sherry, absently surveying the room.

As he had expected, his reverie was soon interrupted by a shout.

" 'Ere, Mr Bucket! 'Ere!"

It came from one of the blackened boxes extending outwards from the back wall. Turning, he saw a horny hand reaching high and beckoning him across. He went, leaned over the central table and shook the hand.

"This was just what I wanted," he said, a wave from his plump hand encompassing the room, "just the ticket."

As Bucket had hoped, Hardacre was not alone. Alongside him were Alfred, the meek gardener's lad who had hovered in the background that afternoon; a pale young man who turned out to be Vincent, the under-butler, and George, the groom with whom he had passed time as he had left that afternoon, taking the trouble to congratulate him on the grandeur of the black stallions he was hitching up. Bucket would be the first to admit a woeful ignorance about the merits or otherwise of horses but he did know such men and the pride they took in their charges.

The welcome was warm. Hardacre was proud of his acquaintance. Alfred and Vincent were wide-eyed and awestruck by the proximity of one of those famous Scotland Yard detectives and George was impressed by the man's appreciation of the finer aspects of livestock.

As he had also hoped, the four men were well ahead of him with their intake from their pewter mugs of stout, so he was able to accept their insistence that he have another with them before pressing them to try something a little stronger in his honour. Soon, all were merry. Very merry.

Even Jeremiah Hardacre, the grizzled old gardener, became quite animated, despite the fact that his experience of the gentry who visited Praxton House (on whose antics much of the hilarity depended) was more limited than that of the others.

Bucket chortled appreciatively at the pretensions of old

Lord Brocket who had so exhausted himself with his primp-
ing and preening in readiness for his portrait that when he
eventually sat down to pose he fell fast asleep and snored
noisily. Then there was the nubile, swooning young Lady
Sarah who always managed to time her swoon so that she fell
straight into the arms of the handsome butler, Sligh.

Mr Bellingham had obviously had to be a very patient
man, remarked Bucket, carefully resisting the temptation to
steer the gossip towards Sligh – knowing it would drift that
way naturally enough.

There was much nodding at this observation. Mr Bellingham, it was clear, had been a very easy-going master. He had
even called them by their first names – except in the presence
of his sitters, of course, who might frown on such familiarity
with the lower orders.

And if any members of their families had been sick he had
allowed them leave to visit and even gave them a few coins to
help with the coach fare or provide calves' foot jelly for the
invalid. A few sly glances were exchanged at this intelligence.
Clearly, their families had been prone to a higher than
average rate of sickness. Which reminded Bucket that he
must enquire into the true state of health of Sligh's father.

Bucket expressed the sentiment that it was a pity that such
a kind and good-tempered employer should be so cruelly
murdered, to which there was much nodding of assent.

"Mind you," Vincent the under-butler suddenly burst
out, "when his temper was roused!"

"Oh, he did have a temper then?" smiled Bucket.

"Oh, aye! Oh, aye!"

The lad was pleased to regain the attention due to being
someone with superior access to the inner workings of the
house. Being so little used to the drink, he was unaware of the
sudden wariness in the faces of his companions.

"You should have seen him when he discovered them
silver Queen's Head studs couldn't be found. He was mad
as a hornet!"

"As I should be. As I should be," said Bucket, then looked
around at the frozen faces of the others. "I think, and I hope

you good gentlemen agree, that it is time for a final round and I hope you will do me the honour." He reached into his pocket but was told to desist. As he had hoped, Hardacre and George the groom went to fetch the drinks.

"And so, did your master find his studs?" he prompted not showing any great interest in the answer.

Vincent shook his head vigorously, then grabbed onto the edge of the table when he realized that such a movement had been unwise.

"No! No!" he insisted, this time thumping the table. "An," he confided in a low voice, "it weren't the first time things had gone missing and that Sligh," he burbled on, "that Sligh even tried to say it must be me or Lizzy the parlour maid that took them! He thought we didn't know about that – but we did!"

Clearly this had caused Vincent great offence which, Bucket guessed, Sligh would soon come to regret.

"And did Mr Bellingham call in the police?"

Vincent shook his head but more gently this time. "Didn't want no scandal. Not with all those toffs coming to the house. Bad for business."

"So, he didn't do anything about it?"

"Oh, yes, he did." Vincent thumped the table harder. "He told Mr Sligh to leave."

Before the final toasts to everlasting comradeship and good-will Bucket regaled the company with tales of murder and mayhem encountered by the stalwart men of the Detective Branch.

By then, the pale young Vincent had become even paler and when he stood up proved somewhat unsteady on his feet. The under-butler was the only member of the quartet to live in at Praxton House. The rest were heading in the opposite direction to the poorer part of the village.

"I'll see this young fellow home," said Bucket firmly. "I'm going his way."

He was now, anyway. The others, who were also weaving about a little, were easily persuaded.

Fortunately, the fresh air perked the lad up, as did his bending over the gutter and relieving himself of some of the poison he had imbibed. This made it easier for the Inspector to steer Vincent through the leafy streets of this part of Chelsea and back onto the topic of Mr Sligh.

"They all know it were him." Vincent thrust his right arm outwards as though to encompassing the whole world but probably only referring to the rest of the household.

They might know it, thought Bucket, but they had kept this knowledge to themselves. Not only, he deduced, due to the fear of being left without a character, but fear of Sligh himself. They doubtless felt that a man so devious and clever would somehow turn the tables on them, particularly since there did not appear to be any evidence against him. Even the persistent loss of small valuables had never been proven.

Vincent admitted that he had no idea just when Sligh had returned on the night in question, being fast asleep under the eves of the house and so hearing nothing. Neither had he nor any of the others ever seen Sligh set foot in the garden, the opinion being that he was loath to dirty his sleek shoes.

As the unsteady pair turned into the avenue on which Praxton House was situated, Bucket became seized by an uncharacteristic melancholy. He, too, was becoming convinced that Sligh had committed the murder after being caught stealing. But he was unable to prove it.

He was distracted from such morose musings by a dark figure emerging from the shadow of Praxton House porch. What was this? The murderer returning to the scene to search the gardens? Or an accomplice of Sligh's? No, he realized, as they drew nearer, it was the butler himself.

Checking that the premises were secure was part of a butler's duty. But he was doing it from the outside and whilst wearing outdoor clothes. Now he was bending down. When he straightened he had a large box in one hand and a carpet bag in the other. He walked towards the garden gate, where he stopped to look about him but paid no heed to the weaving figures approaching down the ill-lit street. He put down his burdens, unlatched the garden gate, pushed the box and bag through, closed it quietly behind him, then bent down again.

Bucket was a portly man but quick on his feet, so that as Sligh drew himself upright again he found his way blocked by the large form of the Detective Inspector, who murmured, "Another midnight walk, Mr Sligh?" as he snapped a bracelet of his second-best handcuffs around the wrist of the startled butler.

The Bucket who made his way to Lilac Villas the following morning was not only a happy man but one newly converted to the benefits of Her Majesty's postal service. Had they not received the letter (from Miss Sutton's hand or no) he would not have revisited Praxton House at that time and the butler would not have taken fright and tried to flee with his loot. So far, the man was insisting he had not hidden any valuables in the garden, declaring smugly that he had put them all behind the skirting board in his pantry where the police had been too stupid to look. But they suspected that this was because more valuables were hidden in the garden, perhaps to be collected by an accomplice.

The air was fresh and the small white villa looked even whiter and prettier in the early morning sunlight. Bucket was looking forward to meeting the dainty Miss Sutton again and expressing his gratitude. Perhaps now she would admit to having penned the crucial missive which had gained him and herself a reward.

He was obliged to ring three times before he heard hurried footsteps echoing along the hall and the door was pulled back to reveal the flustered face of Polly, the parlour maid.

"She's had to go back," she said as though he would know what she was talking about.

Bucket frowned.

"Back? Where to?"

Miss Sutton had not appeared to be a person in transit.

She beckoned him inside then whispered, "To – you know – 'the home'."

Did she mean what he thought she meant?

He sat down on one of the chairs in the hall while she drew the other alongside and sat next to him the better to facilitate a discreet exchange of information.

"She's been a lot better lately so they thought it would be all right to have her back," Polly confided, "but she started to go off again a bit so it was thought best to . . ."

"Off? Oh," he nodded and pointed to his chest. Miss Sutton had intimated she had trouble in that area when explaining why she did not venture out much these days.

"No. No." Polly shook her head causing her already loosely attached cap to slip to one side. "It's the fancies. That's what it is."

"The fancies?"

What was the girl talking about?

"She sees things. Things that aren't there. An' gets fixed on people – like that butler where the murder was." She paused. "She kept saying she saw him doing things in the garden at midnight."

"Well, she *might* have done," said Bucket clinging to his new-found confidence in correspondence. "As a matter of fact . . ."

"She couldn't," said Polly firmly. "She was always tucked up in bed by ten o'clock, an' her room looks out the front."

Bucket brought his fat forefinger to the fore. The girl was obviously unaware that Miss Sutton had been proved right. The butler did it. "She could," he pointed out, "have got up and gone into the drawing room."

Polly shook her head. "Oh, no, she couldn't. We locked the door to stop her wandering about."

Bucket was not usually lost for words but in this instance they did take a time coming.

When they arrived the accompanying forefinger was accusing. "Why didn't you tell me when I was here?"

She lowered her voice. "Well, the family don't like people to know, do they? She seems all right to other people most of the time. But," she lowered her voice more, "I *was* going to tip you the wink before you went but you dashed off afore I could an' . . ." She noticed his dazed expression. "Does it matter?"

He hesitated, then shook his head.

"No," he said. "In fact, m'dear, I'm glad you didn't."

He took out a coin of large denomination and pressed it into her palm. "If you 'ad my case would never have been solved."

Whichever way you looked at it, Bucket decided philosophically when on his way back to Scotland Yard, correspondence *could* be a splendid aid to detection. Hadn't he always suspected as much?

Not Cricket

Judith Cutler

Somewhat restless after completing Bleak House, *Dickens gave a series of public readings from his works, which attracted large audiences and was rapturously received. He would continue to provide reading tours for the rest of his life which, along with all his other commitments, would contribute to his rapidly deteriorating health. These first readings were in Birmingham. Dickens was well aware of the industrialization of the northern towns of England and its effect upon individuals' lives. He had followed the outcome of a strike by workers at one of the cotton mills in Preston in 1853–4. His concern was how the automaton-style demands of industry were turning people into machines and robbing them of individuality and imagination. This was the background for* Hard Times *on which he began work in March 1854 and decided to serialize in* Household Words. *He soon found the pressure of meeting the weekly deadlines exhausting, and though this gave the novel a fluidity and immediacy it also robbed it of Dickens's deep characterization and atmosphere. The book is every bit as austere as the lives of its characters.*

Hard Times *is set in Coketown, a fictionalized Preston. Gradgrind runs a school which produces automatons and represses individuality. Amongst the pupils is Gradgrind's son, Tom, who later develops into a gambler and embezzler. Also at the school is Sissy Jupe, whose father was a circus performer and who is seen as a bad influence, because of her flights of fancy. Tom, though, is fascinated by the circus and uses it to effect his escape from Coketown and England. His father subsequently relents and realizes his approach to education is too rigid and, rather like the transformation of Scrooge, seeks to do good. This, just one plot strand amongst many, is set against the struggle of the workers in Coketown to improve their pay and conditions. The following story returns to Coketown some forty years after the events described in* Hard Times, *and includes a historical but surprisingly Dickensian character as our sleuth.*

Judith Cutler is probably best known for her series of novels featuring Sophie Rivers who, like Cutler, was a lecturer at an inner-city college in Birmingham. That series began with Dying Fall *(1995). With* Life Sentence *(2005), Cutler started a new series set in Kent featuring Detective Chief Superintendent Frances Harman.*

It was Mr William M'Choakumchild who discovered the first outrage, as he took a health-giving spring stroll through Coketown's civic park, generously donated to the town by none other than the victim.

To a casual visitor, the park was not much more attractive than the rest of the town. But at least it attempted to vary the monotony of the smoke-blackened once red-brick buildings, the unarguable green of the grassed areas like old emeralds in a heavily tarnished setting – by no means appearing at their best, but nonetheless gems of great value. The Hands, who chiefly used them (for utility remained a byword despite the great changes to the town), were well on their way to making them their own. On bright Sundays, they were happy to saunter to the strains of music from the green-painted bandstand. The bandsmen were yet other Hands, proudly attired in heavily frogged uniforms and puffing prodigious quantities of air down brilliantly polished brass tubes provided by the Gradgrind Musical Instrument Fund.

During the winter large areas of grass had been scuffed and churned by the Hands' feet in games of football, both official and unofficial. In the far distance lay a cricket field, surrounded by benches and with its centre carefully roped off as a reminder that in the summer games of cricket would be played with all the skill and determination necessary for competing against other counties from across the entire country.

Young Mr M'Choakumchild looked forward with an especial passion to the start of the season, for it was rumoured that early on no less a team than Gloucestershire, with members of the redoubtable Grace family as players, would be visiting. He had no hope of being anything but a lowly twelfth man for Lancashire, but the prospect of even watching WG, the greatest cricketer of all time, was enough to make his eyes sparkle.

The spirit of the reformed Mr Gradgrind beamed benevolently down on the entire scene. He had after all given his name to the park when he had donated the land some forty years ago, saying that now he knew that the heart was more than simply an organ for pumping blood, he hoped to recompense the citizenry for the hard times he had inflicted on them by providing them with altogether more pleasurable ones. But the statue that the grateful Hands had raised to their newly kind patron was not smiling this morning. Or if it was, Mr Gradgrind's sad features being preserved for posterity in the finest marble, no one could see it. Mr Grandgrind's Purbeck head was covered by what the Hands referred to as a "gazunder", since its normal location was beneath the bed.

Mr M'Choakumchild's grandparents, once highly regarded instructors at Mr Grandgrind's own model school, would have been shocked to the core by the discovery. Just as horses or flowers were once deemed out of place on wallpaper, so such an item was out of place on the head, since it was not designed as headgear.

Mr M'Choakumchild, however, was inclined to be more amused than shocked, as were the boys and girls who gathered around him on their Monday morning dawdle to school. However, as a responsible young man preparing to go to university, whose destiny would one day summon him as a missionary to a far-off land where monumental statuary was unknown, he felt he should do no less then shoo the recalcitrant youngsters off to their classrooms and draw the offending object to the attention of the park-keepers, Mr Broadbent and Mr Fowler.

The two gentlemen, resplendent in their civic uniforms and clutching spiked sticks designed for the easier collection of either litter or leaves, stared agog at the statue. Both were old enough to recollect Mr Gradgrind at his most tyrannical, his most dryly factual, and were smitten with a terror that young Mr M'Choakumchild could but dimly apprehend. One was ready to run for the fire brigade, another for a steeple-jack. Both considered the police an absolute necessity. In their panic they did not know which to do first. But the young man recognized that their rhetorical demands – "Who might have done such a wicked deed? And how might he have done the wicked deed?" – were the right questions to ask. A third also posed itself. "And, most of all, how might they retrieve the offending object?"

Mr M'Choakumchild, being of that persuasion rightly known as muscular Christianity, was at least able to provide the answer to the last question. "If I had a ball," he mused out loud, "I might kick it at the article and dislodge it that way."

Mr Fowler raised a finger. "I had cause to confiscate a football only the other day, when some whippersnapper would try to pot it through the window of the great hot house." He slipped away to fetch it, still shuddering at the damage the missile might have done to the supply of fresh fruit to the Gradgrind Infirmary.

Meanwhile Mr M'Choakumchild divested himself of his jacket, rolled up his sleeves, and made several passes at an imaginary ball. When Mr Fowler returned, the youth stationed him behind the statue, Mr Broadbent before it, and after but one abortive attempt the statue was safely divested of its chamber pot, which fell clamorously to earth when Mr Fowler failed to catch it. Mr Broadbent had better luck with the ball.

The local constabulary, however, calling at the M'Choakumchild residence, were not so much impressed by Mr M'Choakumchild's footballing talents as curious to know if he himself placed the article on the benefactor's head.

Sergeant Hardman, who wore his embonpoint with the same gravitas as he wore his silver stripes and ginger whiskers, was particularly suspicious. "You're a fit enough specimen. And you can't be telling me that you would have known how to get it off if you hadn't put it there in the first place," he declared.

Grandmother M'Choakumchild, seated by the cheerful fire burning in her son's hearth, clutched helplessly at a fast-ebbing memory of rigorously taught logic. She could do no more than raise a minatory finger, but perhaps that in itself was enough. The sergeant was one of the scores of little pitchers whom she had inexorably filled with knowledge. To his chagrin he flushed, without reason, and put away his notebook and freshly licked pencil.

Her grandson smiled warmly at the old lady. She had never publicly evinced any grandmaternal feelings, but he had been aware, on the days he had pushed her in her Bath chair around the park, that the experience aroused some emotions in her breast that caused her to smile up and him and reach a gnarled hand for his strong youthful one.

Sergeant Hardman coughed. "So if it wasn't you, my lad, who might it be?"

It was a question on everyone's lips, as the Hands scurried into work, or exchanged illicit snatches of conversation at the mills owned by other than the Gradgrind family, where moderate social intercourse was now positively encouraged. Was it one extraordinarily tall and agile man? Or was there a sinister collaboration, one man holding a ladder for another to climb? In the butcher's shop, one young mother, more imaginative than most, wondered aloud if God Himself had reached down from Heaven with the head-covering, but she was swiftly hushed. Despite the changes in the town, fancy was still not popular amongst the older generation.

For a while, people looked with accusing eyes at each other and especially at strangers to the town, the consensus being that no one who knew the debt owed to the Gradgrinds would have committed such a frivolous crime. Alderman Bitzer, however, declared publicly that the fate was one the canting old hypocrite deserved, but his words caused little more than offence. What further surprised the townspeople was that this son of a man who had risen particularly high in Bounderby's Bank was vocal in his defence of all these stray incomers seeking work.

A veritable image of his father, if cut Mr Bitzer would have been expected to bleed white. His hair – like the rest of him – had progressed from the blond of youth to the white of late middle-age without anyone noticing. In fact his stance on the immigrants made perfect sense. An influx of workers had the capacity to lower wages, a fact that would clearly benefit his bank's clients and thus himself. Moreover, many moved into Bitzer houses, paying Bitzer rents.

Others, more fortunate, lived in the better-built and well-equipped Gradgrind model village, paying more moderate rents and able to supplement their wages by nurturing Gradgrind pigs (though many were referred to by older people as Bounderbys) in sties on their Gradgrind allotments. Amongst these families a great many of the daughters were called either Louisa or Cissie, even Cecilia, but very few sons called Tom, despite the later kindness of Thomas Senior.

But by all, whether they came from Bitzer or Gradgrind families, the chamber pot incident was soon forgotten. They had after all livings to make, and gardens to tend, for recreation looking forward to the humbly named horse riding which was back in town. Though Mr Sleary and his asth-

matic lisp had now joined the great sawdust ring in the sky,
along with most of the men and women who had helped
Thomas Gradgrind come to his senses, the circus folk regularly returned to their quarters at the Pegasus's Arms. Here
they would break horses, practise new acts and refurbish
their bright costumes, all too often a matter of making do and
mending.

Recently the men, walking with legs stiff and bowed from
all the time spent on horseback, and the women, vividly
dressed if negligent in the matter of leg-covering, had been
joined by tumblers and jugglers from overseas. Was it a
matter of surprise that the mighty tiger had to be controlled
by a real Indian fakir? Or that the lions were in the care of a
gentleman who did not need the coal-black make-up that ran
in streaks and could be removed only by ale?

Indeed, the circus had become distinctly international, a
genius who could throw and make a simple piece of wood
return to him alongside a squat man who could make sinuous
creatures called sea lions balance balls on their noses. As in
Mr Sleary's time, however, everyone had at least one other
party piece. The Indian's other talents included walking on
live embers and sleeping on nails, the Australian's shinning
up the central tent pole to attach the tightrope. None of the
circus folk had much to do with Coketown inhabitants except
by way of their profession, preferring a sequestered existence
with sequinned Indian elephants to the mundanity of a mill
town with its melancholy mad ones.

Then another outrage occurred. The drinking fountains with
which Gradgrind had so generously equipped the park ran
with blood, or so it appeared to the man who discovered it,
the clergyman in charge of the New Church, who was
regularly in the habit of imbibing too freely of the commu-
nion wine and whose testimony was promptly rejected. But
red they did indeed run, as the more sober Hands soon
averred, and with dye presumably stolen from one of their
own manufactories. Once again the town was in uproar, not
because the jewel-like colour offended them, ruby enlivening

the grey stone chalices of the fountains, but because the insult seemed to be directed at the Gradgrinds once more, and in particular dear Miss Louisa, who made a point of wearing crimson and other brightly coloured ribbons and of carrying enough about her person to give to any child too poor to buy one for herself. The dye, moreover, left a stinking residue it was hard to shift from the stone.

The constabulary drafted in extra officers to inquire into the affair, but once again they had to admit defeat. No other dye was inappropriately inserted into the water supply, and life once again resumed its even tenor – but not for one young man.

Now the cricket season was beginning, William M'Choakumchild was like a child expecting Christmas. In every moment of his spare time, he was to be found in the nets at the edge of the field, offering to bowl to any of the gentlemen or professionals needing his services and overwhelmed with gratitude when at the end of a long session he was offered the chance to wield the willow himself. He even helped the club steward clean the spectators' benches and whitewash the pavilion. There must be nothing to disgust the great WG, or make him feel that this ground was in any way unworthy of hosting an important match. At last he took himself down to the Grand Imperial Hotel to ensure that sufficient rooms had been allocated to the visitors. Only then did he join other young men of the town at the railway station to welcome their most distinguished visitor and such of his team as were travelling with him.

And there he was – in the flesh! In point of fact, there was a good deal of flesh on WG's superhuman frame: had not most of it been muscle, in his cricket whites he must have looked like an overgrown snowman. There was a good deal of beard, too. Already two greying streaks ran from the source near the firm mouth to the delta at the very tip. Above the beard two bright eyes twinkled, and although today they were benign, affable even, William could see why some critics called them cunning: they said they befitted a man who had all the rules of cricket in his head, but did not always practise them in his heart. But William dismissed the rumours with an idealistic scoff. How could such a magnificent being do anything as human as cheat? How could a man of such generous proportions suffer accusations of being mean with his money?

Today the godlike side of WG was in evidence. To the amazement and delight of the young men like William who surrounded the great man's carriage, WG suggested that while his team-mates might wish to refresh themselves at the Grand Imperial, he himself would like to see the ground where he was to play on the morrow. William truly believed that if the great man had asked them to unhitch the horses and drag his carriage to the park, none would have baulked. However, his progress, though god-like, was a good deal more sedate.

There they were at the ground at last! To their horror they found their passage impeded by a distraught groundsman, who almost prostrated himself before Dr Grace.

"Sir – Your Honour – please, it wasn't my doing! Not any of it!" He wrung his hands, tears flowing down his manly cheeks.

As well they might.

The sacred square, protected, nurtured and guarded like a tender infant, had been violated. Divots of earth had been taken up apparently at random, with blue and red dye staining the wounds.

WG spread his hands – they were all to stand back. Towering almost head and shoulders above most of the Coketown denizens, he could see what they could not. The dye filling the missing clods enabled a keen eye to pick out letters – this was no chance assault on the turf, but the spelling out of a message.

REVENGE!

But even WG was unable to distinguish the scrawl after that. Some thought it might be the letter T, others G. Some said it was a combination, the two entwined, as on a gentleman's signet ring.

But surely no gentleman – no, nor any professional cricketer either – had committed the vile deed.

WG pressed a finger to his lips; he was deep in thought. At last he straightened. "It is clear to me," he said, "that you have a dangerous man loose in the town! A man who would commit such a vile act as this would not hesitate, in my opinion, to commit murder."

William stepped boldly forward. "If you please, Dr Grace, this is not the first offence to be committed in Coketown. To be sure, the others were less serious, but occurrences there were."

"And have the police been informed?"

"They have indeed, sir. But they have apprehended no suspect."

"And how hard did they try?"

William could not vouchsafe an answer – he spread his hands in despair. But his anguish turned to pure gold.

"Young man, you seem to have more sense than most," WG declared. "Let us adjourn to that pretty pavilion there and you can tell me what you know. Meanwhile, I believe that our friend the groundsman here will do his best to repair the damage. I cannot think the pitch will be playable this week, but with careful rolling and filling it may recover for the end of the season."

"But the match, sir—"

"I believe that there is another ground, not far from here, on the Trafford Road. We will use that." Clearly the great man was in no doubt that should any other fixtures have been scheduled for the ground they would be summarily postponed.

A boy having been despatched to the nearest outdoor to obtain jugs of the finest ale, Grace and William walked into the little wooden building as if, William felt, into the very halls of Valhalla.

"So Mr Bitzer might well have a grudge against the Gradgrind family, for its ideological violation of all he holds dear?" WG asked, seating himself in the chair reserved for the club president and motioning with an enormous hand for William to sit beside him.

"Mr Bitzer is a very grand man in the county," William was obliged to object. "He owns a good third of the town, and eats good dinners as a consequence. I cannot in all honesty see a man of his status or size sneaking into the cricket ground with a spade and cans of dye."

"But he would have had access to both?"

"What householder in this town would not have been able to lay his hands on a spade? But Mr Bitzer is not a manufactory owner, who would have much readier access to the dye," he said regretfully.

WG raised an eyebrow. "You would have liked Mr Bitzer to be responsible, I fancy?"

Even in such a sturdy young man as William the latter verb still caused a frisson he chose to ignore. "I fear he is not a kind man, sir, and there are many who would like to see him get his come-uppance. He will have nothing to do with any of the improvements to Coketown that Miss Louisa has steadily instituted. Indeed, the kinder she becomes, the harsher his regime at the bank and the more swiftly he forecloses on those unfortunate enough to owe him money. That's the Bounderby Bank, sir. You'll hear the name of Bounderby a great deal about this place, but the originator of the name himself is dead. He lives on in the form of twenty-five pensioners who took his name and take his meat. But they are all old men, and I cannot think that they would have the strength required to deface the pitch."

"And are there any other disaffected folk in the town?"

The young man frowned in his efforts to please his idol. "There is talk of an aristocrat, one Mr Harthouse, having suffered a setback in an affair of the heart, many years ago. It is said – but very quietly, sir, because we all revere and respect the lady in question – that he tried to make love to dear Miss Louisa, then Mrs Bounderby, who sent him to the rightabout. But the day he left town, they say, she returned to the protection of her father, leaving her husband for ever."

"That would be the original Mr Bounderby?" Grace clarified with a smile. "Ah, thank you – you are very kind!" He counted out the money due to the boy who ran in with the ale. As an afterthought he reached into his pocket book and scribbled something on a page which he tore out and presented to the lad. "There, that will gain you free admission into the ground when we play Lancashire."

The boy, who William deduced had been hoping for a silver sixpence for his pains, looked downcast. Recalling with horror those allegations about the tightness of WG's fists, William fished in his own pocket, and the youngster left speedily, clutching the coin.

Puzzled and possibly ashamed, the great man scrutinized William from under his huge eyebrows. "Admission to the ground costs twice as much when I am known to be playing." The implication was that the slip of paper would have been worth far more than sixpence.

William swallowed hard. "Did you not see his shoes, sir? He could not have walked as far as the Trafford Road without them falling to bits. His father works for Mr Bitzer," he added, by way of meaningful explanation.

Brightening, WG asked, "The revenge promised on the pitch could not have been directed at Mr Bitzer?"

William shook his head decisively. "He has no involvement with any of the other incidents."

"Pray, explain," WG demanded, as if he were back in his surgery asking for details of an ache or pain.

"The statue or the drinking fountains, sir – the other occurrences I mentioned earlier, sir. The first I discovered myself." When he told Grace how he had removed Mr Gradgrind's unorthodox headgear the great man threw back his head and laughed.

"I shall have the pleasure of playing against you, I hope."

"I am only hoping to be twelfth man, sir."

The bright eyes twinkled. "You may be more if you are known to have bowled me out during net practice," he said. "But if we have the sacrilege to the statue, and the dye in the water, it does appear that someone wants to make the Gradgrinds ridiculous at best and uneasy at worst. And the violation of the cricket pitch – as we will make clear to those constables I see even now awaiting our presence –

suggests a very sick mind indeed. As I said, I fear its possessor may stop at nothing short of murder!"

The constables' inspection of the pitch was cut short by a sudden downpour, which had the effect of making the pitch look as brilliant as a circus girl's skirt, red and blue curlicues of colour on a dark velvet ground. It also soaked the practice area, so it was clear that there would be no glory in the nets for William that night. The great man frowned and growled at the constables, but more, thought William, as if he were dissatisfied with something else.

At last, tugging on his beard of beards, the doctor said slowly, "William – I trust you allow me to call you by your Christian name rather than by the excruciating conglomeration of syllables that form your surname? – William, you tell me that the children of Bitzer families are very poor, and cannot even look forward to the treat of a cricket match?"

"All too often they cannot afford a bat and ball with which to play, let alone the entrance fee to watch others," the young man said.

"Then they would not be able to afford any other entertainment?" WG bit his lower lip.

William allowed himself a sad smile. "We are lucky enough to have a circus that makes Coketown its permanent base, sir. And on a show night, you may see a row of the seats of badly patched breeches as the wearers peer through slits in the tent wall."

"Can't even afford a farthing for a circus?"

William shook his head.

"And certainly not for a penny bun to cheer the evening along? I am a doctor, William, and I would prefer youngsters to eat good apples rather than penny buns. But I do realize that a treat must involve some sticky comestible, or it is not a treat at all. William, if you undertake to provide the ragamuffins, male and female, I will provide entrance to the circus and the requisite refreshments. No, no thanks – off on your business. We will meet at – what time does this circus of yours start?"

William flushed with embarrassment on the circus people's behalf. "When they manage to assemble sufficient paying people to constitute an audience, sir."

Grace consulted a great turnip of a watch. "Then let it be constituted for seven-thirty this evening."

The tent was crammed by seven-fifteen but, knowing that anticipation would add to the audience's enjoyment, the ringmaster refused to let the performance begin until seven thirty-five. Imagine the terror at the sight of the great wild beasts close enough to touch, and the amazement as acrobats flew through the air! Imagine the delight as clowns threw custard pies or buckets of water at each other, and girls on horseback pirouetted and dispensed paper flowers to the onlookers! Imagine the disbelief as the Indian walked over hot coals, and a thin-faced man threw a stick that curved in the arena and returned to his hand!

William was as thrilled as the rest, and turned, laughing, to thank his host. But their benefactor was frowning, deep in apparently unpleasant thought. Halfway through the entertainment, he got to his feet, motioning William outside.

"William, what colour are the girls' dresses?"

"Red and blue, sir."

"A familiar red and blue?"

"All too familiar, now you come to mention it."

"And with what do the unfortunate clowns gather up the evidence of the elephants' parade?"

"A spade." William saw the drift of the great man's questions. "But you cannot think that any of the circus folk would desecrate anything pertaining to the late Mr Gradgrind! They became his friends – they saved his son's life!"

"And how did they do that?"

"Tom was a wanted man. They managed to prevent his capture and ensured that he was sent to the colonies, where, it is said, he died."

"*Is said*!" Grace looked excited. "And how old would he be?"

"Somewhat younger than Miss Louisa, sir. That is to say, in his fifties or sixties."

"That cock won't fight, then," Grace muttered. "And yet
– and yet – Tell me, where does this Miss Louisa live?"

"Close at hand, sir, since she always loved the circus. At
Rose Cottage – down there." William pointed down the lane,
to a picturesque dwelling from which a curl of smoke rose
through the evening light.

Dr Grace might have been a big man, but he was remarkably fit and very swift on his feet. William was hard put to
catch up with him, but the smell of smoke leant wings to his
heels. In Coketown there were always plenty of people ready
to join a pursuit, and though no one could have explained the
nature of their urgent errand many were already crying,
"Stop thief!" or "Murder!" as Rose Cottage came in sight.
In the event neither was entirely apposite, but it was true that
a window hung open on bent hinges and that flames were
biting hungrily into the thatch.

"On my shoulders, William!" Grace cried in a mighty
voice. "And get into that room!"

William did as he was told, hardly understanding even yet
the urgency in his mentor's voice. He was met by the sight of
Miss Louisa, apparently dead upon her bed.

With a superhuman effort, he heaved himself into her
bedchamber and, driven by the ever louder crackle of burning straw, seized her, dropping her body without ceremony
into the waiting arms of the good doctor. He perched on the
windowsill, waiting anxiously for the good people of the town
to find a ladder for him to climb down or a strong blanket for
him to jump into. As for the Coketown Fire Brigade, that had
been summoned, and he could see the horse pulling the
tender four streets away.

From his vantage point, he could also see but one person
running away from the fire, and not towards it, a man who in
his effort to escape the notice of the mob curved in and out of
alleyways but always heading towards the circus, just as the
boomerang had returned to the Antipodean's hand. Even as
William's eyes filled with wild surmise, even as he pointed to
the bolting form, his ears caught the sound of a dreadful
creaking. The roof would fall in at any moment!

No ladder! No blanket! And the fire appliance still a whole street away!

William jumped, hoping and praying for a safe landing.

But it was not to be.

The great man was the very first to visit William in the Gradgrind Infirmary, where he and his broken legs were anchored to the bed.

Dr Grace checked his pulse, laid a professional hand on his brow to check for fever, wiggled the exposed toes. At last he declared, "You're doing very well, my lad. What's more, you can congratulate yourself on saving Miss Louisa's life."

"She lives, sir?"

"She does indeed. She had been choked into unconsciousness by our foul miscreant, who hoped that everyone would believe that she had died in an accidental house fire – a fire, it goes without saying, he himself had started. Did I not tell you that a man capable of digging up a cricket pitch was capable of anything?"

William helped himself to one of the grapes Dr Grace had placed beside his bed. "But what made you react so quickly, sir?"

WG found a chair and settled himself on to it, looking for all the world like a coconut on an egg-cup. He spread a ham of a hand and counted off each point on his fingers. "You pointed directly at something, William, before your fall, something or someone. You certainly pointed in the direction of the circus tent. Now, at the circus, we find a man who is agile, and what demands more agility than shinning up a tent pole? We find a man who has access to dyes of various hues, and how else do the circus women fettle up their clothes than with commercial dyes? We find a man with a spade. We find a man whom everyone assumes will stay in the tent for the remainder of the performance but is able to sneak out and speedily return. But most of all we find a man with a grudge, however misplaced."

"A man with a grudge?" William repeated stupidly.

"A man with a grudge," Dr Grace replied firmly. "A man

whose father committed a terrible crime, allowing someone else to take the blame for it, but who always bore a grudge against those he had wronged. A man whose father may have died with his sister's name on his lips but whose father had never done other than covet her riches and blame her for the discovery of his crimes. A man, in other words, William, whose mind was poisoned. Although he was brought up in Australia, part of our glorious cricket-loving empire, he still plotted the very word he inscribed on your cricket pitch – revenge."

William blinked. "But who?"

"Did you see the man with the boomerang? That polished piece of wood, William, that apparently returned at its thrower's behest. I have visited Australia, my boy—"

"Indeed, sir – in '73, '74! I read about your adventures in the papers, sir."

WG looked a touch embarrassed. "And I must confess I nearly killed my cousin with one of the damned things. Apparently they appear nowhere else. Where else should the younger Mr Gradgrind have been sent, except to Australia?"

"But the Indian, the African—" The young man's mind was reeling.

"– speak so little English it is not worth mentioning. No, William, rest assured; we have the right man – Thomas Gradgrind the Third, as our American cousins would call him."

William's eyes widened. "A third Thomas Gradgrind? Our benefactor's grandson – Miss Louisa's own nephew?"

"Exactly so."

"But how was he apprehended?"

"Not without a struggle, believe me. The constabulary tried to set their dogs on him, but he turned his aboriginal instrument on the nearest hound, causing it to expire on the instant. We had stalemate, William. But – like you, my boy! – I am no slouch with what is a potentially lethal missile myself. A cricket ball, hurled at a man's temple, could kill him. And I was determined that he should be taken alive. At last, in desperation, I grabbed a custard pie from one of the clowns and hurled it with all my might at his face. It did him no lasting harm, but rendered him temporarily blind. As he scraped the pie shards from his face, the constabulary did the rest. He is in police custody as we speak. Indeed, he has confessed all."

"And what will happen to him?" William asked.

WG pulled his long beard, now making him look like an Old Testament prophet. "I cannot say whether he will serve the prison sentence he deserves. I have doubts as to his sanity, and Miss Louisa is notably soft-hearted."

"But he has committed a serious crime – she might have died!" And William could not forbear to think of his lower limbs.

"It is of that that I have managed to persuade her. I believe a dear friend of hers has endowed a hospital for the criminally insane—"

"Indeed. The Cissie Mildmay Home. The patients are encouraged to make music and paint and grow flowers and I know not what else."

"Excellent. Exactly what he needs. So all's well that ends well, eh, my boy?"

William tried hard to nod positively. But he was scarcely more than a youth, after all, and though he was delighted that the miscreant would cause no more problems about Coketown, he had indeed problems of his own. Not only would he not be twelfth man in the match he had so long dreamed of, it was possible that he would never play again. Involuntarily, he let his eyes drift towards his legs.

"Well, well," Grace said, with the sort of smile that William had seen on his lips when he had proposed the treat for the Bitzer children, "suppose that the moment you are deemed fit to travel you come down with me to London. Agnes would enjoy looking after you, and I could take you to a few matches. How would that be?"

William knew he must protest. "My studies, sir—"

"Forget them for a while. Remember what that ringmaster says, William: people must be amused."

Tom Wasp and the Swell Mob

Amy Myers

Dickens's next novel was Little Dorrit, *which began to appear in monthly parts from December 1855. Its title, which bears some resemblance to Little Nell in* The Old Curiosity Shop, *does indeed refer to an angelic young girl in somewhat similar straits. This is Amy Dorrit who had been born in the Marshalsea Prison where her father, William, is the longest serving debtor. Dorrit eventually wins his freedom through an unexpected inheritance but discovers that money is not the answer to everything. Dickens was clearly exploring episodes from his childhood and his father's own incarceration in the Marshalsea.*

Amy Myers uses the London of the street urchins to illuminate the background for Little Dorrit. *The story is filled with the street vernacular of the day, most of which is self-explanatory. The phrase "the Swell Mob", used to be used by the poor about the rich, but over time it came to be used of pickpockets and others who dressed fashionably in order to rob the well-to-do. By dressing well it helped them escape detection. Amy Myers is probably best known for her stories featuring the Edwardian sleuthing chef Auguste Didier which began with* Murder in Pug's Parlour *(1986), but she has also been developing a series featuring an East London chimney sweep, Tom Wasp. Several stories will be found in her collection* Murder, 'Orrible Murder *(2006), whilst the first novel in the series is* Tom Wasp and the Murdered Stunner *(2007).*

"Wasp! Come 'ere!"

I obliged. With Dolly Dunks, this was advisable, even though the crumbling chimneys of the Tabard Inn were not my first choice for work. It's said that pilgrims once gathered in the old part of the tavern before they set off to Canterbury. If they'd seen it today with its rotting stairs and galleries, they'd have been even more glad to leave. Even my old Smart's cleaning machine is afraid to go up those flues. The brush comes out at the top – if at all – with a sigh of relief. But with Dolly you don't say no. It's more a case of forget about your threepence and have a plateful of yesterday's dog's dinner in payment.

"There?" I asked hopefully, looking at the newer part of the inn on the right of the yard – newer meaning only a hundred or two years old.

Dolly ignored this question. "You come with me. I got pigmen here."

That was nothing unusual at the Tabard, but the police seldom required a chimney sweep. Not my place to question Dolly, though, so I followed her broad figure and dirty red petticoat trailing through the yard. Hobbling over the cobbles behind her, I was too busy avoiding the wagons and delivery men to wonder where we were off to, until we went past the old part of the inn and through the passageway to the rear yard, which services the stables and some tumbledown dwelling houses for Dolly's workers. She was heading for the old hop warehouse at the far end, and I could see a young pigman, looking most imposing in his swallowtail coat and top hat, with his rattle at the ready in case I tried to rush him.

"What's 'e want?" he asked suspiciously as we reached him.

"Friend of 'ers," Dolly replied, brushing him out of the way like a bluebottle and marching inside.

Hers? What was going on here, I wondered, as the smell of dried hops greeted me.

And then I saw her, lying on a pile of hop pockets, eyes staring upwards, her tongue forced out, and her lovely face all bluish-purple and blood-stained. There was no mistaking her, no mistaking little Alice Dear. Someone had strangled her and left her here like so much unwanted rubbish.

I felt my eyes misty, then the salt of tears mixing with the soot.

"Why come to my place to get herself done in?" I heard Dolly say at my side, sounding most aggrieved.

I heard the pigman talking to her about one of these new detective plainclothes gentlemen on his way to deal with it. I let them get on with it. I had plenty to think about.

Top of the list was how I was going to tell Mr Dickens.

I usually visit Mr Charles Dickens to clean his study chimneys in Tavistock House. The first time was late in 1851. He'd just moved in, and was not pleased to see me. As I came through the door with my tuggy cloth, he clutched his head, demanding to know when he was ever going to get a moment's peace to write again. Another workman, he shrieked. Papers had flown everywhere as he leapt up from his writing table, knocking over a pile in his agitation. In the process of helping him to pick them up I had received no thanks, owing to the sooty marks my fingers left, but suddenly he gazed at me, threw back his head and laughed.

"A sweep," said he. "There should be a wedding. By heavens, *Bleak House*. My Ada *shall* marry Richard."

It is now May 1855 and I have been his regular sweep ever since. He took the news of Alice's death badly, although he had only known her just over three months. He grew very pale and sat for a long time staring out into the garden beyond, while I fixed my eyes on the knick-knacks on the writing table beside him. At last he said: "I need her, Tom. She was my inspiration. How can it be that she has died?"

"She was murdered, sir."

He gave a sort of groan, then jumped up again and gripped

my hand. "It was through no fault of hers, Tom. Did you know that her father was thrust most cruelly into the old Marshalsea prison for debt? And when it closed, was the fair light of London to see him again? No, he was sent to the King's Bench gaol. Had it not been for Alice he would have died many years since. Did you know that poor child sold flowers in the markets to earn a meagre pittance to keep her father alive?"

"No, sir," I said truthfully.

"She was an angel, that child."

"She was twenty-two, sir," I ventured.

He brushed this aside. "A child at heart. An innocent. And a mere child when she struggled to earn a crust or two for her father in the Marshalsea. Was she not an angel, Tom?"

"God sees into all our hearts, sir," was all I could say.

"He does, He does. The pure in heart shine out as His chosen ones. Was she not an example to us all?"

A question I could answer with sad truth. "She was, sir."

"How shall I ever write again?" Mr Dickens asked mournfully.

"By remembering her, sir," I said firmly. "Just as I shall."

"There are terrible deeds done in the dark alleyways of London. *Still*, after all I have tried to do."

"They are the chimneys of life, sir," I said helpfully. "They need to be swept."

He rose magnificently both to the occasion and his feet: "Sweep them now, Tom. Find out who killed my Little Dorrit."

I would do so, not only for his sake but for mine. I'd a great liking for Alice Dear – not for the angel Mr Dickens believed her to be, but for Alice herself, who had laid aside her wings more often than our Lord might tolerate and certainly far in excess of what Her Majesty's pigmen would. Alice was no flower seller. Since the age of seven when her dad went into the Marshalsea, our young angel had been a member of the Swell Mob, as it's known now: high class dippers into ladies' purses and gentlemen's pockets.

The Swell Mob don't bother with the markets or everyday streets like Mr Dickens' Oliver Twist under Fagin's cruel rule, but are highly trained to act as a gang in the better-class areas round the theatres and banks. Young Alice with her innocent child's eyes would steal at the lady's side, her little hands delving into the pockets of the full skirts, so far away from the lady's person that she never felt a thing. With the crinolines of today her task is even easier. A member of the gang is in front as protection, one to each side, and one behind as well in case of trouble. But there never was trouble when Alice was working, so she told me with pride.

She was lying, though, as so often. As a youngster of eight or so she was all but caught, but Kidsman Joe, the gang leader positioned in front of her, nipped back to take the blame; he went to gaol and she escaped. I saw it all. I was sixteen then, and already well established in my trade. She saw me watching and gave me a wink. I'll know you again, young lady, I thought, and I did. Four years ago, I was seeing my wife Mary to her rest in St George the Martyr's churchyard in the Borough, when she – meaning Alice – won my heart by coming up to me.

"Cheer up, Mr Sweep," she said. "Your baby, was it?"

"My wife," I answered.

"Then," she said sweetly, "she's in heaven, Mister Sweep, at the top of her chimney at last."

That was Alice. She had a heart, but usually you'd never know it. After that, I saw her from time to time and we became quite friendly. I knew all about the Mob, and about Kidsman Joe with whom she lived in Lant Street, not far away from St George's or from the old Marshalsea, whose wall still borders the churchyard.

It was another churchyard, St Paul's, where in late January of this year I met Alice by chance. Kidsman Joe's mob likes dipping there. Mothers and children, smart gentlemen, lords and ladies, everyday workers, all flock to it, mostly shopping or on their way to Doctors' Commons, that rotten apple of a law court that has ruined so many people's lives. Here scavengers hunt for wills in dusty registers, in the hope of tracking down some prey, here bitter divorce cases break people's hearts, and yet here marriage licences are granted for those who would wed in haste. Everyone in St Paul's Churchyard, whether they are in search of a wife or a pie from the pastry-cook's, has his mind on other things than purses, and so waiting in the confectioner's or coffee house are the Swell Mob, spying out new victims and lusting after new swag.

On that raw January day, however, even the Mob, let alone the shoppers, had something else to chat about. Mr Thomas Toodle, the well known radical member of parliament, lawyer, associate of Mr Dickens and wealthy philanthropist, had been found murdered here the previous morning. The patterer's chat was that he'd been knifed by a drunkard who had staggered out of a doorway and struck him down, although some said it was a dark deed by Her Majesty's unpopular Tory government, currently in such disarray. I was there to clean the chimneys of Doctors' Commons, where Mr Toodle used to hear law cases – an odd place to work for one so keen on reform. I had turned from the churchyard carriageway into the narrow street of Paul's-Chain, and saw Alice arguing with a gentleman ahead of me on the right, down by the arched entrance to Doctors' Commons.

I recognised her immediately in her poke bonnet and heavy shawl, looking so demure. She wasn't her usual self, though. As I came closer, I saw she was looking anxious, and was arguing with Mr Bob Cheery. He was the senior clerk working in the Prerogative Office at the Doctors' Commons, and I had always found him a pleasant gentleman and highly religious. He must be about forty years of age, and had done well to reach such high office – but then everyone at Doctors' Commons does well, except for the poor souls they serve.

"Good morning to you, Tom. The Lord be with you," he greeted me. He would need the Lord to be with him too, if he had dealings with the Swell Mob, I thought. If Alice was here, the Mob couldn't be far away.

"Trouble?" I asked Alice, seeing her look appealingly at me.

"With the Mob," Bob answered for her.

"I've left Joe," Alice said defiantly. "Bob's been looking after me, but I'm afraid. I want to live somewhere else."

I could see she meant it – or thought she did. "What does Joe think about this?"

I was troubled, for Joe has a nasty temper on him. He must be about thirty by now, which is getting old to run a gang, and there were dogs snapping at his heels for taking over the mob. Buzzer Bill for one, who is a nasty sort of villain, determined with his sturdy brutish strength to run the gang himself and have Alice along with it. He didn't stand a chance against Joe, who is a crafty cove and has had some sort of education. He came to the Mob after his father dropped down in the world in two short months from businessman to docker to a magsman swindling people in the streets. Buzzer Bill on the other hand was born in the Nichol like me, the rookery not too far away from Her Majesty's Tower, but I doubt if she ever looks out of her back windows with a telescope. Then there's Edie, who has no plans for leadership. As a former judy, she's only too pleased to have a job – that is how the Mob sees their work. Next in line for running the gang is Charlie, who adored Alice from afar, but had never dared to cross Joe. Like Alice he behaves like an angel but can be a devil. His name is really Daniel, and he gets his nickname from the old watchmen, that being his role in the Mob. He guards from behind – a good place for him.

"Joe doesn't know where she is," said Bob grimly. "But he soon will if she leaves me."

"You know that Mr Dickens, don't you, Tom?" Alice said eagerly. "He helps fallen women."

"I told you, Alice," Bob said firmly, "you are no longer fallen. God has forgiven you."

"He'll find me, Bob." She wasn't thinking of God, but of Joe, of course, and avoiding Bob's eye. He was looking most put out. I assured him I would take care of her, and, after extracting a promise from her that she would return that evening to tell him what had happened, he reluctantly returned to work.

"Well, Alice," said I, "here's a nice chimney you're asking me to sweep. *Are* you a fallen woman?"

She was most indignant. "I ain't never been on the streets yet, but I can lie about it, can't I?" Then she tried to laugh, looking so angelic my heart was melted. If I hadn't seen her once kick an old woman lying in the gutter out of her way, I'd almost have believed her. But I knew she was only a part-time angel, as most of us are, working the hours she chooses.

"Help me, Tom," she went on to plead. "Take me to Mr Dickens. I want to get away from the Mob and from Bob. He wants me as much as Joe. One wants my body, the other my soul. I can't breathe."

These words sat strangely on Alice's lips, and she was fidgeting with her bonnet strings, so I could see something was wrong.

"But what if Joe finds you?" I asked. "Or Buzzer Bill or young Charlie?"

It was then she turned her face towards me as we walked, and I saw it was full of fear. "I'm afraid, Tom. Afraid for me life."

I had in mind she might become a scullerymaid or perhaps even a shop girl, although I would tell Mr Dickens the full truth about her. No sooner did we walk through the study door later that day, however, than Mr Dickens was spellbound.

"Mary Ann!" he cried to my surprise.

"Well, sir . . ." I was ignored.

"If you please, sir," said Alice, looking her trembling sweetest. "I'm Alice."

"No," he said gazing at her transfixed. "Little Mary Ann. I had a playmate once, Mary Ann Mitton – I called her Little Dorrit. Tell me about yourself, Little Mary Ann. . . ."

And so she did. It was a self I'd never heard of but every time I opened my mouth to correct her, Mr Dickens gave me a reproachful look. Then he recalled they needed their kitchen chimney swept and I was promptly despatched. Not that he touched her, so she told me later, and I believe

her. He was too busy recreating Little Mary Ann out of Little
Alice and turning her into Little Amy for a character in a new
novel. As I left the room, I heard the word Marshalsea and I
knew I was needed no longer. Dolly Dunks had told me that
Mr Dickens' own father had been in the Marshalsea for a
short time, and he himself, a child at the time, had lodged in
Lant Street to be nearby.

Mr Dickens found Alice a job at a flower shop, a good
distance from St Paul's, and set about freeing her father of
debt so that she could live with him, and the Swell Mob
wouldn't find her.

But somehow they had, and one of them had murdered
her: was it Kidsman Joe, full of jealous rage that she'd left
him for Bob Cheery, or Buzzer Bill or Charlie? Or was love
nothing to do with it? Was it that she had betrayed the Mob
by leaving it?

The Borough isn't London and it isn't the country, wherever that might be. But it *leads* to the country, which lies
along the Dover Road, and so once across London Bridge
it seems a distant land. Where I live in East London, the
river is our escape. I can leave the nightmares of the
Ratcliffe Highway and Rag Fair, hurry through the horrors of Nightingale Lane, where every entry holds an
unknown threat, down to the docks. Beyond them the
river Thames is flowing; having deposited upon our mud-
banks the muck she has picked up, she disdainfully passes
on to the sea. This city is my home, but I like knowing the
river's there.

Wagons are coming and going all day along the Dover
Road, pulling up in the yards of the many inns and pubs
lining the High Street down to St George's church: the old
George with its galleries and handy time clock, the White
Hart, the Catherine Wheel, the Tabard and many more. The
Marshalsea prison closed thirteen years ago, when Alice was
nine, and is now an ironmonger's; although it hides its face,
the prison's grim buildings still linger on. Opposite it, huge
warehouses tower over little shops struggling for a living, like

the pie shop where Alice told me she used to buy pies for her father in the Marshalsea.

There is a hum in the Borough air. Always something doing. Some wagons are glad to leave the fog and smoke of London while others are fighting their way into it. I'd choose to be one of those coming *in*, with the thrill of London town lying ahead. The hustle and bustle of the city sweeps you up in the chimney of its arms, although it would squeeze you to death if the Good Lord did not protect those whom He chooses. As He did Alice, until she went her own way.

I walked through the gateway into the Tabard yard the next evening to begin my journey to the truth over Alice's death. One of their cheap entertainments was on, as its great days are long over and the tavern needs all the custom it can get. The Bearded Lady of London and the Giantess of Japan were to be followed by a twenty-minute play, *Murder at the Tabard*. This is an old favourite, but trust Dolly to show it tonight. This murder was about a girl called Mary White, not my Alice, but Dolly wasn't telling folks that. I knew I'd find Kidsman Joe's mob there. It was their usual meeting and gambling place in the evenings before the night's work.

As I walked into the yard, I could hear the hurdy gurdy playing and the roar of voices that a lions' den of drinkers and gamblers can produce. It was only a day and a half since I had seen Alice's dead body lying a stone's throw from here, but I knew there'd be no trace left. It was yesterday's news, today's story, and tomorrow would be forgotten. Life moves fast in the Borough. I wished Alice might be buried in St George's, but the churchyard is closed now. Besides, Mr Dickens said he would take responsibility for the funeral, which is a difficult task. The churchyards of London are overflowing because of the cholera which swept so many away through the sewers of life last year.

I had to do what I could for Alice, so I made my way through the smoke and dirt and, sure enough, spotted the Mob tucked away at a table groaning with tankards. Joe had a natty waistcoat on, with a kingsman spilling out of his pocket, and was ruling the roost. Buzzer looked his usual unmerry self, Edie seemed troubled, and Charlie – well, he was just watching the proceedings. He must be about the same age as Alice was, but he didn't have her courage to use the wits he was born with – not openly, that is.

"Evening, Joe," I said, having bought myself a pint of porter.

They hadn't seen me for some time, but my black face usually announces who I am. For all I wash every few weeks, the soot gets engrained.

They stopped talking immediately, and all four of them fixed their eyes on me, dangerous-like. Edie and Charlie were obviously leaving it to Joe to decide what angle he would take, although Buzzer's expression left little doubt as to what his would be.

"Well," Joe chortled (so that was the line), "what can we smell here?" He delicately held his nose and the other three obediently roared their heads off.

"The smell that stays," I replied carefully, "till we get to the bottom of this."

"Yer booze?" Joe sneered, cuffing my beer-mug with his outstretched arm and laughing as its contents spilled over my working jacket and trousers.

"That's better," growled Buzzer brightly. "At least the porter smells good."

More laughter. Until I said, "Alice," very quietly. "Have the pigmen talked to you?"

"We don't talk to pigs round here," said Edie anxiously. "You know that, Tom." She kept stealing glances at Joe to see if she was doing right.

"Then you can talk to me," I said cheerily. "Who did this to Alice?"

Seeing it was one of them, I didn't expect an answer, and I didn't get one. Not a straight one, anyway.

"What's it to you, sweep?" Buzzer Bill growled.

"Mr Dickens wants to know, and so do I."

That silenced them, not because they were great readers – probably only Joe could read at all – but because they'd heard of Mr Dickens in the way one does, and realized that Alice's death wasn't going to pass unnoticed.

"Who killed her?" I asked again, watching their angry faces.

No one spoke, until Charlie was suddenly inspired. "It could have been Micah Muggs."

All four nodded vigorously, but I didn't believe a word of it. "Why would Micah Muggs want to kill her?"

"He reckons she swindled him. Good at that, were Alice," Joe said approvingly.

I could believe it. She would fix you with that innocent eye and you'd trust her with anything. Trouble was that sometimes she actually meant it, so you couldn't always disbelieve her. Micah Muggs was the biggest fence in London and an unsavoury piece of work, but I realized I'd have to talk to him. Usually the Swell Mob avoided him, getting rid of its own ill-gotten gains, but sometimes it was forced to use his services for the long-tails, the high-value banknotes.

"Anyone else?" I enquired. "What about Mr Cheery?"

Another silence, then Joe said viciously, "He got his roger into her all right."

"I'll do for him, if he knocked her," Buzzer growled, while Charlie burst into tears. A useful trick I've seen him pull when the Mob does a job.

"When did you last see Alice?" I asked patiently.

Another look was exchanged between them. "Pigman said she was killed about ten on Tuesday night. We was up west, working," Joe explained virtuously, by which he meant dipping the theatre crowds at the Haymarket and then moving on to the night life of Piccadilly. If so, it wasn't likely any of them would have been back here in time to murder Alice, but I knew none of them would split on another.

"When did you last see her?" I repeated even more patiently.

"We ain't seen her at all," Joe growled. "She had her own lay."

This wasn't right, and I spoke out. "Alice worked in a flower shop up west."

"Did," he sniggered. "Sacked her."

"How did you know that, Joe?" I asked. So he *had* seen her. My heart sank. I should have realized Alice was in touch with the Mob again. "Was she living again with you, Joe?"

"Nah. With her dad," he said. "Dunno where, though. Might have seen her once or twice, I suppose. She said she couldn't take that Bible stuff of Cheery's," he sneered. "She wasn't with the Mob no more, was she?" He looked at his fellow villains for support.

"No," they all chimed in together, to my mind a little too quickly.

At that moment Dolly Dunks loomed up before us. "Oh, it's you, Wasp. Buzzing around again." Roar of laughter at this witticism, in which I joined as though this joke over my name was the first time I'd heard it. I left buzzing – pickpocketing, that is – to Buzzer Bill. I had important business with Dolly however.

"Did you see Alice in here Tuesday night?" I asked.

"Nah," she said promptly. "But then," she added, looking at the Mob and winking, "my eyesight's not that good."

"Back entrance to White Street open, was it?" I asked. There was a path leading from White Street into the Tabard's rear yard at the side of the row of dwelling houses.

Dolly caught on immediately. "Always is. Think I want them dirty hop wagons coming through my nice clean yard?"

Clean? All I'd ever seen was the filthy muck left until the next rainstorm came to make it less smelly.

"Why should Alice have gone to the warehouse?" I asked of Dolly and the Mob.

"Not to see us," said Charlie, tears springing out to order, at which Dolly came over all motherly. The rest of the Mob quickly agreed with him.

"Unless she was killed somewhere else and brought here," I said, with Joe's lodgings in mind. They all stared at me with great suspicion.

"Why?" asked Buzzer, speaking for them all.

"She must have been with someone she trusted," I said hastily. "One of you or Mr Cheery."

"Bob Cheery," said Joe immediately, and again his three supporters agreed heartily that this was the solution. I couldn't see it. Why would he bring her here to kill her, when he lived up Holborn way, and why kill her anyway?

I began to walk back to London Bridge, and would be glad when I reached it. The Borough smelled of Alice for me. Here I'd first seen her, here she had stood by me in the cemetery, here she had lived with Kidsman Joe, but here she had died as well, and the air seemed rank. For all the noise from the taverns, they were tucked away in yards well away from the High Street, which made it an eerie place by dark, and I felt uneasy especially as I heard someone behind me.

Sweeps are not usually attacked for their financial worth, so I turned to see who it might be. In the small pool of light from the gas lamp I recognized Kidsman Joe and Buzzer Bill, and such was their menacing look that a throb of fear turned my stomach over.

"Here we are again, Wasp," said Joe softly.

"Something about Alice you've decided to tell me after all?" I asked brightly.

"A warning to impart," said Joe, pretending to be gentlemanly as they strolled up to me. His fists were clenched and Buzzer Bill stood with brawny arms akimbo which made it clear gentlemanly behaviour could not be expected.

"Forget about the Swell Mob and Alice, see?" Joe pushed his face up against mine.

"I'll try to, Joe," I said reasonably. "But suppose I can't?"

"Then your legs are going to be even more crooked, Wasp."

"I don't need legs to take me to heaven, Joe. How are you planning to get there?" I asked bravely.

"Yeah," put in Buzzer, who didn't have any idea what we were talking about.

"Alice pulled a fakement on Micah Muggs and that's it," Joe told me forcefully. "Understand?"

"No snitches in the Mob, see," Buzzer informed me helpfully.

I saw all too clearly. "I'll be back," I promised them more cheerfully than I felt. If Alice had been risking her luck with Micah Muggs, she could well have been in trouble – and so could I be.

"*On* your back," sniggered Buzzer with a wit I hadn't credited him with. The way he stuck his jaw out suggested he meant it.

Most dippers and toolers never have to go near Micah Muggs, owing to the high level he deals at. Micah is dressy too, sporting fine Newgate knockers and working in a tail coat. He was even wearing court breeches when I saw him once at the Eagle Tavern. He's not so swell when it comes to money though, taking an uncommon interest in it. His establishment is by Bleeding Heart Yard in Greville Street near Hatton Garden, and from outside looks a genuine gold and silver business.

"No sweeps in here," he roared as soon as he laid eyes on me next morning. "Even you, Wasp."

"Suits me," I roared back from the doorway. "I've come about Alice Dear," I roared even louder.

Quick as a cracksman, he was out from behind the counter, I was pulled into the shop by my jacket and the door was slammed and locked behind me.

"What about her, little man?" he hissed, pulling me even closer to him, then obviously regretting it, and letting me go in a hurry.

"She's dead. Three days ago. I'm looking for her murderer."

His jaw dropped, and he hastily stepped back, as though I had the strong arm of the law up my sleeve.

"It weren't me," he babbled, forgetting all about his swell English.

"Who said it was?" I asked reasonably, and he looked more comfortable.

"She came here Monday morning to sell—" he hesitated "—her christening spoon and mug. Said she'd seen Joe Sunday morning," he added meaningfully. Then, (forgetting he was an honest trader) "she tries a fakement, palming me off with dub finnies and long-tails." I could see why Micah was aggrieved. "I told her I'd put the word around that Kidsman Joe's Mob was a bad 'un."

I could see Joe and Buzzer wouldn't like that. They had a reputation to keep up, and having Micah put the finger on them could do their trade a lot of harm. If he was to be believed, was Alice acting on her own or under Swell Mob's orders?

"Alice pleaded with me on bended knee not to tell any-one," Micah continued, "only it wasn't her knee she was offering me." A salacious gleam in his eye. "Said she did it for her old dad and she could say goodbye to her life if it came out. I told her her dad could buy his own lush, and anyway he was in clink. She said no, he was out, courtesy of that writing cove."

"Mr Dickens," I supplied.

"She told me her dad spent more than she could earn," Micah continued savagely. "I believed her. He came round here later roaring drunk, caught me from behind and wal-loped me. Said he'd tell the pigmen I was a snide if I didn't cough up. If you're looking for who killed Alice, Wasp, don't look my way, I'm a respectable businessman, as you know. Look for old Jacob Dear."

I enquired where old Jacob Dear might live, in order that I might visit him, and he supplied the address all too eagerly. I was getting very interested in Alice's dad.

"But don't forget the Swell Mob," he said darkly. "I told 'em about her, I did."

I wouldn't, I assured him. Guessing I wasn't about to wallop him myself, he fervently shook my hand, and I set off into another dark alleyway.

This one took me right back to the Borough. Ram's Head Court was off Clink Street between the two bridges of London and Southwark on the Surrey side. I was being sent from gas standard to gas standard in my search for light over Alice's death, but I had hopes of this one, because it was not far from the hop warehouse where her body had been found. The court was one of those holes where greedy landlords do nothing for as much rent as they can get, and consequently they are full of stinking cesspools and misery. Why was Mr Dickens' money for lodgings spent on this, I wondered? The door was open, but I tapped politely on it. It was answered immediately.

"Damn your eyes!" came the merry growl from inside.

"Tom Wasp, chimney sweep," I shouted back, stepping in and closing the door.

I saw the gentleman who wished me so well slumped before an empty grate, bottle in hand, waistcoat unbuttoned, collar only half attached to the grimy shirt. He opened one bleary eye:

"My name it is Sam Hall," he continued his song untunefully, no doubt in his belief that he was the great W. G. Ross of the Cyder Cellars.

"Mr Jacob Dear?" I enquired politely.

He nodded cautiously. "Are you the new turnkey?" he asked me doubtfully.

I wasn't sure how to reply to this. I was no prison turnkey; nor was this a prison, save a prison of drink. It was easy to see how his benefactor's money was wasted, in addition to Alice's. Beer and gin bottles tastefully adorned the floor, the table and the only other chair, together with an equally tasteful half-eaten eel pie. Fortunately, he looked happy.

"Welcome to the Marshalsea," he greeted me grandly. "A newcomer to this place?"

"I am, sir," I replied. "Through your daughter Alice."

He blinked. "Poor Alice, poor Alice, dead."

"I am truly sorry, sir. She was your one support, I suppose."

In a trice the bleary eyes had cleared. "You call a shilling a day *support*? A mere trifle sir. A bagatelle. How can a man live on such a sum? Alice deprived me of my rightful inheritance, you know."

"I didn't, sir," I replied cautiously. Could this be the reason that Alice now lay in a mortuary?

"Then you shall," he promised me darkly. He poured himself a glass of beer, but none for me, though I should have welcomed one. "She stole it from me, her own father. My mother, a rich woman, died without a will. I was her only son. I was the heir, the lawyers told me so. My father was long dead. Naturally people advanced me money on my coming inheritance. I spent it merely to please them. And then a cousin of whose existence I knew nothing came out of the blue; he fought the case in the Doctors' Commons, who awarded everything to him. Naturally I could not repay my creditors, who most unfairly placed me in the Marshalsea."

This sounded a strange legal decision to me, but I have never studied law.

"Certificates!" He solemnly wagged a finger at me. "Always keep your certificates, young man. Alas I was born many years before the law requiring central registration, and my dear parents wed even earlier – naturally. No certificates could be found, nor entries in parish registers in the guardianship of the Archbishop. This fiendish cousin produced a case that I was – my dear sir—" Tears began to roll down his cheeks, as he finished in a whimper "– born out of wedlock. In short, that I was a bastard. How could I prove otherwise? Indeed, sir, I could not prove I was born at all."

He continued to weep, and I could see that it was indeed a predicament if a man cannot be said to be alive unless he can produce a document to verify it. I could not, I realized, be alive myself, but as no one would have left me an inheritance save the stink of the Nichol I need not trouble myself about it.

"The case came before the Prerogative Court," Mr Dear continued. "My cousin conducted his own case before himself as judge. Not unnaturally he won. It would be strange indeed, had he lost. My dear Alice considered my fate was hard, particularly when I was not at fault." He reached for another glass of beer.

"But you say *she* stole your—"

"It was her fault," he interrupted angrily. "My own daughter. Alice informed me she would see the case reopened in the Doctors' Commons."

"How could that be?" I asked. "Alice could not run a law case." Then I remembered Bob Cheery was the senior clerk there. He might have known the way.

Mr Dear looked impatient. "Through Mr Toodle, of course," he answered.

"The murdered member of parliament?" I asked surprised.

"The murdered *villain*," he said savagely. "My cousin. He who claimed my mother's estate, he who fought his own case through the Doctors' Commons, he who *died*," he said with satisfaction.

I backed hastily out of this particular flue. There was a puzzling gleam in Alice's dad's eye which I did not take to. Especially as I recalled the rumour that it had been a drunkard who had murdered Mr Toodle. There was plenty of soot in this case already, and adding the flue of Mr Toodle's death would be a step into the dark that I did not welcome.

Mr Dickens left Alice's funeral immediately after she had been laid to rest, being busy creating his memorial to Alice in words, he told me. I took this to mean he was hard at work on his novel. The Mob was present in force, however, and Mr Cheery too, although keeping well apart from them.

"It was good of you, Mr Cheery," I began, hazarding a guess, "to get Mr Dear's inheritance case looked at again."

He shook his head sadly. "Although Mr Toodle did not always display the integrity he professed in parliament, when it came to matters of his own financial affairs, he was meticulous. Poor Alice could not be dissuaded that he had somehow misconducted himself in the case of Toodle versus Dear. After his death I enquired in the hopes of finding the missing register entries and certificates which Dear maintained had existed. I found nothing. For Alice's sake, however, I will search again."

"That's good of you, sir. I met Alice's father, who is most eager for the case to be reopened—"

"Lost to the demon drink, poor man."

"Like the drunkard who killed Mr Toodle."

He looked at me sharply. "There are plenty of drunks in London, Tom. You think it was Jacob Dear?"

I said nothing, and he heaved a sigh. "Alice feared he was guilty. He could so easily have believed that if he killed poor Mr Toodle the money would come to him."

"Do the pigmen know about this?"

"Alice was too loyal."

"Could he have killed his daughter?" I pressed him. "To stop her talking?"

"That could be so," Bob said reluctantly. "Alice came to my home only two evenings before she died, and I tried to persuade her to return to our Lord. Alas, she had returned to Joe instead, so she told me. She had seen him that very morning. The flesh is weak, Tom, and the Mob could have killed her for it."

Unfortunately the Swell Mob had overheard, and Joe, a striking figure all in black, showed an unseemly fist both to me and Bob Cheery. "It's a lie," he snarled. "She never came back, not like that. I never touched her after you got your dirty hands on her."

I thought of what Alice had said, one wanted her body, the other her soul. "You saw her, Joe, didn't you?"

He glared at me. "Not to screw," he said. "We passed the time of day, that's all. Keep away, you creeping Jesus," he added to Cheery who was listening to all this.

"I don't plan to attend any more funerals with you," Bob replied with dignity.

"Except your own," Joe said menacingly. "Think about it."

Bob obviously did for he hastily walked away. Joe spat on the ground. "Pretending to be saving her soul when all he wanted was to ruin her body," he muttered.

"You still think he could have killed her?" I asked.

"Maybe," Joe said carefully.

"Not Buzzer or Charlie?" I pressed my advantage now he was being co-operative.

"Any of us would have killed *him*, not her," he growled.

But he wouldn't meet my eye, nor would Buzzer, Charlie, or
even Edie. There was something they were keeping back, and
for the life of me I couldn't see why. The Swell Mob must be
protecting its own but, if so, why not put the finger well and
truly on Cheery or Jacob Dear, like they'd tried to do with
Micah? And then the beginnings of an idea came to me. An
idea that made me feel most uneasy.

I walked over London Bridge again that night, pausing
between two gas standards to look down at the Pool of
London. You could hardly see the old River Thames below,
there was so much shipping there; but, being dark, there
wasn't the usual throng of dockers and merchants scurrying
here there and everywhere, only the occasional drunk matelot
rolling back to his ship. I thought of Alice with her evil streak
and her loving heart. Joe, Buzzer, Charlie and Edie all loved
her in their own way, even though one of them might have
killed her. So could have her father. So could Bob, if he had
reason. But even if Alice had been hoping to get that case
reopened, I couldn't see it would profit Bob, and I couldn't
see he would be so set on saving her soul that he would
despatch it early to our Lord.

We have many fogs in London, but the only path I could
see through the one shrouding me was this one idea of mine,
which explained why the Swell Mob weren't speaking out.
Suppose on Sunday evening Bob had succeeded in making
Alice see the light? Suppose he had persuaded her to go to the
pigmen who would dearly love to know how to lay their
hands on the Mob? And then suppose all four of the Swell
Mob acted together to murder her to punish her for betraying them? With four of them there she would have felt safe.
They could easily have taken her through the back gateway
saying they were going to the tavern, then bundled her over
to the hop warehouse. The Mob sticks together. However
fond they might be of Alice, they wouldn't take betrayal
lightly.

Alice's death was a many-flued chimney, however, and
some of its flues could be awkwardly horizontal. There's just

been a special cleaning machine invented for such traps, so perhaps I should use one in my hunt for the truth. What about Jacob Dear? Was he in on it with the Mob? And was Alice still pursuing that inheritance question? I'd have to talk to Bob Cheery about that. If Alice's dad had killed Mr Toodle, then he could well be mixed up with this bag of soot; perhaps his job was to lure Alice to the hop warehouse where unknown to her the Swell Mob would be waiting.

As the fog began to lift, and the light of day arrived, I decided that I would go to see Mr Dickens, because I couldn't sweep the Toodle flue by myself. I waited two hours before he could see me, losing a shilling for unswept chimneys while I did so. I managed to take a sleep in the basement of Tavistock House, as the housekeeper had explained her difficulty: as a visitor I should by rights have been shown into the morning room but the chairs, she said, might object to my clothes upon them.

Mr Dickens was delighted to see me. He told me excitedly that he had just begun the first instalment of his new novel, which would be published later in the year in his magazine *Household Words*.

"I am calling it *Nobody's Fault*," he crowed. "Is that not a splendid title? Ironic of course. It is somebody's fault even if it is everybody's."

I could not follow this, and so I reminded him of Alice Dear, whose death might be several somebodies' fault.

"Little Dorrit," he said absently.

"Mr Toodle," I began firmly, before he began on his novel again.

He looked surprised. "A colleague in the fight for justice in parliament. His death was a grievous blow to the cause."

"Any suspicion how he acquired his money?"

"He was of impeccable reputation." Mr Dickens looked shocked, then followed my drift. "Or so I have always presumed," he amended.

"But what if he got his money by dishonest means? Say by forging or suppressing evidence."

"Tom, this is not a matter for you," he said kindly.

"Alice's death is."

"How can the two be linked?"

I hadn't the heart to tell him Alice was part of the Swell Mob, so I pretended it could all have been Jacob Dear's doing: he'd killed Mr Toodle, and then Alice. At first I was informed I spoke rubbish, but unwillingly he agreed to look into the matter. There were, he admitted, doubts over the efficacy of the Doctors' Commons, and talk of replacing it with a court of probate and a secure repository for registration records.

Even as I walked away from Tavistock House, however, I sensed I was in the wrong chimney again – or, rather, I *was* in the right one, but couldn't get it clean. In any case, I had to wait until Mr Dickens had made his investigations.

What he discovered cleaned it well enough to lay before the detective pigman. I still couldn't tell Mr Dickens the whole story, not wanting him to think any ill of Little Alice, so I went alone to the Metropolitan Police. I carried a letter from him so they would take notice of me, and presented my story to the sharp young sergeant called Williamson, who had been looking into the case.

You can never tell in this life. The Swell Mob had had nothing to do with Alice's death after all.

Bob Cheery put up a good performance, when Sergeant Williamson came to arrest him with a police wagon and uniformed constable.

"Gentlemen, I did not kill Alice Dear," he told them with dignity. "I was protecting her from the villains she used to work with. They are the ones you want. When I saw Alice on the Sunday before her death, she was intending to tell you –" meaning the policemen "– where the Swell Mob could be found. I had at last persuaded her that was God's wish."

Bob Cheery had never been on God's side, however, for all his splendid words. With Mr Dickens' evidence, together with missing parish register pages and certificates found in Bob's home, he was arrested, not only for Alice's murder but for Mr Toodle's as well. Sergeant Williamson explained to

me that when Bob had become inquisitive about the Toodle–
Dear case on Alice's behalf he had found the missing evidence in Toodle's office, and been threatening Toodle with
disclosure in return for money. They must have fallen out
and, with Toodle about to expose his wickedness, Bob killed
him. Unfortunately for him, Alice had realized what he had
done, so he had to kill her too.

This explanation troubled me. I had one advantage over
Sergeant Williamson. I had known Alice, and knew her
wings did not always work. How, I asked myself, had she
acquired so many long-tails to produce to Micah on that
Monday morning? From Bob Cheery, I answered myself,
when she had met him the evening before. She had been
trying Bob's own trick of demanding money for her silence.
But why had those banknotes turned out to be faked? And
that led me to have another talk with Sergeant Williamson.

Cheery denied it all, but the evidence was found in the
Doctors' Commons in the form of the will Mr Toodle had
drawn up – in Bob's favour. It turned out to be a forgery,
something Bob was rather good at. Not too bad at faking
banknotes either. It turned out he'd been producing them for
some time. The Sergeant and I decided that Alice had taken
them to Micah to change, found out they were false and
stormed back to see Bob at Doctors' Commons. Bob convinced her he would bring the true money to her on the
Tuesday evening, but to the Tabard rather than her home so
that her father didn't see how much money he was handing
over.

All tied up very nicely. So why was it I *still* felt I'd come
down the wrong chimney, like I did once when I was a
climbing boy? After all, I now knew why Alice had been
afraid for her life last November. It wasn't, as I had thought,
that she was afraid Joe would seek her out and kill her for
leaving him. It was because she knew Cheery had killed
Toodle for the inheritance money. She only came back to
demand money for herself because he'd told her earlier that
when Toodle died her father and she would get the money.
Instead, Cheery laughed at her and told her he had it all. She

threatened to split on the fact that he'd killed Toodle, and he made the mistake of paying her in faked notes. Once she knew that, all was clear to her. And she lost her life, because instead of running away, she went back to face Cheery.

I knew all this. What I didn't know was what the Swell Mob had been hiding from me.

There we all were, them sitting at the same table at the Tabard, but me with them this time. That was a favour. I even got my beer paid for. Even Dolly thanked me. I decided the reason must be something to do with Joe, and I thought I knew what it was.

"You came here that Tuesday evening, didn't you, Joe? That's what you wouldn't tell me."

They all looked at each other, and then Joe said, a bit too eagerly. "Yes, that's it, Tom. I came here to meet her, and she was dead already. I knew who'd done it of course, but I had to scarper quick."

He was lying. He would have put the finger on Cheery good and proper when his name was first raised. So what was it they were hiding? Everyone was watching me now, as I groped my way up this narrow chimney to the truth. I had a feeling I wasn't going to like what I found at the top – and I didn't. I could have wept. I'd thought it was Cheery who wanted Alice's soul, and Joe her body, but I'd had it the wrong way round. Joe really loved that girl.

"You were protecting Alice, weren't you?" I addressed all four of them, not just Joe. "Even after her death."

Joe blushed a bit, and Buzzer shuffled his feet. Edie pursed her lips together, and Charlie didn't cry. He just sat watching me stumble towards the answer.

"Bob Cheery killed Alice all right, and you all knew it," I said. "But you also knew he hadn't murdered Toodle. And nor had Jacob Dear."

Even then I hoped they'd deny it. But they didn't, so I had to go on:

"Alice killed him."

A long silence, and then Joe said awkwardly, "She came to

see me after she got the sack. Told me all about it. Bob kidded her that when Toodle was dead, her father would inherit the money, which meant she'd get it too. So when she told Toodle she wanted the case reopened and he laughed in her face, she killed him."

"She didn't know what she was doing, bless her," Edie cried.

"That's right," Joe agreed.

"Yeah," said Buzzer.

So it was left to Charlie or me to point out that when she went to meet Toodle she'd taken a knife with her. Neither of us did.

Oh Alice, little Alice. What am I going to tell Mr Dickens? Nothing.

It's not nobody's fault, Alice. It's everybody's because life put so much soot in your chimney. But it was you who took that knife. So I was glad that Mr Dickens changed his mind and called his novel *Little Dorrit*. That's the Alice I'll remember.

Miss Havisham's Revenge

Alanna Knight

Between completing Little Dorrit *and commencing* Great
Expectations, *Dickens's life once again became turbulent.
He had acquired Gad's Hill at Higham, just outside
Rochester, which became his final home, and he entertained many guests there, including Hans Christian
Andersen, who rather overstayed his welcome. Dickens
continued with his theatrical company, even performing*
The Frozen Deep, *a play he had written with Wilkie
Collins, for Queen Victoria. It was the first performance of
this play that brought Dickens in touch with a young
actress, Ellen Ternan, with whom he soon became infatuated. Dickens had for some years grown estranged from
his wife, Kate, and Kate believed that Dickens was having
an affair with her sister, Georgina. Dickens managed to
keep his relationship with Ellen Ternan secret, but was still
able to go through with a formal separation from Kate in
the summer of 1858. Dickens established separate homes
for Kate and Ellen in London while he settled into Gad's
Hill.*

*Needing to keep himself occupied, Dickens began an-
other round of public readings, and also determined to
wrest* Household Words *away from his publisher, Brad-
bury and Evans. He succeeded, after an acrimonious*

struggle, and then promptly merged it with a new maga-
zine he had just launched, All the Year Round, *which*
began with the serialization of Dickens's new novel, A
Tale of Two Cities. *Other family problems pressed upon*
Dickens at this time. His eldest children had left home, his
brother, Alfred, had just died and Dickens suffered a real
sense of loss. Amongst his other essays and stories at this
time, Dickens turned once again to visit his childhood and,
by way of therapy, to rewrite it.

Great Expectations, *which began in* All the Year
Round *in December 1860, is Dickens's last major novel*
and one of his best and we have two stories here which it has
inspired. It tells of the young orphaned boy Philip Pirrip,
known as Pip, raised by his tyrannical sister. Pip helps a
convict, Magwitch, who has escaped from a prison ship,
though he is later recaptured and transported to Australia.
The years pass and Pip is summoned by the elderly Miss
Havisham, a rich but unforgiving woman who has turned
against all men since she was jilted at the altar by (Pip
later learns) the villainous Compeyson, a former associate
of Magwitch. Miss Havisham has raised as her ward,
Estella, with whom Pip gradually falls in love despite the
fact that she taunts him and is heartless towards all men, a
trait encouraged by Miss Havisham. Although Pip is to be
apprenticed as a blacksmith he learns he has a secret
benefactor, whom he believes is Miss Havisham, and sets
up home in London to be educated as a gentleman. He
befriends Herbert Pocket, who calls Pip by the pet name,
Handel. It is only later that Pip learns his benefactor is
actually Magwitch, who has made his fortune in Australia
though has returned illegally. Pip and Herbert hide Mag-
witch, who now goes by the name Provis, but Magwitch is
betrayed by his former companion Compeyson and the two
fight to the death. Pip confronts Miss Havisham over her
deception and learns that Estella is to marry the odious
Bentley Drummle. He also learns that Estella is Mag-
witch's daughter. Pip and Herbert eventually make their
way in business and become successful.

Great Expectations *has one of Dickens's most intricate but most rewarding plots. It contains so much that the following two stories, whilst both drawing upon the book, do not overlap in any way. In the first we discover the full story of Estella's marriage from her own perspective. Alanna Knight has had a long and successful writing career since her first book,* Legend of the Loch *(1969) won the Romantic Novelists' Association's best first novel award. She is known as an expert on the life of Robert Louis Stevenson and has written* The Robert Louis Stevenson Treasury *(1982) and other books about the man. This provided her with considerable background on Victorian Edinburgh from which she developed her series featuring Inspector Faro which began with* Enter Second Murderer *(1988). The following story has been adapted and extensively revised from her novel* Estella *(1986).*

Even as I record these events, I fear my fate remains in the balance. If my husband dies, his mother and cousin will endeavour to have me accused and hanged for his murder.

My name is Estella, my strange destiny began when I was adopted by Miss Alicia Havisham, not from any tender impulse to adopt an unfortunate orphan but merely the grim determination to rear a pretty female child as a breaker of men's hearts.

To avenge the bridegroom who had betrayed her.

The room I first entered at Satis House did not terrify me then as it was to do in later years when its true significance became clear. Beyond the candles high in their sconces, seeping through tight closed shutters, a hundred birds in a hundred trees greeted the still warm autumn sunlight while inside the candlelight glittered remorselessly upon a scene of decay and corruption.

A grim charade, with a corpse-like woman whose faded unhealthy skin had not felt God's wind or rain or the blessing of sunlight for a quarter-century, wearing her fusty yellowed bridal gown, all withered and rotted like the obscenity of skeletal bridal flowers, their petals long returned to dust. And dominating that ghostly wedding banquet, the crumbled tower once a wedding cake now woven through and through with curtains of cobwebs, the crawling spiders and the mice who scampered, squeaking into retreat at our footsteps.

"You are not afraid of them, Estella," said Miss Havisham.

I shook my head and a ghastly smile of satisfaction revealed yellowed teeth. Dismissing Mr Jaggers, her lawyer, who had brought me, she patted my arm, her hand once beautiful, now a skeletal claw. "Good, dear child. They are our companions. That is your first lesson."

I was to be given every luxury, treated like a princess in a fairy tale who did not possess a heart to give love or show emotions. Provided with a maid, a poor girl inappropriately surnamed Jolly, under Miss Havisham's watchful eye my lessons in bullying and humiliation began.

The main object of my cruelty was Pip Gargery. If she beheld him near to tears, she would cry out: "If she favours you, love her. If she wounds you, love her. If she tears your heart to pieces, love her. I adopted her to be loved."

My formal education at Dame Clarissa's School for Young Ladies was completed at Mme Chauvez's finishing school in Paris. There the heartless princess had to endure the odious attentions of a spotty eighteen-year-old son and his portly father who possessed between them as many pairs of lecherous hands as the more worthy spiders of Satis House possessed legs. Mme Chauvez, convinced that Mlle Estella was intent upon seducing her innocent son and her dear husband, demanded that I leave immediately.

My return was followed by an immediate encounter with a distinguished young gentleman so elegantly clad I could be forgiven for failing to recognize the blacksmith's boy Pip. My once despised companion and whipping-boy now had great expectations of a fortune on condition that he retained the name of Pip and did not seek to know the identity of his mysterious benefactor.

As I showed Pip out, he smiled. "I can recount every

meeting we ever had together, the very first when you brought out food for me at the back door like a beggar."

"And you pretended you had helped some wretched convict in his escape from the Hulks just to impress me."

"It was true, Estella, although I cannot prove it and I expect he is dead long ago."

Watching him leave as I had done so many times and through so many changes, suddenly I wanted to call him back, for at the mention of Mr Jaggers, to be his guardian until he came of age, our eyes had sought Miss Havisham and we truly believed that she intended us for each other.

Instead it was Bentley Drummle who entered my life. Introduced by a mutual friend of Pip, and looking as if he had stepped down from one of the heroic paintings I had admired in the Art Galleries of Paris. Warriors of a bygone civilization might well have been the model for this English gentleman with expectations of a baronetcy in Shropshire.

Black hair and eyes, a sallow complexion with brooding heavy-lidded gaze, a large man, whose slightly ungainly physique suggested power. He walked like a wrestler, forward on the tips of his toes, moving his head slowly from side to side, as if he were on the defensive.

After the first bowing over my gloved hand, his manner was of the utmost detachment, even of boredom. Not even when we parted did he deign to look my way in the interests of politeness.

This was indeed a new and intriguing state of affairs for Estella Havisham, already recognized by male acquaintances as being worthy of a second glance. Could I be losing my looks so soon? Panic gnawed at me fiercely, for I had to confess a secret attraction to his outlandish looks.

My guardian now decided that having kept me too long as companion since completing my education I was to proceed to Richmond and in the house of Mrs Matilda Brandley, her one time close confidante, I was to be brought out and presented to society.

There I discovered that my activities were no longer limited to breaking men's hearts only, for the urgent matter of finding a suitable husband was predominant in Mrs Brandley's curriculum.

Pip was elected to escort me, not unwillingly I might add, to Mrs Brandley. A little dainty bird-like woman with an unmarried daughter, past thirty; as colourless as her mother shone pink and white, as staid and dull as her mother was youthful and flighty. Most men, one felt, given a straight choice, would opt for the sprightly widow rather than the sullen daughter.

Mrs Brandley's sole conversation about clothes and cards soon palled, as did her tinkling laughter, while her dedication to be young at all costs set my teeth on edge.

"We must be ready to give of our best at all times, my dear Estella. We must never be tired or cross. Frowns are for age, but smiles are for youth."

My patience was sorely tried at being a mere exhibit in her matrimonial showcase, where marriages were based on dowries and hard-headed calculations, and Romance belonged between the printed sheets of novelettes rather than the bridal bed.

And my price tag was high, for Mrs Brandley had spread the word that I was ward to the wealthy Miss Havisham and had expectations of a great fortune. Admirers came from far and wide. In all shapes and sizes and ages and conditions they descended upon us. The very young, to middling young, mature to downright elderly. Even hopeful old widowers hid in their ranks, on the lookout for a little extra capital to comfort their declining years, the added attraction a girl, young, healthy and strong enough to act as companion and nurse. Tall and short, fat and thin, bald and hairy, moustached or clean shaven, there were none who bowed over my hand whose names I wished to remember.

"Moths and many kinds of ugly creatures are attracted to the flame of a candle." I remember my words to Pip when, hearing of my success, he accused me of heartless flirtation and I can still blush at the memory of my supreme self-gratification. Let that be so, since emotions of passion presented certain difficulties for one bred without any heart.

Into this stultifying atmosphere, the presence of Bentley Drummle at an unusually tedious soirée was an exceedingly agreeable diversion. Even as I smiled and postured as required, striving to recall every detail of the elaborate rigmarole my guardian had so carefully laid down for a breaker of hearts, Mrs Brandley was ushering him over, her manner purposeful.

Extending my hand, I found myself oddly tongue-tied. "We have met before."

He stared at me frowning. Horror of horrors, what humiliation. He had forgotten entirely.

"It was at Rochester—" I began.

"Hmm," he interrupted, looking over his shoulder in the manner of one who desires instant flight, but there was no evading Mrs Brandley.

"Mr Drummle, sir, you will oblige me by escorting Miss Estella Havisham into dinner." Trapped, we regarded each other desperately. But perhaps to make amends for our forgotten earlier encounter and in a supreme effort to be gracious, offering his arm he led the way into the conservatory.

It was a cold blustery evening. The cold collation spread on a white cloth amid tinkling crystal frowned upon by curtainless windows which also seemed to shiver, served to remind me uncomfortably of Miss Havisham's wedding feast in its heyday before the spiders and mice moved in. The glazed cold meats, chicken, ham, turkey and lobsters had a funereal appearance and the banquet before us resembled more a lying-in-state than an occasion of cheerful social refreshment. As for the heavily decorated desserts, the ices and jellies, there was a toothache in every bite.

"Permit me to help you to a little roast fowl. Some lobster – no?"

Armed with our plates, we retired to a sofa overhung by indoor plants that the nervous diner might have been pardoned for considering with great caution, paying due attention to their fat glossy leaves and suspiciously predatory looks.

Having seated me speedily, Mr Drummle began to eat with such uncommon interest and vigour that again I was overwhelmed by the bleak despair of my own insignificance. How to compete, how to come between a man and his food? That small matter was also absent from my guardian's curriculum, a salutary warning that breakers of hearts lost their powers when confronted with the brute needs of the male stomach.

Believing all was lost, my pride was saved by the arrival of a young gentleman, extremely thin of face, body and hair who had been casting admiring glances in my direction all evening. Now he hovered, plate in hand.

"Do please join us." While I proceeded to devote my attentions to the newcomer, rasping sounds of cutlery were the sole sounds of life from Mr Drummle's third of the sofa, scraping his plate with a vigour and determination that threatened the destruction of its pattern of roses. Satisfied that no morsel had escaped him, a look of thunder had descended upon his brow. Could he possibly be jealous or was it merely indigestion?

After the food came the dancing. Like many big solid men, Bentley Drummle was light upon his feet, giving the quadrille his undivided attention. Indeed I might have been a statue he held for all the attention he paid me.

The guests departed. I was acutely aware of failure, expecting reproach, but instead Mrs Brandley gushed over me. "Mr Drummle has asked to be permitted to call upon you."

At our next meeting, my sharpened senses became aware of an atmosphere subtly changed as Drummle ushered me into the garden. A pale moon had arisen above the trees and an owl's hoot touched the scene with melancholy. As he towered above me, untouched by moonlight his eyes became black hollows in a face spectral and sinister. I must confess that I shivered and not entirely from cold when he ran a finger down my cheek, tracing it slowly from eyebrow to jaw then cupping his hand around my chin.

"Estella. It means little star and fits you to perfection, my dear."

My eyes snapped closed as his lips, very thick lips, warm

and sensuous in such a stern unyielding face, gently brushed
my own.

"You are a very exquisite creature. And I mean to have
you. Remember that."

This remark, which set so many carillons of joy ringing in
my poor head, abruptly ended as Mrs Brandley and the rest
of the party erupted into the garden.

Drummle refused to be sociable and took his departure
upon the thinnest of excuses while I prepared for bed in a
positive haze of delight, telling myself that one day soon I
should be Lady Drummle, living in a castle, and it had all
been so terribly, terribly easy.

A week passed without further communication and sadly I
decided that he had either been merely flirting or had imbibed too much wine when I received a letter from my
guardian.

The words stood out: "He has asked that he be allowed to
address you with marriage in mind. As you are aware he
stands to inherit when his grandfather, Sir Hammond
Drummle, dies. I urge you, dearest child to accept his
proposal promptly, for I have selfishly kept you by me too
long."

Then the warning note: "I do not expect, if you paid due
heed to my instruction, that you are in the slightest danger of
giving your heart to Drummle, or to any other man. I further
entreat that you continue to be guided by one who has
suffered greatly and bearing in mind your early training
and expensive education, remember that successful marriages are based not upon emotions of sentiment but upon
Property and the establishment of the Family. Come and
visit me as soon as you can. Your affectionate Mother-by-
adoption, Alicia Havisham."

At our next meeting which I expected to be extremely
romantic, Bentley informed me that arrangements for my
dowry were already in the hands of Mr Jaggers. A brief visit,
and preparing to leave he turned and said that I was to inform
Pip that his visits to Mrs Brandley's cease immediately.

Pip was a frequent visitor, my true friend, the one man

who loved me always, while the lips of Bentley Drummle who wanted me for his wife remained sealed upon that subject. As yet he had not uttered one syllable that might be interpreted as a declaration of undying love and I knew that Miss Havisham's instructions were wise. I was not in the least danger of loving Bentley Drummle.

I did a simple test. If I never saw him again my pride would be hurt, but if I never saw Pip again, the heart I was supposed not to possess would ache – and ache, for ever. Ah Estella, there lay the answer, but fool that I was I did not listen or learn until too late the dread path I had chosen.

Jolly should have taken me to Satis House for the last time. She would have cheerfully laid down her life for me, although I had already decided to discard her. Bentley insisted on a French maid, so Jolly was to be abandoned at Richmond along with my outworn clothes and other possessions too shabby for my new life in Drummle Towers.

However, Miss Havisham had elected Pip to escort me, which admirably suited her sly purpose of throwing him into my society on every possible occasion. Now selfishly concerned that the bride's side of the church would be empty, I had no male relative to give me away and Bentley would not allow Pip's presence, although I knew that had I asked, Pip would have come to please me, despite the agony of seeing me lost forever as another's bride.

As we entered Satis House my mother-by-adoption awaited. She hugged and kissed me eagerly, not forgetting to turn to Pip and ask as always: "And how does she use you?"

I saw too late the reason for her unholy glee. She was about to torture Pip with the knowledge that Estella had broken his heart: the coup de grâce my marriage to Bentley Drummle. Pip's role in her diabolical drama was at an end and he too, like Jolly, could be discarded.

Poor Pip. I knew that he had never entertained a moment's doubt that his benefactor was Miss Havisham. The vital link was Mr Jaggers, his guardian, and until she had approved Drummle's proposal, both Pip and I had imagined that when he came of age she would reveal her identity and that my hand in marriage would be offered, Pip's just reward for enduring my small cruelties and torments so nobly over the years.

Now I was painfully aware that in those ghostly upstairs rooms where nothing changed, today she could not get close enough to me. As I tried in vain to detach myself from the unpleasantness of this smothering affection, she demanded: "Are you tired of me?"

"Only a little tired of myself." I did not exaggerate. At that moment, for the first time, I was observing my true character reflected in all its disagreeable intensity and, ashamed of the emptiness of the role I had played throughout the years, I would be glad to leave Satis House for ever.

Angered, Miss Havisham struck her stick on the floor. "Cold, cold heart!"

This was too much. "You reproach me for being cold. I who am what you have made me."

Pip stood watching us without a word. God only knew what his thoughts could have been.

"Look at her, so hard and thankless on this hearth where she was raised. Here I took her to this wretched breast when it was first bleeding from its wound. Here I have lavished years of tenderness upon her."

"When have you found me false to your teaching?" I reminded her. "Who praised me when I learned my lessons?"

Suddenly I was aware of Pip's silent presence.

"Estella." The word came out like a pistol shot. "Tell me it is not true that Bentley Drummle is in town and pursuing you."

"It is quite true."

Another pause while he sought for words. "You cannot love him, Estella. You would never marry him? Such a mean brute, to fling yourself away on – a mean and stupid brute."

"That he is not. He is a fine, cultured gentleman. His family is noble, well bred." And conscious of my guardian's hand strongly on my arm, I said miserably: "Why not tell you the truth? I am going to be married to him."

Pip dropped his face into his hands but not before I had glimpsed his expression, like a man condemned to the scaffold. Even my mother-by-adoption stirred uneasily.

"Estella, I beg you not to allow Miss Havisham to lead you into this fatal step. Put me aside for ever but bestow yourself on some worthier person than Drummle. Miss Havisham gives you to him as the greatest slight and injury that could be done to many far better men who admire you and to those who truly love you. Take, for God's sake, one of them and I can bear it for your sake."

My compassion was quickly usurped by anger at his unjust remarks.

"Why do you hate him so?" I asked, knowing only too well. "What has he ever done to you, other than offer for my hand?"

For a moment he regarded me tight-lipped, silent. "Very well. He is an unmerciful bully to those smaller and less fortunate than himself. And dishonest, for I have seen him blatantly cheating at cards."

I lowered my head suppressing a smile.

"And why does that amuse you?" he demanded sharply.

"Gentle folk have to keep the lower orders in their place," I said sternly, for I had been encouraged to bully tradespeople as well as the unfortunate Jolly. "Besides, everyone cheats at cards," I added, for, in order to maintain my superiority over Pip, I had been doing so since our first game in Satis House.

Pip shook his head. There followed a catalogue of small meannesses and dishonest actions as observed by his fellow pupils which I interrupted by regarding him impatiently. "The preparations for our marriage are being made. The life I have led has few charms for me and I am willing enough to change it, although I doubt I shall be a blessing to Mr Drummle."

"Oh, Estella, Estella. May God bless you and forgive you."

Unable to face the anguish in his voice, I bowed my head. When I looked up, the door had closed. He had gone from my life.

My guardian did not bother to gloat either. She sat with her hand covering her heart as if it meant to proclaim its existence and deny the falsity of her play acting.

"What have I done? What have I done?" she whispered. "He held up a looking glass and showed me what I once suffered. Until this moment, I did not recognize how I had wronged him – and you, dearest child. Can you ever forgive me?"

I assured her of my forgiveness. My marriage would go ahead. But the writing was already on the wall for I did not love Bentley Drummle, except in the mercenary way of what he could provide for me.

All too soon, I was to learn the folly and the dangers of the role I had chosen. To live unhappily ever after with a man who wanted only my dowry and a child I was unable to provide would bring a new and sinister meaning to "until death do us part".

It was soon evident on our honeymoon in Paris when he disappeared for hours on end and returned smelling of a woman's cheap perfume. By the time we took up residence in Drummle Towers some forty miles from Richmond, I had learned that it was the fate of Miss Havisham's breaker-of-hearts to be broken as ruthlessly as the china ornaments which he hurled to the floor in his fiendish rages, increasingly frequent on certain days each month when it was obvious that his gross attempts at paternity were once more to be frustrated.

When at last I became pregnant, any idea I had that this would make him love me was soon proved wrong. As the months passed so did my longing for my childhood become an obsession. I asked that Jolly be sent for; I longed to make amends for the shabby way I had treated her, but this request was refused. The French maid, impersonal but efficient, had been chosen by Bentley's mother, whose ambition that he should marry his cousin Ruth, her devoted companion, had also been thwarted. I was soon a prisoner in Drummle Towers, at the mercy of two women who hated me and about whom Bentley would not listen to one word of criticism.

Harm me? It was my imagination, he declared. Why should they do that? This was nonsense, all part of my condition.

Out of my misery and loneliness grew a desperate yearning for my mother-by-adoption. Perhaps I had a premonition that I was never to see her again in this life for, as winter drew its curtains and snow isolated us from the world beyond the parkland, Herbert Pocket, Pip's close friend brought us the news of Miss Havisham's death.

As she dozed in her chair, a spark from the fire touched the skirt of her bridal gown, so old and dry it blazed like a tinder box. Had Pip not still been on the premises after one of his visits, then the whole of Satis House would have been a blazing inferno. As it was, he had been severely burned attempting to rescue her. Added to this tragedy, Pip had learned that his benefactor upon whom he had such great expectations was naught but a scoundrel in trouble with the law.

Mr Jaggers would be in touch, for I had inherited Satis House. A bitter inheritance indeed, for I was unable to go to my guardian's funeral and Bentley represented me, his account a mere chronicle of those present. He did not remember seeing Pip

Soon the weeks I had been counting turned into days and on one such although I knew that women suffered in childbirth, expecting extreme but bearable discomfort, I was unprepared for the onslaught of such pain followed by searing agony that tore my body apart and I prayed only to die – and quickly.

At the end of many hours, my son was born and, exhausted, I slept.

When I awoke Bentley was at my bedside. Watching him jubilant with delight with his son in his arms, I tried not to remember how during that long and hideous labour his main concern had been with Doctor Bidwell, shouting, "The child, for God's sake, tell me about the child. Surely the child will live. You must save the child. At all costs."

It seemed that in his eyes, I had become a mere vessel to produce an heir to Drummle. Memory prompted no husbandly comfort or concern for the wife who almost died giving him a son. All his attentions were centred upon "young Hammond" and as the sound of drunken noisy celebration drifted upstairs from where he caroused with his gambling cronies, I realized that, my purpose served, I might no longer have existed and I had my first terrible suspicions that my fate lay in the hands of the two women who, curiosity satisfied, found no reason to sit at my bedside.

Bentley appeared only as a hovering shadow anxiously gazing into the cot or as host to a group of grinning companions, staggering in to hiccup their chorus of admiration for his son and heir before dragging him back to the gaming table where he was losing all that remained of the dowry I had brought him.

Only his old grandfather Sir Hammond, whom he longed to see laid in his grave, was my constant visitor. Propped up in a chair carried between two servants, he visited me faithfully. Holding my hand, he told me how proud I had made him, that I was a grand little filly and scarcely even glanced at his new great-grandson in his befrilled cot.

But all was not well. Suddenly I felt desperately ill, sick and fevered. The thought that I was being poisoned slipped into my dreams. The doctor summoned came to my bedside. I was unable to feed Hammond who cried hour upon hour while I drifted, delirious and far from the world, towards the gates beyond which there was no more pain. When at last I regained strength enough to open my eyes it was to find both the doctor and Bentley staring into Hammond's cot.

"The child is dead."

Those were the words that brought me back to life, to the agony of living after the cool serenity of dying.

"I do not believe you. It is not true – it cannot be true," Bentley was shouting. "You insane old devil, it is all your fault. I shall have the law on you for neglect."

"Control yourself, sir," said the doctor. "Such behaviour will not bring the child back again. I beg you find solace in the fact that your wife still lives. You must concentrate all your energies on seeing her restored to health – consider yourself extremely fortunate that you have not lost them both—"

Bentley pointed down at me. "It is her fault that my son died. She would not feed him."

"I advise you to watch your words, Mr Drummle," said the doctor angrily. "That she could not feed him was through no fault of her own. I well understand your grief, but your wife is still gravely ill—"

Bentley threw off his restraining arm, his brooding gaze on me. "Presuming that she does recover, how soon will she be ready to bear another child?"

Even the doctor was a little taken aback by this heartless rejoinder. Smiling apologetically at me, he said: "Mrs Drummle is young and in God's good time, I dare say she will present you with many strong healthy sons and daughters."

My tears were a river of endless grief for little Hammond while Bentley proceeded to be inebriated at luncheon and incapable at dinner, rarely finishing a meal without some calamity of broken dish or spilt wine or shouting drunken abuse, calmly received by his mother and cousin whose reproachful looks said that it was all my fault. His inheritance on the eagerly awaited death of his grandfather, my only friend at Drummle, failed to cheer him and as the months passed I reached a stage of being grateful when the servants put him to bed. Love was a stranger between us and even trying to understand, I found it hard to forgive his punishment, his brutality on those melancholy occasions each month when I was forced to confirm that his gross and humiliating attempts to father another son had again been unsuccessful.

Such was the pattern of our lives when, having long given up hope, to my astonishment I discovered that I was again pregnant. Only optimism bordering on idiocy might have expected news of my interesting condition to improve my husband's irascible and terrifying behaviour, his constant insobriety and physical abuse. Bruises which I could seldom conceal from the scrutiny and satisfaction of his mother and cousin.

The successful birth of a son and heir united us briefly. Bentley's miraculous return to forgotten geniality almost persuaded me that all was not lost and that he might yet become a gentle loving husband and I a devoted wife.

Dear God, how I needed such consolation. And so much more. Clasping my son to my breast, the bruising marks of birth still upon him, again and again as I kissed his tiny face, it began to undergo a rapid change, a strange bluish colour.

Suddenly I screamed, shook the tiny body as one might a watch that had stopped ticking. And even as my wails of terror echoed through the house, the tiny heart beat no more and his head lolled, eyes still open, but oh so still, against my arm.

Any words to describe that bitter grief would be inadequate. Bentley locked himself in the library, drowning his sorrows in a doleful procession of wines carried up from the cellars by the servants. I pleaded with him but he pushed me savagely aside, and as I fell to the floor and lay there, I knew there no longer existed any hope for our marriage.

One day Dr Bidwell called. The library door flew open and Bentley who had been shaken into sobriety had seized this unique opportunity to shake the poor doctor.

"What is it you are saying, man? Unlikely – unlikely that Lady Drummle will ever produce a living healthy child." He turned to me a scowling mask of fury and hate.

The doctor explained that some malformation in the infant's blood circulation was at fault. "In many cases, the first child survives but subsequent ones die at birth, or soon afterwards."

His anxious glance took in Bentley's mother and Ruth. "You must take good care of yourself – exceedingly good care, Lady Drummle." And I heard the warning in his voice.

There had been cholera that long hot summer and my

sickness was presumed to be the last dregs as other members of the household were unaffected. My inability to retain what little food I ate was aggravated, alas, by fear and destruction of the spirit.

Bentley had removed himself to another bedroom at the outset of my illness and for this small mercy I was grateful. Soon I would be thirty, middle-aged, my life half over, a prisoner in Drummle Towers. As the instrument of Miss Havisham's vengeance, I had failed in that too. The breaker of hearts had been broken indeed.

Then something happened to change my mind regarding the true nature of my illness. Dr Bidwell, who had faithfully served three generations of Drummles, had been replaced by Dr Fraser, new to the area. Called in to attend Ruth's sore throat, to this day I can still see the two men in earnest conversation and hear Bentley's voice, which he had never learned to lower, echoing up the staircase.

"Regarding my wife, doctor. She talks constantly of doing away with herself, putting an end to her life. We are all greatly distressed and keep a careful watch."

The doctor laid a hand on his arm. "Perhaps it will pass, sir. Otherwise we can have her committed – there are asylums for such conditions."

"She talks of putting an end to her life." I had never said such words. "Asylums for such conditions." Over and over, the words echoed as I clutched the banister and watched Bentley. It was as if I could see clearly into his mind as I relived the monstrous chronicle of his small cruelties throughout our marriage and perceived that my inability to produce an heir for Drummle Towers had driven him to the threshold of murder. Or worse than my death, the living death of an asylum for the insane.

The drawing room door opened and his mother beckoned him, her gesture furtive and significant. That night, unable to sleep, I heard a sound in the corridor. Opening the door, from Bentley's room, a figure emerged. It was Ruth and there was one obvious conclusion. Although I had long suspected he had a mistress among the ranks of our hard-living neighbours, it had never occurred to me that he would consider his cousin in that role. My observations were rewarded by the interception of many fond glances and lingering touches between Bentley and Ruth. On his mother's face I saw a flicker of triumph and gratification.

I could not pretend feelings of outrage. If Bentley found comfort in his cousin then I had least cause to object, since I no longer fulfilled, or wished to fulfil, my role as his wife. Indeed I soon discovered that I was a beneficiary under this new tide of guilty love. Gone were the indifferent servants; my mother-in-law and Ruth were suddenly solicitous for my well being, tucking rugs about me, bringing cups of herb tea, vile-tasting but with assurances of health-bringing strength.

Bentley's guilt extended to a birthday present, an occasion which he had ignored throughout the years of our marriage.

Kissing my forehead, he said: "Come, I have something to show you." And he led me into the garden where the stable boy held the rein of a fine chestnut mare.

"Her name is Star – and she is yours."

"Mine?" I cried in delight

"Of course. That is why I named her Star – for Estella."

"Oh, Bentley, this is so kind. But – but—" The mare looked valuable but I could hardly reproach him for such extravagance, remembering that he was perhaps also mindful of my dowry squandered at the gaming tables.

"Nothing is too good for my wife. I thought we might resume our old habit of an early morning ride before breakfast." With a deep sigh: "Now that we must reconcile ourselves to being childless—" And, cutting short my apologies, he said: "You have done your best, you have suffered greatly both in mind and body, but that is all over. Now we must grow old together as good companions. Would that not please you, Estella?"

"I would like that."

"I thought you would. Fresh air and exercise will soon bring the roses back to your cheeks. You must get strong again soon, my dear, to please your old husband."

This new smiling Bentley was irresistible. Could hallucinations wrought by melancholy illness have convinced me of a conspiracy in the household to do me harm? Now grasping at straws, I was ready to make excuses for everybody, eager to make a fresh start, to live again.

When Star threw me on that first ride, although I was unhurt, my confidence was shaken. She had an uncertain temper and was much harder to handle than the gentle old mare sold during my sad childbearing days. Now Bentley assured me that Star was a little spirited but I must prove myself her mistress. "She will soon obey you. Come, we will race to the parkland boundary and back."

The autumn morning was dour, the park shrouded in mist which would turn to rain before midday. I regarded the big mare with trepidation as she loomed above me. Far from happy about racing her, I allowed Bentley to assist me into the saddle, less alarmed at being thrown, as an experienced horsewoman, than of throwing him into one of his sullen rages and tantrums that might last for days and thereby lose the little headway we had made.

"Off you go." He slapped Star's rump with his riding crop and as we galloped into the parkland, I saw that I was well in the lead. Was he letting me win, humouring me by holding back his own mount? The movement of glancing over my shoulder made the saddle slide dangerously. The next moment I was sliding—

Falling . . . out of control.

The ground came violently up to meet me and, screaming, I was dragged along by the still-galloping Star. By a tremendous effort I managed to free my foot from the stirrup. I lay where I had fallen, bruised and shaken, grateful for the sound of Bentley's horse approaching.

I sat up, calling to him. I expected concern, not that ferocious expression of anger. In that one sickening moment, I saw that he had no intention of reining in to rescue me. Striking his horse savagely, he was riding me down.

With a scream of terror, in that last instant as the horse towered over me, I rolled aside and instinctively raised the riding crop I still clutched. I struck the stallion in a sensitive area and, with a shrill whinny of pain, the beast kicked up his heels and Bentley shot over his head. He lay still.

For a long time I dared not move, terrified to investigate in case he was merely stunned and we were alone with no living soul in sight, no habitation. If that were the case, I had little doubt that Bentley would finish me off and return to Drummle alone.

I was so cold and he so unmoving, as through my sickened mind raced a procession of his kindnesses lately shown and the true nature for my mysterious sickness. Bentley desperate for an heir, intended to be rid of me, to marry his cousin.

Dear God, that I could have been so simple. And now he lay dead twenty feet away from me. Dead with all my own hopes and dreams. The rain had begun, heavy, drenching. I was chilled to the bone and rose painfully to my feet. With one hesitant look at that still white face, I limped back through the parkland. At the stables both horses had returned riderless and Jim, the stable boy was examining Star's saddle. White-faced, shocked, he said: "Thank God you're all right, my lady. This should never have happened. I'm very particular and fixed your saddle myself. Ask his lordship, he watched me do it."

I told him where Bentley lay and to fetch a doctor and then I staggered across to the house. I hardly heard his mother's screams or saw Ruth slip to the floor in a dead faint.

I sat at the foot of the stairs and waited until they carried Bentley home and laid him on the sofa in his study. No one came near me. I might have disturbed a gallery of marble statues. It was not merely that I presented the picture of a drowned rat stumbling torn and dishevelled into the hall but that I was not the one they expected to return alone from that ride. And a part of my mind still alert, considered their guilty faces. They told me all I wanted to know. That they also were in the plot for my death.

Doctor Fraser arrived. Bentley still lived. "Alive, but I fear the injuries to his spine are grave." He turned to me. As I assured him that I was unhurt, his mother shrieked:

"If my son dies, mark my words, doctor, that woman is his

murderess. She wishes to destroy him and leave me, his mother, and his poor orphaned cousin without a roof over our heads."

The doctor spoke soothingly to her; his embarrassed nods and anxious glances in my direction said that I was not to take such hysteria seriously. As for the orphaned cousin, her screams that night alerted the whole house as she miscarried of a male child: Bentley's son.

As for myself, chilled to the bone, I thought I would never be warm again.

From the maids' whispers, attending sluggishly to my needs as I weakly summoned them with the bell-pull, I learned that Bentley was paralysed and speechless. The master would never walk again.

Each day I grew weaker and no doctor came, but as the fever took me, I ran down a long tunnel and Pip was waiting for me in the light. We were in Satis House but I tormented and tortured him no longer, for I loved him and was his.

"They are going to let you die." The words were spoken clearly in my ear, unmistakably Miss Havisham. "Don't let them, Estella. I didn't rear you for them to destroy. Fight them! You can win, dearest child."

I opened my eyes. I had been dreaming. I was alone and the fire long turned to ashes, had not been relit. But the billowing curtains suggested that someone, tiptoeing in after dark, had thrown open the windows, allowing the cold damp air to add to the icy atmosphere.

"She talks of putting an end to her life. Asylum for the insane."

All seemed lost. A prisoner, my only hope lay with Mr Jaggers, but how was I to reach him? I prayed for strength. and my prayer was heard. Strength came from a most unlikely quarter as one afternoon I opened my eyes to behold a smiling angel at my bedside. A guardian angel in the unlikely form of Jolly, my once ill-used maid

"Drink this, Miss Estella."

No one had addressed me as Miss Estella in years. I was dead and in Paradise, along with those who had loved me long ago. As for Jolly, she was almost as insubstantial as the wraith of Miss Havisham who had summoned my feeble being back to life.

My shoulder was seized none too gently. "Wake up, Miss Estella, dear. You must take this, just a spoonful. It will make you feel ever so much better." A strong hand behind my head, warm liquid in my mouth. "Another sip, there's my good lady. And another. You're fair starved, thin as a winter rabbit."

I no longer needed urging. "So good, Jolly, so good." I was tired, tired yet content. Safe. I had been sent a friend.

"Don't go to sleep yet, Miss Estella. The housekeeper has come back. She's here and she going to throw me out if you don't speak up for me."

"Jolly is to remain, my personal maid. Let me remind you that I am mistress here and could send you packing this instant." At the force of my words, the housekeeper stepped back. Her guilty looks said she was also in the plot and had received instructions to find me dead when she returned.

The sustained effort had taken all my strength. Clutching Jolly's hand, I whispered, "Please stay with me."

As Jolly again flourished the soup spoon I learned that she had left Mrs Brandley soon after my marriage to take care of the great-aunt of her young man, whom she had met at Richmond Fair.

His name was Jim, stable boy at Drummle Towers.

"Wardham is only two miles from here and when my kind lady died her house went to a cousin. They didn't need me so Jim says why not try Lady Drummle? He loves the story of Miss Havisham's strange goings-on but I said you wouldn't need me, you'd have a French maid now. But Jim insisted." She shook her head. "I still don't know where I found the courage to come – Sounds daft, I know, but I felt as if – as if Miss Havisham was whispering in my ear—"

I gave her a startled look. Perhaps Miss Havisham was in charge of my guardian angel and, if I were to believe the experiences of Jolly and myself, she who had willed me to live would have found it an easy matter to propel Jolly down the drive to Drummle Towers.

"They were starving you to death, maybe even poisoning you. When I saw you lying in a freezing room, I was never in any doubt about that." Then in a frightened voice she whispered: "The maids are saying that if his lordship dies then his mother means to have you taken for his murder."

Those words chilled me to the bone and I sobbed. "You saved my life, Jolly, but for how long, just to be hung on the gallows?"

"Never, Miss Estella. But we have to get you away from here. My Jim's clever, he'll find a way."

I had to believe her; she was my only hope. And what she lacked in stature, she made up for in strength and determination, I soon discovered, when later that day with an air of triumph she ushered in Dr Fraser.

To my murmured, "At last!", he replied: "Not from lack of trying, my lady. On daily visits to Sir Bentley, I am told you are not at home. This seems mighty odd considering his lordship's concern over your mental state. Before the accident he considered having you committed."

He cut short my cry of protest. "Today Miss Jolly was lying in wait as I took my departure. She has told me enough to make me realize that you are in mortal danger and you must leave this house immediately. Make no delay. My advice is that you deliver yourself into the hands of a Mr Jaggers, an excellent lawyer who is known to me."

He smiled when I told him of my connection with that gentleman and, assuring him I felt perfectly fit to travel with Jolly, arrangements were swiftly made for us to board the stagecoach which stopped on the London road at midnight. Dr Fraser's last word was a warning to take only a small valise containing essentials.

"Remember by the laws of property relating to married women, everything you own from Miss Havisham's jewellery to the clothes on your back belong to your husband and you could be charged for theft."

Never have hours passed so slowly but at last darkness fell

and we crept down the drive out to join Dr Fraser's carriage driven by Jim. While we awaited the stagecoach, I was profuse in my thanks to this trio, for to them I owed my life.

Dr Fraser looked pleased. "In our profession we are used to investigating cause and effect and it is in my nature, I must confess, to relentlessly pursue truth. That being so, the two riding accidents, linked with Miss Jolly's suspicions suggested that some person or persons had your death in mind. The two ladies were in London to visit their dressmaker, his lordship here with his two nurses and you, so ill, in the care of the housekeeper, who seized the opportunity to visit relatives in Wardham."

He shook his head. "It took only a moment's speculation to realize that they hoped on their return to find that you had passed away and, of course, as they were not on the premises no suspicions could be attached to them. Jim's dismissal also took on a different meaning when he told me that he had observed Sir Bentley fiddling with your horse's saddle. Otherwise why should his lordship, never known to be generous, thrust a sovereign into his hand 'for minding his own business'? Jim suspected that he was being bribed for something, but it was not until your horse came in riderless that he guessed the reason why."

Pausing he smiled ruefully. "All this is evidence, a police matter, but if we attempted to bring it to court, Sir Bentley has friends in high places, and who would take the word of the local doctor and a dismissed stable boy? Let us keep it between us for now."

The stagecoach lumbered up the hill and while Jim and Jolly exchanged farewells, briefly for they would soon be reunited, the doctor handed me aboard and brushing aside my thanks, he smiled and said: "Take your life back, my lady, and live it well."

Safe thus far, travelling swiftly into an uncertain future, I saw so clearly the bitter irony of Miss Havisham's revenge. For it was I who she loved and not Pip, fated to be her hapless victim while Bentley, my murderous husband, became his own executioner.

The Prints of the Beast

Michael Pearce

Our second story follows the exploits of Pip and Herbert Pocket as, towards the end of Great Expectations, *they travel and set up business in Egypt. Michael Pearce is best known for his stories about the Mamur Zapt, or head of the secret police in Egypt at the start of the 20th century. The series began with* The Mamur Zapt and the Return of the Carpet *(1988). More recently, with* A Dead Man in Trieste *(2004), set in 1910, Pearce has begun a new series featuring the exploits of Sandor Seymour, a British Special Branch officer whose expertise takes him to various European embassies and consulates, describing a world inexorably spiralling towards war. All of Pearce's books are written with a dry humour and a keen understanding of the ironies of life.*

I t was the best of times, it was the worst of times, for such a thing to happen. Christmas Eve! When for the first time since, after the collapse of all my expectations and I had joined Herbert in the Counting House in Cairo, we had managed to take a break together, intending for once to celebrate Christmas in the traditional English style. And now this! The bottle was nothing. Even the mysterious footprints in the sand could surely be explained. But the dead man in the barn –

"Handel, old fellow," said Herbert, calling me by that pet name he had always used, "something must be done!"

It certainly must. Someone in the village must be told, no doubt the Pasha's men would have to be informed. In no time the house would be crawling with people.

But.

This was Christmas Eve. *Our* Christmas Eve, the one we had been planning for so many months. Enough had gone wrong already. And was it now all, at the last moment, to be spoiled?

"Herbert—" I said.

"Yes, old chap?"

"Would it make so very, very much of a difference if the body was not found for a day or two longer?"

"It is certainly very unfortunate that we should come across it just now," said Herbert, "at the very start of our holiday."

We both knew enough of the ways of Egypt to recognize that once the body was declared that would be the end of the holiday we had hoped for. Even though the body was, strictly speaking, nothing to do with us, the fact that it had been found on our property, if only our temporary property, meant that in the eyes of the villagers we would, so to speak, own it. At the very least we would have to tell our story, even if we had no story to tell. And we would have to tell it over and over again. The omda would have to hear it. It was too much to hope that he would only have to hear it once. The whole village would have to hear it. Several times. Officials from the nearest town would need to write it down. The Pasha's men would inevitably become involved and who knows what that could lead to? In their capricious way they might even incarcerate us in some scorpion-infected, plague-ridden hell hole while they made up their minds.

Herbert's mind was clearly running on similar lines to mine.

"We have responsibilities back in Cairo," he said.

"Clara!" I said. "The children!"

"The House," he said, looking grave.

"It would only be a question of postponing," I said. "We would not really be interfering with the course of justice."

"In the end it would make no difference."

"It might even help," I said, "if we were not there."

"How so, old chap?"

"It would mean that they were not distracted by unnecessary complications."

"Complications?"

"The bottle," I said. "Would they understand it? Abstinence is enjoined on them by their religion."

"True, true," said Herbert. "Let us say nothing about the bottle."

"Nor about the footprints."

"Nor about the footprints," agreed Herbert. "They might not believe us."

"It might lead them astray again. For who knows how speculation or superstition might work on their weak minds?"

"It would only be for a short time," Herbert remarked, as we moved the body.

After some deliberation we moved it into one of the outhouses. It was a long low building dug out of the ground and lined with bricks and had once, I think, been an ice-house. It had obviously not been used for some time and sand had drifted in and now filled half the space. Yet, situated below ground as it was, and with the roof so well lined, it was still cool enough to arrest the body's deterioration, which would mean, as I pointed out to Herbert, that the investigation would not be affected.

"True," said Herbert. "True."

He seemed, however, a little uneasy.

"It does mean, of course," he said, "that it will not be possible to bury the poor fellow the same day."

It was the practice in Egypt to bury the dead on the day that they departed; a sensible, hygienic practice in the heat.

"But, then," I pointed out, "that could not have happened anyway. They will have to send for the mamur from Toukh and by the time he gets here and has heard all the depositions it will be Tuesday and by then we will have returned to Cairo."

He still seemed a little troubled, however.

"It is, perhaps, as well, after all, that Clara couldn't come," he said suddenly.

At the very last moment, even as the carriages were being loaded, one of the children had developed a stomach-ache.

"It's just excitement," Herbert had said. But Clara, a connoisseur in her children's illnesses, had shaken her head.

"It's more than that," she had said. She had suspected that it might be the onset of malaria.

"If you think that, my dear," said Herbert, "then we shouldn't go!"

"It seems a pity, though," said Clara, "when you and Pip have been so looking forward to it."

And indeed we had. We had been slaving away in the counting house for nearly two years without a break.

"No, you must go," she said now with decision. "You go and I will stay here with the children."

Of course, we dissented vehemently.

"No," she said firmly, "you must go. I have been thinking for some time that you are both beginning to look rather peaky. And, besides," she had said, with a smile, and putting her hand on my arm, "you will enjoy recapturing the intimacy of those old bachelor days in London!"

"Just as well that she couldn't," I said now to Herbert, and we returned to the house.

Running along the front of the house was a broad verandah, on which there was a table and some cane chairs with cushions. After the sand storm of the previous day the cushions were covered with sand which had drifted in. Herbert raised the cushions to give them a shake and in doing so uncovered a pair of scorpions.

"How very annoying!" said Herbert, brushing them away. "The headman swore that the house had been cleaned!"

It had, indeed, been flooded, as was the usual custom when a house was about to be reoccupied, to rid it of any infestation.

"I suppose their attention did not extend to outside the house," I said.

"Yes, but –"

I laid my finger on my lips.

"Now, Herbert," I said, "did we not swear before we left that we would pay no attention to trifles? That we would put aside all care for the proper discharge of duties in others? Put the Counting House entirely behind us?"

"We did, old chap, we did. And we will!"

He plumped up the cushion and sat down, and I went into the kitchen to find a bottle to replace the one that had disappeared. The sand which had blown in the day before, just after we had arrived, was still there on the floor of the sitting room, and still there were the huge, bestial footprints.

I took the bottle out on to the verandah and poured out two glasses.

"Your health, dear Herbert! And a very good Christmas!"

"And to you, too, my very dear Handel!"

He put the glass down.

"If a strange one."

"You are thinking of your family," I said gently.

"I acknowledge it. Of the children especially. The Christmas stockings, you know."

"We can go back at once, if you wish."

"No, no. Clara would not forgive me."

He toyed with his glass.

"And, besides," he said, "are there not things to be done here?"

"You are still disquieted about the body, Herbert?"

"I am, I must confess. For suppose the body is not to be separated from the strange things that happened last night? If we conceal those things from them, how are they to proceed?"

"You mean, we should disclose –? But I thought we had discussed that, Herbert."

"Yes, yes. And you rightly convinced me that the strangeness of the happenings here might prey upon their weak minds. But you see where that leads to, Handel?"

"That we should tell—"

"No, no. Not at all. That we should investigate the matter for ourselves and present our findings to them when we have all the answers."

The house we had secured was in a remote village, about fifty miles from Cairo in the Damiatta direction. It had once been a farm house and was surrounded by plantations of orange trees and fields of dourah, which is the corn they have thereabouts, and cotton. Being closer to the sea, the air was fresher than it was inland and the temperature slightly lower, a mere 90 degrees in the shade and 120 in the sun. At night the temperature fell sharply and we deliberated whether to sleep outside on the verandah or to retreat indoors where it would be warmer. In the end we decided for indoors.

That night, as I lay in my bed, I could hear through the open window as well as the singing of grasshoppers and frogs the distant cry of wolves, answered occasionally by the cries of jackals and hyaenas. Later, there appeared to be a pack of wild desert dogs circling the house. It was, as Herbert had said, a strange place to spend Christmas.

Clara had entrusted me with a veritable mound of presents, among which I was surprised to find a not inconsiderable number for myself. We opened them over coffee on the verandah. I could see that they turned Herbert's thoughts to home so after a while I crept away leaving him there to muse. He was still sitting there an hour later, when I thought the time had come to direct his mind to other things.

"My dear Herbert—" I said.

He sat up with a start.

"You are right, my dear Handel," he said. "It is time to begin."

*   *   *

The facts, such as they were, were that we had arrived the previous afternoon, just as the sun was setting in a red ball of fire above the desert. Even as we looked, it seemed to darken over.

"Is that a sandstorm?" said Herbert. "How untimely!"

We went round the house closing all the shutters. By the time we had finished, the wind was rising and fine particles of sand were beginning to seep through the slats of the shutters. We knew from long experience that there was nothing now to be done but sit it out. We gave ourselves a hasty supper and cleared the plates away before the full force of the storm hit us – there is nothing worse than sand in your food, in your wine, in your mouth. Then we sat down opposite each other and put blankets over our heads and a bottle of wine on the table in front of us. From time to time one of us would put out a hand and refill the glasses, putting a table mat over the glass as soon as it was filled, to keep out the sand. Then we would retreat beneath our blankets.

And then, I suppose, we went to sleep, for the next thing I was aware of was an exclamation from Herbert.

"The bottle, Handel! What have you done with the bottle?"

"On the table."

"No, it is not!"

I emerged from under my blanket.

"I am sure I restored it to the table. In any case, was it not you who helped last?"

There was a little silence.

"On reflection, Handel, it was. But, then, where the deuce could I have put it?"

"On the ground, perhaps."

Herbert stood up and looked around. I heard him give a startled gasp.

"My dear Handel! Look! Look!"

I stood up beside him. The floor was covered with a thin film of sand. And in the sand were some enormous footprints.

They were of bare feet. They entered from the door, made straight across the room, passed the table and then went out through the door which led on to the verandah.

"He . . . she . . . it took the bottle," said Herbert, in a stunned voice.

It could have been any of the three. The foot was large for a man, very large for a woman. Which made one think . . .

Some ape-like creature? But what ape-like creature existed in the wastes of Egyptian desert? A jackal? Of that size? Preposterous! A hyaena? Ridiculous! It was not to be thought of.

A man, then. That was most likely. The bottle argued for that, too. But, then, would any man round here have a taste for the best Cypriot wine? Would not wine have been against his religious principles? Unless, of course— But the bare feet argued against the presumption that he was an Englishman or a European.

We followed the tracks out on to the verandah. The storm had died down a little now although a thin wind put grit into our mouths and stung our faces. The footprints led to the edge of the verandah and then down and across the yard. In the darkness we had no inclination to follow them.

But the next morning they were still there on the verandah. Out in the yard, however, where the sand had blown more freely, we quickly lost them. There was a new, thick layer of sand which covered everything. Whatever footprints there had been had disappeared.

Around the farm, enclosing the buildings and the yard, was a six-foot-high wall, a barrier against the wild dogs and other unwelcome creatures. Part of the wall was sheltered by one of the outhouses and on that part we found traces of intrusion. The man, or creature, had obviously placed its hands on top of the wall – we could see the marks, although they were less clear than the footprints. The sand on top of the wall was disturbed, as if someone had clambered over. And, down on the other side, where the outhouse still gave shelter against the wind and the sand, just for a few yards, were the footprints again. Only not going away from the house but coming towards it.

*   *   *

So much we had seen on that first exploration. But that was not all. For, as we returned to the house, going round the side of one of the out-houses, back in the yard, we came across the body of a man lying face down in the sand. The sandstorm had blown over him and left a layer of sand all over the body. From its undisturbed thickness and from the stillness of the body we had known that the man was dead.

And had been content to leave it so. In Egypt the sight of a dead body is not uncommon: a beggar expired in the street, an infant baby dead in childbirth or abandoned shortly after birth by its mother. After a while you become hardened. You do not normally enquire too closely.

But perhaps Herbert was right. The circumstances were so strange in this instance that inquiry into them could not responsibly be left to others.

"My dear Herbert—"

It was time, yes, to begin.

The first thing to be done was to identify the dead man and the manner of his death.

"Need we?" But Herbert answered himself. "Of course, Handel. You are right."

Which meant revisiting the ice-house. We pulled the body out into the sun and examined it. It was that of a middle-aged man, a fellah – that is to say, a peasant – from his clothes and general appearance, possibly from the village nearby.

"Where else, out here, could he be from?" asked Herbert.

But that, in my view, raised once more the question of informing the villagers, who, if, indeed, he came from the village, would be able to identify him at once.

There was, however, a powerful argument against this. Examination revealed a savage wound in the neck. The flesh was so badly torn that it was impossible to tell how it had been inflicted. A knife, perhaps? But used with an astonishing degree of violence. What, however, could not be ruled out was . . .

"I am afraid so, my dear Handel."

A bite.

And if so, a bite perhaps from that strange creature – if creature it was and not a man, which would have been stranger still – that had invaded our privacy two nights before.

But what effect might this have if it were revealed to the village? Would it not cause alarm and despondency? Terror, even? Might it not lead to acts of despair in a people lacking Christian philosophy?

"No, Herbert. Better to remain mute until we can present them with the answer as well as the question."

But how to advance beyond the question in the first place?

Herbert bent over the body.

"Handel."

"Herbert?"

"Do you smell what I smell?"

I forced myself to stoop closer.

"He had been imbibing."

From his lips, where now the flies buzzed incessantly, came a faint smell of alcohol.

"And consider the fingers, Handel."

"The fingers?"

They were abraded, as if he had been scrabbling at something.

"The wall?"

We went back to the wall, to the place we had found. What we saw now, inspecting it more closely were faint smears of mud, dried out, of course, but still perfectly clear.

"Handel."

"Herbert?"

"The fingers, again. Did you see the nails? They were packed with mud."

"And the knees," I said. "And the feet. Muddy also."

"A potter, perhaps?"

"Or someone working on the canal?"

The fields around the village were irrigated by a system of canals which drew water off the Nile and fed it over the surrounding land. The system worked well and to it was due the astonishing abundance of the fields. But the abundance came at a price. The canals had to be maintained as they quickly became choked with sand. Every year, in the dry season, after the Inundation, gangs of labourers descended on the system and worked to make it good again, digging out the sand, repairing the sides, and re-piling the earth on the raised banks which protected it against the wind and the sand.

The work was heavy and was not done voluntarily. A corvée had been introduced by means of which villagers were compelled to give their labour. Although the work was in their interest, the villagers saw the benefit as going largely to the Pasha, and it was bitterly resented.

We walked down to the village, passing women hoeing in the fields. One of them, an unusually tall black lady, straightened her back and looked at us. The others continued their labour indifferently.

The canal was on the other side of the village. What we had hoped to see, I do not know. What we saw were men up to their chests in water digging out sand and throwing it up on the sides while others went along moving the sand back and forming banks. Behind them, patrolling steadily, was a man with a long whip, the overseer, usually the Pasha's man, exercising the whip whenever he thought fit.

We went back to the village. It was a small one, just a few houses clustered around an open space which served as a square, one or two tebaldi trees and beneath them a well. Women were dipping a bucket into the well and filling their pitchers, and, not far away, a group of men were sitting, the village elders.

One of them rose as we went past. It was the village omda, the headman, whom we had met when we arrived. He asked us if the house was to our liking. We said it was; only the sand had blown in during the storm. He said he would send a woman up to clean through the house again. She had done it earlier, he said apologetically, only at this time of year, when there were frequent sandstorms, it was hard to keep it like that.

I said that to us, after Cairo, the village seemed very peaceful. He said that all the men were away working on the canal. He hoped they would not be away for too much longer as there would soon be a need for them in the fields.

We asked him if he found it difficult supplying the necessary labour for the corvée. He shrugged.

"They know it has to be," he said.

I asked if any of the villagers tried to evade it. He said that if they did it would fall upon the family and on the village, so on the whole people didn't.

Herbert asked if anyone at work ever tried to slip away. Seldom, said the omda, for then the whole gang was flogged. He seemed about to add something, then stopped; then burst out that in fact it had happened only a few days before. A man had disappeared. "The wound is still fresh in our minds," he said. He pointed to a woman filling her pitchers alone by the well. The other women had departed.

"That is his wife," he said. From now on, he said, or at least until he gave himself up, his wife would have to fill her pitchers alone.

"And what if he never comes back?" Herbert asked.

The headman did not answer directly. He said only that the Pasha's reach was wide.

We walked back up to the house in silence.

"We know now, at any rate, the identity of our man," Herbert said, throwing himself into one of the chairs on the verandah.

And yet the mystery had only deepened. We now knew who the poor fellow was. But how had he met his end? And for what reason?

We could now understand, we thought, the explanation for his presence in the farm. He had fled from the gang working on the canal and, seeking refuge, climbed over the wall, believing the farm-house to be still deserted. There, at least, he would be safe from the wild beasts outside.

Was it not possible, however, that in doing so he had come face to face with a creature wilder than any of those he feared?

There were other questions. Had he been pursued to the farm? Or had he come there and inadvertently stirred an inhabitant who, or which, had turned on him perhaps in panic and killed him?

All this seemed possible and likely. What did not seem possible or likely was the tale told by the footprints: that some one or thing should enter the room while we were actually in it, our heads covered, it is true, but nevertheless there, pick up the bottle and then walk calmly out with it and disappear into the sandstorm.

Later in the afternoon, after we had enjoyed the splendid Christmas lunch that Clara had prepared for us, the woman that the omda had promised came up to clean the house again. It was the woman we had seen on her own beside the well. Perhaps the omda had sent her up in pity, knowing that without her husband she would be in need of any recompense that we might offer.

She was a sturdy peasant women in her thirties, bare-legged and bare-footed, though without her face covered, as it would perhaps have been in the town. While we were enjoying our coffee and brandy, she set to work in the kitchen and soon had swept it clean. Then she came into the dining room with her brush. She saw the footprints, there, still in the sand that covered the floor, and stopped.

Then, without a word, she swept the floor clean and afterwards moved on to the bedrooms.

"There goes our chance," said Herbert quietly, "of keeping this from the village."

When she had finished she went home. Herbert and I sat out on the verandah wondering what we should do. If she revealed what she had seen, the whole village would be up here. They would rout around and almost certainly come across the body in the ice-house. And then, as Herbert pointed out, it would not look good for us. We decided that in the circumstances we would have to revise our plans. We would go to the omda first thing in the morning and disclose the presence of the body.

That night I found it hard to get to sleep. Inside the house it was insufferably hot so I moved my bed things out on to the verandah; but there the bright moon light made it almost as clear as day. I lay awake, listening to the cries of the jackals and the wild dogs, and the distant cry of a hyaena.

In the end I could stand it no more and got up. I did not wish to disturb Herbert but walked out into the yard. In my mind were strange memories – the memory of someone else who had once been fleeing from bondage and in his flight had come across a small boy. From that boy he had received a helping hand and that helping hand had stayed with him for the rest of his life. It had transformed his life, made it different not just from what it was but from what it might have been. It had put a light into the darkness of his mind, an *ignis fatuus*, perhaps, a false light, like those marsh gases or corpse lights that dance in graveyards, but nevertheless a light, and, on reflection, I would not have had it otherwise.

Now my mind was turning over uneasily another poor creature who had fled from bondage: for was it not bondage, where work was enforced with the whip?

Flight, flight: did we not all flee from pain? And hadn't I, too, eleven years before fled from pain by leaving England? But was not that flight a false light, too? I had thought to distance myself from a cruel but broken woman. But can one ever distance oneself from one's own heart? I knew now that if I had my chance again I would not distance myself but try, in whatever way I could, to mend what was broken. But chances, I have learned, do not come twice.

Thus musing, I turned on my heel, and, as I did so, I caught what seemed to be a movement in one of the out-houses. For a moment my blood froze. Could it be that our visitant of the first night had returned?

I roused Herbert and together we went over to the barn the noise had come from. There it was again! Something was definitely moving inside.

There were two doors. Herbert went round to the one at the rear while I stood by the main entrance. Something was coming towards it. It came very quietly, a soft padding of bare feet. It came through the door. I seized it and called for Herbert's aid.

It was not as I had expected. Smaller, softer. Weaker. It struggled in my grasp. Herbert came running. I shifted my hands to get a better grip.

And then I nearly let go! The form beneath my hands was unmistakeably that of a woman.

I pulled her out into the moonlight. Herbert came rushing round the corner of the barn, saw her and stopped.

It was the woman who had been cleaning the house for us earlier.

"What are you doing here?" he said sternly.

She spat at him.

I dragged her towards the house. She resisted for a moment and then suddenly submitted.

On the verandah she sat silently and at first would say nothing.

Then she burst out:

"Where is he?"

Herbert and I looked at each other. Could we tell her?

"Who?" I said, temporising.

"My man."

"Your husband?" said Herbert.

She nodded impatiently.

Herbert and I looked at each other again.

"He is gone," said Herbert.

She sat there still for a moment. Then –

"So he is gone," she said. Her whole body seemed to slump. "So he is gone," she said again. She shrugged. "I knew it," she said bitterly, "I knew it when I saw –"

She stopped.

"He was not a good man," she went on, after a moment. "He used to beat me. Especially when he had been drinking. He went with other women. I complained to the omda and the omda told him he would have to leave the village if he couldn't mend his ways. But still he drank, and still he went with them. One especially. I told him I would denounce her to the omda and he would have her stoned. He begged me not to. He swore he would put her aside and be a good husband to me in future. He cried. He always cried after he had been drinking. And he said he would mend his ways. He had said it before, but this time I believed him.

"And I was right to, for he did try to put her away. And she was angry and taunted me, saying I was no good to a man, that I would never bear him children. And then she taunted him, saying that he was not a proper man. Still he would not go with her; but he went back to drink. He could not do his work properly. The Pasha's man berated him and whipped him, and one day he could stand it no longer and ran away.

"He came home to me and I said: 'If you stay here, they will find you. Hide yourself in the old farm-house and I will bring you food.' But then I heard that you had moved in, so I dared not. But when I came up this afternoon I brought food for him. But I could not find him. I thought perhaps he had fallen asleep somewhere, so tonight I came again. But again I could not find him. And now you tell me he is gone."

"Handel, old chap—" began Herbert.

I knew what he was thinking. We could not continue with our deception. It was cruel to this unfortunate woman. Let the consequences be what they would, we would go to the omda in the morning and declare all.

The first thing in the morning we went down to the village and asked to see the omda. The villagers had sensed that something was toward and had begun to gather. The omda came out of his house and sat down on a bench in front of it. He had chairs brought for Herbert and myself. As the crowd grew deeper I grew more and more concerned about what we had to say.

But then something surprising happened. The cleaning lady stood up first.

"Omda, I have come to declare a fault," she said.

THE PRINTS OF THE BEAST

"Speak on."

"I helped my man when he fled in fear from the Pasha's man."

"So?" said the Pasha's man, who was standing at the back of the crowd, fondling his whip.

"He came to me at our house and I said: 'If you stay here, they will take you. Go to the old farm-house and hide there.' I meant to take him food."

"And did you, Amina?"

"No. At least, I did: but I could not find him. Because by then he had fled."

"Fled, Amina?"

"Yes, omda. With this woman."

She was pointing at a woman in the crowd, the big, dark woman we had noticed among the hoers.

"I?" said the woman. "I?"

"Yes, you, Khabradji."

"But I am here!"

"And he is not. But you know where he is, Khabradji."

She looked at the omda.

"That is what I have come to declare, omda," she said, and sat down.

Hands pushed Khabradji forward.

"She lies, omda. It is not so!"

Amina rose again.

"You were in the house with him."

"Not so!"

"It was so. I saw your footprints."

"What!" said Herbert and I simultaneously.

"They will confirm it," said Amina, turning to us.

I stood up.

"Certainly, we saw footprints in the sand," I said. "But whose they were—?"

"We thought they might be of some strange beast!" said Herbert excitedly.

"Strange beast?" said the omda, raising an eyebrow.

"They were large and—"

"Large, certainly," said the omda, looking at Khabradji.

Everyone laughed. She looked self-conscious. Evidently her size was a by-word in the village.

"—but no strange beast!" said the omda.

The crowd laughed again.

Herbert stood up.

"It was a mistake," he said. "And yet in that mistake truth lies. Khabradji, you were certainly in the house. We saw your footprints. You came right into the room where we were sitting. And now, Khabradji, I have a question for you: did you take the bottle?"

"Bottle?" said the omda.

"Bottle?" said Amina.

Herbert turned to her –

"I know, alas, that you are familiar with bottles, Amina. Because of your husband. But was not Khabradji, too? So let me ask my question again: did you take the bottle that was on the table?"

"I – I –" stuttered Khabradji.

"I think you did, Khabradji."

"Well, what if I did?"

"What did you do with it?"

"Do with it? I – I drank it."

There was an amazed laugh from the crowd.

"No, you didn't. You took it out and gave it to Amina's husband."

"What if I did?" muttered Khabradji. "What if I did?"

"Where is he, Khabradji? cried Amina suddenly. "Give him back to me!"

Khabradji seemed to shake herself.

"Give him back?" she said. "That I cannot."

She sat down, as if she had said all she was going to.

I rose from my place.

"But, Khabradji," I said, "that is not all, is it? You gave him the drink, yes; and then what?"

"I do not know," muttered Khabradji.

"I do. When he had drunk and was stupefied, you killed him."

"Killed him!"

There was a gasp of horror from the crowd.

"Killed him?" cried Amina, and made to throw herself at her rival. Hands held her back.

Khabradji now rose in her turn.

"Yes," she said, calmly. "I killed him. With my hoe. While he lay dulled and sleeping." She looked at Amina. "I was not going to let you take him back. While I was in the field, I saw him running and guessed where he was going. That night I went to the farm-house myself and found him. I pleaded with him to come back to me. But he would not and spoke bad words. I was angry and rushed from him. But then I looked into the house and saw the bottle and the evil thought came to me: why should not I be revenged? So I took the bottle to him and let him drink; and then I killed him."

As we were leaving, I heard one villager say to another:

"What was all that about a beast?"

"There wasn't one."

"Odd that they should think there was. Strange minds these Englishmen have!"

"Superstition," said the other villager. "That's the problem."

All in all it was an odd Christmas indeed. But it had one effect that was lasting. It had taken my mind back to another time when my life had become strangely bound up with that of a poor fugitive. Indeed, it was that which had ultimately led to my flight to Egypt. Reflecting on that, I realised that I had left unfinished business behind me. It occurred to me that the time had come to return to England and address it. Perhaps, too – I confess it – it was the children's Christmas stockings, bringing home to me that there was more to life than work in a Counting House. Anyway, I went back to England, expecting not great things now but very little: finding, however, when I got there more than I had ever dared to expect.

The Mystery of Canute Villa

Martin Edwards

Throughout his career as a magazine editor Dickens had a fruitful, if at times difficult, business relationship with Elizabeth Gaskell. They first met in 1849 when she attended a celebration dinner that Dickens held upon the publication of David Copperfield. *Dickens later visited Mrs Gaskell and her husband at their home in Manchester and Mrs Gaskell occasionally asked Dickens for his help in assisting people whom she believed were in need.*

She held Dickens in high regard but did not always approve of the way Dickens would meddle with her manuscripts, nor did she approve of his separation from his wife. Nevertheless, Household Words *serialized much of her best work, including the novel* North and South *and various episodes that became* Cranford, *whilst* All the Year Round *serialized her novel of murder and guilt,* A Dark Night's Work *(1863). The following story is set at the same time that Mrs Gaskell completed that novel. You will also encounter a name in this story that we will come across again.*

Martin Edwards is a solicitor in Liverpool, just like the main character in his noted series of books starring Harry Devlin which began with All the Lonely People *(1991).*

Several of Edwards's short stories will be found in Where
Do You Find Your Ideas? *(2001) and he has also edited
several anthologies including a series for the Crime Writers' Association, starting with* Perfectly Criminal
(1996).

"WWhy should an innocent and respectable lady of good
family and in her late middle years, never touched by
a breath of scandal, be haunted by a mysterious stranger
whose name is entirely unknown to her?"

The woman in the railway carriage nodded. "You have
expressed the problem in a nutshell."

Her companion tugged at his beard. "It is a tantalizing
puzzle, I grant you, my dear Mrs Gaskell."

As the train rattled round a bend, she said, "I only hope
that I have not called you up to Cheshire on a wild goose
chase."

He gave a little bow. "Your summons was so intriguingly
phrased, how could any man fail to hasten to your side?"

"Of course," she said, "I am profoundly grateful to you for
having agreed to spare me a little of your precious time. I
realise that there are many calls upon it."

More than you know, dear lady. Charles Dickens suppressed a sigh. It had been his intention to evaporate – as
he liked to describe it – from London to spend a few pleasant
days with Ellen Ternan. However, as no doubt she had
calculated, Mrs Gaskell's telegram had fascinated him. Within an hour of its receipt, he was on the train heading north to
Manchester. He had an additional motive for racing to her
side, being determined to seize an opportunity to improve
relations between them. Once they had been on first class
terms, but ever since their wrangles over the serialization of
North and South, she had displayed a stubbornness unbecoming (if not, sadly, uncommon) in any woman, let alone
the wife of a provincial clergyman.

He smiled. "Do you remember why I used to call you
Scheherezade?"

She blushed. Not, he was sure, because her memory had failed, but rather from that becoming modesty that had entranced him in the early days of their acquaintance.

"You must recall my saying I was sure your powers of narrative can never be exhausted in a single night, but must be good for at least a thousand nights and one. Besides, your message was so teasing that no man with an ounce of curiosity in his blood could possibly resist."

She permitted herself a smile. "You have not lost your gift for flattery, my dear Mr Dickens."

"Charles, please." He gave an impish grin. "Scheherezade."

As if to cover her embarrassment, she looked out of the window at the fields and copses flying by. "We have reached Mobberlcy. Soon we shall be arriving."

He clapped his hands. "I eagerly await my first sight of Cranford! Tell me, meanwhile, more about your friend Mrs Pettigrew."

"Ah, dear Clarissa. It is difficult for me to think of her by the Major's name. To me, she will always be Clarissa Woodward or, at a pinch, Mrs Clarissa Drinkwater."

"You have met her second husband, Major Pettigrew?"

"Only once, at the wedding."

"You do not care for the Major or his habit of bragging about his service in India?"

"I did not say that."

"And I did not ask if it were true," he said briskly. "I asserted it as a fact, inferred from your manner whenever you have mentioned the fellow's name."

Elizabeth cast her eyes to the heavens, but managed to suppress a sigh of irritation. "I suppose I can hardly complain if, having been enticed here by the invitation to conduct yourself as a detective, you start to play the part at every conceivable opportunity."

He laughed. "We have that fascination for the work of a detective in common, do we not? I recall that splendid little piece you wrote for me on disappearances. *Let me say, I am thankful I live in the days of the Detective Police. If I am murdered, or commit bigamy, at any rate my friends will have the comfort of knowing all about it."*

"Your memory is remarkable."

"So is my inquisitiveness. Why have you not seen fit to inform the local constabulary of Mrs Pettigrew's distress?"

"For no other reason than that, in her letter, she pleaded with me not to do so."

"And why, pray, do you think she was so reluctant for the matter not to be investigated?"

"I suspect that her husband would not approve. She appears to be reluctant to do anything without his permission."

Dickens peered out of the window. "The station approaches!"

His companion gazed out of the window. "The coming of the railway has made such a difference to Knutsford. The embankment divides our old chapel from the rest of the town."

"The march of progress, my dear Scheherezade!"

They were to be conveyed to the Royal George Hotel, where Elizabeth had booked quarters at the rear overlooking the Assembly Rooms. The journey was short but, with his characteristic zest for exploration, Dickens insisted that they be taken the long way round, by way of Princess Street and the Heath, so that he could imbibe the air of a town he had known hitherto only from the pages of his companion's novel.

"That is Clarissa's home," Elizabeth said, pointing towards a grey and forbidding double-fronted house standing in grounds that overlooked a large tract of open land. "Canute Villa takes its name from the ancient king who is supposed to have forded a river here. It is one of the finest houses in Knutsford."

"A splendid situation. She and the Major can have scant need to practise the elegant economy which I associate with Cranford."

"I prayed that she would be happy." She spoke with such soft sadness that Dickens needed to strain to hear over the clatter of hooves on the cobbles. "But when she wrote to me, her terror was evident. I was appalled. Clarissa has known her share of tragedy, but her spirit has always been strong enough to enable her to face the vagaries of Fortune."

Dickens nodded. "Merely to read the letter is to recognize the fear instilled in its author by the events she describes. You have known her since childhood?"

"She is seven years older than myself, but our families, the Woodwards and the Stevensons, lived a few doors apart from each other and were always on good terms. My brother John was friendly with her twin brother Edgar."

Dickens knew a little of John. His death had been one of the tragedies of Elizabeth Gaskell's life. He was a seaman who had sailed the Seven Seas but been lost when his sister was seventeen; some said he was drowned, some that he had been set upon by brigands in the sub-continent, and there was even a picturesque story that he had been killed by pirates. Elizabeth had drawn on her grief when writing; disappearances haunted much of her finest work.

"She married a man called Drinkwater, you say?"

"Thomas was a solicitor, a man fifteen years Clarissa's senior. He was thought to be a confirmed bachelor, but on meeting my friend at a party, he was quite swept off his feet. Clarissa could have had taken her pick of men, but she saw in Thomas a steadfastness that she found admirable."

"To say nothing of a handsome income?"

Her eyes blazed. "Charles, that is a scurrilous thing to say! Thomas was a thoroughly decent man. I know that you entertain a certain scepticism about members of the legal profession, but I really . . ."

"Please forgive me, Scheherezade," he said quickly, and with unaccustomed humility. "I did not mean to cast aspersions on your friend's integrity."

"I should hope not indeed! The fact is that the marriage was one of the happiest I have known. When he died of apoplexy three years ago, she was heartbroken."

"There were no children?"

"No, to the dismay of both Clarissa and Thomas."

"And what of brother Edgar?"

"He died ten years ago. Poor fellow, his heart was always weak. He was the last of the male Woodwards."

"Thus she was left not only alone but also very wealthy?"

As the carriage pulled up before the stables in George Yard, Elizabeth Gaskell slowly inclined her head.

Over afternoon tea in the comfortable public room of the hostelry, Dickens summarized the essentials of the conundrum that Clarissa Pettigrew had posed.

"Since her second marriage, your friend has become a virtual recluse. By nature she is charming and convivial, popular because she has always been not only attractive in appearance but generous and thoughtful. Nowadays, however, she and the Major shun neighbours, friends and even relatives. Your opinion is that this is at his insistence."

"I refuse to believe otherwise."

"Very well. According to your observation, the Major is not only considerably younger than Clarissa, but also appears to lack independent means."

"He is a fine figure of a man, but at the wedding, there was gossip that he had not a penny to his name until he took her for his wife. Some folk said he'd run into trouble while he was serving in India and that if he hadn't left the army, he would have been disgraced."

Naturally there would be gossip; this was Cranford. However, Dickens kept the thought to himself. He drained his cup of tea and helped himself to a slice of gateau.

"The effect of the marriage is, as you will appreciate, to transfer into the Major's name your friend's inheritance. The house, her first husband's investments, everything. A scandalous state of affairs, in my opinion. Nevertheless, that is the law."

"Indeed." Elizabeth's face was a mask.

"Still, although the two of you had enjoyed only limited contact by way of correspondence since the wedding, you had no reason to believe that anything was amiss until you received the letter."

"Friends in the town had informed me of their sorrow, that Clarissa and the Major appeared to be cutting them off. Nobody could believe that was Clarissa's wish. Everyone blamed her new husband. Rumour had it he once blacked her eye when in a drunken rage. But who would dare to come between man and wife? I felt helpless until she wrote and asked for my aid."

"Did you know that she had been unwell?"

"Not at all. You may imagine my dismay when she told me that for several weeks illness had confined her to the house."

"She speaks of a malady affecting her nerves."

"Which is quite unlike Clarissa. As a girl, I rather idolized her. She was blessed not only with a delightful personality but a robust constitution and ready wit. Very far removed, if you will forgive me, from a Dora Copperfield."

"According to Clarissa, on Monday last she spied a stranger lurking outside Canute Villa. An unkempt tramp in a battered hat and coat, hiding amongst the trees at the far side of the Heath. At first she paid him scant attention, but on the following day she noticed him again. He appeared to keep watch on the comings and goings of the household."

Elizabeth eyed him sharply. "You say *according to* Clarissa. Do you imply scepticism concerning her veracity?"

"We cannot rule out anything."

She flushed. "Well, I can! Clarissa would never dream . . ."

"If we are to stand in the shoes of members of the detective police," Dickens interrupted, "we must refuse to be swayed by personal loyalties or affections. Without logic, Elizabeth, a detective is lost!"

"Please proceed," she said, struggling for an icy calm.

Dickens cleared his throat and launched into the story, with as much gusto as if reciting *Mrs Gamp* or *Sikes and Nancy*.

"In ordinary circumstances, she would have approached the man and shooed him off. However, when she ventured from the door at the side of the house, he vanished. Later that night, however, when noting that the housemaid had drawn the curtains imperfectly and left a gap between them, she caught a glimpse in the moonlight of a dark figure loitering on the edge of the Heath and subjecting Canute Villa to intensive scrutiny. She could not see him clearly, but he was wearing a low-brimmed hat and she was sure that the tramp had returned. Fearing burglary, she informed her husband, but although he went out to inspect the grounds of their home, he could find nothing.

"On his return, he accused Clarissa of succumbing to flights of fancy and went so far as to question her state of mind. She came close to believing that she had indeed imagined the whole episode, but the following day, through the window she caught sight once more of the mysterious stranger. When he saw her looking at him, he disappeared from view. The Major was out of the house at the time and when he returned and she told him what had happened, he consulted the housemaid, a girl by the name of Alice. She denied having seen the apparition and the Major lost his temper – not, I gather, an unusual occurrence – and said that Clarissa was imagining things and that if she did not have a care, she would soon find herself confined to an asylum."

Pausing for breath, he considered his companion. Elizabeth was fidgeting with the edge of the tablecloth.

"Why did her husband not believe her?" she murmured, as though wrestling with an abstruse mathematical problem.

Dickens gave a shrug of the shoulders. "At all events, the next morning saw a further development. While the Major and the housemaid were out of the house, she found a crudely scrawled note tucked under the door of the house. It read simply: *Please meet at nine o'clock behind the Lord Eldon*. And it was signed '*Datchery*'. A name unknown to Clarissa. Having lived in the town all her life, she is certain that no local resident is so called. Frightened by the message, she showed it to her husband to see if he was familiar with Datchery, or could otherwise make any sense of the message. Her candour proved unwise. The Major flew into a fury and accused her of indulging in an unseemly association with another man and concocting a tale about a mysterious tramp to conceal her illicit relations with a lover. With no one else to turn to, Clarissa wrote in haste to seek the wise counsel of her old friend and confidante Elizabeth Gaskell."

"You have seen the letter. The trembling script indicates that Clarissa's nerves are in tatters. She says she fears for her sanity and I can believe it." Elizabeth took a deep breath. "This is what marrying the Major has done to her."

Dickens said grimly, "I look forward to making the acquaintance of the unhappy couple. You have explained that I shall be accompanying you on your visit?"

Elizabeth nodded. "Even though she begged me to come and see her, you will recall that she implored me to say nothing in reply that might antagonize her husband, as he always insisted upon reading correspondence that she received, and she had concealed from him the very fact that she had written to me. I composed my response in terms of the utmost diplomacy, saying merely that I would call upon them while taking you around the sights of Cranford. She has always loved your writing, Charles, and I doubt whether even a bully such as the Major could easily object to our visiting them."

Dickens beamed. "An enthusiast for my work? That settles it, Scheherezade. Poor Mrs Pettigrew is most certainly not in danger of losing her mind."

The two of them strolled the short distance from King Street to Canute Villa by way of the Lord Eldon, an old coaching inn close to the livestock market at Heathside. Dickens insisted upon inspecting the alleyway where, he presumed, the meeting with the ruffian who called himself Datchery was supposed to have taken place.

"Hmmm." He tapped a walking stick on the cobbles. "An interesting spot for a rendezvous. Quiet and not overlooked. Convenient for the Pettigrews' house, so it would be easy to slip away and meet someone here covertly before returning home. There is a good chance that a brief absence would not be noticed."

"Why would this man want to meet Clarissa?"

"My dear woman, the first question is whether it was Clarissa whom he wanted to meet."

"You think the note might have been intended for the Major?"

"Or even the housemaid."

Elizabeth said thoughtfully, "I had not contemplated the thought, but now that you mention it . . . Alice is as obliging as she is pretty. She has been with Clarissa since Mr Drinkwater was alive."

"Are there other servants?"

"At the wedding she mentioned a manservant called Bowden, who was rather sweet on Alice. However, in her last but one letter to me, a fortnight ago, she said that the Major had given him notice and not appointed anyone to take his place."

Dickens wagged a finger playfully. "Ah, elegant economy is practised in Cranford after all!"

"I gained the impression that the expenses of the household were mounting. She said that the Major found it most satisfactory to have a home overlooking a racecourse. No doubt he likes to make a wager from time to time."

"Let us speak plainly. If the craze for gambling has seized him, then the assets of the late Mr Drinkwater risk being squandered in all too short a time." Dickens shook his head. "Come, let us make our visit."

As they followed a path across the Heath, Elizabeth pointed out the site of a grandstand that a new company proposed to erect to accommodate spectators at the races.

"This afternoon the place may be deserted, but they say that with the coming of the railway, the races will attract thousands."

He rubbed his chin. "The world is changing, Scheherezade. Yet people, at heart, do not change."

"I'm not much of a man for reading," Major Pettigrew harrumphed.

Dickens favoured his host with a smile so cordial that it bordered on the oleaginous. "You are a man of action, sir. A pair of humble scribblers such as Mrs Gaskell and myself can do nothing but look with awe upon a soldier who has seen service in far-flung and dangerous corners of the world."

Pettigrew eyed his guest suspiciously but, unable to find obvious fault with the compliment, nodded towards the door leading back into the house and muttered, "We must return to the ladies. As I sought to make clear when you were introduced, my wife is a sick woman. It is most important that she should not over-excite herself."

They were standing in the garden to the rear of Canute Villa. A square lawn was fringed by rhododendron bushes, climbing roses and ancient copper beeches. After the demure housemaid had admitted the visitors to the presence of the Pettigrews, conversation was stilted. It was plain from the Major's brusqueness that he did not welcome guests in his home. However, he could hardly expel such illustrious visitors without observing the common courtesies.

Dickens had convinced himself that, if they were to help Clarissa at all, it would be essential for Elizabeth to speak to her in private. Thus, from the moment they were led into the large and immaculate drawing room, Dickens had chattered without drawing breath before glancing through the bay window looking out on to the lawn and expressing his admiration for the garden in fulsome terms before begging to be allowed to inspect it at close quarters. Elizabeth managed to suppress her amusement at his effrontery and Pettigrew had, albeit with a show of reluctance, consented to show Dickens around the grounds. Once outside, Dickens had talked endlessly about the privations of life as a writer while his host shifted impatiently from foot to foot.

Obediently, Dickens trotted after his host as they returned to the drawing room. Pettigrew was tall and erect in bearing and boasted a splendid dark moustache. Dickens could imagine him charming an older woman, if he put his mind to it, but his chin was weak, and a petulant note was apt to enter his voice when he made even the most commonplace remark.

On entering the presence of the ladies, Dickens caught Elizabeth's eye. She frowned and gave an almost imperceptible shake of the head as he spoke.

"Mrs Pettigrew, may I compliment you? Your garden is as delightful as your charming home."

Clarissa's lips twitched; it seemed to be as close as she could come to offering a smile. Her face was deathly pale and her frail body trembled in the brocaded armchair.

"You are – very kind," she said in a voice so faint that it was barely audible. "To think that we should entertain a guest as distinguished as . . ."

"Yes, yes," her husband interrupted. "Dickens, it is good of you and Mrs Gaskell to have stopped off from your travels to call at our humble abode, but as you can see, my wife is dreadfully fatigued. I do believe, Clarissa, that it would be best for you to go to bed. Come, my dearest, remember what the doctor said this morning. You must not tax yourself. It could be dangerous."

" '*Come, my dearest*'," Elizabeth quoted scornfully when they had repaired to the sitting room at the Royal George. "The man is a hypocrite. He does not care for her one jot."

To see her old friend in such a sorry state had hit her hard. Dickens was tempted to clasp her hand and murmur words of consolation, but a moment's reflection persuaded him of the unwisdom of such a course. He would not wish his good intentions to be misinterpreted. Women could be such fearful creatures.

"What did she tell you?"

"Nothing of value. She insisted that she had been mistaken. Her husband was right and the mysterious stranger was indeed a figment of her imagination."

"What?"

"She apologized profusely for having allowed a momentary nervous turn to summon us on a fool's errand. However much I pressed her, she remained adamant. As for the note from Datchery, she had dreamed it. Stuff and nonsense! I know Clarissa too well. Something quite dreadful must have happened in order to reduce her to such a pitiable state, to cause her to lie to one of her oldest friends."

"You are convinced that she did receive the note she described?"

"Most certainly. The question is – what has happened in between her writing to me and this afternoon to prompt such a crisis of confidence that, even when free of her husband's malign presence, she would not admit the truth even to me?"

"I suspect that . . ." Dickens began.

"Surely the answer is obvious? Pettigrew has intimidated her into denying the truth. For some reason, he is anxious that nobody should know of the tramp, or of Datchery – although I believe that they are one and the same."

"There is an alternative hypothesis, Scheherezade. If the tramp does exist, what is his purpose? Could it be that the Major has instructed him to haunt Canute Villa?"

"To what end?"

"So that his wife comes to believe that she is indeed mad?"

Elizabeth passed a slim hand across her face. "Oh, Charles, what are we to do?"

That question remained unanswered as Elizabeth and Dickens drank coffee after dinner that evening. The venison had been excellent, but their appreciation of a fine meal had been dulled by concern for the woman trapped in such unhappiness behind the bleak façade of Canute Villa. Each time Dickens came up with a fresh notion for confronting Pettigrew, Elizabeth dismissed it, pointing out the difficulties of coming between man and wife. They risked making matters even worse for Clarissa, she warned. But when Dickens demanded to know what she proposed to do to assist her friend, she confessed to being at an utter loss.

"Only one course remains open," Dickens said at length. "We must track down the tramp and press him for the truth."

"But where might he be?"

"This is your home ground, Elizabeth. Where do you suggest a man might seek to hide, or make a temporary home?"

She frowned. "The woodland bordering the Heath is quite dense. And there is the Moor, of course."

"The Moor?"

Elizabeth nodded. "It is the marshy valley below King Street. Tatton Mere peters out into tall reed beds and folk call it the Moor. It has a special place in my affections, since I used to play there for hours on end as a child. Certainly that area is as wild as anywhere in the neighbourhood. I remember when we were young . . . my goodness, Mr Tompkins, what is the matter?"

The proprietor of the inn, a ruddy-faced man of equable temperament, had burst into the room. The colour had drained from his face and he was gasping for breath.

"Mr Dickens! Mrs Gaskell! We spoke earlier about your friend Mrs Pettigrew and her husband the Major!"

"What is it?" Elizabeth asked in a tremulous voice. "Has something – happened to Clarissa?"

Tompkins stared at her. "Oh, no, Mrs Gaskell. At least . . ."

"Come on, man!" Dickens was shouting. "Tell us what brings you rushing in here as though you have seen a ghost."

"I have – I have seen no ghost," Tompkins stuttered. "But I have seen the body of a man. It is Major Pettigrew, and his eyes were almost popping out of his head. He has been most foully murdered."

Not until the next afternoon did Dickens manage to secure an interview with Sergeant Rowley, the detective charged with investigating the most sensational crime to have been associated with Knutsford since the hanging of Highwayman Higgins, whose exploits had inspired Elizabeth to pen a story for *Household Words*. To his dismay, Rowley was scarcely an Inspector Field or a Sergeant Whicher. Broad-shouldered, ruddy-faced and short of breath, he made it clear that he was not to be impressed either by the fame of his visitor or a close acquaintance with London's principal detectives.

"You will forgive me for keeping you waiting, sir," Rowley said, without a hint of apology in his demeanour, "but the murder of Major Pettigrew is a most serious business and I have been fully occupied in seeking to ensure that the malefactor is brought swiftly to justice."

"I wish you every success," Dickens said. "I thought it might help if . . ."

"Bless you, sir," Rowley said, failing to conceal smug satisfaction, "it is generous of you to offer assistance, but we have already apprehended the culprit. The constabulary of Knutsford may not be as eminent as its counterpart in the metropolis, but I can assure you that our dedication to our work is second to none, the length and breadth of the British Isles."

"There is talk in the town that you have arrested someone already."

"Indeed, Mr Dickens. A fellow by the name of Bowden. He used to work at Canute Villa, but the Major gave him notice two weeks ago."

"You think that Bowden would have waited so long before taking revenge for his dismissal?"

Rowley shrugged. "There is more to it than that. Young Bowden was hoping to marry the girl who works for the Pettigrews."

"Did she throw him over?"

"Not exactly, as I understand it. But the Major was a ladies' man, God rest his soul. There is talk that he had taken a shine to young Alice."

"But she had worked for Clarissa for years!"

"Even so, sir. The Major's a fine figure of a man and it doesn't take much sweet talk to turn a pretty young woman's head."

"So Bowden killed him to make sure he didn't lay his hands on Alice?"

"You're a man of the world, sir, so you won't mind my saying that I'd wager he's already laid his hands on that young lady a time or two. Of course, she won't admit it, any more than Bowden will confess his guilt. But that's where the truth lies, sir, you mark my words. The fellow is a hot head, this would not be the first time he has been involved in a brawl."

"A crime of passion?"

"Indeed."

"Mr Tompkins tells me that Pettigrew had been strangled."

Rowley frowned. "Extraordinary how fast news travels in this town! And how exactly did he know that?"

"He has a friendly rivalry with the landlord of the Lord Eldon and had called upon the fellow to discuss a business proposition. While they were talking, a lad started shouting outside. They went to see the cause of the commotion to find him standing over Pettigrew's body."

"Have you traced the ligature?"

"Not yet. We believe that the crime was committed with a thick cord or rope of some kind. It was pulled viciously around the Major's neck, cutting into the flesh so much that it bled."

"Did you find such a cord on Bowden?"

"No, but he'll have disposed of it somewhere."

"So you are adamant that the man is your murderer?"

"Oh, he reckons to have an alibi. Claims he was drinking at the Angel, and has half a dozen witnesses to prove it, but the Angel is only five minutes from the Lord Eldon. It's my belief that he slipped out while no one was looking."

"And do you suppose the Major would have agreed to make an appointment with the man whom he had given notice?"

Rowley drew himself up to his considerable height. "Rest assured, it is only a matter of time before the details emerge. It is my belief that Bowden lured the Major out there on a pretext, perhaps under a false name."

Dickens looked at him sharply. "Do you have any evidence of that?"

"As yet, sir, none. But we'll find it, you mark my words."

"The fellow is an ignoramus," Dickens said to Elizabeth an hour later.

"I take it that he has never read one of your books?" she replied demurely.

Dickens snorted. "He has a single idea in his head and is determined to stick to it. I have been speaking to Tompkins and he tells me that young Bowden is well-liked in the town. Sergeant Rowley may find it more troublesome than he would wish to break that alibi."

"I have been talking to the staff here during your absence." Elizabeth nodded. "They describe the young man as a hot-head. His temper has got the better of him more than once and he has given one or two other fellows in town a bloody nose. But nobody believes there is real harm in him. So you think that he is innocent?"

"I can accept that Pettigrew wished to seduce the housemaid, and thought the task easier to accomplish with her young man banished from the house. And I can imagine that Bowden might resort to violence. But would he commit murder by strangulation? I would have thought a blow to the head was more likely. Besides, if Bowden is guilty – what of Datchery?"

"Perhaps Datchery is a *nom de plume*?"

"No doubt. The name is uncommon, though frankly appealing – I may steal it for a character one day. There is much here that makes little sense. Suppose the message which Clarissa told you about was intended for her husband, not for her. Why should the Major fulfil the rendezvous twenty-four hours late? Why, indeed, should he wish to meet the mysterious Datchery at all? These are real puzzles. Was Clarissa able to cast any light upon them when you called on her?"

"Naturally, she is deeply shocked by her husband's death and I did not think it right to interrogate her. Do you have a theory that will explain the mysteries?"

Dickens leaned closer to her and whispered. "Certainly."

"Tell me."

He chose his words carefully. "Consider this. What if Datchery were the pawn in a wicked plot on the part of the Major to drive your friend insane? But something went awry with the scheme. Before the day is done, I shall endeavour to discover the truth of the matter."

"Charles, please. The Major was murdered in a most terrible fashion. Promise me that you will have a care."

He beamed, relishing the tremor in her voice and the hint of admiration it conveyed. "Never fear, Scheherezade. If I succeed in identifying the Major's nemesis, think what a story we will have to tell!"

It was easier said than done. Dickens scouted around the Heath methodically for an hour or more, but could find no trace of the mysterious stranger whose appearance had so distressed Clarissa. None of the people he spoke to had seen a man answering Datchery's description and, as the minutes ticked by, Dickens began to lose heart. The theory he had formed – and which he had taken good care not to share with Elizabeth – was outlandish and he could find no evidence to support it. Reluctantly, he found himself wondering if the tramp had any existence outside Clarissa's imagination.

As night fell, a chill settled on the town. Even wrapped in a heavy coat, he could not help shivering as he strode towards the Moor. For all its proximity to the bustle of King Street, it struck him as an uncommonly lonely place. Squelching along the soft, muddy track that people had trodden between the tall reeds, he could hear the rustle of wind in the trees and the scuttling of a fox. Otherwise the Moor was graveyard-quiet.

He regretted his lack of candour when speaking to Elizabeth, but he felt he had no choice. Her sole concern was for her friend's well-being and it would never do to voice his suspicion that Clarissa might have played a part, however unwitting, in the death of her husband. Besides, even if he was right, the chances of learning the precise truth were slim. Tomorrow, he must return to the capital, and make arrangements to spend a few days with Ellen. If he failed to find Datchery tonight, he would have no choice but to leave the Mystery of Canute Villa – as his good friend Collins might like to term it – to be solved by others.

It was slow going with the pathways – such as they were – so treacherous underfoot and visibility fading. Much as he enjoyed walking in the darkness, the terrain was unfamiliar and he needed to take care to avoid slipping into a ditch or streamlet. Every now and then a branch would graze his cheek. It would be so easy for one of them to put an eye out. He found himself yearning for the lights of London at nighttime and the warm, reassuring consciousness that, even though invisible, teeming humanity was always close at hand. The countryside was so isolated. Who knew how much wickedness lurked here?

Suddenly, as he trudged towards a small copse, he thought he heard something. A cracking of twigs, succeeded by a cough. Dickens froze, straining his ears. Within a few moments came another sound. A low, painful groan.

Was this a trap? Did someone intend him to suffer the same fate as the Major? He peered through the gloom and thought he could make out the faintest shape amongst the trees. Perhaps it was wishful thinking; too often his imagination mastered him.

Another groan, louder this time, and then another, quite prolonged. He did not believe this was a hoax. Nobody, surely, could counterfeit such a noise of pain and despair.

"Who is there?" he hissed.

No answer. He advanced to the edge of the copse. The darkness was quite impenetrable and a branch grazed his cheek, making his eyes water.

"Datchery?"

This time he heard another sound. Was it a man, dragging himself through the undergrowth? Dickens took a stride forward.

"Datchery! I am a friend of Clarissa. We must speak."

Suddenly, he felt an arm wrap itself around his neck. The shock of the attack knocked the breath out of him for an instant, but there was no strength in the attack. After a brief struggle Dickens thrust his elbow into the midriff of his assailant. Winded, the fellow lost his footing and Dickens seized his chance. Before the man could right himself, Dickens knelt upon his chest, and gripped his captive's wrists as though his life depended on it.

"Listen! I do not want to arrest you. I just want to talk."

The man said nothing; although strongly built, there was no fight left in him. He was wearing a ragged coat and had a beard and, although in the darkness it was difficult to make out his features, his breath smelled foul. This was the tramp Clarissa had described in her letter to Elizabeth, of that Dickens had no doubt.

"I am Charles Dickens. Do you know my name?"

"Dickens?" the tramp gasped. "What – what are you doing here?"

"I am helping my friend Mrs Gaskell to . . ."

"Mrs . . . Gaskell?" The tramp's shock was palpable.

"Yes." Dickens leaned over the man's face. "You know of her? She is a well-known author from these parts and her friend is Mrs Clarissa Pettigrew of Canute Villa."

"Not Pettigrew!" the man hissed. "Do not call her that!"

"Ah!" A thrill of triumph coursed through Dickens. His guesswork – no, his deduction! – must be correct. "You know Clarissa?"

"I . . . I knew her. Long ago."

"And you ventured to renew the acquaintance?"

"No – I wanted to save her from that beast Pettigrew. That is all."

"Did she recognize your name, Datchery?"

"Of course not. She knew me as someone else."

A shiver of excitement ran through Dickens' body.

"You dared not tell her your real name. What is it?"

The man groaned. "Mr Dickens, I am dying. Let me leave this world in peace."

Dickens frowned in the darkness. It took no more than an instant for him to make up his mind.

"I believe I may hazard a guess at your true identity."

A soft gasp. "You cannot!"

"You are John Stevenson, are you not? Elizabeth's brother."

A long silence. "How . . . how did you know?"

Dickens could not resist a smile of triumph. "Murder by strangulation is a crime often associated with the sub-continent. I wondered if the murderer had learned his craft

there. He might have been a past associate of Pettigrew's, but
I also remembered that Elizabeth's lost brother spent time in
India. And if John had by some miracle remained alive – that
might explain Datchery's apparent familiarity with the town
and his interest in Pettigrew's wife. As well as explaining why
Clarissa, having met him secretly, tried to throw us off his
scent."

"Dear Clarissa," the man whispered.

"As for your sister . . ."

Stevenson raised a trembling hand. "She must never
know."

Within a few minutes Dickens had teased out the whole
story. John had been a free mariner on the private vessels
working the Indian Ocean, but one terrible day in the winter
of 1828, shortly after arriving at the port of Bombay, he had
been attacked by the bosun, who had conceived a deep dislike
for him following an argument over a game of cards and had
started drinking heavily the moment they reached dry land.
A brawl ensued and, in falling to the ground, the man had
cracked open his skull and died. Two of the bosun's cronies
had accused John of starting the fight and, terrified that he
might fall victim to summary justice, the young man fled into
the back streets of the city. There he quickly discovered that,
in order to survive, he had little choice but to become much
more ruthless and dangerous than the cheerful, God-fearing
young fellow that Elizabeth, twelve years his junior, had so
admired. He became a creature of the shadows, coining the
name Datchery as a mark of his decision to become a
different man.

Stevenson said little of what he had done over the years,
but gave Dickens to understand that the bosun was not the
only man who had died at his hands. He had learned the
technique of strangulation favoured by the murderous Thugs
prior to their suppression. Twelve months earlier, he had
finally worked his passage back to London. Whatever crimes
he had committed, they were too serious for it to be possible
for him, even after such a lapse of time, to dare to assert his

true identity. When he learned, with much astonishment, of his sister's celebrity, it made him all the more determined not to bring dishonour upon her by revealing that he was still alive. Although Dickens protested fiercely, the old man was adamant. Elizabeth might have been heartbroken by his supposed demise, but at least she entertained nothing but good thoughts of him. He could not contemplate shattering her faith in his decency.

The privations of a misspent life meant that he fell sick with increasing frequency. On one occasion he collapsed in Covent Garden and a nurse had assisted him. He gathered from her that his heart was fading. A relapse might occur at any time, with fatal consequences.

Thus he had decided to make one last journey to the North. Not to see his sister, that was impossible, but someone whose memory he had cherished for more than thirty years. He had always worshipped Clarissa, but had been too shy to make his admiration known to her. Now it became a matter of obsession for him to look upon her one last time before he died.

After journeying north to Knutsford, he quickly discovered that the woman he had for so long adored was kept virtually as a prisoner in her own home by an avaricious and violent husband. A husband, moreover, of whom he had heard tell during his years in India. Pettigrew had, after a drinking bout, raped a servant girl. Although his superiors did their utmost to hush up the scandal, the story became well-known and Pettigrew was forced not only to leave the sub-continent but also to resign his commission. Stevenson resolved that he would at least do one last good thing in his life. He would free her from the brute.

It took a little while to pluck up the courage to talk to her. He kept watch on the house and eventually hit upon the idea of asking her to meet him. She had not kept the assignation behind the Lord Eldon on the day he sent her the message, but the next evening, terrified lest her absence be discovered by her husband, she dared to venture out. His faith in her innate bravery had been vindicated. Stevenson said that, once she had recovered from the shock of meeting a man she had believed was long dead, she had begged him not to do anything rash. But his mind was made up.

He had lured Pettigrew out of Canute Villa the previous evening by the simple expedient of a scrawled note saying *I know the truth about your time in India*. The stratagem succeeded. Stevenson had confronted his enemy, but on his account the Major lashed out at him. Illness had ravaged Stevenson's body, but the urge to save Clarissa had given him the strength to overcome Pettigew and slowly squeeze the life out of him.

"You must come forward," Dickens insisted. "An innocent man is under arrest for the crime. Besides that, your sister and Clarissa must know the truth!"

The ailing tramp shook his head. He had lost all his strength now and Dickens had to bend forward to catch what he said.

"No. You swore you would keep the secret, Mr Dickens. And you must."

"But . . ."

The old man raised a knobbly hand. "No. I shall not leave Knutsford, Mr Dickens, never fear. Soon they will find me here, dead, and in my coat they will discover . . . this."

He withdrew from inside his coat a thick, knotted cord.

"You see that stain? It is Pettigrew's blood, Mr Dickens, from when I pulled it so tightly around his throat . . ."

Suddenly he made a strange rasping noise and slumped to the ground, still clutching, at the moment of his death, the means of murder.

Dickens insisted that Elizabeth accompany him to Canute Villa the next morning. It was his impression that there was a faint touch of colour in the widow's cheeks. Her voice sounded stronger and her carriage seemed more erect.

"I hear that Bowden has been released from custody," she said. "I have already said to Alice that I am willing to take him back in service. I was distraught when my . . . my late husband gave him notice."

Elizabeth shook her head. "Is there any doubt that this tramp whose body was found on the Moor is the murderer?"

"None." Dickens held Clarissa's gaze. "It has been a dreadful business. And yet – perhaps some good has come of it."

Clarissa gave the slightest nod. There was a distant look in her eyes and Dickens was sure that she was thinking about the man who had loved her without acknowledgment, let alone hope, for so many years, and how he given her the most precious gift of all. Her freedom.

"How sad," Elizabeth said, "that a man should become so depraved that he should commit a mortal crime for no rational cause."

"Who knows what his reasons may have been, my dear Scheherezade?" Dickens said. "Clarissa has given him her forgiveness and so must we."

Elizabeth nodded. "Poor man. To die, unloved."

Dickens cast a glance at Clarissa and said, so softly that only she could hear, "Perhaps not unloved at the very end."

Watchful Unto Death

Hilary Bonner

And so we come to Dickens's last completed novel, Our Mutual Friend, *released in monthly parts from May 1864. It is one of the gloomiest and bleakest of all of his books, making the squalor, stench and pollution of London almost tangible. In common with others of his recent novels it also explored the influence and corruption of money. Although it has another labyrinthine plot, the basic story-line is simple. John Harmon is the son of a wealthy "dust contractor". Harmon is to inherit his money but only if he marries Bella Wilfer whom, at that time, Harmon had never met, so Harmon decides to conceal his identity at first in order to learn more about her. However, as he is arriving by boat in London, Harmon is attacked by a sailor in whom he confided. In the struggle the sailor is killed. His body is found in the river and, because he is wearing Harmon's coat, is mistaken for him. With Harmon believed dead his father's fortune passes to a former employee, Nicodemus (or Noddy) Boffin. Harmon takes on the identity of John Rokesmith and becomes employed by Boffin, who has also adopted Bella Wilfer. However Boffin is being blackmailed by the street-vendor Silas Wegg, whom Boffin had employed to read to him. Wegg had discovered that Harmon's will had been altered in*

*Boffin's favour and believed this had been Boffin's doing.
Boffin is actually a kind and friendly man who has not
only taken in Bella, but the orphan Sloppy, and a disabled
girl who makes dresses for dolls, Jenny Wren. It is thanks
to Sloppy that Silas Wegg's blackmail is discovered and
Wegg dealt with. At length, alongside a myriad other
plots, Rokesmith learns that Bella truly loves him and so
reveals his identity and inherits his fortune. Despite being
disinherited Boffin remains on good terms with Harmon
and they all live happily together. Or do they? There is at
least one thread that remains unresolved and Hilary
Bonner takes that to its conclusion.*

Hilary Bonner was a former showbusiness editor for the
Mail on Sunday *and* Daily Mirror *before she turned to
full-time writing in 1994, though she continues to work as a
columnist. Most of her novels, starting with* The Cruelty
of Morning *(1994), are psychological thrillers.* No Reason to Die *(2004) is a novel based upon the tragedy at the
Deepcut army barracks where four soldiers died of gunshot
wounds. That book, as with the following story, seeks
justice and closure.*

Yet again she heard the tapping behind her. Yet again
when she turned around there was nothing. Neither
man nor beast.

She peered into the murky night. There was virtually no
lighting in the dark lanes leading east by Blackfriars Bridge.
They darted off like the legs of a spider, their angles awkward
and winding, leading, it seemed, only into black nothingness.

The salty mist from the river merged there with the smoky
fog of the city. The air was thick like treacle, only icy damp.
It chilled to the bone, and she could see only a foot or two
ahead. This was a particularly bad night.

She was shivering. She did not know whether it was from
cold or from fear. Certainly she could no longer deny that she
was afraid.

The cobbles beneath her feet were wet and treacherous,

but she hurried along, thinking only of her mission and the disgrace of discovery. Then she lost her footing and would have fallen had she not managed to grab hold of a post set into the wall by her side. The tapping grew louder, closer. There was an opening in the wall, right before her. A gateway. The gates stood ajar. Without further thought she slipped through them.

At once the smell of death overwhelmed her. An acrid stench of stale dried blood. She guessed she might be in a tanner's yard, or at the back of a butcher's shop. She stumbled against a pile of unsavoury waste of some kind. Once more she nearly lost her footing. But this time she slipped, not on a wet cobble, but some slimy remnant of something that had been discarded in this unpleasant place. She was desperate to leave, but dared not. Instead she cowered there, gazing into the wall of fog, ears pricked, listening, all her senses alert.

The tapping seemed to have ceased. Or had it? She could not be sure. The fog so muffled the sound.

After a few minutes she could stay in that stinking yard no longer. She made her way cautiously into the narrow cobbled lane again and, looking around her all the time, staring wide-eyed into the cold treacle though she could see nothing, began to continue her journey, still walking at a brisk pace, though more mindful now of the treacherous nature of the ground.

Then she heard it again. Tap. Tap. No mistake this time. Behind her. To her right. Or was it to her left? The fog was all powerful. It distorted everything. She could not even work out the direction of the tapping. But there it was. Tap. Tap. Tap. And this time so close she could not believe that she couldn't see the cause of it. Scared beyond measure, she swung round on her laced leather boots, right round in a circle, flailing at the dense air with her arms, her little fists tightly clenched.

Still she could neither see nor feel the source of the danger she felt sure was right there with her. Such was her terror that she even thought she felt the breath of another upon her face.

She took off then, at a run, her feet slipping and sliding in all directions. Once she took a wrong turning and had to quickly double back. But the will to reach her secret destination safely and to leave behind that lurking danger, in whatever form it took, propelled her onwards.

Bella and John Harmon still lived in the beautiful house that the Boffins had bought when they'd thought that they'd inherited John's father's fortune, believing, as all London did, that the young man had been murdered.

Mr and Mrs Boffin still lived there too, a tribute to both their good honest nature and that of John Harmon and his young wife. For the Boffins had gladly handed over the fortune to which they felt they had no right, and welcomed back wholeheartedly the man whom they'd cherished as a boy, while he had embraced them as the family he'd never really had.

Also there lived with the Harmons and the Boffins two young people whom they not only felt it was their duty to care for, because of their loyalty and steadfastness, but had also grown to love. One was Sloppy, a strange but stout fellow with a heart of pure gold, Mrs Boffin said, and the other was Jenny Wren, a young woman with a bent body but the straightest and sharpest of brains, who made dresses for dolls. To the delight of the Boffins and the Harmons, these two, with whose pasts they were so entangled, had recently married.

Sloppy was coachman and Jack of all Trades in the Boffin–Harmon household, and Jenny Wren, while still a doll's dressmaker, officially acted as a kind of lady's maid to Bella. But in reality, she was just what she had always been. Bella Harmon's best and closest friend.

It was a fine and happy household. There was also a cook and a parlour maid. And it was this parlour maid, whose name was Polly Martin, who was giving Mrs Bella Harmon such cause for concern that day.

Bella had never ceased to wonder at her own good fortune. Brought up in extreme, though genteel, poverty by a half-broken but still delightful father, whom she had adored, and a pompous overblown mother she had never quite managed to love as she knew she should, Bella had married for great love alone and then found herself rich beyond her dreams. She was a content and fulfilled woman, wife to a kind, fair, and generous man, mother to a toddler, little Bella, and to a babe of just a few weeks, little John. Her life was almost too good to be true. Certainly so much better, Bella felt, than she had ever deserved.

All of this could, as she had once so feared, have turned her into a selfish grasping person. In fact the effect had been quite the opposite on Bella. She wanted all around her to be as happy and as well provided for as she was.

It irked her that life was so cruel. That good men and women died on the streets from cold and hunger rather than risk the dubious mercies of the Poor House. That children were turned into beggars and thieves by the harshness that was all around them, and that they grew up without any real hope of improving the accident of their birth, the vast majority never even beginning to learn to read or write.

But Bella was a young woman brought up within the strict confines of Victorian England and it did not occur to her, even in her dreams, to attempt in any way to change the world she lived in. Nor did it occur to her that she, nor indeed anyone else, could change the way things were. All she was able to do was to ensure, to the best of her ability, the well-being of those around her, her family, her family employees, and her small circle of dear friends.

Thus it was that Bella had begun to fret so over the well-being of Polly Martin.

Polly was probably a pretty girl, certainly she had lovely dark curls and black eyes which looked as if they should be dancing, but most of the time her eyes were dull and her features drawn. She had been with the Boffins and the Harmons for nearly six months now, hired by Bella and Mrs Boffin as much out of compassion as anything else after a recommendation from the Reverend Milvey, to whom Polly had come for help upon the recommendation of someone the reverend could not quite recall. She had been presented to them as a young woman alone in the world following the death of her father, eager to maintain her respectability and independence, and looking for a place in service.

The Harmons and the Boffins had spotted an injured soul and found themselves incapable of not doing their best to allow that soul to mend. Although at first wary, certainly cautious, Polly had quite quickly come to be at ease with those fine people and had shown herself to be both hard working and fundamentally good-natured. She had even learned to smile again, just occasionally.

But over the last few weeks Polly had smiled less and less. It seemed that she had lost her appetite. Certainly she had lost weight. Indeed she was thin to the point of being emaciated. Her face was pinched and there were dark circles beneath those lifeless black eyes. And, as she went about her work in the drawing room early one morning, she looked as if she hadn't slept for at least a week, nor eaten.

"Are you sure you are quite well, Polly dear?" asked Bella, for the umpteenth time.

Polly was shining the brass fender which stood on the stone hearth of the big fireplace, rubbing it with a polishing cloth so vigorously it was as if her life depended upon it. She did not pause.

"Polly, do you hear me, dear?" Bella persisted.

Polly turned her head towards her mistress then, but still did not for a moment cease her polishing.

"I am quite well Mrs Harmon, thanking you," she replied.

Not for the first time Bella was struck by how well spoken Polly was, for a girl of her apparent station.

"You do not have to work if you are ill, Polly," she remonstrated. "Not in this house. You should know that. Why don't you rest and let me call out the doctor for you. Mrs Boffin and I can always turn our hand to a little house-work. Indeed, I sometimes think Mrs Boffin would be happier doing more in the house. I'm not at all sure how at ease she is with being waited upon and having servants about the place, really I'm not."

The girl finally stopped her polishing then, and turned full round to face her mistress.

"I really am quite well," she repeated, this time managing a wan smile.

But Bella noticed that Polly's face that day was paler and more drawn than ever and the circles around her tired eyes were deeply etched.

"Then something is severely troubling you, Polly," she said. "Please, dear, won't you tell me what it is?"

The girl stared at her for a moment, and it was as if Bella could almost reach out and feel the pain in those dull black eyes. For a moment she thought that Polly might be going to confide in her, share a secret perhaps. But no.

"There is nothing troubling me, Mrs Harmon," said the girl flatly, and she returned at once to her polishing.

Bella stood anxiously watching her for a moment or two more. Then she heard her baby boy's cries from the nursery. He had woken hungry as usual, and was calling for his mother. With one last anxious glance over her shoulder at her parlour maid, Bella left the room.

That night when she had finished her duties Polly set off again on the secret journey that took her to Blackfriars and then through a series of dark and unsavoury lanes, beneath the tall shadow of the Tower of London, and on to a small and not particularly welcoming house close by the river.

The blend of rank city fog and salty river mist was even thicker and denser than the night before. Polly could see less than ever as she made her weary way. She coughed wretchedly. She was bone tired, and her lungs could barely cope with the lethal mixture, yet once again she forced herself to walk as fast as she possibly could. She was in an even greater hurry than the previous night to reach her destination, because she was, as Bella Harmon had suspected, severely troubled – consumed by the greatest anxiety she had known. Greater by far than anything inflicted on her by the drunken father of whom the Boffins and the Harmons knew nothing, and greater even than when she'd had to face life alone after the loss of her darling man.

None the less Polly's ears were pricked for the sound of tapping, particularly as she passed the north end of Blackfriars Bridge where she had first become aware of it. But this time she heard no tapping. And, anyway, she was in so much of a hurry and so worried about that other matter, which was of far greater importance than any danger to herself, that she did not pause once to make sure.

Instead she hurried even more, until she reached the third in a line of plain terraced houses, each one just like the other. And such was her haste to get inside that she did not even glance over her shoulder as she knocked on a door which quickly opened allowing her to immediately enter.

However, if she had done so she still may not have seen the man with the wooden leg through the fog and the mist, although he was very close by. He had pressed himself against the grey stone wall, rising directly from the cobbled lane, which formed the front of the row of houses.

Indeed so smoky and dense was the fog and such was the speed with which Polly had entered the house that he may not have seen her do so were it not for the flickering candle light from within which had illuminated her as the door opened.

He waited until the door was closed and she was safely inside before approaching. The window to the right of the door was roughly curtained, but the ragged drapes had not been properly drawn. Through a narrow vertical strip of uncovered glass he could see clearly into the room within, which was illuminated just enough by candles and a stuttering fire.

What he saw there greatly cheered him. It was as if someone had handed him a musket loaded with the ammunition he had been seeking in order to revenge himself against those he hated most.

He looked again, pressing his face against the window pane, carefully taking in the scene. Oh, there could be no doubt of it, surely. No doubt at all. You only had to look at the girl to know. The love in her eyes. The furrow of concern in her brow. It could only mean one thing.

He backed off then, and made himself as comfortable as he could in the doorway of an ironmongers' shop across the street, from where he could still see the door to the house. Then he settled down to wait, smiling slyly to himself.

Ever since Silas Wegg had been made to give up any claim to the fortune left by John Harmon's father, which he had tried to win by means of blackmail, he had hated the entire Boffin–Harmon household with a terrible venom and dreamed only of avenging himself against them.

He considered that the Harmons and the Boffins had humiliated and destroyed him, and truly loathed them. This in spite of Mr Boffin setting him up again with a street stall – selling items ranging from ginger bread to apples, and also ballads that Wegg himself roughly composed – which to Wegg, actually served only the purpose of providing the means to live long enough to achieve his revenge.

Now he congratulated himself on so swiftly grasping opportunity when it presented itself. He had seen the girl often enough at the Boffin–Harmon house, because Wegg had taken to passing by there whenever he could, concealing himself from the casual eye, becoming aware of all who lived and worked inside, and taking in as much as he could about them in case it could be used in the future.

He had seemed to make little progress, really, and indeed on his last spying mission had been chased away by that Sloppy character and informed that if he were seen again thereabouts the master would set the police on him for what he'd done before.

But then fate had played its part. And returning to his Blackfriars lodgings one night he had spotted Polly Martin passing by, in a hurry, her pale features fraught with anxiety. It had been an unusually clear night, and Wegg, momentarily unsure what to do next, had merely watched her pass. Watched and wondered.

He kept a bit of a look out from then on, though, stepping out of his lodgings at about the same time each evening. A couple of nights later he saw her again, and under cover of the fog had successfully trailed her for more than half an hour. But he feared the tap of his wooden leg must eventually have given him away, because she'd suddenly taken fright and run off so fast that he'd had no hope whatsoever of keeping up with her.

Tonight he'd had another chance. And this time he'd been ready for the chase. Chuckling to himself he glanced down at his wooden leg. The end was wrapped in a thick woollen sock, which seemed to have done well its job of muffling the sound of the tap tap tap.

She was inside the house for what seemed like an eternity. It was actually just over two hours. A long time indeed for a man with a wooden leg and only a doorway for shelter on a bitterly cold, damp foggy night.

He watched as she made her way out into the narrow street, turning to retrace her steps homeward, and walking steadily towards him until she came level with his doorway. Then he pounced, propelling himself forward onto his one good leg so that he was in front of her, blocking her path.

She gave a little cry and lurched to one side, desperately trying to find a way around him. He reached out and grabbed her, locking strong gnarled fingers around her stick thin arm.

"Be still, girl," he hissed. "Do as I say and no harm will come to you!"

He tightened his grip on her arm, and allowed his tone to become even more menacing. "Nor to any that are dear to you. Do you understand?"

She tried to nod but could barely move her head. There was terror in her tired eyes.

"Do you understand?" he repeated.

Somehow she managed to mutter that she did.

"Right," Wegg responded, his gap toothed mouth stretching into an ugly leering grin. "Then I will tell you what it is that you must do for me, dearie."

That night when John Harmon came home from business in the city, Bella shared her worries about Polly with her husband.

He listened with care and responded kindly, though Bella noticed that he was rather more concerned with dandling his new son on his knee than the possible troubles of their parlour maid, for which, she felt, she could hardly criticise him.

"You know, my dear, how much I respect your desire to care for those around you," he said eventually. "But you cannot carry the whole world's trouble on those narrow shoulders of yours."

Meanwhile Polly, exhausted after yet another sleepless night, and half out of her mind with worry following her encounter with Silas Wegg, went about her work as best she could, but with such a heavy heart. Polly was more sorely troubled than ever. Polly had a secret and it was one for which she expected no sympathy.

Indeed she expected that if her secret were ever to be known that she would not only lose her job but everything that she held dear – including the secret itself.

Polly's secret was that she had a child. And she'd never had a husband. It was the child, suddenly sick with a fever, that she had been visiting late at night each time Silas Wegg had spotted her around Blackfriars. She had been content to visit her child, in the care of a waterman's wife, just once a week on her afternoon off until the little girl, named Mary after Polly's mother, had become so ill.

Polly handed over virtually her entire weekly wage to the waterman's wife, a woman well known for hiring herself out to look after other people's bastards, but she fretted all the while that little Mary was not being properly cared for.

In the previous week she had set off four times on the long walk through the night to that sorry little house by the river, in order to see her child and make sure, she hoped, by her very presence, that Mary was well nursed and nurtured, and that the money she handed over was indeed being spent on the baby girl's welfare. Last night the waterman's wife had told her that she had taken Mary to the doctor's shop that day, and had asked Polly for yet more money, but she'd had little to report back and Polly was not sure that she believed her.

But Polly was so weary and so distraught that she could not think at all clearly. The arrival of Silas Wegg in her already unfortunate life had taken Polly Martin closer to total despair than she had ever been before.

She wanted only to lie down and die. But always there was Mary, her own dear sweet child, and the little girl's very existence ensured that her mother would not and could not give up.

However, she could hardly bear to contemplate what the man with the wooden leg had asked of her. It was surely something she could not do. But Silas Wegg had discovered Polly's secret, grasping it with total accuracy just by seeing mother and daughter together. And poor Polly was sickeningly aware of the consequences were she to disregard Wegg's instructions.

All that had mattered to Polly for a very long time now was the welfare of her daughter. For the first time she even considered handing her over, as an orphan, to a good and well-off childless couple so that Mary might have the chance of a far better life than her mother could give her.

But poor Polly dreaded the very thought of never seeing her child again, of her daughter growing up without having any knowledge of her mother. And in any case she did not even know how to go about such a thing – or at least, not without exposing her own vulnerability and her child's bastard status, she didn't.

She told herself there must be a solution, but was far too tired and empty to even imagine what it could be. However, her child had seemed a little better the previous night, so for the next two nights Polly slept gratefully in her bed, praying for some unknown salvation. On the third night she embarked once more on her long and wearisome walk across half of London. She had not in any case dared to leave it any longer. Wegg would have been expecting her before, and she knew without doubt that he was angry with her for letting him down.

In the park that afternoon, wheeling another child, little John, her mistress's baby son, in the brand new baby carriage

the whole family were so proud of, with her mistress alongside holding the hand of her toddler daughter, and with the
faithful Sloppy in attendance, Polly had spotted Wegg lurking amidst a copse of small trees. Then toddler Bella had
excitedly pulled her mother across the grass towards some
ducks on a nearby pond, and Sloppy had danced his ever
eager attendance, leaving Polly and baby John alone on the
gravelled path.

Wegg had instantly shown himself and proceeded to approach Polly and her tiny charge quite boldly, moving as fast
as his wooden leg would allow. But, just as she was becoming
sorely afraid of what Wegg might intend, Sloppy, happy,
carefree Sloppy, turned on his heel and began to lope,
laughing, across the grass back towards Polly and little John..

Wegg backed off at once. Sloppy was stronger than he
looked, and had a toughness born of his early street urchin
days. Wegg had already learned that, and had no wish for
another confrontation with him. He remained just concealed
enough by the copse of trees so that Sloppy would not yet be
able to see him.

But, from the path, where she stood in a state of panic,
almost rooted to the spot, Polly could see Silas Wegg clearly
enough. And she could certainly hear the words that he
hissed menacingly at her. He mouthed them, stretching
his lips exaggeratedly, so that she would have known what
he was saying even if she had been unable to hear anything.

"Tonight, or else!"

He disappeared then, backing off out of sight behind the
trees, still unseen by Sloppy who was by then at her side,
cooing excitedly over baby John.

And so that night Polly set off grimly, knowing that Wegg
would be waiting for her at Blackfriars, waiting for her to
pass on her way to visit her own child, her very life. Waiting
for her to report back, like the spy he had made her, waiting
for her to conspire with him in a plot it almost broke her heart
to even contemplate. But only almost. If she were to lose her
dear, dear Mary then her heart really would break.

The tapping once again alerted her to his presence. But

this time Wegg did not lurk in dark corners and doorways. He appeared suddenly in front of her in that way of his, so surprisingly fast for a man with one leg, like some sort of ghostly spectre. And a truly evil spectre, she thought.

"So when is it to be?" he asked her, his face twisted into an unpleasant leer again.

She shook her head. "I don't know." she murmured. "I'm not sure . . ."

"Haven't you found a way yet? Haven't you found a way to do. as I bid? If not it will be all the worst for you."

"I don't care what happens to me any more, truly I don't." She spat the words at him. Only a fool could but believe her.

Wegg was momentarily taken aback by the fire in her. But he had a sly quickness about him. "Maybe not, but you care about that bastard child of yours don't you?"

Against her will tears filled Polly's tired eyes at even the thought of her dear poor Mary.

"What would happen to that child without its mother to provide for it?" Wegg continued. "No respectable household will employ you when they know your dirty little secret. And do you think that old woman would care for the bastard without your money? At best it'd be the Poor House for the mite, at worst, well . . ."

"Stop it, stop it, I'll do as you bid." Polly shouted the words at him, not knowing if she would or could fulfil her promise, but not caring either. She would have agreed to anything to stop him saying such awful frightening things.

"Tomorrow night then?"

"Yes, yes."

"So, you'll bring the baby boy here, at about this time. You'll slip out of the house unnoticed, just as you've been doing all this past week, but tomorrow night you'll bring young John Harmon here. To me."

Polly nodded. Suddenly all the fight had gone from her.

"You won't hurt him will you?" she pleaded. "You wouldn't harm the dear child?"

"Not if his high and mighty father pays up the modest sum

I shall ask for. And he will, he will. He won't take no risks
with his precious son and heir. And you Polly, you will take
back a note and leave it in the baby's bedroom. Then, if you
choose, you can make it look as if someone has broken in and
stolen the child from its bed. Mr John Harmon will bring the
money and leave it where I ask, I know he will. Then his
child will be returned. Mr and Mrs High and Mighty will
never know who took their child, and for me a debt will be
repaid, albeit only partially. Justice, eh, pretty Polly? Justice."

"And you'll leave them alone after that, Mr and Mrs
Harmon and me too?"

Wegg twisted his mouth yet again into that now familiar
ugly leer.

"I shall never leave the Harmons alone. Never. One half of
everything they have should be mine. At least. That's what
was agreed. And as for you, dearie. Well, we'll have to see,
won't we? There could be advantage in this for you, Pretty
Polly, if you do well. Maybe we can work together, you and I.
For your child's sake, of course. For your child, dearie."

Polly felt a shiver run the length of her body. Surely she
could not be a party to any of this? It was wicked. Inhuman.
Yet what choice did she have?

"'Til tomorrow, then," murmured Wegg.

Polly nodded her head. Yet again words would not come.
She backed away from him, then turned and began to run
once more towards all that remained worthwhile in her life.
Her baby Mary, her darling Mary.

Thoughts of her tragic past and her lost future raced
through her head. None of this would have happened and
sweet, sweet Mary would have had a proud loving father but
for the cruellest turn of fate.

Thomas Vickery, her intended, had one fateful day refused
to allow her to live with her drunken father for a second
longer. Arriving to find Polly nursing a bruised and swollen
face thanks to yet another beating at her father's hands, he
had whisked her away to his lodgings. Thomas was a fine
craftsman, a carpenter, and his prospects were good. A

wedding date had already been set, and engulfed at last by kindness instead of abject cruelty, Polly had seen no reason to deny Thomas any longer.

She shared his bed just the once. A night of tenderness she would never forget. Then the next day Thomas had left early for his work, as usual, and he'd never returned. Her lover, she was told, had stepped right into the path of a bolting horse. He had been killed instantly by a blow to the head from a flying metal-shod hoof. And Polly had often wondered if the accident would have happened had Thomas not been, she was sure, every bit as euphorically happy as she, his bride to be, with his mind far more likely on the night before than the day ahead.

It soon became clear that she was with child. There was no point in turning to her father for help, and, in any case, as it happened, he succeeded in his apparent aim of drinking himself to death just before his first grandchild was born.

Thomas had been an orphan. Polly had no living siblings. In desperation she sought out the only surviving relative of which she knew, her father's sister, who lived in the country just outside Chertsey. Grudgingly the aunt, who had no love for her brother or his offspring, had taken Polly in, purely out of a sense of Christian duty, she'd made it clear.

There had been three conditions. The first: that the presence of the pregnant Polly and later her child was to remain as much of a secret as possible. The second: that Polly would earn her keep, which she most certainly had done. She had cooked and scrubbed, fetched and carried, and washed and mended, virtually all day long. The third condition had been that after giving birth, as soon as Polly and the child were strong enough, the aunt would consider that she'd done her duty by both God and her errant brother, and Polly would have to leave to make her own way in the world.

It was the aunt, who, through a mutual acquaintance, had introduced Polly to the Reverend Milvey – without mentioning Polly's bastard child, of course – as a young woman without family who was desperately in need of a domestic position in a good household. Now this was a position Polly feared she was about to abuse in the most horrible way imaginable.

The Harmons and the rest of their curiously assorted household, the Boffins, Mr Sloppy and the Doll's Dress-maker, were the only people who had shown her kindness since the death of her gentle mother five years earlier. Apart from Thomas Vickery, of course.

Life had not been so bad while her mother had lived. Polly's father, although always a cold and distant man, had not been unkind in those days, as far as she remembered, and certainly not violent. He had been a good provider too. He'd held a management position in a tea house. The family had lived comfortably in a well-appointed home, and Polly had been educated by her mother, an unusually accomplished woman, who had taught her to read and write well. She had never known which had come first, her father's excessive drinking or his losing his job. Or maybe the two had gone hand in hand.

At about the same time her mother had died from con-sumption. Her father's drinking and his temper had both become excessive and unpredictable and the rest of Polly's years growing into young womanhood were steeped in mis-ery. Until Thomas Vickery had so briefly provided salvation. A salvation that had ultimately led to the position Polly found herself in that grim night. A frightened young woman, keeping the very existence of her own child a secret. A young woman being cruelly blackmailed into conniving in kidnap-ping the child of the only people left in the world that she cared a jot for – excepting her own dear little Mary, of course.

For Polly Martin had indeed come to care greatly for the Harmons. And as she hurried along the unsavoury lanes of darkest London Polly's mind was in a fervent turmoil.

The next day Bella Harmon noticed at once that Polly looked worse than ever. The circles around her now red-rimmed eyes were blacker and deeper, and her hands, as she at-tempted not all that successfully to busy herself about her work, were shaking quite dreadfully. Bella was quite sure that the girl had been crying. She made one last attempt to find out what was wrong.

"Won't you trust me, Polly, dear?" she coaxed. "I desire only to help you in any way that I can."

And that was too much for poor Polly, because she knew it was true. She ran from her mistress's presence, and Bella was well aware that she was weeping, because she could clearly hear Polly's sobs and see her shoulders heaving up and down as she fled.

She did not go after the girl. Bella felt that all she could do now was to wait and hope that Polly would eventually confide in her, as she so wished.

There was, however, no hope of that any more. Polly had made her decision. It was approaching midnight, the whole house by then cloaked in silent darkness when, moving as quietly as she could, Polly slipped out of the house, just as, in the words of Wegg, she had done several times before, and made her way through the front gates into the street. Little John's beautiful new baby carriage made her exit trickier than usual. One of the wheels had developed a squeak. Polly slowed her pace, hoping to keep the noise down.

Once safely away from the Harmon house she bent over the carriage and tended the little bundle within, adjusting the pillow, smoothing the covers, before hurrying onwards.

Polly's face was tearstained, and her eyes even more red-rimmed than earlier. But her hands no longer shook and she didn't feel the slightest bit tired any more. Nor so afraid. She knew beyond any doubt that she now had no choice but to continue with this course of action she had decided on.

It took her almost an hour to reach the place in Black-friars where she knew Wegg would be waiting for her. The night was clearer than it had been for days, the river mist reduced to salty wisps, and no fog at all to speak of, just the occasional billow of smoke wafting from the thousands of city chimneys.

Nonetheless the man she now feared more than any other

still managed to take her by surprise. He appeared before her suddenly again, a horrible apparition materializing out of nowhere as she stepped into a shadowed alleyway.

"Well, well, my dear, so you've brought him to me," he murmured, looking down at the new baby carriage. "My passage to riches. My revenge for injustice. He is here then, at last."

"As you see," murmured Polly. Her head was spinning. The plan had seemed so simple, so straightforward, earlier in the day. And above all, inevitable. Now she feared that her courage had departed her.

Wegg moved forwards surprising quickly again for a man with one leg pushing Polly aside, so intent was he on getting his hands on the tiny creature he saw as nothing other than a replacement for his stolen fortune. He bent over the shiny black carriage, peering at the little bundle within.

"Well then, my beauty, my pieces of silver, my grandest finery, all of my riches, let old Silas have a look at you, my chicken, my lovely young chicken that will lay such a golden egg for me."

Silas leaned still closer to the bundle. With one gnarled hand he tugged at the blankets in order to get a better view. Then he cried out quite loudly, both in surprise and anger, straightened up, turned round, and half threw himself at Polly.

"Where is he? Where is my passage to riches? Where is the child Harmon? What trick is this? And who are you, girl, to think I'll allow you to get away with such a thing?"

Silas grabbed Polly's shoulders with both hands and began to shake her. His face was even more twisted and contorted than she had seen before. Greed and jealousy had surely made him a truly evil being. His hands slipped upwards until they were around her throat.

Was he so mad that he intended to strangle her? She would never know for Silas Wegg was not to get the chance. Polly lifted her right hand and plunged the long sharp carving knife it held deep into the soft flesh beneath his rib cage and up into his cold and avaricious heart.

Silas Wegg died at once, slumping immediately to the ground, the knife still imbedded deep in his flesh. He didn't scream, merely grunting slightly as he fell. Bella looked down at him and at the blood on her hand and all over the front of her clothing.

She felt no remorse. She made no sound. Perhaps she was beyond any reaction.

It had been her absolute intention to kill Silas Wegg. She had guessed that he would bend to check on the child he had demanded that she bring to him, and she had intended to use the knife she had secreted among the folds of the heavy winter coat the Harmons had provided her with, to stab him in the lower back, on either side of the spine where she knew that the flesh was soft and all manner of vital organs lay within.

But when the time had come she had been unable to kill in cold blood, instead standing frozen to the spot until he came at her. Only then did she find the strength and the courage, if that is what it had been, to do such a dreadful deed.

And now, afterwards, she felt quite at peace. She was not even really a murderess, she felt. Not in God's eyes, anyway. After all, ultimately she had surely killed in self-defence.

She looked around her, squinting into the night. There was nobody in sight. If anyone in that Godforsaken place had seen or heard a peep they were, it seemed, too wise to intervene.

Silas Wegg lay dead like a dog on the cobbles.

It was almost over now. There was just one avowed task left for Polly Martin.

She turned back in the direction of Fleet Street and the Temple, then left onto Blackfriars Bridge.

Once she had reached the middle, where she deemed the mighty Thames to be at its deepest, she climbed onto the great bridge's iron balustrade and, without pausing even for a second, allowed herself to fall into the swirling river below.

Bella found Polly's letter early the next morning, right after noticing that little John's baby carriage was missing.

"If you are reading this note, my dear, dear, kind Mrs Harmon, then I will have done the dreadful deed and, most probably be dead," the note began. "Last night I learned that my beloved daughter Mary had departed this earth, dying of a fever she would almost certainly never have developed had I been able to care for her and provide the home that a mother should.

"The only good to come of this might surely be that I am now free to prevent a terrible wrong, and that I can rid the only people alive who have shown me compassion of an evil thing. But in order to do so, I have to do evil myself . . ."

By the time Bella had finished reading the letter she was in tears. Polly had told of her plan to murder Silas Wegg, she had told of her ill-fated love, of her cruel father, of the even more cruel loss of her husband-to-be, and of her near desperate intent to maintain her apparent respectability and to provide properly for her daughter. An intent that had ultimately led to her downfall and threatened the well-being of her most kindly employers.

"I had no wish to bring my shame upon your house," she wrote.

Bella put the letter down on the table before her, and buried her face in her hands.

"My poor, dear Polly," she said, talking only to herself. "Can it be true? Can you really have done this dreadful thing? And for us?"

It was true of course. Silas Wegg's body was found the next morning and Polly Martin's dredged out of the river the following day.

Polly had made only one request of the Harmons. It was, she said, her dying wish. She had left all that remained of her wages and her few shillings of savings, with the letter to Bella. She said that she wanted nothing for herself but asked that her little dead daughter should be given a good Christian burial, as an orphan, and not, whatever happened, be labelled in death as a bastard child.

Bella and John Harmon carried out Polly Martin's wishes to the letter, and went further. After consultation with their lawyer, Mr Mortimer Lightwood, and his barrister friend, Mr Eugene Wrayburn – who had himself once protected the man who'd maimed and tried to murder him simply in order not to compromise the respectability of the young woman he loved – it was concluded that there was nothing that would link poor tragic Polly to the murder of the monstrous Wegg, as long, of course, as no attempt was made to reclaim little John's shiny new baby carriage.

Therefore they decided that just as Polly Martin's adored daughter should not be labelled a bastard, neither should little Mary's mother be labelled a murderess. Instead they instructed reputable undertakers to take possession of Polly's body, and meanwhile spread about the story that the poor girl must have slipped to her watery death while running an urgent errand for her mistress which had called for her to take a riverside path after dark, something for which her mistress would always reproach herself.

And so Polly, who had so craved respectability for herself and her child, was also given a good Christian burial, and finally laid to rest in a carefully chosen plot close by her dear Mary.

The Harmons, the Boffins, Mr Sloppy, the Doll's Dressmaker, Mr Wrayburn and Mr Lightwood all attended the funeral and genuinely mourned for poor Polly.

"She did it for us," whispered Bella to her husband. "So that we would be rid of that awful Wegg."

"Aye," responded John. "And so that she would not bring shame upon herself and, as she believed, upon us too."

Bella found herself moved then to pose the kind of question that had never occurred to her before.

"But, dear John, what kind of world do we live in where a decent, kind, young woman can be so afraid of losing her respectability that she is driven to such deeds?"

"It is our world," John Harmon responded. "And the only solace, my sweet, is that some time in the future it will change, I am quite sure of it."

Bella clasped his hand tightly, yet again thanked God for
her own good fortune, and for the sake of every Polly and
Mary Martin left alive, prayed that her husband would one
day be proven right.

The Tidal

Michael Ryan

It was while writing Our Mutual Friend *that Dickens was involved in a serious accident in which he could well have been killed. He had been staying in France with Ellen Ternan and her mother and was returning to London by train, known as the Tidal Train, because it operated according to the tides. There had been works on the line which were incomplete and the train crashed near Staplehurst in Kent. All but one of the carriages tumbled to the River Beult below the embankment. Dickens's carriage remained coupled to the engine, though it hung precariously over the embankment. Nevertheless, with remarkable bravery and presence of mind, Dickens set about helping the injured and dying. He even climbed back into the carriage to retrieve the manuscript of the next episode of* Our Mutual Friend. *Although only 53 at the time Dickens was already in poor health, but disregarded his own pains to help others. The shock of the crash did not affect him until the next day and ever after he found it difficult to travel by train. Many have suggested that the stress shortened his life.*

Michael Ryan takes this incident as the starting point for a story of mystery and intrigue and it's interesting to see another of Dickens's contacts becoming involved.

Ryan is currently an English Lecturer at North Devon College. He has written a range of drama for stage, TV and radio and compiled and edited over 50 published educational texts. He is the author of the Brother John mysteries, Where There's a Will *(2005) and* John Tracy Casebook *(2006). Michael has also acted in and directed more than 20 stage plays and has been co-chairman (along with Derek Wilson) of the Cambridge History Festival.*

On Friday the ninth of June, in the year 1865, I was travelling to London on the South Eastern Railway. The tidal train was a scant twenty minutes out of Folkestone when, with a sudden application of the brake, I was hurled into a corner. My companions and I were unhurt. The carriage we travelled in did not plummet as so many did, but went off the line, nearly turned over a viaduct and, caught aslant upon the turn, hung over the bridge at Staplehurst in an inexplicable manner. When all was still, and I realized that the danger *must* be over, I at once became calm and, clambering out of the carriage window, stood upon the step and gazed around. The bridge was so broken as to be almost gone and, some dozen or so feet below, lay most of the carriages, telescoped together in the bed of the stream and on the grass banks bordering it. In all directions lay dead and wounded, so that the ground was like a battlefield. At once, I rushed back inside, helped my companions to safety, then took out my travelling Brandy flask and top hat. I hastened down the bank, filled my hat with water, and did what I could among the dying and dead.

At first, there being so many needy souls, I was at a loss where to begin. Among them was a woman, scarce more than a child, whose body lay in what remained of an overturned carriage, her eyes and mouth frozen in a look of absolute terror. The sight was almost too much for me to bear. I braced myself for further horrors and hurried on when, almost at my feet, there came the pitiful cries of one in agony. Looking down I beheld a man of middle years, with florid complexion and full whiskers, struggling to raise himself from the ground. His head was horribly gashed across and his body contorted upon its side. Kneeling, I turned him as gently as I could and laid him on his back. Splashing water on his face, I was gratified when his eyes flickered open and a weak smile came to his lips. Gently, I parted them and poured in a little Brandy. The poor fellow swallowed with obvious difficulty then, looking me full in the face, said simply, "I am gone." His head lolled to one side and his breathing ceased. I almost wept, but had no time to linger for, as I gazed round, my eyes lit upon a figure propped against a nearby oak.

Stumbling across the uneven ground, I came upon a woman of mature years, decked simply in sombre grey, her only concession to ornament being a choker and brooch of jet. Her face was covered in blood but her eyes were open, gazing up at the vault of heaven. For a moment I feared that she, too, was dead but then she coughed, a dry bitter sound that chilled my heart. Dipping my kerchief in the small store of water, I mopped her brow. Again the Brandy, again the agonizing wait. Then, when I was near to despair, her eyes met mine. She whispered a hoarse, "God bless you, sir," and smiled; such a warm, kindly open countenance that my very soul cheered to see colour returning to her cheeks. Her gloved hand found mine. The slightest hint of pressure, then her fingers slipped and she seemed to rest. I felt for her pulse. It was erratic but strong enough. She would live! My resolve strengthened, I left her, hurrying to and fro, doing my best to revive and comfort every poor creature I met who had sustained serious injury. Yet, alas, despite my best endeavours, the task seemed impossible. My heart grew heavy and something akin to panic seized my mind.

Increasingly weary, my halting steps led me to a pile of masonry and iron rails. I was about to rest upon a large block of stone when I heard cries from deep inside the ruin. I clambered up and, with bare hands, frantically tore at the pile of shattered stone and twisted metal until, at last, I uncovered the head and shoulders of a young man. Jammed in upside down, he was bound in every direction. His face was covered in dust but I judged him to be no more than five and twenty at most. He was bleeding at the eyes, ears, nose and mouth and I feared that unless he could be rescued promptly, he, too would die. Since he could move neither hand nor foot to aid himself, and my own powers were insufficient for the task, I gazed round desperately hoping for aid. In the distance, a gang of men moved slowly among the wreckage, but they were too far off. Nevertheless, Fortune smiled. One of the guards was within earshot. "Hey!" I cried. "Pray stop. I need assistance here!"

At once he halted. "Sir?" he asked.

"For God's sake call some of those labourers and help me to rescue this young man!"

"At once, Mr Dickens!" he cried, doffing his cap. Soon a half-dozen burly workmen were clearing away the debris. Progress was painfully slow until heavy tools were summoned to break up the carriage that surrounded him. Then, he was free! With the aid of one of the labourers, I assisted him to the side of the railway and administered Eau de Cologne and Brandy, which speedily brought him round. Just then the guard rushed across with an elderly gentleman. "Make way," he wheezed. "I am a surgeon!"

"Thank God," I cried.

"From Ashford," he continued, examining his patient closely the while. "I heard of the crash and made best speed. Sadly, too late for some poor wretches. This young man, at least, appears to be in no immediate danger. In such cases, however, there is always the fear of damage to the vital organs, haemorrhaging . . ."

"An emergency train is on the way from Charing Cross," the guard interposed.

"Then a place must be found upon it," the doctor said, straightening up.

"Any expense," I cried, "I will defray. Not a single other soul shall perish if I can prevent it!"

It was at that moment I remembered the poor lady I had found earlier. I urged the surgeon to accompany me and together we found her, as before, gazing up at the cloudless sky.

"Madam," I said, "forgive me. I had not intended to neglect you so long. But, see, I have fetched . . ." As I drew close, I perceived that the rosy hue had deserted her cheeks, that there were marks upon them I had missed in my earlier attempts to aid her. Anxiously, I reached out and touched her face. It was cold and waxy. "But how?" I cried. "She was breathing, reviving. I would not have left her else!"

The doctor knelt at her side. After a few seconds, he glanced up at me and shook his head. "Come, man!" he said, gently, "you have nothing to reproach yourself for!" Yet I could not refrain from wondering if I had not been remiss in failing to recognize the seriousness of her injuries. I was berating myself thus when a voice in my ear cried: "Oh, sir, I beg you . . . Have you, perchance, seen my wife?"

I turned. A few feet away, a tall, thin, pale man, of indeterminate age between twenty and forty, stood wringing his hands. "Your wife?" I asked.

"We were returning from our honeymoon," he continued. "And in the crash . . . I was thrown free. I have only lately regained consciousness. But my darling Betsy . . . I cannot find her in all this . . ."

"And you, sir," I replied, "hurt, I see." His garments were spattered with blood and his face and hands laced with small wounds.

"A few scratches, only."

"Your bride. I may have encountered her . . ."

"You would be sure to know, sir. Petite, with such pretty ringlets, the sweetest most innocent face, and a gown and bonnet of the palest blue . . ."

I was struck by a sudden awful realisation. Unable to speak, I led the way to one of the shattered carriages. On the floor, her head towards me, lay the young woman I had discovered during my descent from the bridge. No sooner did the poor groom see her than a long low cry of pain and disbelief escaped his lips and rent the air. Before I could stop him, he rushed, heedless, round and round the little meadow, his hands above his head, emitting such a piteous wail that I felt my heart, too, must burst. Then, as he drew near, he dropped in a dead faint. I hastened to his aid and, for a moment, feared that he, too, had expired. Then, he stirred, opened his eyes and said, "Mr Dickens, is it not? I am in your debt, sir!"

"By no means, young man," I retorted, as gently as I could. "You have the advantage of me. Your name, I pray."

"Stephen Bardock, sir. Of Clapham," he replied, taking the flask and swallowing a little Brandy. "Forgive me. It is such a shock. To lose one so fair, gentle . . ." He fell to weeping, his hands beating the air, the ground, his own chest, with rapid fury. I did my best to soothe his grief, to restrain his wilder movements. Finally, his sobs subsided. He became quiet, almost supine. As I raised myself to my feet, and stooped to assist him, there came the sound of a whistle somewhere above, the hiss of steam and steady click click of wheels. At last! "Come, sir," I said. "We can do no more, here." With a deep sigh, he allowed himself to be led up the slope to where the emergency train from London was slowing to a halt. It was only then I realized that, in my haste, I had abandoned Mr and Mrs Boffin, Mr and Mrs Lammle, Miss Bella Wilfer and so many others, in their manuscript form, in the pocket of my overcoat. I clambered back inside the carriage and, despite the alarming sway as I walked, quite calmly rescued *Our Mutual Friend* from the seat where it had fallen. Then, overcoat and Gladstone bag in hand, I descended once more and joined my fellow passengers for the journey to town.

Aided in no small measure by the intervention of the surgeon from Ashford I managed to acquire a carriage for myself and a few others, including my travelling companions and the young man trapped earlier under the wreckage. He had revived, somewhat, and was able to speak, announcing himself as Mr John Dickenson, a commercial traveller from Epping. As we sped towards the Metropolis, he became more animated and proved to be a charming, cheerful fellow of easy disposition and ready wit. Yet, as I watched him regaling our fellow passengers with tales of his adventures on the roads and byways, I discerned that his eye was a little too bright, his skin had taken on a greyish hue, and his lips were more than usually rubicund. My fears for his health and well-being grew and it was with heartfelt relief that I greeted our approach to the terminus at Charing Cross.

There was such a hullabaloo at the Station that I was more than usually glad to see my dear faithful assistant, Wills, who hailed me as I stepped on to the platform. With his usual efficiency, he had procured a carriage and in it, with his assistance, I placed my young charge. From there we travelled the short distance to the nearby Hotel where I was fortunate to secure rooms for him. By then the impact of recent events was more evident. Mr Dickenson was, he confessed, "suffering from palpitations and a general lethargy of spirit, aches in all my joints and a sensation of weakness in my limbs." Urging rest, and promising to visit him after the week-end to assure myself of his progress, I returned to my quarters in Wellington Street North. It was as I climbed the stairs that my self-possession and calmness deserted me. Now, safe in London, I felt quite shattered and broken up. I had a sudden vague rush of terror and started to shake all over. Even a strong draught of Brandy could do nothing to dispel the vivid images of the crash from my mind, the overwhelming sensation of horror. Again and again, the faces and cries of the dying and dead rose up to haunt me. So anxious was Wills to see me thus that he insisted on sleeping in the next room in case I needed him.

By the morning, I was a little recovered, though the sense of dread remained with me. I took a hansom to the Station. Again, visions of the accident plagued my sight. I felt faint and sick in the head and even the noise of the carriage distressed me so that, by the time I boarded the slow train to Rochester, I was much the worse for wear. My voice seemed to have deserted me as if I had unaccountably brought someone else's out of that terrible place. The journey was well nigh unbearable. At every slight jolt I was almost in a state of panic. More than once I fell into a paroxysm of fear, trembled all over, clutched the arms of the seat and suffered agonies of terror. I saw nothing for a time but that most awful scene. In particular, my vision was haunted by the sight of the poor woman I had encountered under the oak. Her face was so clear I could see the livid bruises there and upon her neck. Indeed, such was my state of nervous apprehension that when asked how I did by the landlord at the Falstaff Inn, I said, in all earnestness, "I never thought I should be here again." My dear son, Charley, sought to distract me with a ride in the basket-carriage. Yet, ever the fear was upon me. "Go slower, Charley," I cried, even when we came down to foot-pace.

I had neglected many letters since my return from France and was grateful, that weekend as never before, to be doing something practical and useful to turn my brain from its constant obsession with those dreadful memories. I was determined that I should not on any account be examined at the inquest into the disaster. I could not bear to relive those events in so public a manner. In the event, the high esteem in which I was held, and the intercession of friends and acquaintances with influence in such matters, meant I was not called upon to give evidence though, I was subsequently informed, my attempts to assist the unfortunate victims were recorded. Indeed, some few weeks later, The South Eastern Railway Company honoured me with a piece of plate in recognition. Be that as it may, I fretted at home while the proceedings took place at the Railway Hotel in Staplehurst itself.

Ever again, as I sat at my desk or strolled in my beloved garden, my mind would be filled with doubts. Why had I not observed those marks, done more to assist the poor creature? Why had I abandoned her when her very life, it seemed, was in the balance? I berated myself roundly at what I judged to be my neglect of a fellow creature. How often, I reflected bitterly, had I enjoined my own children to aid those in distress? And yet it was I, the great moralizer, who had proved so inadequate. Over dinner, Charley furnished me a full account of the inquest. He would have given me chapter and verse but I prevented him. "I beg you," I said, "just the bare facts. My nerves are shattered enough without more of the grisly details." Obeying my injunction, he rendered me a creditably detached report of the proceedings, concluding with the verdict that all ten poor souls who perished had been feloniously killed by the gang foreman on the line and the district inspector. The neglectful pair were to appear before a special magistrates court at Cranbrook in all probability to be committed for trial at the Kent Summer Assizes.

Charley's calm and measured tones did little, however, to ease my sense of guilt. Such was my agitation and, I freely confess, self-loathing, that sleep eluded me. I lay in my bed, returning again and again to my own failure. To not notice! I who was ever alert to the tiniest details in those around me, who laboured so diligently to apply those lessons in the creation of the characters who peopled my stories. How could I have missed such obvious signs? And then, in a moment of sudden clarity, somewhen in the dark recesses of the night, I knew. I had not seen them because they were not there! Not then, when I first found her. If that were so then it followed, inexorably, those injuries had not been caused by the accident itself, but by some event thereafter. By some person. Her murderer! And in that moment of certainty I vowed, to the spirit of that poor woman, that I would seek out that murderer and bring him, or her, before the bar of Justice. I could, in all conscience, do no less.

Yet there were so many people on that fateful train who could have found her resting there and hastened her end. How could I even begin to trace them all? The Railway Company would have no list of passengers. There were labourers on the track, guards. Even among those who had rushed to the scene from the neighbouring area there could have been someone with opportunity enough among all that chaos to take her life. If murder had indeed been committed, by whom and for what motive? I summoned all the detail I could of the events following the crash but could find no clear pattern to aid me in my quest. The task seemed impossible.

Once again in London, I set about keeping my promise to young Mr Dickenson. In seeing how he fared, I might, perhaps, glean from his recollections of the dreadful events of the previous week some small detail that might aid me in my quest. I found him propped up, colour once more in his cheeks, and a twinkle of merriment in his eye. Congratulating him, heartily, on obvious signs of progress, I sat beside his bed for some hour and fifteen minutes, chatting amiably, for the most part, and finding myself warming more and more to his open and frank character. His memory of the crash was, alas, still insubstantial. He recalled, vividly, the moment of impact then could conjure nothing until he woke up with the anxious surgeon bending over him.

Not wishing to tire him further, I bade him a fond farewell. Fearing the return of the shakes that had so held me in thrall I decided to walk rather than risk another journey by hansom, so arrived at my offices in Wellington Street shortly before noon. Wills was at his desk, poring over submissions for the next issue of *All The Year Round*. "Ah, Charles," he said, "how are you? A restful weekend, I trust?"

"Alas, no. So many letters! As for my health, it mends, but slowly."

"You are strong enough, I hope, to attend to a visitor? She has been waiting some little while but . . ."

"A visitor?" I exclaimed. "I was expecting no one today."

"No," Wills replied, quietly. "I have told her how busy you are at present. What with the magazine and *Our Mutual Friend* but she will not be deterred. She must consult you on a . . . personal matter and will brook no refusal."

"Indeed? I am intrigued. And by what name am I to address this visitor, pray?"

"My apologies. I should have said. Miss Alice Mullender . . ."

The woman who stood as I entered my office was tall and of such a bony and angular appearance, with such a stoop of her narrow shoulders and such a pinched expression, that I at once thought of the witch in Hansel and Gretel. Yet when she spoke all such thoughts melted away, so rich and musical was her voice.

"Mr Dickens?"

"The same, ma'am. Please, resume your seat. You wished to see me?"

"Indeed. I was at the inquest. In Staplehurst."

"Aah! As an interested spectator?"

"As a relative, sir, of one who died in that awful tragedy. You tried to save her, I am told. My cousin. Miss White."

At once, the features of the lady under the tree returned vividly to my sight. "A very pleasant, soft-spoken lady of middle years?" I asked.

"Fifty-three, sir, though many accounted her much younger."

"As I myself would have done, ma'am. You have no idea how much her death pained me. I had thought her recovering . . ."

"Then you will be moved, as I was, by her last letter to me," she interjected, drawing a small white envelope from her reticule and placing it on the desk in front of me. A cursory examination showed it to be of the finest vellum, likewise the three sheets of notepaper within. As I unfolded them, there was the faintest hint of lavender. Miss White's hand was precise, her style confident and well judged. Of the contents there was little to remark until the penultimate paragraph, which I read and reread until I was sure I had not misinterpreted its import. There, at the end of an easy flowing narrative detailing recent events in the life of a much younger relative came the intriguing words: "She will admit nothing but the most extravagant praise of his virtues. Yet my heart misgives me. I fear his motives are far from pure, sinister even. Pray God my doubts are misplaced."

"Of whom does she write, may I ask, Miss Mullender?"

"Lydia, Caroline's nearest living relative. When the sweet little thing lost her parents, she took her into her own household, as her companion."

"And the other person she mentions?"

"A leech, by all accounts. George by name. In trade, I believe."

"And your cousin's tragic death. I confess I fail to see a connection . . ."

"As did I, Mr Dickens," she interjected. "Until the inquest!"

"Yes?"

"He was there! In sombre black, looking for all the world as if his mother's milk was scarce out of him. But I saw, Mr Dickens, when the verdict was given out. Such a smile. Grim, smug satisfaction. I knew then, as certain as there is breath in my body, that he killed her, sir. I swear it!"

"And what can you tell me of him?"

"Little, I fear. I saw him but once at one of Caroline's entertainments, paying court to dear Lydia, but we were not introduced. A slight young man, with dark hair and paler eyes, I seem to recall, spectacles, olive skin, something of the foreigner about him. Italian, I thought, or French perhaps, but I did not gain a very vivid impression."

"Vivid enough, ma'am. But nothing beyond the physical that might identify him?" I asked, imagining how many Georges there must be in these islands.

"There was one singular event. The singer for the evening, a wonderful soprano, had just stepped up to the pianoforte and the company were falling silent when I heard him say something about a floating academy. The meaning is obscure to me but I turned at the sound, and it was clear from his expression that he had not intended the remark to be over-heard."

"No, indeed he might not," I said, increasingly convinced that my earlier suspicions were well founded. "Yet, Miss Mullender, I am at a loss as to motive," I continued, after a brief pause. "Why should this George, however unpleasant he may seem, wish to take your cousin's life?"

"Greed, sir, shameless naked greed! Caroline was a wealthy woman, a spinster. Some ten days ago, I visited her at home in Clarence Place. I found her pale and agitated. 'Oh, Alice,' she cried, 'what am I to do?'

" 'Pray, compose yourself, my dear,' I said, taking her trembling hands in mine. 'What troubles you?'

" 'They are fled,' she continued. 'Eloped! To Venice. The maid, it seems, was party to the plan. I had to be round with her to elicit the truth but there is no doubt. Lydia's bed has not been slept in, her boxes are gone. She is ruined! And for such a scheming wretch! Oh, it is beyond endurance!'

"At that point Queedy, the butler, entered, letting Caroline know that the carriage was outside and her cases were ready. At once, Caroline rose and made for the door. 'Where are you going?' I cried.

" 'To bring her back, before . . . You know how frail she is. Her poor heart. All this . . . turmoil . . . and dissension . . .' She was clearly struggling to find words to describe her fears. Yet, after a few seconds, she said, her tone calmer, more resolute: 'I have instructed Browndress to draw up a new will in my absence. Whatever else happens, that man will not profit by this . . .' "

"And you think, Miss Mullender, that he killed her before she could sign the document?" I asked.

"There is no doubt. Under the terms of the existing will, which I myself witnessed, apart from a few small personal bequests, the bulk of her estate was left to Lydia."

"And may I be so indelicate as to enquire as to the value?"

"In land and property, securities, around two hundred thousand pounds."

"Indeed a sum for which an unscrupulous man might commit murder! But if you are correct in your apprehension, why come to me? Surely, you should more profitably report your suspicions to the police . . ."

"I have tried, Mr Dickens. They would not listen. They call it wild speculation, a woman's hysteria. But a man in your position, with such a reputation, influence . . ."

The events she described only served to confirm my own fears. I promised to do what I could to spur the authorities to act but, for much of that day, was absorbed in more pressing matters of business and could not make good my words. By evening, I was too tired to return to Gad's and determined,

instead, to remain once again in town. I passed a fitful night
and, on the morrow, set out to find my old friend Inspector
Field before whom I laid all the facts, as I knew them.
Though retired, he remained active in the role of Consultant
Detective to the Metropolitan Police. He was as bluff as ever
and, in his customary bustling manner, said, at last, "As neat
a tangle as any yet, Mr Dickens. A poser an' no mistake! A
wealthy lady rushes orf to Italy in search of 'er love-struck
niece. A few days later, same lady travils from Folkestone on
the Tidal an' ends up done to death, or so it seems, by person
or persons as yet unknown. And you think this George has
had a hand in it?"

"I am inclined to Miss Mullender's opinion, I confess.
And you, Inspector?"

"Could be," he said, his eye roving about the room,
searching every corner in the constant expectation that the
villain might be lurking even there. "He sounds a cunning
cove, I will say that. Floating academy, eh? Man o' bisness,
you say? Not the type to bandy words like that in polite
society. And what, I asks myself, does he want to go a-talking
about prison hulks for in the first place. Served a stretch
himself, p'raps?"

"If he's as cunning as he seems," I retorted, "he'd be too
wily to get caught."

"Maybe. Me and the lads'll do a bit of snoopin' around.
See if we can't get a bit o' nose, beggin' yer pardon information, on 'im! Don't worry, sir, we'll have 'im yet!"

With the Inspector's confidence ringing in my ears, I took
a leisurely stroll back to my offices, purchasing a copy of *The
London News* on the way. Wills was still at luncheon and,
feeling lethargic, I idled my way through its pages until I
came to the account of the Staplehurst disaster and subsequent inquest. Charley's description of proceedings had been
sufficient for me to skip much of the detail on the events
leading up to the crash. It was only when the unfortunate
victims were enumerated that I paid particular close attention. There was poor Miss White, described starkly as
"Female, 53, Spinster", and alongside the names of her nine

companions in death. I scanned the list: Hippoilite Mercier,
Cook; Hannah Condliff, wife of Martin, Hotel Keeper;
Adam Hampson, Surgeon. Then, one entry made my blood
run cold. I read it over and over again, images of the dead
suddenly before me. Then, in an instant I saw the whole
fiendish device. There had been not one, but two murders at
the least. And I had, unwittingly, aided the felon in concealing the crime.

I then debated whether to take up the newspaper, hail a cab
– with all its attendant terrors – and relate what I now knew
to the sagacious Inspector Field. To delay might allow the
murderer even more time to elude justice. Set against that
was the strong probability that he would not flee. If, indeed,
he was hoping to gain control of Miss White's fortune, he
must needs await the interminably slow processes that followed the death of such a wealthy individual. There would be
a funeral, a decent period of mourning, the reading of the
Will, and endless other formalities. And if he was as cunning
and cool as he appeared, he would be content, nay eager, to
say and do nothing until that wealth was firmly in his grasp.
That gave those pursuing him time, also. "No," I concluded,
there was no urgency. "Better," I mused, "to let him believe
himself safe." So, instead, I busied myself for an hour or
more with the pleasures of a mutton chop and a glass or two
of Porter, drawing up the while what I hoped would be the
instrument of his undoing. By the time Wills returned at two
of the clock, I was ready to present my compliments, once
again, to my fortunate friend, Mr Dickenson.

I found a remarkable transformation in his condition. He
was out of bed and, indeed, about to take a short stroll when I
encountered him in the lobby of the Hotel.

"I would be honoured, sir, if you would accompany me,"
he said, when we had exchanged greetings.

"By all means," I replied, readily slowing my normal gait
to his more halting steps.

By no conscious decision, our slow progress led us towards
the River. The heat was less oppressive than the previous
day, though there were ominous signs of a storm to come in

the louring clouds. A stiff breeze off the water sent shivers through my young companion.

"I fear I need to rest a while, Mr Dickens," he sighed. "I am still too much the invalid, alas, and you who are so vigorous must find my pace wearisome."

"By no means," I replied, helping him to a nearby seat. "I should be glad of the opportunity to pause, also. The days since the dreadful accident have been very trying on my constitution and I confess to pains in my left foot. I have not fully recovered from an attack of frostbite earlier in the year. Too much walking in the snow after Christmas, I dare say. Now, tell me, dear sir," I continued as we both took our ease, "a little about yourself. There is a young lady, perhaps, upon whom you have set your heart . . ."

"By Jove, Mr Dickens, how did you know?"

"A chance speculation, nothing more, my young friend. But, pray, enlighten me. Your affections, are they reciprocated?"

The gaze he fixed upon me was more eloquent than any words he could have uttered. There was joy in those eyes, a deep contentment, a certainty and yet, for a moment, a cloud passed across his vision, some hidden fear, perhaps. Then, sighing, he said: "Indeed, I am the most fortunate and happy man in the whole of this great Metropolis, nay in the entire British Empire. Becca, Miss Nash, has honoured me with her heart and I have obtained her father's consent but . . ."

"Yes," I asked, gently, after a brief pause.

"Ours will be a long engagement, I think," he said, wrily. "Though we are of one mind about the future. God willing, we intend to emigrate. To the New World. We would like to have our own business, in a modest way, a shop perhaps. But that is some years in the future. For the present, we are content to save a little money towards the happy day." There was a yearning in his voice, one that echoed my own feelings as a young man. For a long painful time I was visited by a Spirit. It wore blue drapery and I thought (but was not sure) that I recognized the voice of the most perfect creature that ever breathed. My emotions were so intense at that moment that they threatened to overwhelm me. I was strangely glad when I heard Mr Dickenson say, "But I trust in Him who ordains all things. He will speed our union, sir, I know it!"

He spoke shyly, but with quiet determination. I glanced sidelong at him: jet-black hair above a narrow visage, tanned from exposure to the summer sun, a plain but honest face, slightly Continental in appearance but no less pleasant for that. "Yet," I reflected, "what lies behind his or any other such face? Kindness, truth, all manner of virtues? Or hidden malice, coldness, cruelty even? How to judge! Ay, there's the rub!" Suddenly aware I had been neglectful, I turned to him again. He was shivering so, fearful for his health, I suggested we retrace our steps. "I confess, he said, "that would be most agreeable."

We said little as we strolled until a remarkable occurrence as we were approaching the Hotel. A hansom, one among many, clattered alongside us. I chanced to look up, straight into the eyes of the passenger who, in an instant, drew back and called out: "Drive, man, as if your life depended upon it!" At once the vehicle picked up pace and was soon disappearing into the distance. I turned to Mr Dickenson, to comment upon the strangeness of the man's behaviour but the sight of his face, ashen and drawn, stopped my mouth. He staggered, suddenly, and almost collapsed into my arms. "My dear, sir, I said when I had restored him to the perpendicular, "what ails you?"

"Oh, Mr Dickens, it is he, the very Devil incarnate!"

"Who? The fellow in the cab? There was something familiar . . . His name?"

"He has many, none true, I dare say. Some call him Thomas Gospel, others Jonathan Ferry, Stephen Bardock, Robin Why. All I know is he is the coldest most black-hearted villain . . ."

"What? Bardock, you say? Of Clapham?"

"You know him? But how?"

"No matter. For the moment. Pray, relate to me the circumstances of your acquaintance. And omit no detail, however trivial," I said, sensing that, at last, I might have started in earnest upon the trail I had neglected thus far. The tale he told matched in so many tiny details the one Miss Mullender had related that I had not a scintilla of doubt but that the George she described was one and the same man with the heartless fiend who had done so much to blight the lives of young Mr Dickenson and his intended bride. When he had concluded his narrative, I rapidly sketched for him my surmises concerning the Staplehurst disaster and then asked: "Do you feel strong enough to hazard an adventure that will rid the world of this villain?"

"Indeed, Mr Dickens, I am. Though I fear I may be of poor use in a tight corner, should matters come to that."

Our compact made, I bade him farewell, then hastened to my office to find Wills pacing the floor in a most agitated manner. "Ah, there you are!" he cried as I entered. "I have had a visit from a Police Constable not ten minutes since."

"Oh?" I replied. "And?"

"Inspector Field sends his compliments and asks if you will be kind enough to meet him at St Giles's Station House at nine tonight. The Constable will return within the hour for your response."

"Splendid!" I cried. "I will compose it this very instant!"

I scribbled a brief note of gratitude and then turned my attention to other matters. The afternoon and early evening were slow, dull affairs, leaving me ill at ease and dissatisfied with my own attempts at writing. After a mediocre supper, I made my way eagerly to St Giles Church where the clock was just striking the three-quarter hour. Mr Dickenson arrived shortly thereafter and we were soon attended by a Detective Sergeant and a Constable, both of whom greeted us most cordially on the Inspector's behalf.

Presently, Mr Field himself joined us. I introduced Mr Dickenson and, as we walked, the young man regaled our escorts with what he knew of our villain. In turn, we were given to understand that a fellow answering to the description provided by Miss Mullender had been spied that very afternoon leaving a low lodging house in a street known as Rats' Castle. Not fifty paces from the Station House, and

within call of Saint Giles's Church, we found our senses
assailed by a compound of sickening smells as we picked our
way among heaps of filth, all around us tumbling houses and
in the light from the Constable's lantern, a host of lowering
foreheads, sallow cheeks, brutal eyes, matted hair, and
ragged figures who scuttled into the gloom at the sight of
us. Some, however, the more brazen perhaps, closed in round
us forming a silent, sullen cordon which threatened to im-
pede our progress. At the sight of two other Constables on
duty who had followed us, however, they did as instructed
and "hooked it", sneaked away, as Inspector Field shouted,
"Close up there, my men! Keep together, gentlemen; we are
going down here. Heads!"

At the end of a lane of light, made by the lantern, was a
dilapidated door. The Sergeant barged it wide; we stooped low
and crept down a precipitous flight of steps into a dark close
cellar. There was a fire, a long deal table and several benches.
The room was full of company, chiefly young men in various
conditions of dirt and raggedness. Some were sleeping, each on
his foul truckle-bed coiled up beneath a rug. Others were eating
supper and looked up, alarmed, at the sight of the Inspector.
Clearly, he was a well-known figure. Every thief cowered
before him. A tall grey, soldierly-looking elderly man whom
we understood, later, was the Deputy who ran the lodging-
house, suddenly called out in a loud, strident voice: "Why, Mr
Field, I hope I see you well, Mr Field?" At the sound of the
name, a heap of rags in the corner at once started up and,
scuttling past us, bolted up the steps to the street above.

"It's him," yelled Mr Dickenson at my side.

"After him!" the Inspector barked, but the Deputy, surprisingly agile for his age, barred the entrance, holding up a
flaring candle in a blacking-bottle and asking: "Do you want
to see upstairs? I'll be pleased to show the rooms!"

"So, you would play the confederate, would you, Grout?"
the Sergeant said, thrusting him away. "I shall be a-visiting
you again!"

The threat had the desired effect. He moved aside and we
left him to the ministrations of the denizens of his cellar and

set off in hot pursuit of the pile of rags. "This Bardock is a nimble cove," Mr Field said, as we emerged into the street. "But I have the hand that naps his. Quick, my lads, this way! A rat needs flushing out. And no use a-waitin' till he's safe in his drain, eh, Mr Dickens?"

We were about to set off when my young companion seized me by the arm. "I cannot keep pace, sir," he said, ruefully, "My legs remain weak . . ."

"Hah!" the Inspector said, "Green, a hansom for the gentleman!"

"And the address, sir?" the young Constable asked. A hurried whispering, the nodding of heads, a shrill whistle, the clip-clop of horses' hooves, and Mr Dickenson was safely stowed and on his way.

"Now," Mr Field said, "for our quarry!" He led us down a maze of streets and courts, lit only by the lanterns the Constables carried. Here and there, a chink of illumination would be furnished by the curious opening of a shutter or the passing of a candle behind a grimy window pane but, for the most part we stumbled and dodged as best we could in the gathering darkness. At last, we turned a corner and beheld Mr Dickenson, standing nervously outside a sequestered tavern. In the bar, among ancient bottles and glasses, men in sailors' garb sat, smoking pipes and listening to a sentimental sea song. The landlord, a tall rotund man, sauntered over to us and greeted the Inspector freely and good-humouredly.

"Bardock?" you say, he asked when informed of our purpose. "Thin dark cove about so high?" He extended an arm just below Mr Field's shoulder.

"The very same! His room. Smartly now. He can't be long on our heels. Green, Rogers, set a watch!"

The landlord whipped away the Constables' uniform jackets and supplied them with aprons. They soon melted into quiet corners, no doubt with a good view of all the ways in and out of the crowded room. Then, he showed us up a flight of rickety stairs under the watchful gaze of many in the company. "Don't you worry, Mr Dickens," the Sergeant said. "They'll not meddle. The Inspector's done more than one a good turn and sailors has long memories!"

We had barely settled ourselves in the narrow dingy cell than there was the rapid pitter-patter of light feet on boards outside. The Sergeant motioned my young friend and I to flatten ourselves against the chamber wall either side of the entrance while he and the Inspector took up their stations to forestall any attempt at escape through the casement. My heart beating fast, I watched as a thin figure hurried in from the corridor. He had barely crossed the threshold when I slammed the flimsy door shut and pressed my back against it. Rapidly scanning the room, and realizing he was trapped, he drew a knife from somewhere in his clothing and brandished it. "The first one as tries to take me I'll drop where he stands, so help me!" he cried.

For a moment, no one moved and I was able to observe him more closely. He had discarded the bundle of rags he was wearing in Rats' Castle and was clad in much more respectable garb. Gone was the pale, thin, grieving bridegroom whose plight I had felt so much for at the Staplehurst disaster. In his place a swarthy, grim-faced fellow stared balefully round, calculating, no doubt, the forces ranged against him. Out of the corner of my eye, I saw young Mr Dickenson step cautiously forward. Fearful that the villain might observe his motion and lash out with the knife, I said: "Mr Bardock, we meet again. Or perhaps you would prefer Mr George Whitby since it is in his guise, I believe, that you stand before us?"

"Ah, the great novelist, Charles Dickens, eh?" he sneered. "To set my eyes on such an august figure once in my life was a singular honour. Twice, sadly, is not!" With that, he lunged at me. As he did so, there was the whish of a cane and he lay sprawled upon the boards.

"Oh, well done, Mr Dickenson, sir!" the Inspector cried as he and the Sergeant pinioned the seething murderer and wrestled the knife from his bony fingers. Then, thrusting him hard upon the bed and fastening his wrists with bracelets, they turned him to face me.

"And what great fiction have you concocted to ensnare me?" he hissed.

"Oh, this is no invention of mine," I replied. "The web in which you are now caught is of your own weaving. In brief, you wooed the naïve and impressionable Miss Lydia Kimber, won her heart with your smooth lies, in order to obtain the fortune to which she was heir. In the face of resolute opposition from her aunt, you convinced the poor creature to escape with you to France where you promptly married her. By the time her relative arrived to forestall you, your new bride had already glimpsed something of your true character and regretted the match. Secure in the knowledge that Miss White would go to any length to resuce her niece from your clutches, you readily agreed to a handsome settlement to have the union set aside. Am I correct, thus far?"

"An interesting fairy story," he retorted coldly.

"Then," I continued, "a little over twenty minutes from Folkestone, there occurred the Staplehurst disaster. As the train derailed, you grasped the chance for more than the part-share in Miss White's fortune to which you had agreed. Attacking the poor woman as she fell, you thought to give her a mortal wound. But, and here I confess I am speculating, your blow was deflected . . . by the doctor accompanying her, Mr Hampson. In your fury, you struck him so forcibly that, when I came upon him a few moments later, he promptly expired where he lay. Then, the carriage plunged into the stream below and you set out to ensure that Miss White was indeed dead. But she was very much alive and I tending her. Watching from some hidden vantage point among the wreckage, you waited until I had moved away then, cool as ice, strangled her where she lay. In the struggle, you sustained the scratches I see remain upon the backs of your hands."

"Yet more creations from your fantastical brain, Mr Dickens. Ingenious, I grant you, but were I to have indeed committed the crimes you lay to my charge where is the evidence that would convince a court? And what of dear

Lydia? Is it your contention that she also died at my hands?" he asked, fixing me with a baleful stare.

"Ah, no," I said. "There, I fear, nature is the villain. Should her body be examined I have no doubt but that the coroner would conclude that she died of a diseased heart. Yet it was the shock of seeing your murderous attack upon her aunt that, I believe, brought on the seizure that so tragically ended her young life. So, morally at least, you have three deaths to account for."

"And account you will, while there is breath in my body," the Inspector declared as he hauled the villain from the bed and thrust him out the door.

True to his word, Mr Field delved until, at last, he was able to draw all the strands of the case together and provide enough evidence to convince a jury. The man known as George Whitby was convicted, sentenced to death, and hung at Tyburn. When I read the reports of his death, I confess to a smile of grim satisfaction. As for Mr Dickenson, in due time – being some twelvemonth after the events described here, he was married and, on this eighth day of August, 1869, has embarked with his young bride for New York. For myself, I am glad to have had some small part in aiding his progress and to have returned to writing once more, brimming with ideas for a new novel. It will be a mystery, with a murder at its heart.

Author's Note: The story is based on the rail accident at Staplehurst on 9 June 1865 in which Dickens played the part, largely as described. The names of the dead quoted are from the official record of the inquest, though I have created the links between Miss White, Dr Hampson and Mrs Whitby and, of course, the crime itself.

The character of Mr Dickenson is entirely mine, though a young man of that name was rescued by Dickens from the wreckage. That Dickenson was, in fact, later Major S. Newton Dickenson of the 19th Regiment. At the time of the crash he was 18 years old (not in his mid-twenties as I've described him). Charles Dickens treated him, in many respects, like his own son and did take an active interest in his career until their last meeting some time in late 1867.

By a strange coincidence, a John T. Dickenson did emigrate with his wife to New York but probably not until around 1882 when they asssembled with others from England to organize a migration of their families westward. Four families out of the twelve eventually made their way to Missouri where they founded a colony. In 1888, John T. Dickenson built a huge new store building in Eglinton, Missouri, and later established a new post office, named after the English writer of whom he was very fond – Charles Dickens. That office was discontinued in 1952 but still goes by the name of Dickens. It is that foundation that led me to create the possible future for the Dickenson character I built in the story.

The Thorn of Anxiety

Edward Marston

After completing Our Mutual Friend, *Dickens threw himself into his round of public readings, both in Britain and in America. They were financially very rewarding, as they were to his ego, as he always delighted in public adulation, but they took a severe toll on his health. It was a man in great pain who picked up his pen to start what would be his final novel,* The Mystery of Edwin Drood.

It is set in Cloisterham, the name Dickens gave to Rochester in Kent, near his home at Gad's Hill. Edwin Drood and Rosa Bud are an endearing young couple promised to each other in marriage by the terms of their respective parents' wills. Unknown to Edwin, he has a rival for Rosa's affection, his uncle and guardian, John Jasper, her music teacher. Jasper is the Cathedral's choirmaster but is also an opium addict, acquiring the drug from an old woman called Princess Puffer. Helena and Neville Landless, dark-skinned orphans from Ceylon, are sent to Cloisterham by their guardian. Neville is to be tutored by the Dean of the Cathedral, Septimus Crisparkle, while Helena joins Rosa and the other pupils at Miss Twinkleton's Seminary for Young Ladies. As soon as he meets her, Neville falls in love with Rosa. He therefore takes offence when Edwin appears to be indifferent to his betrothed. A fierce row develops between the two men. John Jasper arrives to calm them down yet he later provokes a quarrel between them. On Christmas Eve, Edwin and Neville go down to the river to watch a storm raging. And that is the last anyone sees of Edwin Drood.

Dickens died on 9 June 1870 when he had only completed about half of the planned novel, so we never discover what happened to Drood or, if he was murdered, who the culprit was. It has remained an enduring literary mystery and many have attempted their solution to the crime.

Edward Marston is just one alias of the prolific author and playwright Keith Miles. He is perhaps best known for his Domesday series, set in the years after the Norman conquest, which started with The Wolves of Savernake *(1993), but has also written the Nicholas Bracewell series of Elizabethan players that began with* The Queen's Head *(1988), plus a series of maritime mysteries written under the alias Conrad Allen that began with* Murder on the Lusitania *(2000).*

Cloisterham was never particularly well lighted. When the strong wind blew out some of the lamps and, in some cases, shattered the glass, it was gloomier than ever in the cathedral city. The darkness was augmented and confused by flying dust from the earth, dry twigs from the trees, and great ragged fragments from the rooks' nests up on the tower. When they got to the river, Edwin Drood and Neville Landless could *feel* the storm far more clearly than they could actually see it. An occasional flash of lightning in the distance illumined the scene for a brief moment and allowed them a glimpse of trees being bent to and fro, of bushes threshing wildly and of water being churned up into angry waves by the blast. From behind them came the sound of chimney pots being toppled into the streets and of slates smashing on the cobbles. A stray dog barked in fear.

Cowed into silence by Nature's deafening symphony, they stood side by side. They had come to establish some sort of reconciliation but neither of them felt able to make the first move. Another storm was raging inside Neville's head and Edwin was also deeply troubled. Each of them was so locked up in his own private thoughts that he seemed unaware of the presence of a companion. As the tempest roared on, and as Christmas Day inched nearer, there was no festive spirit to cheer them. They were as unsettled as the weather.

At length, Edwin made a supreme effort to speak, turning to Neville to offer him the hand of friendship. But the other man was no longer there. He had vanished into the darkness.

"Neville!" he called. "Where are you, Neville?"

There was no reply and, though Edwin explored the river bank in both directions, he could find no trace of Neville Landless. Giving up his search, he began to walk back towards the city, unaware that he was being stalked. When Edwin least expected it, someone came out of the gloom behind him and struck him hard across the back of the head with something cold, solid and unforgiving, sending his hat cartwheeling across the grass. As the victim fell to the ground, other blows rained down on him with relentless power until Edwin Drood plunged irretrievably into oblivion.

Hiram Grewgious, that lawyer of incorruptible integrity, had his chambers in one of the two irregular quadrangles that formed Staple Inn. There was no irregularity in his office, however. It was a model of sublime order. Every account book, document, strong box, legal tome and item of correspondence was in its appointed place so that the lawyer could put his hand on it at a moment's notice. When he was shown in, the visitor marvelled at the sense of overwhelming neatness and regulation.

"Sit down, sit down, my dear sir," said Grewgious, shaking his hand. "Thank you for coming so promptly." His visitor lowered himself into a chair. "You received my letter, then?"

"Yes, Mr Grewgious," said the other, "and the case intrigued me. A man cannot disappear off the face of the earth without assistance. That assistance, of course," he added, "could conceivably have come from the elements, though I think it highly unlikely that Mr Drood was blown into the river by a blast of wind then carried helplessly away. Some trace of him would surely have been found."

"Search parties were sent out on the following morning. They scoured the river for miles." He heaved a sigh. "What a way to spend Christmas Day – looking for a dead body!"

"If, indeed, he *is* dead."

"What do you think?" asked Grewgious. "You are the detective."

"The balance of probability is that the young man is no longer alive. What must be discovered is whether he died by his own hand or by that of a person or persons unknown."

"Do you believe you *can* discover it?"

"I'm certain of it."

"Six whole months have elapsed," warned the lawyer.

"Such an event will stay fresh in the memory for far longer than that. From what you tell me, Cloisterham is a sleepy place where very little happens."

"That is why Edwin's disappearance caused such a stir."

"Exactly!" said the detective. "Besides, the passage of time will work to our advantage. People will be able to view the event with less passion and more objectivity than they did at the time. More to the point, Mr Grewgious, the killer – if such a person exists – will be so confident that he got away with it that he will be off guard."

"Neville Landless remains the chief suspect," noted Grewgious, "even though there is insufficient evidence for an arrest. John Jasper, uncle to Edwin Drood, still believes that Neville was involved."

"I will go to Cloisterham with an open mind. Since no progress has been made in the investigation in six months, the killer has either fled from the city or is adept at hiding behind a disguise. I will meet him on his own terms and go there in a disguise of my own."

"A capital idea!"

"When I have taken lodgings," promised the detective, "I

will inform you at once. Should you need to contact me by letter, refer to me by my assumed name."

"And what that might be, dear sir?" asked Grewgious.

"Datchery – henceforth I am Dick Datchery, a single buffer, of even temper, living idly on his means."

"How soon do you expect to have gathered evidence?"

"Very soon," said the detective airily. "You have given me the necessary facts. You have described all the personalities involved. In other words, I have a flying start." He got swiftly to his feet. "The case will be solved within a month. I have no doubt whatsoever about that."

Dick Datchery was as good as his word. Barely three weeks after being commissioned by Hiram Grewgious to look into the baffling mystery of Edwin Drood, he returned to the office in Staple Inn with a confident swagger. The lawyer was overjoyed to see him.

"You've come back already!" he said, beaming. "I trust that you bring a full report."

"I do, indeed, sir," replied Datchery, pulling a sheaf of papers from his pocket like a conjurer producing a rabbit from a hat. "I think you will find it admirably comprehensive."

"Then let's hear it straight away." He waved his visitor to a chair then resumed his own seat behind the desk. He became aware that his clerk was hovering at the door. "You'd better stay, Bazzard," he went on, indicating that the clerk should close the door. "My clerk is cognisant of everything that's passed between us regarding this case, Mr Datchery. You've no objection to his presence?"

"None at all," said the visitor, concealing the fact that he found Bazzard a particularly objectionable character and wondering why Grewgious employed someone so dull and melancholy. "I am your humble servant, sir. If you wish to summon a large audience for me, I'll be happy to divulge my findings in front of them."

"Privacy is essential here. Bazzard and I will therefore be your only listeners. Are you agreed, Bazzard?"

"If I'm ordered to stay," said Bazzard gloomily, "then I will."

"Bless me!" cried Grewgious. "It's not an order that I'm issuing. It's an invitation."

"In that case, I don't care if I do."

"Then it's all arranged."

They were a strange pair. Hiram Grewgious was a dry, sandy-haired individual with a face so ashen and expressionless that it looked as if it had been carved out of balsa wood in a drunken stupor by a blind man with a blunt knife. Bazzard also lacked animation. His dark hair and dark eyes were thrown into sharp relief by the deathly pallor of his cheeks. Though he was much younger than Grewgious, the clerk seemed to have an inexplicable power over him, as evidenced by a deference shown to him by his superior.

"We are ready, Mr Datchery," announced Grewgious after first checking that Bazzard was comfortably ensconced. "Pray, proceed."

"Yes," said Bazzard in a monotone. "Proceed, Mr Datchery."

"Then I will do so under my rightful name," said the visitor, "and that, as you well know, is Richard Cherry, born and brought up in Datchet. For the purposes of disguise, I shortened Richard to Dick and lengthened my surname as compensation by using my birthplace as a suffix. Datchet and Cherry thus became Datchery. Having shed my false name," he continued, reaching for his white mane, "I do the same with my false hair."

So saying, he pulled off his wig with a theatrical flourish and put it beside his feet where it lay like a contented albino spaniel. The transformation was extraordinary. He lost fifteen years in an instant, his eye took on more lustre and his face more definition. Dick Datchery, living idly on his means, became Mr Richard Cherry, private detective, alert, eager and wholly impressive. Grewgious let out a gasp of approval.

"The secret," Cherry resumed as he tapped his sheaf of papers, "was to infiltrate Cloisterham and win the confidence of its citizens. I befriended the excellent Canon Crisparkle, I lodged with the estimable Mr and Mrs Tope, I broke bread with Durdles, the stonemason, I dined with Thomas Sapsea, the Mayor, I ingratiated myself with Miss Twinkleton and I achieved as much familiarity with Deputy as it is possible to do with a wild boy compelled to throw stones at all and sundry. In short, sirs, I became one of *them*."

"One name remains unmentioned," observed Grewgious.

"I'll come to him in a moment," said the detective with a confiding smile. "First, let me deal with the young man supposed by some to have murdered Edwin Drood."

"Neville Landless?"

"The very same, Mr Grewgious."

"You have proved his innocence?"

"Without a shadow of doubt," affirmed Cherry.

"But he was the last person to see Edwin alive."

"That gruesome privilege was reserved for his killer, a fiend who did not – I repeat, did not – answer to the name of Neville Landless. Yes," he hurried on as the lawyer raised a hand in protest, "I know that a certain amount of evidence points to the boy. He was impulsive, hot-blooded and had even confessed to harbouring thoughts of murdering his cruel stepfather. Neville and Edwin had quarrelled violently. On the night that they went down to the river together, Neville was carrying a walking stick, stout enough to knock out a man's brains. All this is true, I'll not deny it. What is equally true, however, is that Neville Landless was given to spontaneous action and I discern guile and calculation in this crime. That absolves the boy at once."

"Yet a certain person is absolutely convinced of his guilt," the lawyer reminded him. "John Jasper has dedicated himself to the task of seeing Neville Landless convicted of murder."

"A clever ruse, sir," said the detective.

"A ruse?" repeated Bazzard.

"Of the most devious kind."

"Pray, Mr Cherry," said Grewgious. "Do please explain."

"What better way to deflect attention from oneself than by leading the hue and cry after someone else? John Jasper knows that Neville Landless is completely innocent because it was that same respected choirmaster who actually committed the crime."

Hiram Grewgious was shocked and he turned to his clerk to gauge his reaction. Bazzard gave nothing away, hiding whatever thoughts he might be having and whatever emotions he might be experiencing behind his usual bovine stare. Referring to the first page of his report, the erstwhile Dick Datchery surged on.

"I ask you to consider these points, gentlemen," he said. "First, that John Jasper was an opium addict. He patronised a London opium den run by Princess Puffer, an old woman I chanced to meet in Cloisterham. I need hardly tell you what effect that drug may have on a man's brain. Septimus Crisparkle recalls a time when, recovering from the effects of opium, Mr Jasper leapt up from his couch in a state of delirium, neither awake nor asleep but occupying some region between the two where self-control does not exist and where a type of madness has free rein."

"You had this from the Dean?" asked Grewgious.

"From his very lips, sir," said the detective. "Much of what I am about to divulge came to me from Mr Crisparkle, though he was unwilling to draw the conclusion that John Jasper could be a killer."

"Mr Jasper loved Edwin Drood and did so excessively, by all accounts. What possible reason would he have to kill a nephew on whom he doted?"

"Jealousy."

"Jealousy," echoed Bazzard.

"He loved Edwin but he loved Rosa Bud even more and he could never possess her while his nephew was still alive. The obstacle between him and his intemperate desire had to be removed."

"Rosa Bud would never marry Mr Jasper," said the lawyer. "She told me so in this very room. He frightens her. When he declared his passion for her, it sounded more like a threat than a proposal. That's why she fled to London."

"He will stalk her wherever she is," said Cherry, "but I digress. Let me give you more evidence. Two, Mr Jasper provoked a quarrel between Edwin and Neville Landless. When the two young men were at such odds with each other, the sensible thing was to keep them apart. Instead, John Jasper invited them to dine with him and mixed a mulled wine of such strength that it was bound to inflame them and stir up their differences. Three," he added turning over a page, "our cunning choirmaster told everyone about the animosity between the two fellows and he even showed Mr Crisparkle an entry in his diary, indicating his fear that Neville Landless's resentment against Edwin would explode sooner or later."

"Jealousy," noted Bazzard.

"Jealousy, perhaps," conceded the other, "but it was tempered by strong protective feelings towards Rosa Bud. Her betrothed, as he then was, spoke of her unkindly and her new admirer could not bear that. He felt that Rosa deserved better from her future husband."

"So she did," said Grewgious sorrowfully. "You have done well, Mr Cherry, and I congratulate you, but I have to admit that I've yet to hear any conclusive proof of Mr Jasper's involvement in the crime."

"Bear with me," Cherry assured him, "and you will. Four, there is the night that Mr Jasper visited the stonemason among the tombs. I had to chisel this information out of Durdles and Deputy and, though neither of them is wholly reliable on his own, their testimony, when put together, leads to a startling revelation."

"Why, dear sir – what happened?"

"In brief, the facts are these. Mr Jasper expressed much interest in the tomb of Ethelinda Sapsea, late wife of the Mayor of Cloisterham, and not only because he advised Mr Sapsea on the wording of the inscription to be put on the tomb. He had brought drink with him and offered it to Durdles. No sooner had the stonemason poured it down his throat than he lapsed into a sleep, long enough for his companion to deprive him of the key to Mrs Sapsea's tomb."

"Why ever should he do that?" said Grewgious.

"In order to formulate his plan."

"Jealousy," intoned Bazzard.

"I fancy that it was lust that impelled him," said Cherry, turning over another page. "Lust for Rosa Bud, lust for power, lust for the world of sensation he had glimpsed in his opium-induced trances. He entered the tomb and when he came out – Deputy swears that he saw this occur – he took something from his pocket and pressed the key into it. I believe that Mr Jasper was making a wax impression so that the key could be later copied by a locksmith. There was something else that the boy witnessed. Durdles had already shown his visitor where the quicklime was kept and told him of its properties. Deputy, albeit coaxed with a little money, remembered watching Mr Jasper return to look at the quick lime and stand in a meditative attitude for some time. He only moved from the spot when the boy knocked off his top hat with a well-aimed stone."

"This is all very intriguing," said Grewgious, sucking his teeth, "but I wish that you could call upon more convincing witnesses than a drunken stonemason and an untamed street urchin."

"Don't you realise what Mr Jasper was doing?" said Cherry.

"Paying his respects to the dead, that was all."

"Then why do it so late at night, Mr Grewgious? Why not visit the place in daylight where he could read the inscriptions and find his way around without the aid of Durdles? What he was doing," said the detective, finding a new page, "was searching for a means of disposing of the body."

"But we know how it was disposed of," argued the lawyer. "It was flung into the river. Mr Crisparkle found Edwin's watch and shirt-pin at the Weir. They must have become detached during the struggle and were carried downstream. To rescue them, Mr Crisparkle had to risk life and limb by plunging into the icy, turbulent water. As for the body, it must have been washed out to sea."

"That is precisely what John Jasper *wanted* us to believe."

"Are you saying that he put those items at the Weir?"

"Dick Datchery is certain of it and so am I. In a sentence," said Cherry, inflating his chest as he reached the climax of his report, "the truth is this. Knowing that his nephew was out in the storm that night and aware that Neville Landless had been his companion and could therefore be made to look like the villain, John Jasper murdered Edwin Drood, carried his body to Mrs Sapsea's tomb, opened it with the substitute key then destroyed the corpse with quicklime."

"Ingenious!" exclaimed Grewgious.

"What about the ring?" asked the lugubrious Bazzard.

"A perceptive question, sir," said Cherry, genuinely surprised at this flash of intelligence from the clerk. "Mr Grewgious told me about the ring of rubies and diamonds, delicately set in gold. It had belonged to Rosa Bud's mother and he instructed Edwin to place it on the girl's finger as a token of his determination to marry her. In fact, Rosa wanted to call off the engagement and have Edwin as no more than a good friend, a situation to which, I suspect, he readily complied. Now, sir," he went on, turning to the lawyer, "was the ring returned to you?"

"No," replied Grewgious. "Edwin must have kept it."

"Unbeknown to John Jasper," the detective pointed out. "His uncle knew about all the other jewellery upon Edwin's person. He chose to detach the watch and the shirt-pin. Of the existence of the ring, he was totally unaware."

Grewgious jumped to his feet in excitement. "I think I see where all this is heading," he said. "Edwin's body may have been dissolved by the quicklime but it could not consume rubies and diamonds. If your supposition is right, they should still be there in the tomb."

"They will be," said the detective with confidence. "That is why you and I will return to Cloisterham at once and, witnessed by policemen, have that tomb opened for inspection."

"Splendid work, sir! What do you say, Bazzard?"
The clerk rolled his eyes. "Jealousy."

They caught the next stagecoach to the cathedral city and spent most of the journey wishing that a railway station would soon be built in Cloisterham, making any visits to and from the capital speedier and more comfortable. Bazzard accompanied the two men and Richard Cherry, now disguised once more as Dick Datchery, was in such high humour that he did not resent the presence of the mournful clerk. The detective's patient work was at last on the point of fruition and nothing could rob him of his exhilaration.

Arriving at their destination, they summoned two policemen then conducted them to the tomb of Ethelinda Sapsea, into which the lengthy and sanctimonious inscription devised by her husband had now been carved with reverential finality. Stony Durdles was hauled out of the vault and, without any explanation, ordered to open the tomb. He showed great reluctance, warning them that the Mayor would hear of this outrage and might well take legal action against those who disturbed the peace of his dear wife.

"That peace has already been disturbed," said Dick Datchery, tiring of the man's resistance and snatching the key from him. "When we enter this tomb, you will find proof positive of a heinous crime and you, Mr Durdles, will realize that you were an unwitting accomplice of the devil who committed it." He turned the key then flung open the door. "Behold, gentlemen, evidence of a foul murder."

And that is exactly what they did behold. But it was not the tell-tale ruby and diamond ring that met their gaze nor was it anything else that might have been connected with Edwin Drood. What lay on the cold stone floor in front of them was the corpse of an old woman with a necklace of dried blood to show them exactly where her throat had been cut from ear to ear. It was left to Deputy, the ragged boy with his pockets full of stones, to identify the murder victim. Pushing between the two policemen, he needed only a glance at the haggard face and the lifeless body.

"Princess Puffer," he said. "She runs a Hopium den in London."

John Jasper was coming around Minor Canon Corner when he saw the posse approaching. His nerve failed. The sight of two policemen, a lawyer and his clerk, a stonemason and a boy, all of them led by a dark-haired man waving a luxuriant white wig in his hand, was too much for the choirmaster. Abandoning all decorum, he turned on his heel and ran for all he was worth. To the following pack, it was a clear confession of guilt. The chase was on. Grewgious waddled, Bazzard loped, Durdles lumbered, the quondam Dick Datchery managed a respectable sprint and the two policeman blew their whistles as they bounded along.

Once again, it was Deputy who came to the fore. Outstripping all the others, he hit their quarry with such a merciless volley of stones that Jasper sank to his knees and covered his head with his arms. He was soon surrounded. Because he was panting less than anyone else, Richard Cherry became the official spokesman, using the stern voice he had cultivated when working as an Inspector in the Metropolitan Police Force.

"Seize him!" he ordered and the policeman obeyed, taking an arm apiece and hauling the prisoner to his feet. "John Jasper," said the detective, pointing an accusing finger at him, "you are under arrest for the murder of Princess Puffer, whose body you concealed in the tomb of Ethelinda Sapsea until you could dispose of it with quicklime. You killed a poor, weak, defenceless woman of advanced years."

"She was a manipulative old hag," snarled the unrepentant Jasper. "She only came here to blackmail me."

"That does not excuse your crime," said Cherry, replacing his wig so that he became Dick Datchery once more. He smiled at Jasper's obvious consternation. "Yes, my friend, you recognize me now. You remember all those confidences we traded. I met Princess Puffer and I know you were a client of hers in London, a dope fiend who made some incautious remarks while in the grip of opium. My guess is that those remarks concerned your nephew, Edwin Drood."

"Ned!" cried Jasper. "I miss my dear, sweet, lovable Ned!"

"He was not dear, sweet and lovable when you took his life on Christmas Eve and tried to pin the crime on someone else."

"I never touched Ned – I swear it!"

"The evidence is irrefutable," said Grewgious. "I employed a detective to find out who the real murderer was and he has done so."

"No!" protested Jasper in desperation. "I admit that I cut the throat of that vicious harpy, Princess Puffer, and I'll go to the gallows for it. There are other crimes on my conscience that will be removed by the hangman's noose. But," he pleaded, "I swear by all that's holy that I did not harm Ned in any way."

Datchery was not persuaded. "Where have you hidden the ring?" he demanded. "That will attest the truth."

"What ring?"

"The ruby and diamond ring that was in Edwin Drood's pocket. When you destroyed all trace of him with quicklime, the ring would have survived. You were bound to see it when you made a second visit to the Sapsea tomb with the corpse of Princess Puffer."

"I saw no ring," said Jasper. "I have no ring. This is the first that I ever heard of such a ring as you describe. Search me, if you wish. Search my lodgings from top to bottom. Until this moment, I had no idea that Ned had ever possessed a ring."

He spoke with such patent honesty that everyone accepted his word. With tears running down his cheeks, he went on to insist that he had not murdered his beloved nephew but had devoted his life to the pursuit of the real killer.

"And who is that?" asked Grewgious.

"Neville Landless, of course," retorted Jasper.

"I am satisfied that Mr Landless is innocent."

"But he killed Ned on Christmas Eve."

"That is a figment of your imagination, Mr Jasper."

"Is it?" asked the choirmaster, shaken by the notion that he might, after all, have been mistaken. "Well, *someone* killed poor Ned. If it was not Neville Landless – then who was it?"

There was a protracted silence. Hiram Grewgious did not know the answer and neither did the two policemen. Durdles was baffled, Deputy was confused and even Dick Datchery, who removed his wig absent-mindedly to revert to Richard Cherry, could not muster any suggestion. The silence was eventually broken by Bazzard.

"The Reverend Septimus Crisparkle," he grunted.

"Never!" said Grewgious in utter disbelief. "You dare to name Mr Crisparkle, Minor Canon, early riser, musical, classical, cheerful, kind, good-natured, social, contented and boy-like Mr Crisparkle?"

"Yes," said Bazzard, smiling for the first time in a decade. "Find the gentleman and I guarantee you will find the missing ring."

Septimus Crisparkle held out the ring so it could catch the light from the window. The rubies shone brightly, the diamonds glistened and the gold glinted. Rosa Bud, young, lovely and impressionable, was overcome with the beauty and significance of the object.

"I can see that it is my beloved mother's ring, Mr Crisparkle," she said as she tried to stem her tears. "How ever did you come by it?"

"It was given to me for safe-keeping by Edwin, my dear," he told her, twisting the ring between his fingers so that it dazzled her eyes. "He was given it by Mr Grewgious with the instruction that Edwin should pass it on to you to seal your engagement. In the event, you had already decided to break off that engagement so the ring did not even leave Edwin's pocket."

"Why did he not return it to Mr Grewgious?"

"Because he hoped that you might one day change your mind," said Crisparkle. "It is a curiosity of human nature that we cannot appreciate the full value of something until we no longer have it. So it was with Edwin. While you were promised to each other, Rosa, he took you for granted. The moment that you ceased to be his, however, he came to see what a loss he had sustained."

"But he seemed so happy for us to continue as friends."

"He was putting on a brave face."

"What will happen to the ring now?"

"The only thing that should happen, my dear," said Crisparkle with a benign smile. "It should be worn by the person for whom it is destined. I know that I am a little older than you but age brings maturity. My judgement is that you are the most adorable young woman in the world and in doing this," he added, easing the ring on to the third finger of her left hand, "I give you a pledge of my love and a solemn promise that I will do everything in my power to ensure your continued happiness." He kissed her hand softly. "Well, my dear?"

Rosa Bud was utterly bewildered. It was disconcerting enough to receive an unexpected proposal from any man. When it came from the Dean of Cloisterham Cathedral, a Minor Canon of unimpeachable probity and in full possession of his virginity, it was all the more devastating. Wanting an affirmative response so that he could draw back the curtain of his desire and show her how much he had coveted her, he took a step closer and broadened his smile into a hopeful grin. To her eternal gratitude, Rosa was spared the ordeal of giving a reply. As she bit her lip in dismay, the door suddenly burst open and five men rushed into her room.

Two were policemen and they immediately seized the lovelorn clergyman. Another was Hiram Grewgious with his clerk, Bazzard, at his elbow. The fifth newcomer was a total stranger to her.

"Allow me to introduce Richard Cherry," said Grewgious, "whom I engaged as a detective to solve the mystery of Edwin Drood."

"There *is* no mystery," insisted Crisparkle. "He was killed by his uncle, John Jasper, and I have been gathering evidence to prove it. Instead of manhandling me, these gentlemen should arrest Jasper."

"They have already done so," explained Cherry, "and he has been charged with the murder of Princess Puffer, the owner of an opium den. He has given a full confession and is now under lock and key. Mr Jasper was not involved in the death of Edwin Drood even though he sought to profit by it. *You* were the killer, sir."

Crisparkle laughed. "What a monstrous suggestion!"

"It was Bazzard who unmasked you," said Grewgious, giving his clerk a pat on the back. "Tell him how you did it, Bazzard."

"I had this thorn of anxiety in my head," said Bazzard. "Whenever I thought about this case, I felt a sharp prick at the back of my mind. The cause of my anxiety, Mr Crisparkle, was you."

"Tell him why," urged Grewgious.

"It was because he found the watch and the shirt-pin," said the clerk. "They were seen as evidence of foul play. But where did he find them, I ask. It was at the Weir, two miles away from the spot where Edwin Drood and Neville Landless had been standing – two whole miles. Are we to believe that Mr Drood was killed, thrown into the river and that his body, as it was swept downstream, obligingly divested itself of the two items at the Weir? Strong swimmer as Mr Crisparkle is known to be, is it credible that he would plunge into fast-flowing waters to retrieve two small items whose weight would surely have taken them to the river bed? Is it not more likely that the victim was first lured to the Weir by a trusted friend, murdered then stripped of his valuables?" He turned his saturnine countenance upon Crisparkle. "We know you took the watch and shirt-pin from him, sir, so you must also have relieved him of the ring."

"The ring!" shrieked Rosa Bud, pulling it from her finger.

"The ring!" shouted Grewgious, taking it from her to examine it. "It's the very same one that I gave to Edwin Drood."

"With this ring," said Bazzard sonorously, "I thee accuse."

Septimus Crisparkle gave up all pretence of innocence. His head fell to his chest, his shoulders sagged and his knees bent.

As he was hustled to the door by the policemen, he threw a last despairing glance at Rosa Bud.

"I only did it for your sake, my dear," he said. "Edwin Drood was unworthy of you and I was called to take his place."

"Your place is on the scaffold beside John Jasper," said Cherry with grim humour. "Dean and choirmaster will hang there like a pair of discordant bells ejected from the Cathedral in sheer disgust. Take the wretch away!"

The policeman pulled Crisparkle out and Rosa began to tremble with fear. She had received two proposals of marriage in her short life and both had come from murderous would-be husbands. Was there something about her that inspired men to extreme violence? It was a thought that made her shudder.

"Congratulations, Mr Bazzard," said Cherry, warmly shaking the clerk's hand. "You are as good a detective as me. I found one killer and you led us to another – and all because you had this thorn of anxiety."

"Wait a moment," said Grewgious, "I've heard that phrase before. Yes, of course I have!" He slapped his thigh. "*The Thorn of Anxiety*. Isn't that the title of the play you wrote, Bazzard?"

"Yes, sir," confirmed Bazzard.

"And what was your play about?" asked Cherry.

"Jealousy."